A *Wedding for*

JULIA

A Wedding for
JULIA

Vannetta Chapman

HARVEST HOUSE PUBLISHERS
EUGENE, OREGON

A WEDDING FOR JULIA
Copyright © 2013 by Vannetta Chapman
Published by Harvest House Publishers
Eugene, Oregon 97402
www.harvesthousepublishers.com

Library of Congress Cataloging-in-Publication Data
Chapman, Vannetta.
A wedding for Julia / Vannetta Chapman.
    pages cm. — (The Pebble Creek Amish series ; book 3)
ISBN 978-0-7369-4616-2 (pbk.)
ISBN 978-0-7369-4617-9 (eBook)
1. Amish—Fiction. 2. Wisconsin—Fiction. I. Title.
PS3603.H3744W43 2013
813'.6—dc23

2012043877

Printed in the United States of America

13 14 15 16 17 18 19 20 21 /LB-JH/ 10 9 8 7 6 5 4 3 2 1

For my friend,
Donna Marlene Seals

Acknowledgments

This book is dedicated to Donna Seals. She is one of those rare things—a friend you can call any time, day or night. She's also a fabulous proofreader and has helped me through every manuscript. I love you, sweetie.

Thanks to my prereaders: Dorsey and Kristy. They do a fabulous job of catching my mistakes and I value their opinions. Also, I appreciate my family and their encouragement as I pursue my dream of putting stories full of grace into readers' hands. I'm grateful for the help of my agent, Mary Sue Seymour, as well as the superb staff at Harvest House for publishing this story. Kim Moore deserves a very special thank-you for making my job so much easier than it might otherwise be.

I invite readers to visit www.locksoflove.org. They are mentioned in passing in this novel.

I enjoyed this return visit to Pebble Creek located near the real town of Cashton, Wisconsin. If you're ever in the area, stop by, visit the local shops, and enjoy the beautiful country.

And finally...*always giving thanks to God the Father for everything, in the name of our Lord Jesus Christ* (Ephesians 5:20).

Isaac brought Rebekah into his mother Sarah's tent,
and she became his wife. He loved her deeply,
and she was a special comfort to him after the death of his mother.

GENESIS 24:67

⊰ *Prologue* ⊱

J ulia Beechy stood next to the open grave and prayed the wind would stop howling for one moment. Next to her, she could feel her mother trembling. Ada Beechy had turned seventy-eight the previous week, two days before Julia's father had passed. It would have been perfectly acceptable for her mother to sit, especially in light of the mist, the cold, and the wind.

Ada Beechy had no intention of sitting.

But Julia did shuffle one step closer to her mother, so that their sleeves were touching, as the bishop began to read the words to the hymn Ada had requested—"Where the Roses Never Fade." Ada had stared out the window of their kitchen, her attention completely focused on the rosebushes, which had yet to bud, while members from their church sat beside Jonathan's body in the next room. She'd gazed at the bushes and made her request.

Bishop Atlee had nodded, ran his fingers through his beard, and said, "Of course."

Julia tried to focus on the bishop's words as the men—the pall-bearers—covered the plain coffin with dirt. How many shovelfuls would it take? Would Bishop Atlee have to read the hymn twice? Why was she worrying about such things?

David King stepped back, and Julia realized they were finished. Bishop Atlee bowed his head, signaling it was time for them to silently pray the words from the passage in Matthew, chapter six, verses nine through thirteen—their Lord's prayer. Julia's mind formed the words, but her heart remained numb.

"Amen," Bishop Atlee said, in a voice as gentle as her mother's hand on her arm.

The large crowd began to move. Words of comfort flowed over and around her. There had been a steady coming and going of people through the house to view her father's body for the entire three days. Julia had become used to her privacy as she cared for her parents alone. The large amounts of food and the people had surprised her. Some of them she saw at church, but others came from neighboring districts. Those she barely knew.

She and Ada turned to go, for their buggy was marked with a number one on the side. The white chalk against the black buggy caused Julia's heart to twist. They had led the procession to the cemetery. They would lead the gathering of friends away from the graveside.

But Julia realized she wasn't ready to leave.

She pulled back, needing to look one more time. Needing to swipe at her tears so she could read the words clearly.

Jonathan Beechy
11-3-1928
3-6-2012
83 years, 4 months, 3 days

Now she and her mother were alone.

∼ Chapter 1 ∼

Tuesday morning, six months later

Julia glanced around the kitchen as she waited for her mother's egg to boil. Everything was clean and orderly. Why wouldn't it be? It was only the two of them. Except for the days when she baked, there was little to do. Julia was hoping that would change soon, and she meant to talk to Ada about it. Today would be a good day. She'd put it off long enough.

The water started to boil, and she began counting in her mind. Three minutes made for the perfect egg, at least for Ada it did. There were few things her mother could stomach on the days she wasn't well, but a soft-boiled egg was one.

Julia walked around the kitchen as she counted, and that was when she noticed the calendar. She'd failed to flip the page to September. Where had the last six months gone?

Six months since her father had died.

Six months of Ada's health continuing to fail.

Six months that Julia had continued to postpone her dream.

She flipped the page, smiled at the photograph of harvested hay, and vowed that today she would speak with her mother. Returning to the stove, she scooped out the egg with a spoon and placed it in a bowl of water to cool. Slicing a piece of bread from the fresh loaf

she'd made yesterday, she laid it on a plate and added a dab of butter and apple preserves on the side. She set the plate on a tray, which
already held a tall glass of fresh milk. Picking it all up, she turned to
walk to her mother's room and nearly dropped the tray when she
saw Ada standing in the doorway.

"I'm not an invalid, and I don't need to eat in my bedroom."

She weighed a mere eighty-nine pounds. Julia had brought in the
scale from the barn last week and confirmed her fears. Her mother
was losing weight. She was also shrinking. Ada now stood a mere
five foot four inches.

Why was it that the body shrank as it grew older? It was almost
as if it needed to conserve its energy for more important things. Her
mother had attempted to braid her hair and tuck it under her *kapp*,
but the arthritis that crippled her hands made the task difficult. The
result was snow-white hair sprouting in various directions and a *kapp*
tipped slightly to the back of her head. She also hadn't been able to
correctly pin her dark green dress.

In spite of her appearance, the blue eyes behind her small glasses
twinkled with good humor and complete clarity. Her mother's health
might be failing, but today her mind was sharp. Julia was grateful.
Some days sporadic bouts of dementia robbed her even of that.

"*Mamm*, I don't mind bringing it to you."

Ada waved her hand, dismissing the notion. "When I'm too feeble to get out of bed, I'll be praying the Lord sees fit to take me home."

Julia didn't think it was a good time to remind her she'd stayed in
bed three days last week. Ada remembered well enough. She simply
chose to ignore the bad days.

"Let me help you."

Setting the tray on the kitchen table, Julia was relieved to see that
at least her mother was using the cane Dr. Hanson had provided.
He'd suggested a walker, but Ada had insisted "the Lord was her
strength." The cane was a compromise.

Julia inwardly winced as she looked at her mother's hands.
Some mornings the crippling arthritis was better than others. This

morning her hands—wrinkled, and spotted with age—resembled claws. She wondered how her mother would be able to pick up the utensils to eat. She was tempted to offer to feed her, but the last time she'd suggested that had earned her a twenty-minute lecture on self-sufficiency.

Ada must have noticed her staring. Patting her daughter's arm, she murmured, "I know the Lord is always with me. I will not be shaken, for He is right beside me."

"Indeed."

She bowed her head as her mother prayed over her breakfast. While Ada thanked God for her food, Julia prayed for strength and wisdom.

Was today the right day? And how best to broach the topic? Why were her palms sweating?

She waited until Ada had finished the egg and eaten half the bread. Some part of her wanted to believe that if her dream came true, Ada would improve. Another part knew it was only a matter of time until she'd be left alone in the big two-story house beside Pebble Creek.

"My baked goods have been selling well at Lydia and Aaron's shop."

"Ya. That's *wunderbaar*."

Julia nodded but vowed in her heart to push forward with her plan. She'd thought perhaps she should wait until her mother's health improved, but after the visit with Doc Hanson last week, she knew that wasn't going to happen. It was imperative she not wait until winter. The tourist crowds came during the summer and stayed through the fall foliage. If she was going to do this, she needed to do it now.

"*Mamm*, I'd like to expand my cooking business."

"You don't have a business." Ada fumbled with the glass of milk, and they both reached to settle it. "You have a hobby."

Rising and walking across the room, Julia fetched the herbal ointment the doctor had recommended. When she opened the jar, the smell of mint balm filled the kitchen. Pulling her mother's left hand across the table, she worked the cream into the skin, rubbing gently with her fingers to massage the muscles until they were straightened.

"I'd like to make it a business, though." She looked up, peering directly into her mother's eyes.

Why was this so hard? Why was she so afraid Ada would say no?

She was thirty-seven years old, and she was still worried whether her mother would approve of her plans. "I'd like to open a café here in the house."

Ada didn't speak as Julia reached for her right hand and began rubbing the ointment into it. When she'd finished, her mother touched her cheek, leaving the faint scent of mint and summer.

"Dear Julia, how can you open a café in these rooms if you won't be living here?" Behind the glasses were blue eyes filled with calmness, sadness, and determination.

"I don't understand—"

"Do you think your *dat* and I would leave you here after we've gone on? Leave you alone?"

"But—"

"*Nein*, Julia. It wouldn't be proper. It wouldn't be right."

"What..." Julia's heart was racing so fast she felt as if she'd run from the creek. She didn't know which question to ask first. "How..."

"We always hoped you might marry. Your father spoke to you about this on several occasions."

"*Ya*, but—"

"I know your reasons, and I even understand them. The fact remains that you can't live here alone once I'm gone, which according to Doc Hanson will be relatively soon."

Julia jumped up from her chair, walked to the kitchen counter, and glanced outside. Her gaze fell on the rose bushes. They still held some of summer's blooms—a deep, vibrant red.

"So you're deciding I have to leave? Just like that? I have no say in it at all?" Her voice rose with each question.

"You'll go to Pennsylvania. Back to live with my family."

"I don't even know those people."

"They're family, nonetheless. You've exchanged letters with them for years."

"This is my home, *mamm*. You would kick me out of my home?"

Ada bowed her head. She didn't speak for the space of nearly three minutes—long enough to boil another egg. When she looked up, her words were gentle, but they still made Julia want to scream. "God is our refuge and strength, *dochder*."

"The Psalms are not the answer to this!"

"Always you can find the answers in *Gotte*'s Word."

Julia closed her eyes and forced her emotions to calm down. When she looked at her mother again, she saw the same quiet, loving woman who had been beside her every day of her life. What she recognized, in her mother's eyes, was kindness—and it confused her as much as the decree she had just issued.

"There's no changing your mind?"

"*Nein*. The papers were drawn up before your *dat* passed. It's why we agreed to sell the pastureland to Mr. and Mrs. Elliott. This home will be sold when I pass, and the money will be put in a trust for you, to help support you the rest of your life—"

"Support me."

"On the condition you live in Pennsylvania with my family."

"Why are you telling me this now?" Julia's voice was a whisper. How could her life have taken such a catastrophic turn? When she'd slipped out of bed this morning, she never would have imagined that her days in this home, her days living beside Pebble Creek, were numbered.

It was true she hadn't been overly social. She couldn't remember the last singing she'd been to, but then she was not a girl. She was a woman.

Instead she'd waited. She'd done what a good daughter should do, followed all the rules, and waited. For what? So she could be turned out of her home. So she could be told once more what to do.

It wasn't fair.

And she hadn't seen it coming. She had never expected such an answer. She had never dreamed her mother and her father—she mustn't forget *he* had agreed to this plan—would betray her this way.

No, she'd been busy designing a café in the bottom floor of their home. Where should she put the tables she would purchase from David King? What type of sign would best attract customers? What would be the best location for it? Should she advertise in the *Budget*? What design should she use for the menus?

None of those things mattered if she would be living in Pennsylvania.

"Why now?" she repeated.

"Why? Because you asked." Her mother stood, gripped her cane, and shuffled out of the room.

Leaving Julia alone, staring out at the last of the crimson roses.

⪜ Chapter 2 ⪜

C aleb Zook guided his horse and buggy along the road that ran parallel to Pebble Creek. He was headed toward the Beechy place. It was the first Tuesday in September, the weather was cooler, and he should have been in a fine mood.

Except the changing of the weather reminded him he wasn't getting any younger. Who was?

He scrubbed a hand over his jaw—clean shaven. *Ya*. There was the rub. There were things he regretted, and never marrying was at the top of the list. It had started bothering him more since he turned forty last month, but regrets were like the water running beside him, running down Pebble Creek.

He couldn't catch them. He couldn't do anything about them.

It was best to let them go.

Fall in Wisconsin was a thing of beauty. There was a light breeze and the temperature was a pleasant seventy—he'd seen the readout on the bank building as he drove out of town. Afternoon light bounced off the water playing over the rocks in the creek. He might finish up his run for the general store early and put in an hour or two of fishing. Soon enough hunting season would start. Perhaps he'd talk Aaron into a hunting stand a time or two, depending on Lydia's condition. She was pregnant with their first child, and it was due before the end of hunting season. He smiled at the thought of his friend and his young family. Aaron was happier here in Wisconsin than he'd ever been back home. Caleb didn't mind admitting to himself that Aaron had found something he hadn't.

And there was the problem that was scratching at his happiness this fine autumn day. Without fail, winter would follow fall, and winters in Wisconsin were long. One wretched cold night followed another, and the solitude was somewhat depressing.

Caleb hunched over the reins and pretended his horse needed directing. If he were honest with himself, he'd admit that hunting was losing its appeal, as was fishing. Maybe he was sick. Or perhaps he was lonely.

Could be. Whenever he went back home to Indiana, he was surrounded by family, and he thought about staying. His life was here, though. He'd come because Aaron's letters had described a life that held so much promise. And Wisconsin had been all that he'd described and more. It had been all Caleb had imagined and hoped.

Hadn't it?

What kind of life did he have, spending every night alone?

Gotte, *what I need is a friend.* The words popped in his mind. He almost laughed out loud. He had many friends in Pebble Creek, people he could call if he needed a hand. Making the turn toward the Beechy house, he realized his heart was right, though. He needed a close friend, someone who was as alone as he was. Someone he could have long talks with. Someone who didn't have to hurry off because of their own family, their own obligations.

Gotte, *I need a friend.* The words echoed in his heart, and they felt true. His *mamm* used to say that prayer eased the heart by lifting burdens up and into their proper place. He wasn't one for fancy praying, but maybe that didn't matter so much. Maybe it was the asking that counted.

He found himself whistling as he turned again—this time down the lane that led to the Beechys. He slowed his gelding in front of the two-story house and studied the large square structure.

"That would be a fine house if someone took care of it," he said to Red, his sorrel. His father had named Red last year when he came to help Caleb settle. Jebediah had never been accused of having an imagination. He'd gone with Caleb to pick out the horse, who had a reddish tint to his coat. The name naturally followed.

Jebediah had no imagination, but Caleb did.

He looked at the house in front of him, and he saw how it must have looked years ago, before the elder Mr. Beechy had become ill. Before the burden of the place had fallen on the shoulders of Julia.

"Shame," he muttered.

Red didn't seem to have an opinion. He tossed his head and began pulling at the grass in front of him.

"Don't eat a bare patch," Caleb cautioned. "I only have the one box. I'll be back in two minutes."

He knew talking to the horse was ridiculous, but Tuesdays and Thursdays were delivery days. The other three days he worked for the grocery, he helped unload pallets of food and stock shelves. On delivery days, he drove the back roads. Riding the remote routes of their district alone, the quiet could build up and make you long for a conversation. The ride became lonely, even for an Amish man, who was accustomed to quiet. Too much of a thing could make you restless, which was probably why he was looking forward to seeing Julia.

Sure would beat trying to talk to Samuel Gingerich. The man constantly spouted Scripture.

"The Bible says we should devote ourselves to *Gotte's* Word," the older man had bellowed.

Caleb had made the mistake of asking if he had tried fishing recently.

"Fix your thoughts on what is true, and honorable, and right, and pure, and lovely, and admirable." Samuel frowned and stared at Caleb as if he had offended him in some way.

So Caleb had said, "Have a good afternoon, Samuel," and left.

But the lecture from the old guy rankled his nerves. It seemed to him that fishing was lovely and admirable. Perhaps it was even honorable as it provided food for people and did so in a peaceful way.

Besides, he didn't need a lesson from Samuel Gingerich. He read the Bible and didn't need it quoted to him.

All right, he hadn't read it a lot, but he'd read it some. You'd think Samuel would want to talk about something else—the weather maybe or all the tourists who had been through town—but he hadn't. Caleb had been happy to drop off the man's groceries and turn Red back down the lane.

Funny how some people never wanted to come into town to buy their groceries. Some people, like Samuel, didn't care to see other folks. They avoided it whenever they had the chance.

Other folks, like Julia, couldn't get away even if they wanted to. He'd watched her since he'd started delivering groceries a year ago. She was devoted to her parents and rarely left the house. What would that be like? To be completely tied to a place?

Had she ever been over to Wildcat Mountain? How often did she go into town to shop for things a woman needed? Her dedication was something he had a hard time understanding, especially given his history with women—correction, one woman.

Hefting the box of groceries up on his shoulder, he walked up the steps, knocked on the door, and inwardly chided himself. The past was past and he was over it. What he'd been through with Lois had happened years ago, and he didn't feel any bitterness toward her. She'd been young. He was wrong to use her behavior as a measuring stick for how other women might or might not act.

He knocked again on the door.

When Julia's mother answered, he knew something was wrong.

Chapter 3

"Hello, Caleb."

"Ada."

"*Danki* for bringing the groceries."

"Happy to do it." Caleb stood there, uncertain what his next move should be. He'd been bringing groceries to the Beechys twice a month for a year, and Julia had always answered the door. Was she sick?

Ada pushed the screen door open a crack, which was difficult for her to manage, what with her arthritis and the fact she was still clutching the cane. Caleb shuffled the box to his other shoulder and opened the door.

"You can take that into the kitchen."

"Oh, *ya*. Sure thing." Maybe Julia was in there cooking. Something did smell good. Caleb didn't realize how much he'd looked forward to seeing Julia and her smile until Ada had answered the door. The thought of not seeing her again for two weeks made his stomach twist, which was ridiculous. He'd see her at the next church meeting, but that was different. On Sundays the women kept to themselves, especially the single women.

Caleb walked across the small entry hall and through the front room. An *Englisch* family would have used it for a dining room, but

Julia and Ada had filled it with their sewing things. On the far side of the room was a doorway leading to the kitchen.

Cooking on the back burner of the gas-powered stove was a stew, which was what Caleb had smelled. His stomach growled as he set the box on the counter next to the pot—beef vegetable if he wasn't mistaken. No doubt all of the vegetables had been grown by Julia, but where was she?

He turned around and Ada handed him an envelope with the money for her groceries. She didn't need to ask the amount because it was always the same.

"How are you feeling?"

"*Gut!*" Ada's left hand clutched the cane, but she raised her right to illustrate her point. "I will sing to the Lord, for He has been good to me."

Caleb recognized the words from the book of Psalms. Since delivering to the Beechys, he'd become quite acquainted with King David's words. Somehow it didn't bother him quite the way that listening to Samuel Gingerich did. When Ada quoted from the Bible, it was as if she were sprinkling salt on a meal. She was seasoning the day.

"*Gut* to hear, Ada." He moved to his right and glanced into the breakfast area. From where he stood, he could even see a portion of the sitting room, enough to know there was no sign of Julia in the house. Disappointment swelled through him, but he pushed it down. He couldn't expect her to wait around on the grocery man.

"I guess I should be going on to my last stop."

"Your last stop is your *freind* Aaron. Surely he can wait." Ada walked over to the pitcher on the counter. "Thirsty?"

"*Nein.*"

She poured a glass of water anyway. "I wonder if you could take this out to Julia."

Caleb tried not to respond to her words, but he wasn't very successful. By the time Ada handed him the glass, he'd forgotten about the stew and was ready to dash outside. Julia was home. He'd be able to see her. Suddenly delivering Aaron's groceries slipped from his mind.

"She's been working in the garden for some time, and she might be thirsty."

"I'd be happy to." Caleb wanted to hurry back out the front, but he didn't because Ada insisted on accompanying him to the door. He'd never realized how slowly she walked with the cane. He could have lapped the house in the time it took them to walk back through the sewing room.

Ada patted his arm and thanked him again.

"You know your way out, Caleb. I believe I'll stay here by the window."

"All right. You have a *gut* day, Ada." Caleb was nearly out the front door when he remembered to ask, "Same order next time?"

"*Ya*. Same things." Ada waved her hand as she settled in the rocker near the window. She didn't reach for her quilting, though, and why would she? Her hands were knotted so badly it was a wonder she could turn the pages of the worn Bible she picked up from the table next to her chair.

Caleb knew the garden was around the back of the house, but he was surprised Julia had been out there for so long. There was little to do in the fall except harvesting the vegetables that were late to produce. Most of her harvest had been canned already.

Coming around the corner of the house, Caleb stopped abruptly in his tracks. Julia was sitting on the far side of the garden, facing the house. She had her knees drawn up under her dress and her arms wrapped around her knees. Even from where he stood, he could tell she was upset. From where he stood, he could tell she wanted to be alone.

But he was clueless as to what he should do because it was obvious she had already seen him.

Julia stared at him a moment—a moment when neither of them moved. Sweat trickled down his back as he held the glass of water and felt like a complete fool, but then she raised her hand and waved him over.

He couldn't have stopped the grin on his face if he wanted to, and he didn't want to. She was upset about something, but maybe he could help—that's what friends did, right? And they were friends, or at least acquaintances. Making his way around her garden, he joined her on the slope.

Together they stared at the house. After a few moments, he remembered the glass of water he was holding.

"Your *mamm* sent this. She thought you might be thirsty."

Julia sighed and turned toward him to accept it. When she turned her brown eyes up at him, Caleb had the sensation he was falling. That made no sense at all as he was firmly seated on the ground. Maybe he was the one who needed to drink the water.

What was more unsettling was that she had plainly been crying. Her eyes were red and a little puffy.

Caleb had no idea what he was supposed to do, so he pushed the glass into her hands and said, "Um...maybe it will make you...um... feel better."

Julia laughed, but it wasn't a real laugh. It was a sad laugh, like when you wanted to pretend something was funny, like when you wanted to cover up your true feelings. "I doubt it will, but I'll drink it since you were so kind to bring it out to me."

She sipped some of the water, and then they fell back into a comfortable silence. From where he was sitting, Caleb could see Red eating a bare spot into the front yard where he'd left him. The gelding could not be hungry, but he was a creature of habit.

After the silence had stretched on for another moment, Caleb decided he should say something. But what?

Julia was miserable. She was heartsick and she was hot. Worse, she couldn't find a solution to her problems. Now her mother had sent out Caleb Zook. The poor man looked completely lost.

He cleared his throat and said, "Problem with the garden?"

Julia set the glass down between them, put her forehead against her crossed arms, and started laughing in earnest. Unfortunately, the laughter turned to tears.

"It was a bad joke." Caleb patted her on the back. "I can see that your garden is fine. My mouth trips me up when I don't know what to say. I'm sorry."

"*Nein*. It's not your fault." Julia rubbed at her eyes. They already felt as if they had dirt sprinkled in them, and rubbing made the sensation worse. "I'm acting like a child, and I'm making you feel bad about it."

When he didn't speak, Julia peeked over at him.

"You're honestly worried about how I feel?" Caleb gave her a lopsided grin. His dark hair needed cutting, but his face was open and honest. He'd always been kind to both her and her mother.

Her mother!

"I don't know what I'm worried about," Julia admitted. "I had a fight with my mother. Not a fight, actually. More a disagreement. She issued a decree, and now—well, now I don't know what to think or what to do. So I came out to the garden."

"You have a lovely garden."

"*Danki*." She smiled again, this time one that came from her heart and caused a pain all the way down to her stomach. "I've always loved working out here. It's one of the reasons I enjoy cooking."

"The stew inside smelled *gut*."

Julia shook her head. "That's what I mean. Take a single man like you, Caleb. How do you eat?"

"I'm not following. You had a fight with Ada about how I eat?"

"Not exactly, but how do you eat?"

"I eat well enough." He patted his stomach, though Julia noticed he didn't carry much extra weight. "You can tell I'm not starving."

"Would you stay for dinner if we offered?"

Caleb squinted at her. "Are you offering?"

"I'm saying this badly. Describe to me what you eat in a normal week."

"Probably not what you'd consider *gut* meals," he admitted. "A lot of meat, since I hunt and fish. Less well as far as vegetables, unless Aaron and Lydia have me over. I try not to impose on them too often."

Julia nodded. "That's why a café would be perfect for Amish and *Englisch.*"

"A café?"

"Yes! But *mamm* wouldn't even listen. Instead she told me about this ridiculous decision she and *dat* had made more than a year ago, apparently. Had anyone told me? *Nein.* Not until now. Not until the day I finally had the courage to tell her about my dream."

She closed her eyes and fought back the tears that threatened to spill again.

Caleb didn't rush her. He didn't call her foolish or tell her she was acting like a baby, and yes—she realized that sitting in the garden and crying was childish on one level. Instead, he sat patiently beside her and waited. He treated her as a friend would.

How long had it been since Julia had confided in a friend?

She had them—overall, the women in her district were kind. But she wasn't particularly close to any one person. She had no one to run to when she was hurting like this.

"You don't want to hear my problems."

"I don't?"

"And probably you need to go."

Caleb shielded his eyes against the afternoon sun. "The last delivery isn't that important—only a box of things that needs to go to Aaron and Lydia at the cabins." He smiled and even winked at her. "It's no problem."

Julia felt heat rise in her cheeks. Had Caleb Zook winked at her? Was he flirting or just trying to make her laugh again?

"But I should probably see to my horse before he tears all the grass out of your front yard."

"Oh. It's okay if you need to go."

"*Nein.* I'll move him toward the barn. Walk over with me?"

Julia considered saying no, but her choices were to walk with Caleb, go inside with her mother, or stay here in the garden sulking.

Standing, she dusted off the back of her dress. "At least I won't have to mow that spot."

"Mow? If we leave Red there any longer, you'll have to take a hoe to that patch and plant another garden."

They walked toward the front and talked of the fall colors, and of how the Plain Cabins were doing since Aaron and Lydia had taken over their management. Caleb said the cabins were usually full of guests—typically *Englisch* families but occasionally Amish folks from surrounding districts. They also discussed the large shopping center in town, Amish Anthem. Julia told Caleb how much controversy had surrounded the building's remodel, as well as the *Englisch* owner Byron Drake. They spoke of everything except what was burdening Julia's heart.

Caleb untied Red, who nudged at Julia's hand.

When she pulled some raisins out of her pocket and offered them to the gelding, Caleb shook his head in mock disgust. "You're spoiling my fine horse."

For a moment she could almost believe it was another Tuesday afternoon when Caleb had stopped by to deliver groceries and brighten her week.

It wasn't though.

The earlier conversation with her mother still echoed through her mind. It still pricked her heart. As she glanced around the property that she had lived on her entire life, she realized anew that soon she would be leaving her home beside Pebble Creek.

ᗒ Chapter 4 ᗕ

Caleb was aware of the exact moment Julia's mood changed. She had briefly relaxed when she handed the raisins to Red. A smile had even appeared, though it wasn't the smile he was accustomed to seeing.

What could have happened that had upset her so much? And what was this talk about a café?

"So you had a disagreement with Ada."

Julia pulled in a deep breath as they walked toward the barn. Caleb led Red to the western side of the building. Though the sun was headed down, the afternoon was still pleasant. He tied Red to the hitching rail next to the barn.

"I'll be right back." Julia disappeared inside before he could argue. She returned in a jiffy with a small bucket of oats.

"You don't have to do that."

She smiled slowly, and then she turned her back to the barn, leaning against the metal railing and studying the property. Red ate greedily from the bucket she still held. From where they stood, what was left of the Beechy place spread out in front of them. Caleb could see the corner of Julia's garden, which extended down the western side of the house and beyond it by a good ten feet. How did she work such a large plot alone?

The property west of that included what had been sold to Tim Elliott—the *Englischer* who was trying Amish ways, or at least Amish farming ways. He'd stuck with it for more than a year, which was longer than most. That piece of land also included a smaller house. Caleb hadn't seen it himself, but Aaron had told him about it once.

Pebble Creek ran behind the entire property, to the north, and he was surprised to find he could actually make out the rooftops of a few of Aaron's cabins.

"I didn't realize the Plain Cabins were so close."

"Sometimes I can hear children playing and laughing." Julia met his gaze before glancing away. "It's one of the reasons I thought a café would be a *gut* idea. The cabins are doing well, and I think Aaron's customers would like a place nearby that serves *gut* healthy food."

"And you want to provide that here at your home?"

"The house is ridiculously large." Julia waved at it with a hand that said more than her expression. "*Mamm* and I hardly need two floors and nine rooms."

"You'd need help."

"I would, but you know as well as I there are always Amish girls looking for work. I spoke with David, and he has several tables and chairs ready to purchase."

Caleb closed his eyes and walked back through the house in his mind. The sewing room would nicely hold two tables, two more in the breakfast area, and three or four in the living room. She had the space to do what she was describing.

"You'd have the café downstairs and live upstairs."

Julia waited to answer until he had opened his eyes. "*Ya.* Of course, we would eat downstairs, but there's plenty of living space upstairs. We hardly use it now."

"And you have enough money saved to get started?"

"I do, from my baking and our produce stand. And my customer base is right across the creek. I feel I need to start now, though, while everyone is coming to see the fall colors."

"Why didn't you do it this summer?"

Julia glanced back out over the property. "*Dat* had been sick for several years. Selling off the land to the Elliotts wasn't difficult for me. We hadn't been able to farm it for the last five, maybe six years."

She turned to him and looked him full in the face. Once again Caleb had that sensation of the ground shifting, of falling. For some unknown reason, his mind flashed back to Lois, to when he was young and didn't have control over his emotions.

"That was my *dat's* vision, to farm the land and make it productive. I suppose it's every Amish man's dream."

Caleb nodded, more to keep her talking than because he agreed with her. He'd never been much of a farmer himself. He knew how. He'd helped often enough back home, but it wasn't where his heart lay.

"When he could no longer work the land, he was happy to help me with the garden. That's part of the reason it's so large." Julia ran her hand along the metal rail they leaned against. "So we sold the land to the Elliotts to help with the taxes and expenses, and none of us missed it much. *Dat* was too sick by then to do more than nod his approval. *Mamm* quoted something from the Psalms, fifty-five I think."

"Fifty-five?"

"Give your burdens to the Lord...It's one of her favorites. Anyway, I didn't miss it. The land wasn't something I could use, and the other house was a constant reminder that—"

She cut herself off, as if she'd said too much.

"I didn't miss it," she repeated. "And the Elliotts seem like nice folks."

"*Ya*. They do."

The silence stretched between them until Caleb again became aware of Red, waiting patiently beside them. He'd finished his bucket of oats and was nudging the weeds that grew next to the barn.

"I don't know when the idea of a café first sprouted in my heart, but I do know I waited the first year or so because *dat* was sick and the timing seemed poor. When he died last March, I felt I should wait through summer. But this morning, when I looked out my window and saw the leaves turning to gold and red and brown, I knew today was the day I should lay out my plan to my *mamm*."

"And she said no?"

Julia nodded.

"She doesn't want strangers in the house?"

"It's not that at all." Julia reached down and pulled at one of the weeds. When she did, her *kapp* strings fell forward and brushed against his pants leg. A small, unintended contact between them, but it stirred something in Caleb's heart.

"Julia." Caleb waited until she stood straight and looked him in the eye. "Ada's mind is clear, and she has always seemed devoted to your welfare and our community. What was her reason for denying you this dream?"

Two bright spots of color appeared on Julia's cheeks, but she didn't look away this time.

⸺

Julia pulled in a deep breath and repeated the words that had been circling around and around in her mind all day. She couldn't believe she was saying them to Caleb Zook, to a man she knew casually at best, but she had to say them to someone or her head was going to pop like an overripe watermelon.

"She said I couldn't open a café here because I wouldn't be living here anymore."

Caleb had been leaning against the metal rail with his arms crossed, but now he stood up straight and his hands fell to his side. "What?"

"She said she couldn't leave me here alone after she passed. She said it wouldn't be proper, and that this—" Julia's hands came out and she waved at the house, the garden, and the banks of Pebble Creek. "All of this is to be sold."

"Sold?"

"And used to support me, but only if I agree to return to Pennsylvania to live."

"Return?"

"My parents are from there, but I've never been before. I suppose for me it wouldn't be returning as much as moving there for the first time."

Caleb stared at her, and the shock on his face did more to ease the burden in her heart than any words he could have said. His inability to speak helped her to spill the rest.

"She told me to seek God's answers in His Word—beginning with Psalm Forty-Six, 'God is our refuge.'" Having shared nearly everything, she was able to finish. In a lower voice and no longer looking directly at Caleb, she confessed, "They had hoped I would marry."

His laughter was the last thing she expected.

"I see nothing funny about this."

"*Nein*. It's not funny at all, but I can just see your sweet little mother quoting 'God is our refuge and strength' as she informs you that you'll be moving soon. She's a feisty one, that Ada is."

"Easy enough for you to laugh. No one is uprooting you and crushing your dreams."

"True enough, and I'm sorry for your troubles, Julia." Caleb reached out and touched her arm, sending goose bumps all the way up her shoulder. No doubt that was the exhaustion having its way. "Can she do it? Will she do it?"

"*Ya*, my *mamm* is very stubborn, and apparently she and *dat* drew up legal papers long ago."

Caleb nodded as if that made sense.

Julia helped him turn Red around so they were headed back down the lane, and together they walked the rig past the barn and to the front of the house.

She felt better, having shared her problems with someone, though she still had no solutions. Perhaps Pennsylvania wouldn't be so bad. Perhaps her mother would live to be one hundred, though even if she did, it seemed there was no café in her future.

How could she begin something she might have to abandon at any moment?

"You know, Julia, it's plain that Ada does care for you, and she's doing what she thinks is best."

"Which doesn't help me at all, but *danki* for trying to put a rosy face on it."

"I was thinking." Caleb climbed up into the seat of the buggy and smiled down at her. "There is a way you could stay and have your café."

Now she knew he was teasing her, but he had stayed late and listened to her whine, so she smiled slightly and tilted her head to the right. "You don't say. And how is that?"

"Find someone to marry."

With another smile, he called out to Red and trotted off down the lane.

≈ *Chapter 5* ≈

S haron Zook knew she was late for dinner, and her parents did not abide lateness. She jumped from James's battered green pickup before he'd properly stopped it.

"I can take you closer," he hollered over the roar of the muffler, which he'd promised to fix. There was no sneaking in with all of that racket shattering the peaceful Indiana countryside. Though James wore *Englisch* clothes and drove the old truck, his hair was still cut in typical Amish fashion. With one foot in both worlds, even he didn't seem to know if he was merely enjoying his *rumspringa* or whether he was actually considering leaving the Plain life.

"*Nein.* I'll be in enough trouble already." Waving, she ran toward the house. She heard James's laughter as he shifted the transmission into reverse and drove away. The old truck rattled and bounced, but she had to admit it was better than a buggy. It never nipped, and it was bound to be warmer in the winter.

Slipping between the barn and the kitchen door, fall leaves crunching beneath her feet, Sharon didn't want to even think about spending another winter on the remote farm in Indiana. She had to find a way to get to the city. It seemed James was willing to take her there.

"Wash up," her mother said when she tried to quietly take her place at the table.

Eight sets of eyes stared at her—five younger brothers and her baby sister, plus her parents. Sharon bit back the retort she had washed her hands before coming in the house, which she had—in town. There was no sense in arguing, though. It was easier to do as her mother asked.

After she'd sat down again, they all bowed their head for grace. Sharon found herself thanking God for James and his 1972 Ford truck which might or might not make it to Indianapolis. She tried to think of something else to be grateful for, but she couldn't. Was that bad?

Dishes rattled and she realized she was the only one still praying.

Her brothers ranged in age from seven to fifteen. Jonas, the oldest, was now working with her *dat* in the fields because he was finished with school. How did he stand it? Didn't he want more? Obviously not, by the way he talked constantly about crops and animals and manure.

Sharon stole a glance at the phone in her pocket, which turned out to be her fatal error.

"That's pretty," Ruthie said. "Can I see, Sharon?" She dropped her spoon against her plate and attempted to reach for the phone.

Sharon's mother sent her a warning look and the conversation between her *dat* and Jonas stopped.

"Sharon, what is that you're fiddling with?"

Heat began to creep up her neck. She wouldn't lie to her father, but she didn't want a confrontation, either.

"Ruthie needs more milk." Sharon's mother was good at running interference. "I'll get it."

"I asked you a question." Norman stared at Sharon, waiting for an answer. Silence fell on the table like a cloth they might use to cover it with if company were coming.

"It was my phone, *dat*. I'm sorry."

Norman closed his eyes for a few seconds, a sure sign he was attempting to control his temper. "I have told you I will not abide those things in our home."

"I know. I meant to leave it in the barn, but I forgot."

"You forgot."

"I was in a hurry because I was late, and—"

"Forgetting is not an excuse for disrespecting the rules of this house, the rules of our faith."

"Those rules don't even make any sense!"

"Do not raise your voice to me." Norman's palm came down and slapped the table.

When Sharon had been a young girl such a display of authority would have sent her scurrying. Now it made her sad. If he weren't careful, he would break the old rickety table, and then they would need another.

"Hand me the phone."

"What?"

"You heard me. Hand me the phone."

"*Mamm*—"

"Do as your father says, Sharon."

Sliding her hand into her pocket, she pulled out the small, sleek, blue mobile device—her one connection with the outside world. Standing, she walked around the table and placed it in her father's outstretched hand.

"Tomorrow I will return this to the store where it belongs. You need to focus on other things, *dochder*. On the things that matter." Pushing back from the table, Norman stood and trudged out of the room.

Would he take her phone back to town? Or would he leave it in the barn, tucked away on some bale of hay?

Either way, she was trapped.

⤳ Chapter 6 ⤳

C aleb stood beside Aaron, holding the board steady as David hammered it into place. He'd awakened the next morning to the sound of hammering and had been instantly caught up in the building project—one of the drawbacks of living on Aaron's property.

Normally he was off on Sunday and Monday, but someone at the grocery had needed to change shifts. He was off today instead, and he usually spent his off days down by the creek.

Didn't work out that way this morning.

Since Aaron and Lydia had taken over the cabins, they had become quite the success. When Caleb moved to Wisconsin, he'd planned on looking for a place to rent until he could decide where or if he wanted to purchase land. Aaron had admitted they could use a night watchman on the property.

"Watchman" was a loosely used term. Caleb didn't watch much. He did a final walk around the cabins and office buildings before retiring each night. If the guests had a problem, a sign on the office door directed them to his room, which Aaron had built on to the back of the barn. It was snug enough in the winter with the stove they had added, and the summers were perfect.

The cabins had continued to increase in popularity until they

were full nearly every night, except for Sunday and Monday evenings
when they were closed. On Sundays Lydia and Aaron weren't actually on the property, but guests were often still about from Saturday
evening. Lydia made sure they had paid the night before and left
them fresh bread, coffee, and juice in the main office. All Caleb had
to do was unlock the door.

Today's project involved the building where Aaron and Lydia
sold goods from area families. The sign above the door said "Plain
Shop."

Aaron had added it to the property when he took over the cabins,
but it had become something of a problem. Basically, it was too small
and did too much business. It was always crowded, and there wasn't
enough room to keep the stock they needed to display.

"When we put this up a year ago, we had no idea so many people
would want to sell their goods here." Aaron stepped away and swiped
at the sweat running down his face.

"*Ya*, if we'd known that we would have built it bigger to begin
with." David slipped his hammer into his tool belt. "I thought you
were a little *narrisch*, building a store on the property when you
couldn't even attract an overnight guest."

All three men turned and looked at the full parking lot and guests
spilling from the cabins.

"*Gotte* is *gut*," Aaron declared, picking up another board.

"That He is." David walked over to the jug of water Lydia had left
and poured himself a glass. Downing it in one long drink, he ran the
back of his hand across his mouth.

Seeing Lydia walk toward the shop, Caleb hollered out, "Sorry I
was late with the groceries last night."

"No problem."

"Explain to me why you would be late," David said. "You're always
on time, much like the *Englisch* trains."

Aaron laughed. "It's a woman's fault."

"It's always a woman's fault," Caleb muttered.

"I heard that." Lydia waddled into the front door of the shop and turned the sign from "Closed" to "Open." Aaron's wife was far along in her pregnancy, and Caleb was surprised she still insisted on coming to work each day at the cabins. "What is our fault this time?"

Caleb closed his mouth and studied the board they had just finished nailing into place.

"We were saying it's your fault the cabins are doing so well." Aaron's grin widened as he lifted another board. The room they were adding to the shop would more than double the size.

"'Fault' would be an unusual choice of words in that case." Lydia walked back out on the porch and crossed her arms as she surveyed their work. "You're all doing a nice job, so I'll forgive any intended insult. And as I have no customers yet, I believe I'll go help my *schweschder* serve breakfast to our guests."

When she was out of earshot, David said, "Before she returns, catch me up. It's obvious you're too shy to talk around her."

"It's not that," Caleb said. "There's nothing to tell, is all."

"Nothing to tell? When have you ever been late returning home? Usually you're here early so you can put a line in the creek before dark." Aaron's laughter was as clear as the ring of David's hammer against the nail.

"You were late because of..."

"Julia." Aaron nudged Caleb with another board. "Julia Beechy."

David let out a low whistle. "She's a nice-looking woman and available for sure, but I wasn't aware she was dating. In fact, it's been a very long time since Julia has shared a buggy ride for the purpose of courting."

"It wasn't Julia who caused me to be late. Not exactly. It was the conversation we had, which made me stay longer than normal. Plus I was distracted, so I drove past the cabins a few miles before I realized I needed to turn around."

"Must have been some conversation."

"Wait until you hear the details." Aaron's grin grew even broader.

Caleb couldn't fault him. He'd known Aaron since he was a young boy, tagging along behind as Caleb and Aaron's older cousin had gone fishing and hunting. Aaron was too good-natured to hold a grudge against, though he did seem to be enjoying Caleb's misery this morning.

He proceeded to fill in David as they worked, though Caleb corrected him once or twice on minor details.

"So Ada is going to sell the place?" David shook his head. "I guess I should say the rest of the place. Most of it already went to the Elliotts. Real shame. Julia grew up here. We went to school together. Moving will be hard, I suspect."

"*Ya*, and all because she isn't married." Caleb had picked up a hammer and drove the nail a little harder than necessary.

"I told Caleb he should pop the question."

"That's not funny, Aaron."

"I wasn't being funny, my *freind*. I was serious."

"Which isn't funny."

David held up his hands to stop the two. "If I didn't know you were friends from your youth, I would think you were *bruders* the way you argue sometimes."

"Actually, I was closer to Aaron's older cousin. Matthew was two years younger than me. Our parents' farms shared a property line, so we spent a lot of time together. Aaron was a little guy who visited often and insisted on following us around all the time." Caleb climbed the ladder and began working on the roof of the addition.

"I thought you were the oldest cousin." David passed materials up to Caleb as he spoke to Aaron. "You told me that's why you had to come to Indiana to help with the cabins, because you were the oldest."

"I might have said that, but I meant the oldest *unmarried* cousin."

"And look who's married now," Caleb said, laughing.

"Yes, I am, and I'm telling you that married life is pretty nice. You should consider it."

"I don't even know her."

They all paused at that. Aaron picking up a board, David with his hammer back and nail in place, and Caleb perched on the roof.

David was the one who broke the silence.

"That's probably true of most married people. You don't truly know someone until you share your mornings and your nights with them." He shook his head and began hammering again. "I thought I knew Anna when we married, but I didn't. I'm not saying marriage is something you should rush into. Aaron's idea is radical and a thing you would need to pray about, but the truth? No one can completely know another person until they've shared their life."

Caleb was relieved when Lydia came back and the conversation ended. He'd endured a restless night, and David's words left him even more confused.

He wanted to help Julia. He did. But marry her? Was he supposed to go that far?

What stuck in his mind more than the splinter he'd managed to catch in his forefinger were the words he'd prayed as he'd driven up to her house yesterday. Maybe it had been a coincidence. Maybe it had nothing to do with all that followed, but he couldn't help remembering that he'd cried out to God for one thing and one thing alone. He couldn't help remembering how right that prayer had felt. The words still echoed in his mind. He'd prayed, Gotte, *what I need is a* freind.

But friendship and marriage were two different things, weren't they?

Julia pulled gently on the reins to her old Bay Paint mare, Missy, slowing the buggy as she approached Bishop Atlee's home.

Fortunately, her mother hadn't asked any questions when she'd finished the morning chores and said she was going to town. She would never lie to her mother. She'd even prepared a speech in her mind, explaining why she felt the need to speak with the bishop.

Now the speech whirled around under her prayer *kapp*, unneeded and unused. Ada had nodded and resumed tending to the rose bushes, adding, "Do be careful, dear."

The bushes didn't actually need pruning. Julia took care of that, but Ada seemed to enjoy trimming back the dead blooms, often stopping to brush her hand across the newest red buds. The task was cumbersome for her. Some days she could barely work her arthritic fingers into the handles of the pruning shears. Still, she insisted on doing it herself. Watching her work slowly and with extra care, Julia knew her mother was remembering the hymn from her father's funeral—"Where the Roses Never Fade."

How could she be angry with her mother when she was such a sweet old thing? How could she stay aggravated when each day she worried about her mother's health? Each day might be her mother's last. Even today it seemed Ada was a little weaker as she walked from the kitchen, out the back door, and to the row of rose bushes.

When Julia had asked how she felt, Ada had waved a hand and said, "I will sing praise to the name of the Lord."

The Psalms—always the Psalms! Since she was a child it had been so. She'd asked her why more than once, but Ada had simply patted her hand and answered with words from another Psalm. It was maddening.

An evening's rest and morning chores had done nothing to lessen Julia's confusion, and Bishop Atlee Keim might be the one person who could provide answers.

Before she could knock on his door, the bishop walked out of his barn and waved a hand in greeting. "Julia, nice to see you."

"And you, Bishop."

"Is everything all right with Ada?" The skin around his eyes crinkled in concern, and he ran a hand up and over his cheeks—cheeks as weathered as the pages of Ada's Bible.

Atlee had been their bishop for as long as Julia could remember. He had a beard which was mostly white and reminded her of the *Englisch* pictures of St. Nicholas. The hair on the top of his head was also white and beginning to thin. He'd been married, but his wife had passed a few years before. Recently he'd moved into the smaller house—the *grossdaddi* house—on his place, and his oldest son had moved into the big house. Often when Julia saw the bishop, he was surrounded by children -his own grandchildren or the children of his congregation.

"My mother is fine." Julia's hand went to her *kapp*, though she knew it was pinned perfectly. "I was wondering if you could spare a minute to talk."

"Of course." Atlee nodded toward the porch. "It's what the rockers are best for. I'll go inside and fetch us some drinks."

By the time he returned, Julia had gathered her courage and was ready to spill the entire story. She did it a little more succinctly than she had with Caleb, so that she was finished before the bishop had taken two drinks from his glass of lemonade.

"I can see you're upset by this discussion you've had with your *mamm*."

"Of course I am! What they decided is so unfair."

He tipped his head to the right, the way he did during a church service before he was about to make another point. "Fairness is a difficult thing to pinpoint, so I won't speak to that. I do know that Ada and Jonathan love you very much."

She liked that he spoke of her father in the present tense. Julia believed in the resurrection, and she knew her father was in heaven even now, watching over her.

"I'm not sure my *dat* understood exactly what he was doing when he made this...decision."

"Because of his illness during his last year?"

"*Ya.*" Relieved that he was understanding her, she pushed on. "You know better than anyone how addled he could become. Some days he thought I was his *schweschder*. Am I to believe he knew what he was doing when he set this course for my life?"

Atlee didn't respond immediately. Instead he rocked and stared out at the trees, which looked as if they had been colored by a child— their leaves were so bright and attractive.

"You're saying you would follow your father's advice, normally. The problem is you're not sure he was of a clear mind when he made this condition that you must marry to inherit the home here in Pebble Creek."

Julia nodded. It was a slight nod because she wasn't sure if that's what she was saying or not. She did trust her father, but this was all so crazy.

Atlee set his lemonade down and folded his hands in his lap. For a moment she thought he might be praying, but then he raised his wise brown eyes and looked directly into hers.

"I don't suppose you've seen the legal papers Ada spoke of, but Jonathan had them drawn up several years ago while his mind was still quite clear. I know because he asked me to witness them." He paused, allowing time for his words to sink in. "I also know because before he did such a thing he spent many an hour here with me, praying about it."

Julia shook her head, wanting to say something, say anything to make him stop.

"I suppose it's hard to understand how a parent worries over a child, and you are still a child to your parents no matter how old you become. Jonathan's heart was burdened that you had not married." He raised his hand to stop her protest. "He enjoyed having you at home, but he wanted you to have what he had. He wanted the peace of knowing someone would protect you, love you, and cherish you as a husband would. Together, we prayed for this. In the end, he decided that his duty as a parent was to send you back to Ada's family."

"But I'm a grown woman."

"Yes, you are."

"I can take care of myself."

"Yes, you can."

"This isn't fair!"

Atlee's hand came out, dismissing the subject as he had the first time.

Julia took another sip of the lemonade, which now tasted too tart. "What am I to do?"

"The choice you make is yours, Julia. I will pray for you during this time, and any time you would like me to pray *with* you, I'd be happy to do that as well. In the meantime, I suggest you search the Scriptures. Always you will find guidance there."

Standing, she thanked him and walked back to her buggy.

Following beside her, the bishop asked her to give his best to Ada. When she'd climbed into the buggy, he said, with a twinkle in his eye, "The marrying season is upon us, Julia. Is there no one from among our community you'd consider?"

"Just like that? Just marry someone?"

"There are *gut* men who would—"

"Name one."

"Bishop Beiler, on the east side of Pebble Creek."

"He is in his fifties." Julie clapped her hand over her mouth. She would never have said anything disparaging about the bishop, but marrying him? Was Atlee serious?

Smiling, he continued. "Gabe Miller's brother has been visiting. I've heard he means to stay."

Julia closed her eyes, determined not to say another word. The entire world had apparently gone mad. She had known Andrew Miller only a few months, and she'd spoken less than a dozen words to him.

"And then there's Caleb Zook."

Now her eyes popped open.

"Caleb?"

"Sure. He's been here more than a year. Aaron has vouched for him, and I've spoken to his previous bishop as well. He seems like a fine young man."

"Caleb?"

"Zook. *Ya.* You know him. About this tall, longish hair, delivers groceries."

Julia picked up Missy's reins. With a polite but firm smile, she said, "No, Bishop. I haven't given it any consideration."

Then she murmured to the horse and turned her buggy down the lane.

It wasn't until she was halfway home that she realized she hadn't quite spoken the truth. She had given marriage some consideration and with one of the men Bishop Atlee had mentioned. The question was whether she had the courage to do anything about it.

Chapter 7

J ulia sat through the church service and struggled to pay attention. She wasn't having much success, though she'd been at it for several hours. Aaron and Lydia's home was small but cozy. What would that be like? What would it be like to share the most intimate of moments—waking, breakfast, passing each other in the mudroom, even going to sleep together?

She pulled her thoughts back to the worship service.

The singing portion had gone fairly well until they had reached "Where the Roses Never Fade." Why this week? When her memories of her father were so fresh, so muddled, why was this one of the chosen hymns?

The lyrics spoke of their heavenly home and streets of gold. They reminded her of the tree of life. Voices raised around her, singing of roses with eternal blooms. The words of the hymn comforted her, while at the same time stirring in her heart an ache for her father.

Tears threatened, but Julia blinked them away. She'd had more than her share of hugs and warm greetings this morning. It seemed perhaps her situation had been the topic of the Amish grapevine— out of concern and not maliciousness, she had no doubt. Still, she didn't want to begin weeping now. It would be sure to cause more talk and trouble her mother as well.

On Thursday, Ada had taken a turn for the worse.

She hadn't been able to leave her bed for two days. Julia was worried enough to go to the phone shack and call Doc Hanson. He'd come to the house, assessed her mother's condition, and spoken with her about it in the hall outside her mother's room.

"It's her heart, Julia. Same as before. The muscle is old and tired. Perhaps with a pacemaker—"

"My hearing is still *gut*, Grady Hanson, and I believe I've given you my decision on that topic."

Doc Hanson had shrugged, and Julia had gone back to her mother's side. Suddenly she was worried and ashamed she'd spent hours upset at Ada for their conversation about her future. What if the time she'd spent angry were some of her mother's final hours?

By Saturday Ada had taken one of her miraculous turns, and on Sunday morning she woke insisting she was well enough for church.

The episode had done more than shame Julia about her resentment toward her mother. It had convinced her that she might not have long to make her decision. If she wanted to stay in Pebble Creek, she would need to find a way to do so.

But short of marrying, how?

As the hymn singing stopped and the preaching began, they turned in their Bibles to the twelfth chapter of First Corinthians. Julia's attention didn't stay on Paul's description of the spiritual gifts, though. Instead, her eyes drifted across the page to the apostle's words on love.

"Love is patient and kind. Love is not jealous or boastful or proud or rude. It does not demand its own way."

How many times had she read those words? But always with an eye to how she treated others in her congregation or her parents. Never with a mind toward marrying someone she barely knew. Would she actually consider such a thing? And who was to say—here was the real rub, which caused her eyes to fill with tears again—who was to say that someone would be willing to marry her?

It was worse than humiliating.

As they rose to sing the next hymn, she glanced across the room and was startled to see Caleb watching her. Her heart flipped like pancakes on a griddle.

Had he noticed her reaching for her handkerchief? Did he guess what emotions she was struggling with?

And what exactly had he meant when he left her house on Tuesday? He'd said she could stay in Pebble Creek and have her café if she found someone to marry. What would prompt him to say such a thing?

Even if someone from their congregation offered to marry her and she accepted, there was no guarantee he would agree with her plans to turn their home into a café. She would be subject to his decisions. He might not even want to live in the old house along Pebble Creek. What would be the chances that her dreams would be his dreams?

More importantly, what would be the chances that their marriage would be a union of love, one like that described in Paul's letter she had been reading? She was old enough to realize that not all marriages were held together with love. A marriage was a private thing, and what one saw on the outside was not always what existed within—even for those around her, even for Amish marriages.

There was no such thing as a perfect community with perfect families and perfect relationships. She would have no guarantees.

As they were dismissed for lunch, she turned to help her mother stand. Ada smiled up at her. What could she possibly have to smile about? Her hands were nearly clawlike today, her heart unreliable, and she was shrinking before their eyes. Ada never failed to amaze Julia, but then she was learning—daily—that there were many things she didn't understand, many things she had yet to learn from her mother. The question was whether God would grant them enough time.

Caleb was not happy.

Sitting at the picnic table next to Aaron, he hunched over his plate of food and pretended to eat.

It seemed as though a protective barrier was around Julia Beechy, and he was having trouble finding a way through it. Before the church service it had been women—lots of women. Aaron's wife, David's wife, Julia's own mother. When he had arrived at Aaron's house for the morning service, Caleb had tried to catch Julia's attention, but he couldn't make his way through the women who were talking with her.

At one point they actually linked up arms and walked off in a different direction, leaving Caleb holding his hat and wondering what he was supposed to do. To make matters worse, Aaron had laughed and slapped him on the back.

Had the entire district gone crazy?

During church he'd made a concerted effort not to stare at her, but she'd looked so forlorn, not to mention beautiful, that he'd had trouble tearing his eyes away.

When had she started looking beautiful? Last week she'd merely looked like Julia.

Caleb knew what he needed. He needed to spend a day fishing. Things made more sense when he had a line in the water, when he was standing on the bank of Pebble Creek and his thoughts were following an orderly fashion. Since Tuesday, his thoughts had jumped in every direction, and he wasn't sure what to do about it. He needed to make it through Sunday, and then Monday was his regular day off.

Except he'd agreed to work the next day. He'd start early, finish early, and make time to go fishing. Once he put his life back on a normal track, everything would be fine.

First, though, he needed to talk to Julia. So he'd tried again after the service.

This time the table she was watching over was crowded with old people, children, and men, and she was at the vegetable table. No one was ever interested in the vegetable table! Suddenly, Andrew

Miller couldn't have enough of the squash casserole. Andrew, who Caleb had seen swallow more sweets in a month than he personally could consume all year. He ought to take the young man aside and have a talk with him. Andrew was making a fool of himself. But Andrew wasn't the only one.

Apparently every single man in their district, and there were a few, had heard of Julia's predicament.

"Better go and speak with her, Caleb, before someone sweeps her off her feet." Aaron laughed as he stuffed a piece of ham into his mouth.

"Speak with who?" Seth, David's oldest son, glanced around as if he'd missed something.

The boy was growing faster than hay in summertime. He was practically swallowing his food whole, and everyone knew why. As soon as Clara finished working in the serving line, the two would be off walking near the river. Rumor had it that they would publish their marriage intentions soon, which was one more thing to irritate Caleb on this beautiful Sunday afternoon.

"Never mind who." Caleb stood and gathered up his dishes. The crowd around the vegetable table was thinning out. Most had taken their plates to their tables. Andrew remained, but Caleb was certain he could find a way to move him away from Julia.

"Aren't you going to eat that cobbler?" Seth asked.

"Take it." Caleb handed it to him and walked off, the thought of cobbler turning his stomach slightly. It had looked good enough when he'd accepted it from Clara, Lydia's sister. He'd never be able to eat it now.

His hands began to sweat as he covered the distance to where she stood. What was he doing? What was he going to say? Was he actually going to say what he thought he was going to say? Had he fallen down and hit his head sometime in the last week?

Veering away from the food line, he walked to the edge of the gathering and braced his hand on a tall northern red oak. Looking up into its dark red leaves, he calmed somewhat, and that was when he remembered the conversation with his father. After several days of driving past his delivery drops, burning his own dinner, and waking in the middle of the night with a certain woman's face dancing through his mind, he'd finally gone to the office at the cabins and put in a call to Indiana.

His *dat*, in typical fashion, had summed it all up with a few questions.

"Is she a gut woman?"

"Sure, she is—"

"Do you care for her?"

"I care, but—"

"Is she in need?"

"Yes, that's why—"

"Do you feel Gotte has placed you there at this time to provide for her need?"

"Maybe."

There'd been silence on the line, and then his *dat* had said the words that had calmed Caleb then and settled him now as he turned and walked back toward Julia. *"Sounds as if you know what you need to do, know what Gotte intends you to do, and know what your heart is wanting you to do. All that's left is to see if you're willing to do it."*

Good ol' *dat*. He never wasted minutes on a telephone walking around the hayfield. No, he preferred to get straight to the point.

"Hi, Caleb." Julia smiled at him and rearranged two of the dishes.

"Caleb." Andrew grinned in a way that seemed suspicious. Had he already said something to her?

Caleb greeted them both and waited, but Andrew made no move to step away from the table. Sighing, Caleb pushed forward. He hadn't thought of what he was going to say, but he knew he wasn't going to say it in front of a man who was barely over thirty and hadn't even committed to staying in the area.

"I was hoping to talk to Julia alone for a minute."

"Oh. Sure thing." Andrew nodded, his smile still firmly in place. It served to irritate Caleb even more. What was he so pleased about?

"Well, remember the offer stands, Julia. David can contact Gabe anytime."

"Thank you, Andrew." Julia appeared flustered and shuffled the two casserole dishes back to their original position.

What offer? Why was Julia uncomfortable? And why was Andrew grinning as though he were holding a prize brook trout instead of a plate filled with green beans, corn, and squash? Finally, he smiled back at her again and turned to go.

Caleb didn't realize he was scowling after him until Julia cleared her throat and said, "You wanted to talk with me?"

"Oh, ya." He stuffed his hands in his pockets. "But would you like a break? You've been standing here since lunch began."

"I'm not very hungry," she admitted. "I am glad the line's thinned out, though. I've never seen folks so hungry for vegetables."

Caleb was tempted to clue her into the fact that it wasn't vegetables the men were after, but he let it slide. "How about we go for a walk, then? Aaron has made a nice path down to the river."

"I don't know. My mamm—"

"We'll watch after her, Julia." Elizabeth Troyer was standing at the next table—the dessert table. She was Aaron's kin and the former owner of the cabins. When her husband had died, Aaron had moved to town to help with the management. Eventually, he and Lydia had purchased the cabins from her.

"Oh. All right." Rearranging the nearly empty vegetable dishes one last time, she stepped away from the table.

They walked in silence for the first moment or so.

Caleb tried to remember what he was going to say, but his mind had gone blank. Looking around at the house, the fields, and the barn, it occurred to him it was always safe to talk about everyday things. "Aaron's made a lot of improvements here since buying the place."

"You have no idea," Julia said.

Caleb glanced at her and then back at the path they were walking down. "What do you mean?"

"You came after much of the work was done. When Aaron first arrived, this property was a mess and where Lydia lived with her parents..." she pointed to the property next door. "It wasn't much better, though Menno and Ella did their best."

"Menno's illness was bad, even then?"

"*Ya*. Many feel it's a miracle he's still alive. The farmer's lung, it prevents him from doing very much." Julia shook her head. "But he's still able to pray. You should hear Lydia talk about her father... or maybe you have."

"A little. Aaron's very fond of him too."

"He's a special man."

When she grew quiet, Caleb figured she must be thinking about her own father. He missed his family as well, but he could hop on a bus and visit them anytime he wanted. He also received letters regularly. What would it feel like to know you'd soon be left alone?

"Your parents had no other children?" he asked.

"They tried, but my *mamm* wasn't able."

They reached the creek, where Aaron had placed a bench beneath a tree. Julia sat down when he gestured to it, and he sat beside her, leaving a respectful distance between them. It reminded him of their time sitting beside her garden on Tuesday, and that made him smile.

"Does Pebble Creek make you laugh?"

"*Nein*, and I'm not laughing. I was remembering Tuesday."

"What could you possibly find funny about that?"

He took off his hat, knocked it against his leg, and then set it back on his head. "I had no idea what I was walking into, is all. Sometimes your life takes a turn and you have no clue it's about to happen."

She turned to face him now. "And how did your life change?"

"I don't...I don't even know yet. It's only that it feels different. Does that make any sense?" She nodded slightly, so he kept going. "I'm trying to understand myself, but I won't lie to you, Julia. I don't understand. I walked out to the garden with a glass of water and left your house with a dozen questions, none of which I've found the answers to."

"So why did you ask to speak with me?"

"Maybe because I needed to."

Her brown eyes stared into his blue ones for the space of a heart-beat. Had he been too honest?

When she smiled, freckles popped across the bridge of her nose. "I'm glad you're not asking me for answers, because I'm fresh out. I don't have any left at all."

"Sort of like your vegetables."

That started them both to laughing, and Caleb realized the knot that had been in his stomach was gone—finally it was gone. Was it because he was with Julia? Or was it because he'd stopped worrying?

They sat for a few moments, listening to the creek running languidly by.

"The sound of the water is soothing," she admitted. "I should walk down to the bank behind our home more often. I used to, before my mother became so ill."

"That must be hard."

"Actually, it's probably an excuse. We have a bell, and *mamm* would ring it if she needed me. It's easy to forget what things relax you, and easier still to crowd them out of your day."

Caleb had always thought sitting in the shade near a creek was restful. It helped to calm his emotions.

"I suppose I should go back," she said.

"Have you...have you given any thought as to what you're going to do?"

"I've thought of little else." Her voice had dropped to a whisper, so that he had to bend his head closer to catch her words.

"And?"

"And I don't know." When she raised her eyes to his, something hit Caleb in the chest with the force of a baseball driven for a homerun.

"Maybe I can help," he murmured, reaching out and touching her face, trailing his fingers down her neck.

"And how would you do that?"

The words almost didn't come out. He tried once and again a second time. His throat was so dry he had to swallow in order to find his voice. His mind and his heart filled with images of men crowded around Julia's table, men standing between him and her. Then that was replaced by Julia sitting next to him in her garden, her eyes red but smiling as she waved him over. Finally, all he could see was Julia, waiting next to him right that moment.

That image gave him the courage to say, "We could marry."

⇐ Chapter 8 ⇒

J ulia stared at Caleb. She tried to think of a response, but her mind had gone completely blank at the word "marry."

When Andrew Miller had offered to stop by and help her with her fall garden work, she'd been surprised, but this? She gawked at Caleb in amazement and leaned closer because she was sure she had heard him wrong.

"It's not such a crazy idea, Julia. There's no need to look at me as if I asked you to run off to Hollywood to join the circus."

"Did you ask me to marry you? Is that what you just did?"

"*Ya*. I suppose so."

"You suppose. So you're not certain."

Caleb removed his hat and combed down his hair, an expression of confusion replacing the hopeful one he had been wearing. "I'm certain—"

"Because I wouldn't want someone asking me to be their *fraa*, to join them in sacred union for the rest of our lives..." Julia sprang up from the bench and began pacing in front of him, "...if he wasn't exactly sure of what he'd asked."

"Julia—"

"One of these days, you might wake up and find yourself married if you're not careful, Caleb Zook. It could be quite a shock." Julia heard her voice rising as a sort of nervous hysteria took over, but she couldn't stop herself.

A little ways from where they sat, Clara and Seth were walking. As Julia's voice rose, Clara turned to look at her. Seth tugged on her hand, and they continued around the bend of the river.

Caleb stood, blocking the route she had been pacing. "If you want to walk, we can. Or maybe you could sit down and we can talk about this."

Looking into his eyes—which were calm and amused—settled her, reminding her of the time she'd seen her father speak softly and settle a young colt. Julia closed her eyes, pulled in a deep breath, and nodded. She sat down.

"I do know what I asked you, but I didn't know I was going to ask in exactly that way. So I surprised myself as well as you." Caleb pulled her hand away from her lap and held it in both of his. "I'm sorry I'm not very *gut* with words, Julia. I suspect you already know this about me, but it won't change if we do wed. I trip over what I mean to say much as a child stumbles over his first steps, especially if I'm a little nervous. I always have."

His honesty was more than charming. It touched a place in her heart she had long kept guarded.

"Why would you suggest such a thing, Caleb? We barely know each other."

He stared out over the creek, but he didn't release her hand.

"In some ways that's true. I don't know what your favorite pie is or what subject you liked best in school." He glanced back at her, a smile playing at the corner of his lips. "But I know you plant flowers at the end of your vegetable rows, that you quilt with brighter colors than your *mamm*, and I would be blind not to see how devoted you are to her."

She had to look away then.

How much more had he noticed? She'd grown accustomed to him delivering their groceries, but she hadn't realized he'd become attuned to their lives.

She wished he would stop, but he pushed on, oblivious to her discomfort.

"I know how well you are regarded within your community, though I've been here only a year. It didn't take long to understand that the people in our congregation think well of you." Caleb laughed and resettled his hat on his head again, with his left hand because his right was still holding hers. "If Aaron's word on my reputation isn't enough, perhaps you'll want a letter from my bishop back home, though Bishop Atlee has already spoken to him."

"I'm flattered—"

"Don't say that."

"What?" She raised her eyes to his and thought to pull her hand away, but she couldn't. How long had it been since someone had touched her this way?

"Don't say you're 'flattered, but...'"

"I *am* flattered, but—"

"You don't believe, in your heart, that you could learn to care for me in the way a *fraa* cares for her husband?" His expression grew somber as he studied her.

"How can I know, Caleb? This is all so sudden. Everything is happening so fast."

He nodded as if he understood. The strange thing was, Julia sensed he did.

Would he be willing to give up his life as it was to marry her? Could he be the answer she had prayed for? He hadn't said he loved her, but was it possible he might one day?

"I was thinking the same thing. Seems to me at times life moves slowly, like the waters of Pebble Creek at this moment. Other times, it speeds up and the details of our lives change quickly, like when the rains come and the water rushes down the creek. Remember earlier this year in the spring, when we had a long string of stormy days?"

Julia nodded, clueless as to why they were talking about the weather they'd had six months ago.

"The waters rose so fast and so high that they cut out a new bank on a portion of Aaron's property. He feared it was a real tragedy at first, but now you should see it—better fishing, a cleaner bank, and a nicer spot all around."

He glanced at Julia, squeezed her hand, and then released it.

"Our lives are like the river?"

"Maybe." He shrugged. "Or maybe I'm stumbling over my words again. One thing I'm sure of—*Gotte* knew what He was doing then. I suspect He knows what He's doing now."

Julia shook her head. "I want to believe that, but this is such a big step. It's a decision that will last the rest of our lives, all because of some decree my parents made years ago."

"*Gotte* knows our past and our future." Caleb stood and pulled her to her feet.

When she raised an eyebrow, he added, "Something my *grossdaddi* always says."

They were quiet on their walk back, but Caleb stopped short of the group of families waiting at the picnic tables.

"You can tell me it's none of my business, but...was Aaron asking you the same? Asking you to marry him?"

"Aaron Miller? *Nein*. He was offering to work in my garden."

The smile that covered his face caused her pulse to race.

"Take your time deciding, though from what you've said it sounds as if you don't have long. But there's one more thing I wanted to tell you. I don't know if it will make a difference. It's what gave me the courage to speak to you today."

Julia stopped fidgeting with the strings of her prayer *kapp*, and though she felt the eyes of some of her *freinden* on her, she stepped closer to hear what Caleb was about to say. He seemed more embarrassed even than when he'd first brought up the subject of marriage.

"I'm a believing man, Julia. I try to follow the Scripture, and of course I'm baptized and a member of the church. I don't pray as I should, though. I can't say I actually know how to do it well." He scrubbed a hand over his face and stared down at the ground. "On the day I was delivering your groceries—"

"Last Tuesday?"

Caleb looked up now, directly into her eyes.

"*Ya*. Last Tuesday. As I was driving to your house, I was praying. Maybe because while everyone is very friendly..." he waved a hand to encompass the group of people milling about, "I haven't made close *freinden* other than Aaron and David, and they are busy with their families. Whatever the reason, I clearly remember my prayer."

"What—"

"I prayed for a *freind*. That was it. I told *Gotte* I needed a *freind*, and He led me to you, in the garden, with tears in your eyes and a burden on your heart. Maybe, Julia, maybe friendship isn't a bad place for a marriage to begin."

Squeezing her hand once again, he turned and walked away to his buggy.

⌒

Julia didn't mention the conversation to her mother or anyone else. She ate a little cold ham, helped to put up what was left of the food, and stayed close to Ada for the remainder of their time there. The ride home was pleasant in the fall afternoon, but Ada began to shiver next to her on the buggy seat, so Julia called out to her mare and pulled up on the reins. Missy slowed immediately. Once Julia had stopped the buggy, she hopped out to retrieve a blanket from underneath the backseat. It hadn't been cold enough to need one since winter, but Ada plainly could use one now.

"*Danki*."

"*Gem gschehne*." Julia positioned the blanket until it fit snugly around her, and the image flashed through her mind of Anna, David's wife, tucking a quilt around her baby. In so many ways, on so many occasions, Ada was now like a child.

They were silent except for that brief exchange as they continued their journey home. The quiet was peaceful and comforting and allowed Julia to comb through Caleb's words again.

When she'd helped her mother up the stairs, changed her clothes, settled her into her bed, and fed her some soup, she thought to darken the room in the hopes Ada would go to sleep early. The day had worn her out, and Julia wondered if they should have foregone the church service and had their own Bible study at home instead. In such cases, Bishop Atlee was happy to stop by the next day to pray with them. Julia had long suspected it was also his way of checking to see if the people under his care needed anything else in the way of ministering to.

She reached out to pull down the shade. The sun had set, but there was still light outside the old house's window, and she wanted her mother to rest. She tugged on the cord of the shade, but Ada touched her arm, causing her to pause with the shade half closed. The light from outdoors gently bathed the room.

"This is the day the Lord has made, Julia."

"Ya, *mamm*. It is indeed."

"And we rejoiced." Her *mamm* appeared so frail, so small against the white pillowcase. Something in Julia's heart threatened to tear.

"We did."

"I'm glad."

The words of Psalm 118 weren't lost on Julia. She'd heard them every Sunday since she was a wee *kind*.

"I know you are." She bent and kissed Ada's cheek—soft, weathered, and worn. "I am too."

She pulled down the shade and a gentle darkness blanketed the room, though a small amount of light was still visible through the open door from the hall.

"What will you say to Caleb?" Ada's hand plucked at the quilt that had been covering her bed longer than Julia could remember. "How will you answer him?"

Julia didn't bother to ask how her mother knew.

"I haven't decided."

Ada patted the bed, so Julia sat.

"How would you have me to answer?"

"He's a *gut* man, yes?"

"He seems to be."

"Maybe *Gotte* has sent him to us in our time of need."

Julia thought of what Caleb had said, of his prayer asking for a *freind*. She shrugged and remained silent. She expected Ada to spout a Psalm, maybe 145 or 139. They were both favorites. Instead, a smile tugged at her mother's lips, one Julia could barely make out in the light from the hall. Ada's next words caused her to laugh in spite of the weariness spreading through her limbs.

"He does need a haircut, though. If my hands weren't so bent, I'd sit him in a kitchen chair and do it myself."

"I remember when you would cut *dat's* hair."

"Back when he had some on top, it was a twice-a-month chore."

Julia stared down the hall, as memories of her *dat* and then Caleb flooded through her mind and then through her heart. She wasn't surprised at what her mother said next.

"Go read your Bible, *dochder*."

"Yes, *mamm*."

She was nearly out the door again when her mother spoke from the bed.

"Read the story of Isaac and Rebekah. Genesis twenty-four."

An unusual selection, one Julia couldn't remember her mother ever recommending before. Maybe she'd take her Bible and a cup of tea to the garden. There was enough light yet. Maybe that was exactly what she needed after a day with not enough answers and too many unexpected twists.

⤳ Chapter 9 ⤳

Sharon crept back to her house as the eastern sky lightened to pink. It was too close to dawn. Her father would surely be up and working. Her father would see.

Should she go in the front or risk sneaking in the back? Either way she was bound to be caught and there would be a scene. Though the morning was cool, she wiped at the sweat beading underneath her hair.

Her hair! She'd forgotten all about her *kapp*.

Ducking back behind the hot water shed, she hastily braided her hair and pinned it back into a bun before covering the chestnut mass with her *kapp*. James loved her hair. He'd told her so again last night...or was it this morning? Warmth heated her cheeks as her mind flipped through the memories. The evening had been worth it, even if she did wind up in trouble.

And she'd do it again. There was no doubt in her mind she would do it again.

Going to Indianapolis, eating in a real restaurant, seeing a movie, and driving in the old truck with her hair down and her hand out the window—for the first time in her life she had felt careless and free.

She wanted to feel that way every day.

She did not want to feel like a twelve-year-old sneaking home after having skipped school.

Glancing left and then right, she ran toward the front steps.

Her *mamm* would be in the kitchen making breakfast, and the boys would be up readying for school. Better to enter from the front, and maybe she could sneak up the stairs and into her room. She crept through the front door, which was never locked. The smell of coffee from the kitchen almost persuaded her to change her plans. Coffee would be good, but her mother would notice she was wearing the same clothes she'd worn to last night's singing.

Sunday clothes on a Monday?

Nein.

She needed to go upstairs and change. Besides, the *Englisch* clothes she'd worn to the movies were still stuffed in her bag. Best to go to her bedroom first, the room she shared with her baby sister, Ruthie.

She almost made it.

But she stopped to look out the window that was positioned halfway up the stairs. Her brother Jonas was walking from the barn to the field. He looked so happy, almost as if he were whistling. At six thirty in the morning? What could he possibly be so happy about? Why was he content within their community and faith when she wasn't?

Shaking her head, she stepped back to continue up the stairs, and that was when she forgot to avoid the middle of the step. Nearly all of them creaked.

Her mother had been walking from the kitchen toward the front door to throw out some water on the flower bed. When she heard the squeak, she detoured around to the stairs, thinking it was one of the boys, but instead she saw Sharon.

Their eyes met, and Sharon was certain that her mother knew. What Marion couldn't tell from Sharon's disheveled appearance, she would guess.

The question was, how much would she share with Sharon's father?

Marion didn't bring up the matter until they were hanging the second load of laundry. The breakfast dishes had already been done, the boys were off to school, and Ruthie was playing in the leaves at their feet. Sharon's little sister was nearly four, and if there was one thing she'd miss when she left home, it was the little tyke with curly hair who looked at her as if she were perfect.

"What you did was wrong, Sharon."

"Which part?"

"All of it." Marion held up one end of the sheet while Sharon walked the other end down the line and pinned it.

Laundry for two adults and seven children was an enormous task. One line alone was completely filled with Ruthie's clothes. Sharon's little sister was adept at making a mess. Two sets of dresses and aprons a day was not unusual for her. They would be lucky to be finished with the laundry by the time the boys returned from school.

It was one of the reasons her parents had not pressured Sharon to find a job. Her mother could use all of the help her older daughter provided. At seventeen, no one was in a hurry to see her leave, though there had been several discussions about settling down and marrying when the right man came along. Sharon's mind drifted to James, and she had to ask her mother to repeat what she'd just said.

"You told us you were going to the singing."

"We did."

Her mother wagged a finger at her, a clothespin in one hand and the other hand planted on an ample hip. When had her mother gained so much weight? When Sharon was young, she'd been thin and beautiful. She still was beautiful, but—

"We're only having this conversation alone if you speak truthfully. I still plan on speaking with your *dat*, but things might..." She took the clothespin and attached it to a pillowcase. "Things might go better if you aren't in the room at the time. I'll speak to him tonight after dinner, and I'll bake his favorite dessert too. Soften him up some."

"Oh, *mamm*. What difference does it make? He's going to blow the hat off the top of his head either way."

Marion peered at her from between two of Ruthie's dresses. "Why did you do it, Sharon? Why do you keep testing him so?"

Sharon didn't answer immediately. Instead, she continued hanging the laundry as she mulled over her mother's question. When the last piece of bedding was hung, she plopped down on the ground. Ruthie immediately crawled into her lap. Somehow it was easier to speak the things of her heart while holding her baby sister.

"Have you always wanted..." Her hand came out to encompass the laundry, the fields, the barn, and even the house. "This?"

Marion swiped at her hair, pushing it back into her *kapp*. She moved over and sat down on the ground with a grunt that made them all laugh.

"I suppose I did. When I was your age, I thought your father was the best thing I had ever seen. He'd speak to me, and my heart would jump like when thunder claps right next to you. I knew he was all I needed to be happy. More than that, I knew that once I was married to him, I would be living the life I was supposed to live."

"And do you still feel that way?"

Marion sighed and looked out over their farm. "I hear the judgment in your voice, Sharon. My life isn't perfect, but it's not the worst, either. Your *dat* is a *gut* man, and I'm grateful to *Gotte* for him, for all of my life and all of my *kinner*."

Sharon didn't answer. She didn't know what to say, and she was embarrassed by her mother's honesty.

Finally, she pulled at a blade of grass and tickled Ruthie with it. "He made your heart jump like when the thunder claps, huh?"

"*Ya*. Still does some days. Does James make you feel this way?"

"Sometimes."

"Do you think he's the one *Gotte* has chosen for you?"

"I don't know, *mamm*." Sharon focused on Ruthie, who was busy crushing red, yellow, and brown leaves. She'd crumble two fists full, and then she'd sprinkle the pieces over the both of them. "I don't know if I even believe in that."

Marion sighed, put her hands on the ground, and attempted to push herself up.

"Let me help." Sharon moved Ruthie off of her lap, popped up, and grabbed her mother's hands. She managed to pull Marion into a standing position but nearly fell into the clothesline when her mother let go suddenly.

"You did that on purpose." She was laughing as she caught herself.

"A young man can cause your heart to race, as yours did when you thought you were going to fall." She stepped forward and touched Sharon's face. "In life though, falling hurts. I want what is best for you and so does your *dat*."

Sharon shook her head. James wasn't like that. He'd never hurt her.

"Now tell me the rest. I want to be able to explain it truthfully to your father."

So she did. She told about how they had gone to the singing and then left early. She explained about the ride into the city in James's old truck with the other car of Amish kids following. How together they had gone to the late night movie, and how it had been an animated show but with a story line directed toward teens.

"I never knew they could do such things with a computer, *mamm*."

Her mother nodded and motioned for her to continue.

As they walked toward the house, Ruthie tugged on Sharon's hand and demanded, "Carry me, Sharon! On your back!"

So she squatted down as Ruthie moved behind her and wrapped her arms around her neck. Soon she would be too heavy for piggyback rides. Soon she would be off to school instead of playing as they finished the laundry.

Standing in the hot little washing room, she told the rest—about the all-night diner they had found, how different the food was, the ride home, and even the kiss at the end of their lane.

She left out two things, though. She didn't mention the *Englisch* clothes—blue jeans and a purple T-shirt top with lace around the hem, still hidden in her room, and she didn't admit how much she looked forward to doing it again. Something in the pained expression that covered her mother's face told her it would be best to stop short of those confessions.

"I'll speak to your *dat* this evening, Sharon. Perhaps you should go and spend the night with your *grossmammi*. Give him a day to cool off."

After the noonday meal she packed an overnight bag, and her brother Jonas drove her down the road to her grandparents' farm.

Banished from her own home.

It was humiliating. She didn't even have her phone to call James and let him know where she was.

How could her life get any worse?

≈ Chapter 10 ≈

It wasn't Julia's first time to walk into the grocery store in Cashton. She tied Missy to the post in the parking lot, straightened her apron and her *kapp*, and tried to calm her heart, which felt as if it were going to thump right out of her chest.

Why was she so nervous?

She just wanted to ask Caleb a few questions. There was nothing to be afraid of. Her mind understood that, but her body continued to overreact. She had to wipe her hands on her dress, they were sweating so. Pushing her way through the front doors, she was relieved to see that very few customers had arrived before her.

"Can I help you?" A young *Englisch* girl with short blond hair and bright blue fingernail polish stood at the front register.

"*Ya.* I'm looking for Caleb Zook."

"Oh. Sure. He's loading up at the back dock. I saw him when I clocked in. Let me call him for you."

The girl picked up a telephone and spoke into it. To Julia's horror, when she did, her voice came out over speakers on the wall loud enough for all to hear. "Caleb Zook to the front register. Caleb to the front register, please."

Hanging up the phone, she turned back and smiled. "I'm sure he'll be here in a second."

"*Danki*," Julia whispered, wondering if she could flee before Caleb made it to the front.

The girl's voice had been louder than an auctioneer! Why not take an ad out in the local paper? What had she been thinking of when she drove here?

She had been thinking she could quietly pull him aside and ask the questions that had been tumbling around in her mind since Sunday.

"Julia? Is everything all right?" Caleb had walked through the double doors at the far side of the room.

"*Ya*. Everything is fine." Julia glanced from the girl at the register, to the customer she was helping, and back to Caleb.

"It's *gut* to see you..." Caleb stopped and studied her a moment. "Why don't we step outside?"

"Is it okay? You're supposed to be working."

"I have a fifteen-minute break coming. I've been here since six loading." He pulled the front door open and waited for her to walk out first. When she did, he motioned to a bench positioned near the plate glass window of the store, but she shook her head no.

It was all too public. She shouldn't have come to his place of work, but she hadn't known what else to do.

"Did you drive Missy here?"

"*Ya*."

"Let's go see how she's doing."

They walked around the corner to the parking area. Missy was exactly where Julia had left her. Of course she was—she'd been gone less than ten minutes. Caleb reached into his pocket and brought out a handful of raisins.

"I remember when you accused me of spoiling your horse, and look at you. You're carrying raisins in your pocket."

"You never know when they'll come in handy, and my own gelding was spoiled long before you fed him." He smiled as he offered the treat to the mare with one hand and patted her with the other.

"Is this better?" he asked, lowering his voice. "You seemed to want somewhere more private."

"*Ya.* I didn't know the girl was going to shout your name out so loud when she said she'd call you."

Caleb's smile immediately put her at ease. "That startled me the first few times as well. If you work at the store long enough, you grow used to their speaker system."

"I don't think I could."

"It's loud from where you were standing, but in the back, where trucks and other machinery are, it's the right volume."

That made sense. Still, she felt foolish for having had him called out so loudly and so publicly.

"What brings you to town?"

Julia closed her eyes. He had a fifteen-minute break. There was no church on Sunday, and he wouldn't be delivering groceries to their home again until a week from Tuesday. She'd only left Ada this morning because one of her mother's quilting friends had stopped by and insisted on staying until lunch. This moment was the perfect chance to ask him the questions she needed answers to, and she shouldn't squander the opportunity.

"Julia?"

"I've been thinking." She pressed her fingers to her lips. "I've been considering your offer."

"Do you mean my proposal?"

She opened her eyes and stared directly into his. "Yes. Your proposal."

"And?"

"And I think that maybe I will say yes."

She'd gone over a dozen ways to begin this conversation. None of them had included plopping her answer out there, and she certainly hadn't anticipated the slow smile that spread across Caleb's face. She'd actually thought his most likely reaction might be denial—as in he hadn't actually meant to ask for her hand in marriage.

"This is *gut* news."

"Caleb, I said *maybe* yes. We need to talk about this first. I have a lot of questions, and I'm not convinced you understand all you're getting into."

Now his eyebrows shot up beneath his long bangs, and Julia was reminded of what her mother had said about the needed haircut.

"You think I don't understand what marriage entails?"

"*Nein*, but you don't know all of the details of my situation. You can't possibly know the condition of my family's finances, all that needs to be done at the farm, and my mother's—"

Raising a hand, Caleb waved away her concerns, but she stopped him.

"No. This matters. If we are going to begin a marriage without—" she bit off the word "love" before it could escape. "Without the traditional feelings, it's all the more important we understand other things about each other. Plus, we need to decide when and where and what happens next."

A truck trundled around from the back of the shop. Its driver nodded at Caleb and then continued out onto the main road.

"I don't even know where you live," Julia continued.

"I live here, in Pebble Creek." Caleb's voice held a light note, but his eyes studied her seriously. "I can see you've given this a lot of thought, Julia, and I'm glad you have. I realized you weren't a young girl who might jump into something without much prayer and consideration. How about I come over to your house tonight after work?"

"Tonight?"

"Too soon?"

"No, but—"

"We can talk as long as you like. I assume your home would be better because it's probably hard for you to leave Ada alone."

"*Ya.* It is." It occurred to her again that he had noticed much about her life, but she knew very little about his.

"Tonight, then. I'll eat dinner before I come, but if you have any of your famous baking left, I won't turn it down."

"All right."

Caleb helped her into the buggy and handed her the reins.

She glanced back once. He was still standing there, in the parking lot, watching her leave.

⌒

It had been a long time since Caleb had courted a woman. He let his mind slip back through the years, trying to do the math. There had been Lois and then a few feeble attempts after that. His mother had tried to arrange some dinners—not so subtle efforts at matchmaking that had failed miserably. Even then he had known that politeness required him to bring something to The Event, which is how he'd always thought of it.

His heart hadn't been in any of those occasions, though.

With Lois, he'd been enamored and not thinking clearly. He'd been lucky to arrive wearing both shoes. Once he'd even forgotten his hat. The other girls? He had operated from duty. First because he thought he should, and then because other people thought he should. He'd known before the evening started that things wouldn't work out, so it hadn't much mattered what he'd taken as a token gift.

Tonight was different.

Looking at the two items lying next to him on his buggy seat, he prayed he'd chosen well. Julia had looked so vulnerable, almost afraid, standing at the front of the store before she had seen him walking toward her. Caleb didn't know how this was going to end or what God had in mind, but he did know he wanted to decrease Julia Beechy's burdens, not add to them.

He drove straight to the barn because Red seemed to behave himself better there. After releasing the horse from the harness and leading him to a shaded pasture, he walked back to his buggy and retrieved his gifts. By the time he walked toward the front porch steps, Julia was waiting for him.

She looked different somehow, and it surprised him again that he'd never taken the time to notice her before. Her clothes were proper for a Plain woman—but hadn't she always worn the same color? He thought it was a practical gray with a black apron, but he couldn't remember. He couldn't think clearly as he walked up the steps of the porch. Today her dress was a dark green and her apron a light gray. It wasn't the same thing she'd worn to the store, so she must have changed, as he had. He could barely see her hair, which was pulled back. Maybe an inch of chestnut brown showed in front—combed and pinned, but a few curly strands teased out from the nape of her prayer *kapp*.

He'd guess her height to be somewhere between five foot seven and five foot eight—certainly well under his five foot eleven. And though her brown eyes often clouded with worry, he didn't see any lines yet...only the freckles sprinkled across the bridge of her nose.

"Forget something?" she asked.

"No. Why?"

"You're standing there looking as if you left something back in your buggy, or maybe you aren't sure about coming up." The smile teasing on her lips grew.

It eased his heart to see that the tension from earlier in the morning was gone, at least for the moment.

"Let's see." He shifted the flowers to his left hand, the hand still holding the basket, and began patting his pockets. "I did have a list. I'd written down the addresses of houses I could stop at, and I wasn't sure if this was the one or if maybe...say, do I smell oatmeal cookies?"

"You do."

"This is the house then. The one with the beautiful woman, *gut* cook, and fresh oatmeal cookies."

Julia's eyes narrowed, and he wondered if he'd pushed too hard. "Flattery will not get you up these steps, Caleb Zook."

"How about flowers for your *mamm* and fresh raspberries for you?"

"*Ya.* I believe that will do it."

They walked into the house, shoulder to shoulder, and Caleb wondered if that was what it would be like should they marry.

"Where did you find the berries? And how did you know—"

"You like to cook, so I guessed you might like them. Folks put out signs on my route, and Mary Stutzman had more than she could use."

"Mary? You deliver to the east side of Pebble Creek?"

"*Ya.* East and west. I deliver to all the Amish families, and Kendrick uses the truck to deliver to anyone farther out than I want to take Red."

They had made it to the kitchen, and the smell of baking caused Caleb's stomach to rumble.

"I believe he's hungry, Julia." Ada sat at the table. What was left of the evening light shone through the window positioned next to the stove. It fell on her like a blessing. "Feed him. He brought you flowers."

"*Nein.* I've already eaten dinner, though the cookies smell *wunderbaar.*" He set the small bunch of flowers in Ada's hands. She couldn't straighten her fingers, but she pawed at them and leaned forward to inhale their fragrance.

"The berries are for Julia," he explained. "But the flowers are for you."

"Sky Blue Aster—butterflies like this one." Ada pushed her small glasses up so she could see better. Leaning forward, she ran her fingers over the blooms. "Julia, we can dry these and put them in your garden next spring. These taller ones are Spotted Joe-Pye Weed. I haven't seen it in ages. The blooms are such a deep purple. You must have found them growing near the creek."

"Yes, near Aaron's cabins. There's a place that stays moist nearly all the time. I saw them when I went home this afternoon to..." He cleared his throat, not wanting to go into detail about how he'd taken off work early and spent time cleaning up and changing clothes. He was beginning to feel like a seventeen-year-old on his *rumspringa.* "I hope you like them."

"Let's put them in water." Julia slipped a mason jar onto the table and placed the bouquet in it. They stood there in the last of the day's light, a bundle of color against the approaching darkness.

"Honor and majesty surround Him." Ada's voice was softer than the breeze coming through the window. "Strength and beauty fill His sanctuary."

Caleb glanced at Julia, uncertain how to respond, but she shook her head.

"*Mamm*. Let me help you to bed now."

"Is it so late already?"

"*Ya*."

"But the flowers—"

"Will be here in the morning."

He offered to help. Ada was still fairly mobile, though, and she waved him away. Her mind might wander. She might use the Psalms as a sort of guidepost to help her find her direction, but her body seemed determined to continue plodding along each day. She stood, grasping her cane, and walked out of the room in front of Julia. When she reached the doorway of the kitchen, she turned and wagged a finger at him.

"If you decide you want that hair cut, I believe I can still find my scissors."

Before he could respond, she'd crept on down the hall, explaining to Julia she wasn't being rude by offering her services.

Caleb was left running his fingers through his too long hair and staring at the jar full of wildflowers.

$\backsim$ Chapter 11 $\backsim$

Ten minutes later Caleb was sitting on the front porch in one of the rockers. Julia was perched on the other. A plate of still-warm oatmeal raisin cookies sat between them as well as a glass of cold milk for him and water for her.

"Go ahead and eat them. It's plain you want to."

"*Ya*, but I'm trying to be polite and let you go first." Caleb smiled, reached for a cookie, and popped the entire thing in his mouth. Closing his eyes, he allowed the flavors of sugar, oatmeal, nutmeg, and cinnamon to please his senses, reminding him of home and simpler times.

"I'm going to assume by the look on your face that you approve?"

"Oh, *ya*. I approve, Julia. You're a *wunderbaar gut* cook. Where did you learn? From Ada?"

"Some." She drew the word out as she made circles on the arm of the rocker with her finger. "My mother cooked as well as most women, but I could tell from the time I was a teenager she didn't much enjoy doing it. So it seemed natural for me to take over that chore. Baking was something that came natural to me. Soon I was trying my hand at casseroles and other types of dishes. I like old recipes, but I also enjoy experimenting." She hesitated before adding, "It's why I want to open a café. I know I'd be good at it, and I think it would provide us with some financial security. My father left enough money to provide for the two of us, but I still feel I should be contributing."

Caleb downed half of his glass of milk and devoured another cookie. "You've had this dream a long time."

"I have."

"And you're worried that if you marry me, you won't be able to pursue it."

She studied him for what seemed like a long time. As he waited for her answer, he could make out the sound of a chipmunk in the bushes near the porch.

"Will I? If we were..." She stumbled over the next word. "If we were married, would I still be able to open the café?"

Wiping his mouth with the napkin she'd provided, Caleb shot one last look at the plate of cookies. He would have liked to have eaten more, but he sensed they were down to the serious part of their evening. For all he knew, she would need to go in soon to be with Ada.

"If it's important to you and something that financially we could afford to do, then yes—I think *we* will be able to give it a try." When she started to interrupt him, he held up his hand. "I like your idea, Julia. I liked it from the very first moment you told me before I even thought I might be involved."

He studied the old porch, which could use some repairs, not to mention a coat of paint. "But we need to make a list of what our start-up costs would be for a new business, how much money we have, and how much we're willing to risk."

"*Our* start-up costs? *Our* money?"

"Ya. Together we should decide how low we're willing to take our finances before we would admit the café is not going to work—at least for this time and place."

Julia rubbed more vigorously at the arm of her chair. "You sound as if we're already married."

"That's what we're talking about, though. Aren't we?"

"*Ya.* I suppose we are."

"This would be a union in every way. Together we could make a go of it, and I think it would work. But we have to be open to the possibility that it might not." He nodded toward the lane in front of her house. "I see a lot of businesses start up and close in the first few months, usually because people haven't thought out all the possible outcomes. Failure is a possibility, though we'll work and pray for success."

"Our...our marriage would be about more than the café, though. How could you be willing to do this, Caleb?" She had been staring off into the gathering darkness, but now she turned and looked at him directly. "How can you be willing to commit yourself to me and to my mother?"

Caleb hesitated before he answered. He'd asked himself that same question a dozen times, and he still hadn't found the words to explain his answer. "Neither of us is getting younger—"

"So I'm your last chance?" Her voice rose, startling a nearby bird.

"*Nein.* I told you of my prayer—my plea for a *freind.* I didn't ask *Gotte* for a *fraa,* though I remember thinking how lonely I was, how it wasn't *gut* to be alone. But marriage? I stopped thinking of that a few years ago, I suppose. Somehow, in my mind, that wasn't going to happen."

"Surely there were women who were interested back in Indiana."

"*Ya,* but there was always a reason why it didn't work out. How about you?"

Julia put both of her hands into her lap and stared down at them. "The same, at first. Lately, with my father and now my mother, I haven't exactly been marriage material."

"That's not true. I could see at Sunday's luncheon that several men would be interested. Why have you never considered them before?"

She shook her head so hard he could see the strings to her prayer *kapp* stirring in the small rays of light from the sitting room window. "They say they are interested, but they wouldn't be. Once they visited here, I wouldn't hear from them again. I'm not saying they are bad men, but if they saw *mamm* and her confusion, and then took a *gut* look at her hands and this house..."

She paused long enough to also look around the porch, as if she were seeing it for the first time. "I know it looks fine from the road, but up close the years of neglect show. I'm aware of the repairs it needs. *Nein.* They would change their mind, and I half expect you will too."

Caleb scooted his chair so it was facing hers, so their knees were touching, and he reached for her hand. He held it as he had by the river at Aaron's house. "I won't be changing my mind. When I commit to a thing, I stay with it."

Something in Julia's heart flipped over at those words. *"When I commit to a thing, I stay with it."*

Could she trust him? Did she dare?

No doubt he *thought* he meant them, but then people said things they *thought* were true all the time. Time and trouble often proved them wrong.

"Julia, look at me."

It took more strength than harnessing Missy, but she raised her eyes to his.

"Marrying this way is unusual. The one thing we need is to trust each other. You need to trust me when I say I won't run away from your problems."

She jumped up from her seat and walked to the porch railing. She needed to feel the old boards beneath her palms. This house and her parents were all she had known for so long. Now she was supposed to trust Caleb? She barely knew him.

He was beside her before she realized it, his voice low and close. When his hand covered hers, she looked down. The sight of his calloused hand on top of hers nearly took her breath away. This was all happening so fast, and so many things could go wrong.

"I see Ada's hands and also her confusion at times. And while this home needs certain repairs, it's a *gut* solid house. Together we can make a life here, if that is what you want."

Tears filled her eyes, blurring her vision.

"You won't make me move?" The words tore from her heart, scratching at her throat as she spoke them.

"Why would I make you move?"

She shook her head and swiped at her cheeks.

"Let me do that." He reached forward and wiped her tears away with his thumbs.

His hands on her skin sent her emotions scurrying in a dozen different directions. She struggled to remain focused, to control her fears and seek the answers she needed.

"Why would I make you move, Julia?"

"Promise me we can stay in Pebble Creek." Staring into his eyes, she added, "You don't own a home here, or...or back in Indiana. Do you?"

Caleb laughed. "*Nein.* I live in Aaron's barn at the cabins."

"I couldn't bear to leave this place."

"You have my word. Wisconsin, and Pebble Creek, will be our home."

It was all she needed to hear.

It was more important even than the café, though she heard his promise for that as well.

When he took a step forward and softly kissed her lips, she didn't move. Instead, she held her breath, wondering what she was supposed to do. He ran a thumb along her bottom lip, kissed her once more, and said, "We should go in. You're shivering."

They might not love each other, but he was a kind man. He wouldn't desert her.

She knew that as he helped her gather up the dishes and they walked back into the house.

Her life had come down to two choices—living here with Caleb or living in Pennsylvania with people she didn't even know.

Which meant her choice was made.

Together they walked into the kitchen. She excused herself and hurried upstairs to check on Ada, who was fast asleep. She had come back down the stairs and was walking through the sewing room when she spied him, standing next to the calendar on the kitchen wall.

Her hands shaking slightly, she pulled it off the small hook, and they carried it over to the table.

"Fall communion is mid-October, and if I've heard the rumors correctly, there are already many weddings scheduled for the end of the month. Not everyone has published their intentions yet—"

"Then how do you know?"

"When you deliver groceries, you hear things." Caleb rubbed his hand over his jaw. "And you see extra plots of celery growing."

"We're the more progressive side of the district, but many traditions remain the same. Families still make the creamed celery for wedding meals and put it on tables as center pieces too."

"It's the same in Monroe. Lydia's *schweschder* Clara works at the cabins. She's always full of news, and she has talked of nothing but announcements and weddings for weeks."

"I don't hear that much during Sunday meals, but then I am usually serving food or helping my mother. I didn't realize we had that many couples of marrying age."

Caleb nodded, still studying the calendar. "If we consider both the east and west side of our district, I suspect nearly every Tuesday and Thursday from here to here is full." Caleb ran his finger down the daily squares through November.

"We could have two in one day."

"Yes. We sometimes did that in Indiana as well. Or…" He turned the page back and tapped the first Tuesday after fall communion— the third Tuesday in October. "Or we could ask Bishop Atlee if this day would be acceptable."

"So soon …"

"*Ya.* Do you need more time to prepare?"

Julia brushed her palm down the length of her apron, pausing to touch the stitches on the hand-sewn hem. Then she admitted, "I'll only have a few announcements to deliver."

"Same here."

"As far as a dress, *mamm* and I can whip that up fairly quickly."

"Doesn't seem as if Ada can sew with the arthritis so bad."

"True, but she's wonderful at giving me directions while I cut and pin and stitch the seams."

Caleb laughed. "I could have guessed she was very *gut* at directing. She also told me I needed to have my hair cut."

"I'm sorry about that. She shouldn't have—"

"She was right!" Caleb combed his fingers through his bangs, a slightly embarrassed smile playing on his lips. "I've been meaning to take care of it, but there's been no pressing need until now."

Julia again touched the October square. "What of the field work? The crops will be in? Otherwise families wouldn't be able to attend."

"*Ya.* Corn is coming in this week and next—I've picked up some extra work helping. Hay is nearly done as well. According to Aaron, it will be harvested a few weeks early this year."

"We need to ask Bishop Atlee to make the church announcement, and there's no service this Sunday."

"*Gut* point. He could do it the following week."

"*Ya.*" Julia pressed her hand to her stomach, trying to quell the butterflies circling at full speed. She had to suppress the urge to run to the drawer in the kitchen, pull out her pad of paper, and begin making lists. "October then, the third Tuesday."

"A little over a month from today." Caleb's smile told her all she needed to know. They were actually going to do this. "It's a date."

He smacked his hand on the table, as if he'd just won a hand of Dutch Blitz rather than settled on the day of their wedding. "That will give us plenty of time to see to the marriage license."

"I hadn't even thought of—"

"Aaron told me all about it." He explained to her what documents they would need. "And we'll have to go to Sparta."

"Sparta?"

"Ya. That's where the county clerk's office is."

Julia pinched the bridge of her nose. Already there were complications. "How are we going to get to Sparta? It's twenty miles away."

"I'll handle the transportation, but we should go as soon as possible. I can get off early Thursday if that will work for you."

"I suppose I could go then, but I might need to bring my mother."

"No problem. The three of us will have dinner in town together."

"I don't think—"

Caleb stood and reached for his hat. "Our new life is an occasion to celebrate, and it will include all three of us. There will be much work to do before and after. For one afternoon, it will be *gut* to pause and enjoy ourselves."

Julia walked him to the door, her mind dizzy with dozens of details and questions. All of those faded when Caleb stepped out into the night. She thought he'd left, but he darted back across the doorway to squeeze her hand and kiss her once more on the lips.

Without another word he was gone.

She was left standing on the front porch, listening to the night birds, the beating of her heart, and his whistling as he walked toward the barn to retrieve Red.

Chapter 12

Though she was somewhat overwhelmed by the attention, Julia appreciated everyone's kindness.

Bishop Atlee had announced her and Caleb's intentions to marry at the end of the church service that morning. It seemed a fairy tale that their wedding was to take place in a few weeks. Only twelve days had passed since they had spoken on her front porch and she'd agreed to marry this man standing a few feet from her.

Caleb was still being congratulated by the men in their district.

The women had been every bit as excited and had reluctantly left Julia to go and help with placing out the food. It was the last Sunday of September, and though the weather was warm and pleasant—easily reaching into the seventies—there was a hint of fall in the air. Soon they would be eating indoors instead of out under the trees. It seemed fitting that this Sunday the service was at Bishop Atlee's home, the same place she had come to seek answers when she'd first learned of her parents' decree.

"Why aren't you helping?" A young girl, not yet in her teens, with somber brown eyes and brown hair peeking out from her *kapp* stood in front of her. In the crook of her arm she held two objects—her Bible and what looked to be a drawing tablet.

"You must be Grace."

"*Ya.* We live on the east side, but we came to Bishop Atlee's church today because of my cousin. He's my *mamm*'s nephew so I suppose Seth is my cousin." She scrunched her nose at the last word. "Seems as though lots of folks are getting married."

"You don't approve?"

"I guess so, for someone like you." Grace popped her hand over her mouth.

"Someone older."

"That came out wrong."

"It's all right." Julia glanced over at Seth, who stood beside Caleb. There was more than twenty years difference in their ages. Bishop Atlee had made a comment about Seth not having yet turned twenty. Caleb had turned forty a month earlier. Atlee had reminded the congregation to pray for both men, for both couples, as they entered this new phase in their lives. He had chuckled and said there was no guessing when the Lord would steer your path in a different direction.

Looking at both Caleb and Seth, she didn't envy Seth his youth. For Julia that had been a time of heartache and indecision. No, she much preferred the age she was and the man standing beside Seth. She was learning that Caleb was steady and dependable. Both were things she longed for in her life. His age, though? That had surprised her a little. She would have guessed him to be in his mid-thirties, not forty. In the last week, she'd replayed the scene in her mind several times—the moment when they had presented their documents at the county clerk's office in Sparta.

"*Is forty old?*" *The look on Caleb's face said he hadn't given it too much thought.*

"*I hope not. I'm thirty-seven, which is only three years younger. I certainly don't feel old.*"

"*But you were surprised at my age.*" *His smile proved he wasn't offended.*

"*Maybe a little.*"

Caleb reached for her hand and entwined his fingers with hers. They were walking out of the courthouse. Ada was sitting on a bench in the sun, waiting for them. He didn't speak again until they were alone on the sidewalk, and then he stepped closer to her.

"I think you are much more beautiful than the younger women, Julia."

Her eyes had widened at the compliment, and she'd felt heat rushing to her cheeks.

He'd reached out and touched her face. "The age we are? It's the age we are supposed to be. The age Gotte knew we would find each other."

She was certain he would kiss her, there in broad daylight standing outside the courthouse building. He'd wanted to. There was no doubt about it.

But instead he looped her arm through his, patted her hand, and guided her toward the bench where Ada was sitting and watching some children play on the grass across the lawn. While they'd eaten at the restaurant in Sparta and even on the drive home, she'd caught him glancing her way, looking at her differently. She wasn't sure how to react to his expression, one wavering between playfulness and desire.

It still confused her, still sent goose bumps dancing down her arms, when she thought about that day.

Turning to Grace, she aimed for a reassuring smile. "Seth is rather young, but sometimes young is all right. Occasionally people know what they want at an early age."

"That's what my *dat* said. He said *Gotte* has different plans for different people."

Julia had been walking toward a large red maple tree that stood apart from the tables where they would eat. She'd hoped for some time alone and a moment or two of quiet, but she found she didn't mind Grace's company.

"I know your *mamm* and *dat*. At least, I've met them before when they've visited our side of the district, but you've grown since then."

"Ya. My *grossdaddi* says I'm growing faster than a fawn in springtime."

"Indeed."

They walked in silence until they reached the shade of the tree.

All of its leaves had changed to a vibrant red, but they hadn't fallen yet. Their portion of the state would be awash with tourists in the next few weeks, coming to see the beauty of a Wisconsin fall.

"So how did you get out of serving?" Grace held up her pad. "Not that I mind helping when it's my turn, but I'd rather be drawing if I have the chance."

"Oh. I see." Julia didn't answer immediately. When the other women had first pushed her away from the serving line, she hadn't known what to do. Now she realized they probably understood she needed a moment to catch her breath. "It seems when you're about to be married, you're given the week off from helping."

"So everyone can talk to you and tell you how happy they are about your marriage?"

"Correct."

The girl was observant, maybe because she watched what others were doing before she took out her drawing pencils.

"I suppose that's okay, but too much attention makes me squirmy."

"That may be why I decided to take a walk."

Grace's eyes rounded. "Am I interrupting your alone time?"

"*Nein.*"

"My *mamm* needs alone time every once in a while, especially now that Rachel is walking and into everything. Would you like to see a drawing of her?"

"I would."

They sat down together under the tree, and Grace opened up her tablet and began turning pages, searching for a drawing of Rachel. She paused when she reached one of her mother. "I did this one last week."

The rendering was from the back as her mother hung laundry on the line. What was surprising was the detail in the drawing—right down to a rip in the cuff of a pair of men's work pants drying in the sunshine.

"May I?" she asked.

"Sure." Grace shrugged and handed over the tablet.

Julia wasn't sure what she expected to see. A child's drawings, perhaps stick figures, with some shading if she were sophisticated. She certainly didn't anticipate the type of artwork one might see in an *Englischer*'s book sold at Amish Anthem. Had someone mentioned little Grace's drawing ability? If so, Julia hadn't paid any attention. She'd been caught up in her own life.

She flipped through the pages rather quickly, and then she went back to the beginning and moved slowly from one drawing to the next. Julia finally stopped at a page which showed Aaron's cabins. "This is beautiful."

"*Danki*. I like catching the river in different lights. It seems...to me it seems like a living thing. Do you know what I mean? It's like Rachel."

Grace reached over and turned the pages back to a drawing of her sister. It caught the back of the toddler as she attempted to climb up on a chair. "She looks different to me from one week to the next, though I know she's the same. Parts of her are changed, though. When she was born I could hold her in my lap, and now she's scrambling all over the place."

"You love your *schweschder*."

"I do, and I love Pebble Creek too. My *dat* and I lived in Indiana before, and that was nice. This is home, though, and Pebble Creek is one of the best parts. In some ways it stays the same throughout the year. Then again, when I look at it, I have the feeling it has changed from one moment to the next."

Julia glanced toward the tables. She saw Caleb shielding his eyes and looking for her. They were about to say the blessing, and she would need to sit with him today. It was, after all, the church service when they had announced their wedding plans. Her heart skipped, literally jumped over one beat to the other, at the thought.

"We should go back." After she stood, she checked the back of Grace's dress to make sure there wasn't grass and twigs on it. "You're *gut*."

"And so are you, except for those beetles." Grace laughed and pointed to the small red and black critters.

Julia swiped herself clean, and then they walked back toward the group of church members, which was larger than usual—due to the wedding announcements, both hers and Seth's.

"Grace, if I asked you to draw something for me, would you do it?"

"I could try."

"Caleb and I are going to open a café, and we could use some artwork on the menus. Also, I might like some flyers to post around town."

"Sure. I did something like that for Lydia and Aaron."

"*Wunderbaar.* I'll talk with your *mamm* to see if we can set up a time."

Grace stopped and tilted her head. "Is your place near Pebble Creek?"

"It is. Our back pasture goes right down to it."

"And I could draw that too?"

"Certainly."

Grace's smile widened. "Then I can't wait."

Julia thought she would feel awkward during the meal, sitting with Caleb on one side and her *mamm* on the other. She didn't, though. There was so much talking and good-natured teasing taking place that she didn't have much time to focus on her emotions.

How long had it been since she sat in the middle of a group rather than on the fringe? And was it because of the group, or because she had pulled herself out of everyone's circle for so long? Regardless, the faces around her were all friendly now. No one seemed surprised at their announcement, but then why should they be?

The Amish grapevine worked well.

Plus, Caleb had taken off from work twice, and certainly people had noticed that. Once so he could go to Sparta for the license, and another time to pick up a load of supplies he brought to her house to begin work there. His buggy had been filled with paint, lumber, nails, and other items Julia couldn't have named.

When Julia and Ada had gone to Irene Gingerich's home to see if she had wedding dress material for sale, the woman had met them at the door and congratulated Julia before they had spoken a word. Yes, it seemed everyone had already heard about their plans to marry, and everyone approved.

Ada was the happiest of all. She sat in the fall sunshine, a shawl wrapped around her shoulders and her eyes nearly squeezed shut, she was smiling so. Julia and Caleb might still be finding their way, still answering the big questions, but Ada was convinced God had satisfied every need.

With all the excitement, Julia was surprised to glance down at her plate to find she'd eaten nearly everything she'd placed on it. The way her emotions were hopscotching, she'd been certain she wouldn't be able to swallow a bite.

"We need to borrow Julia," Lydia said, rising from the table by pushing both hands down on the seat. Her stomach protruded to such an extent that they'd had to place the bench back a little so she'd fit.

"Borrow me?"

"*Ya*. Wedding details." Miriam patted Gabe's arm as she dumped Rachel in his lap. "Watch this one, would you? She's faster than that new mare you bought."

"My *dochder*? Fast?" Rachel reached up for a handful of his beard and laughed when Gabe kissed her on the cheek. "You can count on us, *fraa*. Three men can watch one *boppli*."

"Hmm. I may have heard that before."

"She only escaped the one time, and we found her sleeping next to a pile of fresh hay."

Miriam waved as she tugged Julia away from the table.

"Where are we going?"

"To talk about your wedding." Lydia linked arms with her on the right as Miriam clasped her hand on the left. "We're practically going to be in-laws because Aaron and Caleb don't have family here."

Julia hadn't thought of that. She should add it to the list she kept, but what would she list it under—become closer to new family?

"And Gabe goes to Aaron's every time he comes to see my *bruder* David. We're all going to be very close." Miriam patted her hand. "Now tell us what you have ready for the wedding and what you need."

"Oh. I don't know. We've finished my dress."

"*Gut*. I'm not much for sewing right now with this stomach." Lydia shook her head. "I can crochet and knit, but sewing seems to fall off my lap. What else have you done?"

"I've written out the invitations, and we'll deliver them this week. Our guest list isn't very long."

"I'm sure your invitations are beautiful," Lydia assured her. "It's been interesting to see Caleb spend his days off at your place. Usually every free hour is spent down on the creek, angling for a fresh supper until it's too dark to see his line. That man enjoys fishing more than anyone I've ever known."

"Is he going to keep working at the store?" Miriam asked.

They had reached the front porch, the same place Julia had sat with Bishop Atlee nearly three weeks ago. Climbing the steps, they each took a rocker. Miriam pulled hers closer so they formed a tight little circle.

"*Ya*. He's going to stay on there at least at first, until we see how the café is doing."

Miriam beamed at her. "So many changes at once. All *gut*, but a lot to digest."

"The next few weeks are going to be especially difficult for him. There's so much that needs to be done at the house to prepare for the wedding and also because we plan to open the café the week after we're married."

"Gabe's crops are in. Maybe he can help." Miriam leaned back in her rocker. "I'll speak to him about it."

"Tell us what we can do." Lydia folded her hands over the top of her stomach. "Caleb told Aaron about your lists. I know you can't have it all done."

"He told—"

Lydia waved away her surprise. "Men talk as much as women do, only somewhat differently. Believe me, I know. I hear them as they work."

"I don't know what you mean."

"Oh, I think I do, but go ahead and explain, Lydia." Miriam set her chair to rocking.

"One moment they'll be discussing us—who they claim not to understand. The next, they'll jump over to a fish they caught last week or the newest type of seed to use in their field. It's not as if we don't matter more than their hobbies or work. It's more as if one naturally leads to the other, and we're all part and parcel of their world."

"So I'm on the same level of conversation topics as a fish?" Julia pretended to be offended, but she couldn't quite pull it off. She was picturing Caleb as he had stared off at the bend in Pebble Creek one evening, and then he went back to working on the side of their barn that had needed mending. She had been able to see the longing in his eyes, but he had chosen to help her instead.

"Pretty much." Lydia rubbed at the right side of her stomach.

"Elbow?" Miriam asked.

"That or he has a pointed head. Now tell us what's left on your lists, Julia."

So she did. She didn't have any trouble remembering. She could close her eyes and picture both pages quite well. There had been several moments of panic when she'd wondered how she could accomplish everything and still care for her mother and deliver the invitations, though there were precious few to deliver.

As she spoke, they divided what was left to do among the three of them. Julia was astonished that neither Miriam nor Lydia balked at the amount of work left to accomplish.

How had she ever thought she could do it all on her own? How had she ever thought she could do it all in time?

She had checked off every item left to do, envisioning it clearly in her mind, when Lydia cleared her throat. Opening her eyes, she saw the look pass between her two new *freinden* and realized now she could call them that—God had blessed her once again.

"What?"

"I'm thinking that we can do all this, but there's the harvest and perhaps you might want to consider..."

"What she's trying to say is you might think about expanding your guest list. We don't want to tell you what to do, but people care about you Julia. They want to celebrate this day with you, especially the people from your congregation." Miriam glanced out toward the folks still milling around the table. "Not that you have to invite them all, but together we make up a family of believers."

Lydia nodded in agreement. "And inviting more guests means more invitations, more food, and more work!"

Julia's heart sank. "It's too much to do in too short a time, isn't it?"

"*Nein.* Not at all." Miriam reached out and covered her hand with her own. "My *mamm* will pitch in, and don't forget I have lots of family here—nieces we can call on to help, plus three *bruders* who have wives."

"My *mamm* will be happy to help as well," Lydia said.

"But Clara and Seth are marrying too—"

"Their wedding is two weeks after yours, and we've been planning it for months. *Nein.* What I'm thinking is that we can cut the work you're trying to do in half." Lydia stood and stretched, placing her hand at the small of her back.

"In half?"

"*Ya,* if you'll allow someone else to take care of the cooking. I know it's what you do, and I know you do it well, but you can't expect to prepare your house and cook for your own wedding. It's not possible."

Julia opened her mouth and then shut it again. Finally she managed, "Who—"

Miriam squeezed her hand. "Let us worry about who. We'll be in charge of the cake and the menu, if you trust us."

"Ya. Of course I do."

"You can jot us a few notes for what you had in mind, and we'll take it from there." Lydia looked pleased at the thought.

"And we'll divide up some of these tasks among the men. Aaron can bring the church pews. Seth can see that the property is nicely mowed and trimmed."

Julia fiddled with her apron, overwhelmed by their offer. It was tradition to have the wedding at the bride's home, and she had thought her house was ready until she'd started looking at it as a guest might. There was much she'd let slip since her father had passed, and probably for years before that. There was too much work for one woman to do, and maybe that was proof also that *mamm* was correct in saying it would have been difficult for her to live there alone.

Once they had set a date for the wedding, she'd realized it meant a lot of work. In her mind if she awoke earlier each day, worked harder, and went to bed later, she could somehow finish it all, but even with Caleb's help she had been falling further behind.

"Are you sure you want to do all of this?"

"We do. That's why we offered," Lydia said.

"Seems like *gut* solutions." Miriam stood as well. "But only if you like our ideas."

Julia pulled in a deep breath and looked from Lydia to Miriam. The thing that convinced her to agree was that she knew they wouldn't run over her. They wouldn't make any decisions she wasn't happy about, and besides, Julia wanted to make it *through* the wedding. In her heart, she was more interested in reaching the other side, in starting a new life together with Caleb.

If, as a group, they could help to make the wedding day a success and her place presentable, that's what she wanted to do. It wasn't that she was prideful, but Caleb had shown her that there were certain areas on the porch that were rotten—unsafe even. And the grounds, other than her garden, had been utterly neglected.

What they were suggesting would solve the problem of preparing for the wedding and also help with meeting the deadline they had set to open the café the week after they were married.

"I'll want to speak with Caleb first, but if he agrees, then yes! I say yes."

⸆ Chapter 13 ⸅

S haron walked along the side of the four-lane road, determined not to cry. The darkness of the night seemed to close around her like a bad dream, and she had no way to tell what time it was. She hoped she was walking the right direction. She hadn't paid much attention when James was driving. She didn't think she had been this way before, at least not recently, and she didn't know what the road names were—she hadn't noticed earlier.

There were a lot of things she hadn't noticed.

At first her anger had kept her tears at bay.

She had been so mad when they had stopped at the convenience store in Romney that tears were the furthest thing from her mind. James hadn't seen her angry before, but he caught a good dose then.

The night had gone nothing like she'd expected. Why had she thought it would be the same as before? Because he'd said it would be, that was why. Because he had lied. She kicked a rock with her foot, kicked it hard enough to feel the impact on her toe.

Now she had to walk with a sore toe. Not very bright at all. In fact, it was stupid! Just like slipping out of her grandparents' window had been stupid. What had she been thinking?

She'd been thinking about his blue eyes. Colossally stupid.

The single night at her grandparents' had stretched into a week. It had been harsh punishment—*ya*. She loved her *grossmammi* and

101

grossdaddi, but they lived so far out in the country, and she couldn't see her *freinden* or speak with anyone her own age. Then there were the pigs she had to help tend—feeding them scraps, changing the hay where they slept, and cleaning their pens. The smell was disgusting. The entire week had been awful.

As bad as it was, she was scheduled to go home the next day. She'd told herself she wouldn't sneak out with James, that she would walk away if he even spoke to her at church...but then he'd stood in front of her and stared at her with those eyes the color of the sky when it was clear and you could see into forever. He'd slipped the note into her hand and whistled as he'd walked away.

Her heart had been thumping so hard, she was sure her grandparents would hear it during the buggy ride on the way home. They hadn't. She'd waited until after she was supposed to be reading her Bible in her room, and then she had pulled out the sheet of paper with his words of love.

All lies! She knew that now.

Though the instructions had been clear enough. She was to meet him on the next farm at exactly nine o'clock. Sneaking out hadn't been an issue because her grandparents fell asleep before eight. No, the real problem had started when she'd opened the door to the old truck.

"What is that smell?"

"I don't smell anything."

Then he'd leaned over to kiss her, and she'd backed up against the door. *"You've been drinking? Already? And you're driving?"*

"Relax, Sharon. You sound like my mamm." He'd dropped her cell phone into her lap, winked, and kissed her again.

She placed the phone in her purse and buckled her seat belt tightly across her lap as he peeled out of the drive. It was a good thing her grandparents were nearly deaf or he would have wakened them, even if he was next door at the abandoned farm. How had he managed to get her phone back? He'd mentioned he knew one of the clerks who worked at the store. She'd love to hear the story—

James reached for the radio dial and turned it up so loud Sharon knew they wouldn't be talking, which was fine with her. She appreciated the return of her phone, but she thought drinking and driving was unbelievably stupid. She hoped he'd had only one. Certainly one couldn't do much harm. She'd watch him, though. If he started driving erratically, she was getting out of that truck, and she would try to take the keys with her.

Instead of turning south onto the highway, James crossed it.

"I thought we were going to Indianapolis," she shouted. When they'd gone before, the trip had taken a little over an hour's drive from her home in Monroe. She couldn't be sure, but it seemed they were going a different direction.

"You thought wrong, sweetheart. I have a surprise for you tonight."

Sharon reached for the radio dial and turned the volume down so he could hear her. "I don't want a surprise, James. I want to go to the movies and the diner. Where is everyone else?"

He grinned, turned the radio back up, and revved the engine, pushing their speed ten miles over the limit as he shrugged his shoulders.

What was with him?

A few minutes later they pulled into a convenience store parking lot. She almost thanked him when he turned off the ignition. The silence was like a balm on her ears.

"I need to run inside for a minute." He hopped out of the truck, glancing left and then right as he did. "Want anything?"

"Nein."

Walking around to her door, he opened it, leaned inside, and kissed her. Although she hated the beer aftertaste, she had to admit his kiss still had the power to send her pulse skipping.

So she sat there hoping—like a child—that the night might improve. When she saw him walk out of the store with the six-pack tucked under his arm, her heart sank all the way past her Englisch blue jeans, which she'd smuggled to her grandparents, to the bottom of her shoes.

"How did you buy that? You're not old enough to purchase alcohol."

"Fake ID. Wanna see it?" James grinned as he popped a top and set the remaining five cans of beer on the seat between them. The cans were still tucked into the plastic ring and cold against her arm. "You can have one if you want."

"No, I don't want. And where did you get a fake ID? Why did you get one? And why are you drinking while you're driving?"

Instead of answering, James downed half of what was in the can, and then he turned toward her, his back against the door of the truck. "You know, Sharon, you're real pretty and I like you, but you're not going to be much fun if all you're going to do is nag."

She was so angry she thought the top of her head might fly completely apart. "Not much fun?"

"Ya, now loosen up a little. I could have brought along my mamm *or* schweschder *if I wanted to be lectured."*

"That's it." Sharon released her seat belt, opened the door of the truck, snatched the remaining beer cans, and slammed the door as hard as she could. The window made a satisfying rattle when she did. "I'm taking this back inside, and I'm telling the clerk you bought it illegally."

"You wouldn't dare—"

She never found out if James started after her or not. Her heart thumping wildly, she'd fled into the store. She'd explained all about the fake ID to the clerk, who had stared at her as if she were one of those cartoon characters they had watched in the movie theater. He'd finally accepted what was left of the six pack—five beers still in the plastic ring—and set it on the floor behind the counter, no doubt to take home later.

Not her problem.

He didn't look stupid enough to drink and drive. What he did in his own home was his business.

Feeling satisfied that she'd handled the situation well, she marched back outside and stared at the empty parking lot.

James had left.

Left her alone at a convenience store in Romney, Wisconsin.

Left her in the middle of the night.

Sharon kicked at another rock, glancing up as fat raindrops began to splat against the asphalt.

It was a good thing she'd had her purse slung over her shoulder when she'd hopped out of the truck. At least she had a little money and her cell phone. Stepping off the road, out of the beam of any oncoming traffic, she checked the display.

No missed calls. No messages. No reason to stop walking.

She turned the phone off, something she'd fallen in the habit of doing to save the battery. Who knew when she'd be able to charge it again?

Where was she? And why was the rain now coming down harder?

Oh, how she wished for her prayer *kapp* to cover her head. The steady drizzle against her scalp left her cold, and she was even more miserable than she had been ten minutes ago. Not to mention the ridiculous *Englisch* clothes she'd worn were clinging to her like wet laundry pinned to a clothesline.

Maybe she should call the phone shack near her parents' home. It was late, though. No one would hear it ring. If she wanted anyone to come and fetch her, she would have to call her friend Joana. She lived two farms down from her parents. She could run down and tell them, or Joana's father could. The thought of involving so many people caused Sharon's stomach to flip up and over.

Maybe she could keep walking. Maybe someone would offer her a ride. Her shoes began to squish as the rain increased.

How could James leave her? And why had he been acting so strangely? She'd heard that boys behaved badly while on their *rumspringa*, but he had changed so drastically since their last evening together. He hadn't been kind or considerate or attentive to her at all. It was almost as if he wasn't sure he wanted her along. Why had he asked her then?

Her tears mixed with the rain and slid in rivulets down her face. She stopped under a streetlight, peering into the direction she was walking and then back at the route she had come. Surely there was somewhere she could wait out the storm, but all she saw was black-top road, and up ahead a flashing caution light. Maybe if she walked a little farther, she could figure out where she was.

She hurried through the storm toward the intersection, wrapping her arms around her middle in a futile effort to keep warm. Thunder rumbled across the sky, and the storm tossed leaves, pieces of hay, and scraps of stray garbage in front of her. At least the wind was at her back. If she had been walking directly into it, she would never have had the strength to continue.

Reaching the crossroads, she peered up at the two signs.

County Road 700 crossed the road she had been walking on for the past hour, the same road the convenience store was on, which apparently was State Road 28. But which road led back to Monroe?

There were no farm houses at this intersection, only fields stretching off in each direction. Sharon began to shake as she realized if she went the wrong way, she might end up walking all night.

Car lights again appeared out of nowhere, washing her in light and nearly blinding her. She jumped back from the intersection and into the safety of the field. The car slowed enough that she could make out the music drumming from the radio, and then it sped off.

What if they had stopped? What if they had tried to force her into the car? What was she doing out walking this road alone?

Her hands shaking so badly she resembled her *grossmammi*, Sharon huddled over her purse, unzipped it, and pulled out her cell phone. Turning it on, she waited for the signal that would tell her if she had service.

As she waited, she prayed. Finally, the screen displayed the words, "Entering service area."

She pushed the number 3 and held it.

Number 1 was for voice messages, and she didn't have any.

Number 2 was the preset number for James.

Number 3 was for Joana.

As her best friend's phone rang, she remembered speaking with her mother as they had hung laundry on the line. Her mother had talked about falling, about how it hurt, and about how she wanted what was best for her.

Staring into the darkness, waiting for Joana to pick up, Sharon didn't have any answers to all the questions bouncing around in her mind, but she did know that this was not the best her mother had in mind.

Chapter 14

Tuesday dawned sunny and crisp. Julia glanced out her upstairs window. The sky sparkled blue, trees blazed with color, and Pebble Creek glittered in the distance. It was the perfect fall day for a wedding.

Her wedding.

Was this actually happening to her? Was she ready for all the changes that would take place? Sitting back on her bed, she glanced around her room. Soon it would be *their* room. Soon everything that was hers would be *theirs*.

She ran her hand over the quilt—a double wedding ring pattern. Ada had pieced it long ago, well before her hands became misshapen by the arthritis. Julia could remember coming in from helping her father in the barn and seeing her mother sitting in the front room, quilting the layers together.

It had gone in the blanket chest at the foot of her bed, buried there with her hopes and dreams. This week they had pulled it out and aired it on the line, and last night they had placed it on the bed.

Had Ada known, years ago, that one day this moment would come? Had she actually believed God had a plan for Julia's life and that it included an October wedding to a man she barely knew?

Julia blinked back tears which threatened to fall and reached for her Bible. This was a joyous day, not one she should begin by weeping.

It was no surprise that when she opened the old, worn book that had been hers since she was a child, it opened straight to the Psalms. Of course it would. Ada had been reading to her from that book's one hundred and fifty chapters since she could remember. Julia often found herself searching other parts of the Old Testament for answers and relying on passages from the New Testament when she needed to feel closer to her Savior. When she needed comfort, though, when she felt joyous, or even when she was afraid—she turned to the Psalms.

She turned to them now.

Her gaze landed upon the fifth verse of the thirty-seventh chapter. "Commit everything you do to the Lord. Trust him, and he will help you."

She could do that.

She might not know how to be a good wife, but she knew how to pray and turn things over to the Lord. She'd been doing that all of her life. How was a marriage any different?

Trusting in Him was the one thing that made sense. Marrying a man she barely knew didn't. Even if he did seem kind and compassionate and—she allowed her mind to caress the word—loving. Trusting Caleb she could learn to do, but trusting God? She had been doing that all of her life.

She'd done it as her parents aged. She had done it while she stood beside her father's grave. And she could do it this morning, as she took Caleb's hand.

A confident peace filled her heart as she finished her prayer, shut her Bible, and rose from the bed. Straightening the quilt, she realized—not for the first time—how interconnected the rings were.

So their lives would be—from this day forth.

Thirty minutes later, after a quick breakfast with her *mamm*, she went to the barn to feed Missy and found Seth King there. A grin spread across his youthful face. He seemed amused that she was surprised to see him.

"Can't have you tending to a mare on your wedding day. No worries here, Julia. I'll take care of anyone arriving and see that Missy is comfortable too."

"*Danki*. I didn't even know you were here."

"Caleb sent me. He asked me two days ago if I would come and tend to things. I don't think he's leaving anything to chance today. He wants to make sure you make it downstairs and to your wedding with no mishaps." Seth tilted his head toward Pebble Creek. "We need to make a bridge. If we did, he could walk over here."

"*Gut* idea. Maybe not today though." Julia hurried back toward the house to change into her new dress.

It was Plain, but it was beautiful nonetheless. She hadn't bothered with new dresses in quite some time, and the bright blue wedding material practically sparkled as she slipped it on. She tried to imagine wearing it to special occasions—others' weddings, Christmas services, maybe even when they went into town for a dinner like the day they purchased their marriage license.

She knew whenever she wore it she would think of this morning, of her new life with Caleb, and of all the hopes and dreams that filled her heart—though there was a small amount of fear there as well. This moment wasn't the time to focus on fear. She closed her eyes, remembered her morning prayer time, and tried to will away the nervousness.

There was no point in being afraid. There was no reason to listen to doubts. And it was too late to back out now anyway.

Her mother waited for her in the kitchen. When Julia reached her side, Ada reached up to touch her face.

Today was indeed a good day. Ada's eyes were clear behind her glasses, and she was able to open her hands and place her palms against Julia's cheeks. Her mother's hands against her skin felt like the softest lamb's wool.

"The blessing of the Lord be upon you, my dear."

Julia had been on an emotional buggy race since the morning Ada had first told her about the decree, but she had never doubted her mother's love. Tears filled her eyes as she realized, once again, that her days with her *mamm* on this side of heaven were numbered. Soon she would be all that was left of her family—or at least the family she knew.

As if reading her thoughts, Ada added, "By this evening we'll be a new family—a family of three again."

Hooking her arm through Julia's, they moved toward the front door, where Miriam and Lydia were walking up the porch steps. Though it was not yet eight in the morning, and almost everything had been readied the day before, the two women had arrived early to help with last-minute preparations.

"Perhaps soon after this day, if *Gotte* sees fit, we'll grow beyond three."

Julia didn't think there was much chance of that. She was thirty-seven years old. While it wasn't unheard of for women her age to have children, it seemed she'd probably missed those years. She'd been worried enough about it to overcome her embarrassment and bring up the subject with Caleb. His response was a pause, followed by a slow smile.

She was learning that was typical.

"We'll have children if Gotte wills it. Ya?"

"But didn't you want—"

"I wouldn't have children at all if I'd stayed single. The way I look at it, my chances are much higher now."

"If you married someone else, someone younger, your chances would be higher still."

They had been sitting down by the creek, watching the fish rise to the top of the water, catching insects for their dinner.

"But I'm not marrying someone else." He'd turned to look directly in her

eyes. "I'm marrying you, and we'll have children if Gotte *wills it. If not, I'll be grateful for the family He's given me."*

She hadn't brought it up again, but Ada's comment reminded her of that conversation and sent her thoughts scurrying toward the evening ahead.

Now her stomach churned with worry. She had no idea what to expect as far as her wedding night, and she hadn't brought up *that* subject with her mother. There were some things she was going to have to learn on her own.

They opened the door, and the quietness of the morning was shattered as Lydia and Miriam oohed and ahhed over her dress. Grace asked if it would be all right for her to draw before the wedding—though no portraits, of course. Soon other women from their church were arriving, bringing box after box of food.

Lydia and Miriam corralled her back upstairs, which they had decided would be the wedding staging area. After one look at Julia's face, Miriam hurried to the bathroom next door and drew a cup of tap water.

"Are we sure everything's ready?" Julia walked back and forth in front of the window in her room. "Maybe I should go downstairs and see if they need a hand."

She felt as if she couldn't pull in a deep breath, as if she'd been running, trying to catch Missy in the pasture—only Missy always came now when called. Besides, Seth was with Missy. Her mare was fine.

Miriam walked in, holding the glass of water. "Here, drink this. It will help calm your emotions. You might be hyperventilating."

Lydia rubbed her back in light circles.

"Why would I do that?"

"Nerves," Lydia declared. "Most people have them. You should see Caleb. He was certain you were going to change your mind. I had to stop him from driving over here last night."

"Me? Why would I—"

"Why would you? Caleb mentioned to Gabe that you might wake up and realize he wasn't good enough for you."

"Good enough?" Julia was starting to feel dizzy from looking back and forth between Lydia and Miriam.

"Men can be insecure, same as women." Miriam took the cup away and pulled her toward the bed, insisting she sit for a moment. "And they aren't always *gut* at explaining their emotions. They're adorable, especially when they're nervous."

The word "nervous" reminded Julia of her worries regarding the evening and what was to come when she and Caleb were alone. She glanced right, left, and finally down at her hands before asking the questions that had plagued her the last week.

Both women alleviated her fears, explaining what she needed to know and promising to be there for her in the future in case she needed to talk again about such personal matters.

"My *mamm* had the one talk with me, before Gabe and I married, and that was it. I felt as if I were consulting a textbook from school. Of course, we don't have anything remotely approaching the subject in our Amish schools, but there are several good books in the public library in Cashton." Miriam walked to the window.

Julia turned to Lydia. "She didn't."

"She might have. Teachers think they can find the answer to anything in a book."

"Where did you learn what you needed to know for your wedding night?" Miriam turned back toward them and pinned Lydia with a stare.

"Oh, my *mamm* will talk about anything. We have a houseful of girls, and she believes we need to be well prepared. I'll admit it's a matter she refuses to speak of unless she is sure no man is within several buggy lengths of the house."

"Excellent!" Miriam clapped her hands. "Three *gut* sources of information—myself, Lydia, and Ella. And the Cashton library, if you're so inclined."

"I would never. And I barely know Ella—"

"You've known her all your life," Miriam reminded her.

"Yes, but—"

"She made your wedding cake. It's a simple frosting design, two layers, and beautiful. You're going to love it."

"Did she make the fruit pies?" Julia allowed herself to be distracted by the thought of food and her guests and what was to take place over the next few hours.

"She did." Now Lydia was standing, rubbing her stomach. "Plus cream-filled doughnuts that she had to practically hide from my *bruder*, Stephen. You'll have plenty of sweets for your guests."

Together they stood at the window, looking down at the lawn where the church pews had been arranged. It seemed everyone she and Caleb had invited—the extended list of guests—had arrived. From upstairs, the women's dresses looked like a sea of rainbow colors, and the men were all dressed in black coats, black pants, and white shirts. They had all arrived early and worn their best. For some reason Julia was surprised. She had thought...

What had she thought? That perhaps they would find an excuse not to come. That her wedding couldn't be an important event in their lives.

There was a light knock at the door, followed by her mother's voice. "Bishop Atlee is ready to meet with you, dear."

Miriam and Lydia each gave her a quick hug before pushing her gently away from the window. She pulled in a calming breath, squared her shoulders, and went to the door. Praying that her stomach would calm, she walked out of her bedroom.

Her life had certainly changed in the last month in nearly every regard. She made her way down the stairs and into the sitting room. The shades had been partially drawn for privacy. Bishop Atlee and Caleb both turned toward her as she entered the room. She tried to decipher the emotions playing across Caleb's face, but it was impossible. She didn't know him that well.

Was he excited? Frightened? Regretting this bold decision they had made?

The bishop suggested they all sit, and then he opened his Bible and began to counsel them. Slowly Julia's fears calmed to a manageable flutter. It was good that together they would begin this day with Atlee's words of guidance and silent prayer.

Julia had been to dozens of weddings in her life.

She had heard the traditional Scriptures read to the members of the church before the two were announced as one—the Scriptures Bishop Atlee would use in a few moments.

But while they had this time alone, he opened his Bible slowly to the book of Genesis. His hand, aged and work worn, moved slowly down the page until his finger stopped at the twenty-fourth chapter and he began to read. He read to them of Abraham, of a father's love and concern for his son. How he sent a servant to do what he couldn't. "'Go instead to my homeland...and find a wife there for my son Isaac.'"

And then the servant trusted that the Lord would guide him. "'O Lord, God of my master Abraham...give me success today.'"

Julia had heard the story before. She recognized it as the verses Ada suggested she read a few weeks ago. This was different, though.

She had never heard the story of Isaac and Rebekah while sitting in her wedding dress, sitting across from Caleb. She had not heard it moments before she was about to be married. As Atlee spoke, it seemed he was stitching each word into the fabric of her heart.

"'Before he had finished praying, he saw a young woman named Rebekah...'"

Rebekah, who woke and walked to the spring not knowing that act would set off a chain of events that would lead to her marriage.

As Julia had not known that day she'd run to her garden, run seeking a place of refuge, that Caleb would be sitting across from her now, the man she was going to marry.

"'Here is Rebekah; take her and go. Yes, let her be the wife of your master's son, as the Lord had directed.'"

A lump formed in Julia's throat as she realized for the first time the role Rebekah's and Isaac's fathers had played in their marriage.

Atlee had stopped reading, and Julia thought perhaps they were done. She heard the singing from outside—their guests, raising their voices in celebration as she and Caleb and the bishop shared these special moments alone. Atlee glanced up at them, this man who so often had a smile playing across his lips, and he had such a serious expression that Julia wondered what could be wrong.

"Your marriage, it is somewhat different, ya? It is starting more like the old ways. You did not court or date or choose each other in quite the fashion our young people do today. The world has moved on, and even though we cling to the old ways as best we can, Amish communities have moved with the world in some regards."

He patted his open Bible, and then he gently closed it and set it on the table next to the couch. "There may be days where you have your doubts because of this strange and *wunderbaar* beginning. When you do, remember Isaac and Rebekah."

Reaching out to her with his left hand and to Caleb with his right, he spoke softly. "'Isaac brought Rebekah into his mother Sarah's tent, and she became his wife. He loved her deeply, and she was a special comfort to him after the death of his mother.'"

When he bowed his head, Julia found herself staring into Caleb's blue eyes. The moments ticked by, and she realized they were to be praying. She tried to look away, to look down, but she couldn't.

She didn't know how this would all end. She couldn't define the emotions dancing through her heart. She certainly didn't know if she would have the kind of love Rebekah experienced.

But the expression in Caleb's eyes gave her hope—hope for their future together.

As they moved outside to be wed, her stomach still quivered and her hands still shook. But those things no longer worried her. As Lydia had said—most people were nervous. The time with Caleb and Bishop Atlee had convinced her that the new life they were beginning would most certainly be one God would bless.

Chapter 15

Caleb tried to focus on the sermon, but his thoughts kept turning back to the moments he, Julia, and Atlee had spent in the sitting room.

The bishop's words weren't lost on him. Though their parents hadn't selected him and Julia for each other, they had approved of their decision. Ada had told him so twice, both in front of Julia and privately. She explained she had been praying for years that God would send someone to care for and love her daughter. She was certain he was the answer to those prayers.

His own parents had been every bit as encouraging. Although they couldn't make the trip from Indiana to Wisconsin, they had made him promise he would bring his new bride to visit soon. Already he had in his pocket a letter from them, a sealed letter, addressed to Julia Zook.

As the wedding ceremony continued, he and Julia sat in front of the rows of benches. They sat facing each other.

Caleb tried not to stare at the woman who would soon be his bride, but it wasn't easy.

He scrubbed a hand over his face, sweat trickling down the back of his new white shirt though the morning was a pleasant fifty-eight degrees. He knew the temperature because he'd checked it on Aaron's outdoor thermometer. He'd wanted to ensure that everything was going to be perfect, as if he could do anything about the temperature.

The day had turned out perfect. October sunshine splashed across Julia's garden.

The yard was in pristine condition, thanks to the work Seth had done. The boy had been a real blessing; only he wasn't a boy. Caleb realized with a start that he would soon be married as well.

Aaron, David, and Gabe had helped with the porch, the downstairs rooms, and the portions of the barn that couldn't wait. There were still things he would like to do before the café opened, but his friends had stepped in and made this morning possible.

Everyone stood and now Caleb and Julia were mere inches apart. Together they joined in one last song. Standing so close, he was able to make out her alto notes, even mingled in with so many voices. It was the first time he had heard her sing. Normally during church they sat on opposite sides of the room and her voice always blended with others. This morning he found himself listening to each word, and he knew he would always be able to pick out her voice now even when they were separated by a room full of people.

They sat again as a deacon came forward to give the second sermon. The first sermon had covered examples of godly marriages through the Old and New Testaments. This time the sermon focused on the love Christ has for the church and how marriage reflects that love. Caleb glanced again at Julia and caught her studying him.

He wiped his hands on his pants, hoping the sweat from his palms wouldn't stain them. He was aware that some thought the Amish weddings, which lasted nearly as long as their church services, were overly long.

Kendrick, one of the men Caleb worked with at the grocery, had teased him about it just last week. "Our weddings last twenty minutes tops. Unless you're a Catholic, and then they can get somewhat lengthy."

Twenty minutes!

Caleb couldn't imagine. He only knew he was grateful for this time—moments to calm his rapidly beating heart, collect his thoughts, and pray he could be the man Julia needed him to be.

Before it seemed possible, Bishop Atlee was signaling them that it was time to come forward. It was time to exchange their vows.

He heard a stirring among their friends as he and Julia stepped toward the bishop. Glancing back, he caught sight of a few grinning faces. It was a blur, though. He was trying not to trip as they walked the few steps to join Atlee. He was also distracted by Julia. She was so beautiful. The morning sunshine fell through the trees and landed on her in a circle of light.

A lump caught in Caleb's throat, and he feared he wouldn't be able to respond to Atlee's questions. Then Julia reached for his hand and smiled.

"Do you, Caleb Zook, and you, Julia Beechy vow to remain together until death?"

"We do."

"And will you both be loyal and care for each other during adversity?"

"We will."

"During affliction?"

"Yes."

"During sickness?"

Caleb was suddenly aware of the breeze on his face, the light smell of jasmine soap on Julia's skin, and her hand shaking ever so softly in his.

"We will."

Atlee reached forward, covering their hands with his own. "All of those assembled here, as your *freinden* and family in Christ, and I, as your bishop, wish you the blessing and mercy of God."

Caleb heard a roaring in his ears, and over that clapping from the people who had come to watch this sacred moment. Julia had tears in her eyes, but she was also smiling. He realized how important that was to him, to see her happy. Sometime in the last month, it had become his dream to see her content.

"Go forth in the Lord's name." Atlee turned them to face their guests. "You are now man and wife."

Caleb didn't think he would be able to eat a thing. As he sat beside Julia at the corner table—the *eck*, he thought he would only be able to glance at her and wonder how he had come to be so blessed.

Then someone handed him a plate of chicken with bread filling. He helped himself to a healthy portion and passed it to his right. Next came one vegetable dish after another, including creamed celery. How could he say no to any of them? Soon food was heaped so high on his plate he had to pass dishes without taking any because there was nowhere left to add servings.

He leaned toward Julia before taking his first bite. "Tell me you didn't stay up late cooking all of this."

"*Nein*. Lydia and Miriam arranged all the cooking—"

"We had to put a lock on the kitchen to keep her out," Miriam declared, as she passed them carrying three more plates of food.

Julia blushed as she denied that. "Not true."

Caleb paused midbite and sneaked another look at his new bride, trying to gauge her reaction.

"I will admit it was hard to stay out of the baking and preparations, but there was no need for a lock. I was busy preparing things in other parts of the house." She blushed prettily. "I will be ready to cook again once the café opens. I've missed it."

"We're fortunate Amish women enjoy cooking." David was seated down the table a few places and across from Caleb. Single men—including Seth, sat on the same side, to his right.

All very traditional. He almost laughed.

The west side of Pebble Creek considered themselves to be liberal, but when it came to weddings things were done the same as they always had been. No doubt they would be shocked to see some of the Amish weddings in Indiana, where the brides actually put flowers on the tables instead of leafy celery stalks in jars. In recent years, the weddings of younger couples occasionally even took place in rented facilities rather than in the house of the bride's family.

None of that mattered to Caleb. Those were minor details. He wanted to enjoy this day that was the beginning of their life together and then dive into the work waiting to be done. He wanted to make Julia happy and erase the fears that sometimes worried her expression.

Aaron pointed his fork at Caleb. "David's right. Amish women cook well. But you, my *freind*, have married a woman who is going to cook all day, most every day. Blessed among men, that's what I would call you."

"I won't be arguing."

"We can share in the fruits of Julia's labor as soon as we start on the bridge, which I think should be next week. I spoke with Tim, and he has some ideas on the design..." Aaron held up his hands when they all put down their silverware and stared at him. "What?"

"You're talking business at a wedding, dear. Eat more, talk less." Lydia stopped at their table with a pitcher of water and refilled his glass.

"Julia was talking of work."

"She said she loved cooking." Miriam strolled by with two more plates. "Completely different."

Caleb continued studying his friends while everyone at his table resumed eating. Julia was answering something Clara had asked—the young girl who was to marry Seth was sitting to her left. All of the young unmarried girls were.

He didn't mind the talk of work. He liked the idea of their two properties being connected by a bridge. Not only would it save time driving and walking around by the main road, it would entice customers staying at the cabins to visit the café.

Glancing toward Pebble Creek, Caleb felt the familiar tug. He was at peace when he was near the water, and families who came to the cabins came there looking for rest and tranquility. Last week, he and Aaron had gone into town to make sure they didn't need a building permit. Because together they owned both sides of the creek and because they were technically outside the village of Cashton proper, no permit was required.

The work could begin next week.

His life would be different now, but surely he would still find the occasional hour to fish along the creek's banks.

He turned to Seth and asked how his wedding plans were coming along.

Within two shifts, everyone had been fed. Their guest list had grown, but it was still small by Amish wedding standards. There were certainly less than two hundred in attendance, though Caleb was happy to see everyone looked as if they planned on staying the entire day.

Already the young people were spreading out across the yard for games of volleyball. The women were passing buckets down the tables—one for silverware, another that plates were scraped into, and a final for stacking the dishes. Some of the mothers and older sisters had placed blankets on the ground under the shade of the trees—babies were going down for naps.

The wedding cake had been set up on a table near the garden, but on the side near the house where it was situated in the shade and protected from the breeze. They would share it after everyone had taken a break from the large meal.

Caleb reached over and intertwined his fingers with Julia's. "Let's go take a walk."

"Walk?"

"Sure. I see our cake has been set out on the table."

"*Ya*. Ella did a *wunderbaar* job. I peeked at it in the kitchen."

"You peeked but didn't taste?"

"Caleb! Of course I didn't—" She stopped and shook her head as a smile spread across his face. "I never knew you were such a teaser."

"*Ya*. My family always said so." They had made it to the cake table. Ella's baking was delicious. Caleb knew that from the items she sent for customers to purchase at the cabins. He thought he knew what she was capable of making, but he wasn't prepared for the large, two-layer cake in front of him. It looked more like something he'd seen in the *Englisch* magazines the cashiers at the grocer sometimes flipped through when they weren't busy.

"Do you like it?" Julia asked.

"Hmm..." Caleb glanced left and right. "I'm not sure. Let's see."

He reached forward as if he were going to run a finger through the frosting, and then he pulled back when Julia gasped in shock.

"You did that on purpose."

"Guilty."

Because no one was near them, he kissed her lightly on the lips. It wasn't their first kiss, but it was their first as man and wife. Julia froze, as if she didn't know how to respond, but then she reached up and cupped her hand around the right side of his face.

"*Danki*, Caleb."

"For marrying you?"

"*Nein*. For everything." She turned away, suddenly interested in the gift table, which was overflowing with many things they would be able to use—both homemade and store bought. All were practical items—a coffeepot for the stove, a set of sheets, a buggy blanket. He realized their friends had thought of everything and probably shared what they would bring, as it didn't seem any item had been duplicated.

"Oh, my." Julia trailed a hand along the table. "I hadn't expected all the—"

"Gifts?"

"*Ya.*"

"People are kind here in Pebble Creek, same as in Monroe." Caleb glanced out across the lawn and saw the couple he'd been meaning to talk to.

"Let's go visit with our neighbors."

"Our neighbors?"

"Timothy and Jeanette."

"Oh. Sure, but I should check on my *mamm*."

"She's sitting with Miriam's mother. You can relax for today, Julia. I believe others will make sure she's taken care of."

Julia nodded. "You're right. It's just that I've grown used to watching after her all the time."

"Like a *mamm* with a *boppli*."

Julia's cheeks pinked instantly.

Was she thinking about the same thing he was? His thoughts had turned several times to the evening ahead, something he didn't want her to worry about, but he didn't think it was proper to broach the topic. So instead he squeezed her hand and said, "Tim's youngest is waiting in line for one of the balloon animals."

"I don't know them well," Julia confessed.

"You sold your land to them."

"*Ya*, but I haven't had much time to visit since then."

"Timothy is the one who is a little shorter than I am and nearly bald."

Julia gave him a don't-be-a-wise-guy look.

"The redhead is his *fraa*, Jeanette." He ducked out of the way in time to miss her playful slap.

"And how do you know so much about our neighbors?"

"Aaron has been helping Tim. He wants to learn our ways, and the *mamm* and *kinner* come into the grocery once a week." He delivered this last piece of information as they reached the *Englisch* family.

The youngest girl had received a pink balloon and was holding it up to her mother. "It's a giraffe, just like I asked for. Did you watch him? Did you see how he did that?"

"I did. It was amazing." Jeanette had bent down to straighten her little girl's dress, and that was when she noticed Caleb and Julia.

Everyone introduced themselves, and Timothy insisted they call him Tim. "Feels less formal."

A look passed between Tim and Jeanette, something that made her smile before she added, "I'm not sure you met our children when we bought the place. Our youngest is Zoey."

"Hello, Zoey." Julia squatted down so she could be on eye level with the girl. She wore her hair in two long braids on each side of her head, with purple ribbons woven into the brown tresses. "I love your hair."

"Mom always does it this way when she has time. I like the ribbons."

"I do too."

"She's six and wants to put ribbons on my workhorses." Tim Elliott rubbed his hand back and forth over his head and smiled at his daughter.

"They like it, Dad."

Jeanette snagged another little girl who had walked up with a yellow balloon turtle. "And this is Victoria. She turned ten last summer."

Victoria had red hair like her mother, which she wore in a single ponytail pulled to the back. She looked from her balloon to Julia and finally blurted out, "That was a long wedding!"

"Victoria—" Tim stepped closer to the young girl, leaned forward, and whispered something in her ear.

"Sorry. I love the games, though. I remember going to a wedding before, but I don't remember games."

"Wess said I couldn't play." Zoey's bottom lip came out in a pout. "He said I was too little."

Julia glanced at Caleb. "Wess is—"

"Our third child," Jeanette explained. "He's seventeen, and I'm not sure where he went."

"Probably to join the volleyball game next to the front porch." Caleb turned the little girl and pointed her in the opposite direction, toward the far side of the garden. "Younger ones are playing that way if you want to join them."

The two girls looked to their parents for permission and then took off running, animal balloons clutched in their hands.

"Thank you so much for inviting us to your wedding." Jeanette stepped closer to her husband. "I know we haven't been very good neighbors this last year."

"*Nein.* I should have been over to visit. My *mamm* has been ill, and my *dat*—"

"Yes, I know. I'm so sorry."

Tim put his arm around his wife. "We will get to know each other better now."

"That would be *gut*," Julia said.

"Aaron has told me about your attempt to farm using our methods." Caleb pulled Julia out of the path of two small children chasing a ball past where they stood. "How are you adjusting to Plain ways?"

"This year has gone better. I was an engineer in my old life. It's taken some time for me to learn how to do things the simple way, but I like it."

"You were an engineer?" Caleb remembered Lydia's admonition about talking business, but he couldn't stop himself from broaching the subject. "Aaron mentioned you might have some ideas to help us in building a bridge across the creek."

He managed to keep the conversation brief. They had other guests to speak with, but it seemed to him that perhaps having this *Englisch* neighbor next door was a blessing.

"Nice couple," Julia murmured as they walked away. Miriam had called out to her, so they were walking back toward the house. She was needed to match up the single guests, anyone over sixteen, to sit together for the evening meal.

Caleb wanted to make sure everything was ready for the young people to have their singing in the barn, which was scheduled to take place later in the afternoon.

As they moved in separate directions, it occurred to him that the day could not have gone more smoothly.

Chapter 16

When Julia woke the next day, Caleb was already dressing. By the time she puzzled through several different emotions—joy, longing, excitement, worry, and embarrassment—he was bending over her and kissing her cheek.

"Off to the barn. Back in an hour." His fingers caressing her face and lingering in her hair drove out all her worries. Perhaps yesterday and last night had gone as well as she thought it had.

Oh, how she wished Miriam or Lydia lived next door so she could run over and have a word with them. It was rare that Julia ever wished for any of the *Englisch* conveniences, but at that moment she would have gladly picked up a telephone to call one of her friends.

Instead she slipped from the bed, took her turn in the bathroom before Ada needed it, and returned to her room to dress quickly. She intended to go downstairs straight away, but her eyes fell on the letter from Indiana, the one Caleb had handed her as soon as they had walked into their room together the evening before.

Her fingers traced her name on the envelope—Julia Zook.

Unable to resist, she pulled out the single sheet and sat in the rocker beside her bed. She remembered well enough what was written on the plain paper. She had read it twice already—once while

Caleb stepped into the bathroom to give her a few moments alone and then again, while he sat beside her on the bed.

He'd described his parents to her then. Jebediah, his father, had recently turned sixty-five but still worked in the fields a portion of each day. Caleb's brothers—three older, two younger—took care of the bulk of the farm work, but Jebediah enjoyed the time outside and claimed it kept him youthful.

"Do you look like your *dat?*" Julia had asked.

"*Ya.* I suppose I do—same height and same build. Though his hair is much whiter."

He'd touched at the place on his scalp that was graying. She'd wondered if he was aware of it. Apparently he was, and it didn't matter to him at all.

"And your *mamm?*"

"Betsy." Caleb's smile said more than his words possibly could. "She's a *gut* cook, Julia. You two will have a lot to talk about. All that cooking, though, for us boys...it's taken its toll. *Mamm,* she never was tall, and she's put on a few pounds over the years."

"Is she...is she healthy?"

His laughter eased the worry that tried to creep into her heart.

"*Ya.* Doc says she'll outlive him, and he's fifteen years younger than she is. *Mamm* is what we call sturdy. It came in handy over the years." Caleb hesitated before adding, "She didn't have any girls of her own. Maybe that's why she tends to take special interest in her sons' wives. You'll probably receive a letter each week."

It was with that image in mind that she reread the words this morning. Dawn's light was a bare tinge on the eastern horizon. The first full day of her married life had hardly begun, but it seemed appropriate that she should pause and take the time to feel Caleb's mother's blessing upon their life.

Dearest Julia,

Since Caleb left Indiana, I have prayed each day for him. Prayed for his safety. Prayed our Lord would guide him. And prayed that

Gotte would care for you in every way. Yes, I prayed for you even before I knew your name, Julia.

I have never doubted that Gotte had someone special intended for my son. Caleb has a generous heart, and you will soon learn that he is a hard worker. His faults are no worse than any others. (Does he still fish every chance he gets? Well, at least it provides dinner.) I will pray you have a full measure of patience to help you deal with his shortcomings. And I will pray that your marriage grows in love, is sprinkled with laughter, and always travels the path our Lord has given. Each day is an opportunity to extend Gotte's love and grace to each other.

Julia glanced up and across the room, out toward the barn where even now Caleb was working, caring for Missy and Red. He had laughed when they had reached the line about his faults. "Just like *mamm* to warn you," he'd said as he put his arm around her.

Julia turned the page over and continued reading.

Caleb has explained enough of your situation so that we will know how to pray. Until you can come for a visit, I would love to hear from you. Please know that each morning and each evening I will lift you, Caleb, Ada, and your home there on the banks of Pebble Creek up to our Lord. I will also remember your new café and ask that the Lord will bless the work you and Caleb attempt together.

This is a time of great change for you both, but also of great joy. Remember, Julia, courage is fear that has said its prayers. Have courage. Pray without ceasing, and write to me as often as you are able.

Lovingly yours,
Betsy

Julia carefully folded the single sheet of paper and slipped it back into the envelope. She walked over to the large oak dresser in the room, which now held both her clothing and Caleb's. Opening the

bottom drawer, she tucked the letter between her winter dresses and
the old aprons she used while cleaning or canning.

She would write back this evening, after dinner.

As far as praying, that she could do while she worked. Though it
occurred to her, as light spilled over the horizon, that perhaps God
wanted a moment or two of her undivided attention. So she stood
by the window, forced her mind away from all there was to do, and
gave her worries to the Lord.

The rest of the week went remarkably well, considering.

They were able to move the downstairs furniture upstairs. Julia
had envisioned turning the third bedroom into a sitting room, and
Caleb had agreed it would be a good idea. This left all of the downstairs open for dining areas.

It worked unless they had a child, but Julia pushed that thought
from her mind. Even if she did become pregnant, they would figure
out something before the baby arrived. Besides, she didn't need to
spend her time worrying about what *might* happen. They had their
hands full with all that *was* happening.

The extra upstairs room wasn't big enough to hold all of the
furniture from the downstairs sitting room and their sewing room.
Some of it would need to be stored in the barn.

"You lap quilt, so we don't need the quilt stand. We only use the
treadle machine for clothes, and Caleb can fetch it when we need it."
Ada patted her on the arm. "It's not a problem."

But Julia nearly wept to see her old black sewing machine carried toward the barn by Seth and Caleb. The barn! With the horses
and hay and manure! Caleb stopped, said something to Seth, and a
moment later they were walking back to her. "It will fit in the basement," he said.

She nodded, relief surging through her heart. The basement

would be a good place for it, and much easier to reach if she had sewing to do.

Crossing the item off her list, she marched back into the house and focused on arranging the tables and chairs David had delivered. Everything fit—barely.

They kept the breakfast area the same and decided this was where they would take their meals as a family. Caleb also set up a rocker and reading table in a corner for Ada.

"She'll need a place to rest, and she won't want to always be upstairs."

He was right. She should have thought of it herself.

What had been their downstairs sitting room held five tables that seated four people each. The front room, the old sewing room, held another three, plus two small tables which sat two and were placed near the front windows. All told, they could feed thirty-six at full capacity.

Things were looking good.

The real problem came with the licensing, which she never would have been able to maneuver through without the help of Jeanette. Caleb had found out about the food handling class from his supervisor at the grocery. Julia had taken and passed it the week before her wedding. And that was just the beginning.

They also had to apply for a business license and tax, zoning, and alarm permits. She had no idea what most of those things were.

"We have a problem," Jeanette declared. She'd paused to knock on the front door, but Julia had waved her inside.

"This place looks amazing!"

"*Danki.*" Julia sank onto a chair at the nearest table and pulled out her list. "A new problem or an old one?"

"A new twist on an old problem." She went on to explain that all of the permits had been approved except for the signage permit.

"What is a signage permit?"

"The sign outside your property has to be approved."

"We don't have a sign yet."

"Exactly. That's part of our problem." Jeanette twisted one of the short red strands of her hair. "You have to be granted a signage permit before your final application can be evaluated. I've found a person in the permit office who says he'll be there until four p.m."

"It's one o'clock now."

Jeanette gave up on the hair twisting and pulled off her purple glasses. After she'd cleaned them with the hem of her blouse, she pushed them back on and stared at Julia. "We're too close to give up now. Where are the guys?"

"Barn. I believe they're hiding. I've had them working since daybreak."

"Let's find them. If they can knock together a sign, I'll take a picture of it with my phone and text it over to the permit office."

"But Grace's drawing isn't finished yet, and then we were going to have it blown up and—"

"Doesn't matter. This is a temporary sign. You can always change it later."

Somehow they did it. Together they found material to create a five foot by five foot board. Mounting it on the fence near the road wasn't easy, but Tim's engineering skills came in handy, and they were able to safely build a support.

It was the Elliotts' teenaged son, Wess, who came up with the idea of using left-over paint from the front porch for the actual words. He also was better at painting letters than they were.

Standing back, they all studied the finished project.

The words "Plain Café" were centered on the board, and he'd painted a white border around it.

"That definitely won't win any art awards," Wess said.

Caleb slapped him on the back. "Maybe not, but anyone who is hungry will know where to stop."

"One more task completed." Julia ticked café sign off her list—an item that hadn't been on the list at the beginning of the day. It was amazing what they had been able to accomplish in one day, thanks to their friends.

"I was happy with it even before Wess put on the border." Jeanette snapped a picture with her phone and then began pushing buttons.

"Are you sending it now?" Julia asked.

"I am. The man in the permit office said he would e-mail back your permit in the next thirty minutes." Jeanette slipped her phone into the pocket of her jeans, high-fived Tim, and then turned to Julia and pulled her into a hug.

Caleb, Wess, and Tim let out a cheer. Zoey and Victoria danced in a circle before stopping suddenly, turning to their father, and asking, "What's a permit?"

Ada pushed up her glasses and hooked her arm through Julia's as they turned to walk back to the house. "Oh, the joys of those who trust the Lord."

"Indeed, *mamm*. Indeed." Julia couldn't help thinking the psalmist was correct, but he probably didn't have to deal with obtaining permits in order to serve a meal to a hungry traveler.

They were halfway back up the lane, headed toward home and relieved to have the day's work behind them, when they heard a horse and buggy turn into their lane.

It was Aaron, and the expression on his face was enough to alert Julia that something was wrong. Her first thought was of Lydia and the baby.

"We need to build that bridge," he said as he stopped the horse and buggy beside them. "Then I could get here faster."

"*Ya*. If the weather remains good, we're starting it next week." Caleb glanced at Julia and then at Tim. "What's wrong, Aaron?"

"I'm not sure, but your *mamm* called. She needs to speak with you right away."

⤜ Chapter 17 ⤛

Sharon stared at her mother and dad. They were sitting around the kitchen table, though it was well past dinnertime. Marion had called her in from the sitting room, where she was watching her little sister, Ruthie, color on a blank page. At her mother's voice, she'd been surprised to glance outside and see the sky was growing dark already.

How long had she been sitting there? Where were all the boys?

"How late is it, Ruthie?"

Her sister only shrugged and went back to her coloring sheet—a scene that included grass and a four-legged animal that was colored purple.

Remembering that plum-colored animal, Sharon wondered if the entire world had gone crazy. She also wondered if the boys were hiding in the barn. No doubt they had all known what her parents were about to say. Everyone had known except her.

"Did you say Wisconsin?"

"*Ya.*" Her father didn't blink. "That's where Caleb and Julia live."

"Who?"

"Caleb, your Aunt Betsy's middle son. You remember him." Marion spoke quietly, gently, as if she were afraid Sharon would bolt from the table.

"It doesn't matter if you remember him or not, Sharon. He's your cousin, and you'll be leaving the day after tomorrow to stay with him and his wife."

"Why?" Panic clawed at Sharon's chest, reminding her of that night, of waiting in the field, of the car that had stopped before her father's driver found her. She pushed the thought away, closed her eyes, and tried to swallow. "What...what have I done wrong?"

"What haven't you done wrong?" Her father's voice wasn't harsh, exactly, but neither was it kind.

There had been a wall between them since that night three weeks ago, since he'd gone down the road to their *Englisch* neighbors and asked for a ride in the middle of the night.

"It's not what you've done, Sharon." Marion reached out across the table, but Sharon jerked her hand into her lap. "We have spoken with the bishop."

"Again?"

"And we think this is best for everyone."

"To send me away?" Sharon stood abruptly, the chair skidding against the kitchen floor.

Her father stared at a spot to the left of her shoulder, his face devoid of emotion. Her mother shut her eyes, as if she were praying or trying to wish the entire thing away. Maybe trying to wish her away.

"I hate you," Sharon whispered. "I hate you both."

Sharon had twenty minutes of privacy before her mother followed her to her bedroom. She could hear her five brothers downstairs now. It sounded as though a pack of pups had been let loose in the house. Laughter, footsteps, someone losing a game of checkers and daring a rematch, and someone else complaining he was trying to finish his homework.

Normal sounds for people who had normal lives.

"Crying won't change anything." Marion pressed a fresh

handkerchief into her hand. "You had better accept what is to be and make the best of it."

Sharon pushed her face deeper into her pillow. The last thing she wanted was to speak with her mother. She understood nothing!

"Why is she crying, *mamm?*" Ruthie lifted up Sharon's arm and pushed her doll under the pillow, down near her face. "Take my *boppli*, Sharon. She'll make you feel better."

Ruthie's voice, concerned and close, was the only thing that could have broken through Sharon's wall of despair. Sitting up, she rubbed at the tears still running down her face.

"Don't cry." Ruthie crawled onto the bed and put her chubby hands on both sides of her sister's face and squeezed. "Okay?"

Sharon laughed, which made her hiccup, and then more tears escaped.

"A cold wet rag will help." Marion stood.

"I'll get it." Ruthie hopped off the bed and ran out of the room.

"Wring it out," Marion called after her.

They studied each other for a heartbeat before Sharon broke the silence: "I don't want to go."

"*Ya.*"

"I barely remember Caleb."

"He's been gone only a little over a year."

"But he's old and..." another sob escaped. "Why do I have to go?"

Ruthie returned with a washcloth dripping water across the bedroom floor.

"Take it back, sweetie. Squeeze the water into the sink." Marion made wringing motions with her hand.

"Ohhhh..." Ruthie dashed back out of the room.

Marion scooted farther onto the bed, until her back was resting against the wall. "It's been three weeks since—"

When Sharon didn't speak but only stared down at Ruthie's doll, her mother pushed forward. "Since you called your *dat*. You're still not eating."

"Is that what this is about? I'll start. I promise—"

"You said that last week and the week before." Marion shook her head. "I don't know what's wrong, Sharon. I don't believe I know everything that happened to you that night. What could have frightened you so? What are you still struggling with? These are questions that worry both your *dat* and me. What we do know is when one of our *kinner* has changed—and you've changed."

"Everyone changes." The words slipped out from a secret place in her heart. Speaking them hurt so much she thought she might be having a heart attack. Could seventeen-year-old girls have heart attacks? Was that medically possible?

Ruthie returned with the cloth, climbed onto the bed, and began patting Sharon's face—forehead to chin, left ear to right.

"*Ya*. That is true. People change, but the changes we've seen in you are worrisome. You've lost nearly fifteen pounds—weight you didn't have to lose."

Sharon began shaking her head, but Ruthie put a hand to her forehead and said, "Hold still!"

"You don't sleep at night."

"How—"

"Do you think anything happens in this house I'm not aware of?" Her mother reached out, touched the top of her head, and let her hand linger there a moment before continuing. "After what happened at church on Sunday—"

"It wasn't my fault."

"Did I say it was?"

Deciding the baby doll needed washing as much as Sharon did, Ruthie pulled it into her hands and sat in Sharon's lap. Singing softly to herself, she cradled the faceless doll and focused on using the washcloth to clean her.

"Change can be healthy. We met with your Uncle Jebediah and Aunt Betsy yesterday. They were the ones who suggested you go to Wisconsin and stay with Caleb and Julia. They have a large home and are opening a café where you can work. Perhaps work, in a new place, is the answer."

"But it's in Wisconsin."

"*Ya*. It is." Marion stood and kissed both Ruthie and Sharon on top of their heads. "Betsy spoke with them today. They're happy to have you."

Sharon closed her eyes. Surely this was a nightmare, like all the others she had been suffering through. Maybe she would wake soon, wake to her old life—the one she hadn't yet ruined.

The squirming sister in her lap suggested otherwise.

Besides, if this were merely a bad dream, it had very realistic people who kept saying things she didn't want to hear. As her mother left the room, she added, "Tomorrow we'll decide what you should take. Your bus leaves early Friday morning."

⌒

Sharon stood next to her mother in the predawn darkness. Her brother Jonas had elected to stay with the horse and buggy, over on the far side of the parking area. He'd only spoken with her once, the day before, and it was plain he was siding with their parents.

Her father hadn't come with them to the downtown station where the bus depot picked up and dropped off passengers. His only words to her had been delivered in a flat, resigned tone. "Goodbye, Sharon. May *Gotte* keep you safe."

She hadn't been able to look at him.

Part of her wanted to cry and beg him to let her stay.

Another part wanted to lash out and remind him she was seventeen—practically an adult. He couldn't just decide where she would go and with whom she would live.

It wasn't right. It wasn't fair.

But instead of pleading her case with tears or arguments, she'd sat there frozen, not even pretending to eat.

Her father had taken one final look at her breakfast plate, shaken his head, and left through the kitchen door. Her last sight of him was with his coat collar turned up and his shoulders hunched against the wind as he walked toward the barn.

Her younger brothers were only beginning to stir as they left.

And she didn't have the heart to peek in on Ruthie, who was still sleeping in the room they shared.

"Bus is arriving in five minutes, folks. Be sure your ticket is handy and your luggage is tagged with your name."

Sharon searched her mind frantically. There had to be something she could say to her mother. There had to be a way she could change what was about to happen. She couldn't leave Monroe. How could they expect her to travel to Wisconsin, and live with people she didn't even know?

"There's Edna." Marion began waving her hand. "We are so fortunate someone from our district was traveling to Minnesota and could change her plans and leave today instead of next week."

"Mamm—"

"Mind your manners, Sharon. Edna's older and she can be strict. She'll be a good chaperone, though."

"Mamm—"

Before Sharon could say another word, Edna joined them. She was probably ten years older than Marion, smelled like the peppermint candies she ate all the time, and rarely smiled.

"Edna, gudemariye."

"And to you, Marion. I see Sharon is ready to go." The woman's false teeth clicked softly as she spoke.

Sharon looked around at the other passengers. Maybe she could dart in between them and escape. But where would she go? None of her friends would take her in. Who was she kidding? She no longer had friends. They all believed James's version of what had happened.

James, who had abandoned her on the side of the road. James, who hadn't really cared for her at all. James, who was the reason she was here being shuffled off to a distant land with people she didn't even know.

"I'm not going." She realized in an instant that no one could force her to leave. Instead, she turned and began to walk back toward their buggy.

"Sharon—"

She could hear the bus pull in behind them. The door made a hissing sound as it opened, and passengers began shuffling forward. There were words of goodbye and the man collecting tickets asked for folks to make a line. Her mother called out her name again, but her feet seemed to have a will of their own. They kept moving toward the parking lot, toward safety, toward home.

Suddenly she felt a hard grip close around her left arm.

"Young lady, you turn yourself around this minute."

"I won't."

"Oh, yes you will. We have already paid for this ticket, and you will use it."

"Is that all you care about? The money?" She'd told herself she wouldn't cry, but her tears were like a faucet, and she was no longer in control of when they were turned on or off. "Admit it. You don't care about me at all!"

Marion pulled back, the look on her face suggesting she didn't know her daughter anymore. That made two of them. Sharon didn't recognize herself when she looked in the mirror. Unfortunately, Marion still didn't let go of her arm.

"Do you think so, Sharon? You think I don't care? Do you think I don't cry at night as I pray for you? Pray over what has happened and what is to come? May you never know the agony of praying for a *dochder* who has gone missing, who returns terrified, who is wasting away before—"

Marion stopped. Lowering her voice, she said, "I love you, and that's why I'm making sure you get on that bus."

"If you love me, let me stay."

"Sharon, get on the bus."

"Please, *mamm*. I'll do whatever you ask, but don't make me go."

Marion was pulling her now, dragging her like a small child and handing her over to Edna. "Get on the bus."

Sharon took one look at the older woman, who had pursed her lips as if she'd swallowed something distasteful.

With a sigh that sounded even to her like a small animal caught in a trap, she turned away from them, squared her shoulders, and moved to the end of the line of passengers. The final few steps to the bus felt like a mile or more. Her mother stepped closer as Sharon moved to follow the others up the steps, close enough that when Sharon turned and spoke, even though it was a whisper, she was able to hear her quite well.

"You don't love me. You don't love me any more than he did. If you loved me, you would never send me away."

Before her mother could answer, she turned and boarded the bus, walking down the long aisle of strangers.

Chapter 18

S haron's a *gut* girl," Caleb said, as they waited outside the feed store for the bus to arrive. "I remember she used to sing in the school program. She has a beautiful voice."

"*Ya?*" Julia cornered herself in the buggy seat so she could better study her husband.

Ada sat in the back, staring out the window at the occasional shopper who was braving the turn in the weather. Julia would have preferred to have left her mother at home because the wind was blowing cold today, but she had known when Ada walked down the stairs that leaving her alone wasn't an option. After one glance at her mother this morning, with her prayer *kapp* on inside out, Julia had known what kind of day they were going to have. She'd asked Doc Hanson about these occasional spells of confusion, and he'd admitted it could be several things—the onset of a cold, mild dementia, or even an unsettling dream that had disoriented her on wakening.

"Be patient with her, Julia. As long as her good days outnumber her bad, be grateful. And if you're ever concerned, bring her into town or ask me to come out. You don't need an appointment."

Ada's confusion had lessened after eating breakfast, but Julia still recognized the symptoms. This was not going to be one of her better days. She didn't want her to be alone in case she fell or became more disoriented.

"There are a lot of boys in my *onkel*'s family." Caleb was explaining. "Sharon and Ruthie were the only girls. Those two had to stick together."

"Sharon is seventeen?"

"*Ya*. Hard to believe. Ruthie, she's a small thing. She was barely talking when I moved to Wisconsin." Caleb rubbed at his jaw where his beard had started growing. "No doubt Sharon will miss Ruthie while she's here."

"Did your *mamm* give you any other details? Other than she needed to be somewhere else for a time?"

"*Nein*. I think maybe in her next letter she'll say more. *Mamm* isn't too comfortable on the telephone." Caleb buttoned his coat and tugged his gloves on as the bus pulled up. "I was surprised she called. I've phoned them a few times, but they've never phoned here. I knew it must be an emergency when they did."

Julia wondered what kind of emergency. She didn't ask. How much trouble could one seventeen-year-old girl be? And it wasn't as if they could or would say no. Family helped family.

The bus was idling near the ticket booth, and the door had opened. Where were the passengers from? And what did they think of this cold, dreary Wisconsin weather?

Caleb glanced over and gave her a reassuring smile as he reached for his hat and pushed it down tightly on his head.

They could use Sharon's help in the café. Caleb would be starting back at the grocery on Tuesday, three days a week. Julia would have her hands full with cooking, serving, and caring for her mother. They had talked of hiring help from the local girls, but Julia wanted to wait and see how many customers they would have, if any. Seth had helped put out flyers at local businesses, and she'd run an ad in the *Budget*. Would it be enough?

As Caleb opened the buggy door to step out and walk toward the idling bus, Ada reached forward and plucked at his coat sleeve.

"'The words of the Lord are pure.'"

Caleb patted her hand and smiled over at Julia. "That they are, Ada. That they are."

Something in Julia's heart opened at that moment. Though she'd been sharing her bed with Caleb for three nights, and though they had been making plans together for nearly two months, there was a part of her she'd been holding back.

There was a part of her that hadn't been ready to completely trust him yet.

It wasn't only because men, or rather boys, had let her down in the past. It was because she'd been used to doing things on her own, and it was frightening to join herself emotionally with someone else. She understood that they were married for life, that their commitment was a permanent one, but she was still coming to terms with exactly what that meant.

And her mother...

Her mother was like her child in so many ways. While Caleb had always been polite and respectful, she still considered Ada to be her responsibility.

Seeing him pat her mother's hand and offer her a reassuring word before stepping out into the cold, and watching him deal with her on a bad day, Julia realized that her husband had already stepped further into this marriage than she had. His kindness toward her mother made her want to follow him out of the buggy, stand beside him in the cold, and wait for Sharon.

Instead, she made sure Ada was covered with the lap blanket. She waited and prayed they could be the refuge Sharon needed.

⌒

Caleb turned his back against the wind and peered up into the bus's windows. It didn't seem that long ago that he'd been the one stepping off the bus and onto the streets of Cashton, stepping into his life in Pebble Creek. He couldn't help shaking his head. Things had certainly changed since then—and for the better!

He didn't know what was going on with Sharon's situation, but he hoped she could find what she needed here among the people of their district.

The bus driver exited through the open door and retrieved a single bag from the underside storage compartment. At least Caleb wouldn't have to figure out which passenger was Sharon, as it seemed only one person was exiting.

From what he remembered, she was an energetic, healthy girl. Chestnut hair, laughing brown eyes, and cheeks that had a sprinkling of freckles across them. He drew a blank after that, but he was praying Julia and Sharon would become close friends.

Slowly an old woman made her way down the stairs of the bus. Caleb immediately recognized Edna Hostetler. She was one of the oldest and sternest widows in their district. He moved forward quickly to help her down the final step.

"Edna, *mamm* didn't mention you were coming."

"I'm not coming to Cashton, Caleb." Every detail of the woman's hair and dress was perfectly in place. No one would have guessed she'd been on a bus since early that morning. "I'm chaperoning Sharon, is all. My destination is Minnesota."

"Oh." Before Caleb could think of anything else to say, a shadow of a girl appeared in the bus's doorway. It was Sharon...and it wasn't.

She had grown at least two inches taller than the last time he'd seen her, and perhaps that was part of the reason she looked so thin. Caleb had the feeling she might blow away in the winter wind. Her clothes draped on her, like a coat on a hook. Dark circles rimmed her eyes. She glanced at him once and then stared down at the ground.

"Hurry, girl. The driver is ready to leave." Edna turned to Caleb. "She only has the one bag. Be sure you write to your parents this evening to tell them she arrived safely. I informed them we would only call if there was a problem. There is no need to use those contraptions every time one feels a need to communicate. A pencil and piece of paper will serve fine."

Turning to Sharon, she sniffed once and then said, "I hope your stay here is better than this morning's beginning."

Did Caleb imagine it, or did Sharon flinch?

Edna turned and climbed back up the steps of the bus.

The bus driver handed the single piece of luggage to Caleb and then followed Edna. In less time than it took Red to eat a handful of oats, the bus was gone.

Caleb waited until Sharon glanced up. When she did, he smiled and said, "Welcome to Pebble Creek."

She didn't even blink, so he gestured to the waiting buggy. She followed him, though he wondered if she would. She seemed glued to the spot, practically incapable of moving. Perhaps the wind had something to do with it.

She crept along behind him, and when they reached the buggy, she climbed into the backseat without a word.

Caleb placed her bag in the compartment at the rear. When he joined the women inside, Julia was attempting to make conversation. He glanced once at his bride, shrugged, and called out to Red. The soothing sounds of his gelding's hooves clip-clopping down the road soon filled the afternoon.

Caleb stretched his arm across the seat, allowing his hand to lightly brush Julia's neck. He had noticed she seemed to relax when he touched her, and he made it a point to do so whenever possible.

The road curved closer to Pebble Creek, and Caleb slowed the buggy so he could watch the water play over and around the rocks. He hadn't fished in several days and could feel the pull, though the temperature and wind today would have been large enough deterrents even if the work at home hadn't stopped him.

"Maybe there will be time tomorrow afternoon," Julia said, following his thoughts perfectly.

"Ya. Fish would be *gut* for dinner."

Ada leaned forward, reminding Caleb of a faithful hunting dog he'd had back in Indiana. Not that he would ever compare his mother-in-law to a hunting dog. It was only that the way she had of popping up out of the backseat made him think of Blaze. Perhaps he should talk to Julia about getting a pup. He'd heard Miriam mention that her father sometimes had a litter for sale.

"'The Lord blesses His people with peace,'" Ada announced.

When Caleb and Julia glanced at her and nodded in agreement, she sat back, satisfied.

Caleb chuckled, realizing their conversation might sound somewhat odd to his cousin.

"Ada's an expert on the Psalms, Sharon." As far as he could tell, the girl still hadn't spoken, but he continued as if she had. "I've learned quite a lot about the psalmists' writing in the two months since Julia and I began courting."

"You only courted two months?"

So she could speak.

"Actually it hasn't quite been two months," Julia murmured.

"No?"

"Just over six weeks."

"You don't say?" Caleb directed the buggy past the new sign, down their lane, and stopped in front of the house to let the women out.

"Six weeks." He glanced back and saw his young cousin staring at them in surprise. "I guess you're right. Sharon, I'll fetch your bag. You all get out here so Ada doesn't have to walk through the wind."

After setting the bag inside the front door, Caleb returned to the buggy and drove it to the barn. He couldn't help smiling over the expression on Sharon's face. Apparently, she hadn't realized the café was in their home. She'd stood in the entryway, staring left and right, as Ada had thumped past her with her cane—mumbling more verses from the Bible and declaring it a good evening for Julia's thick potato soup.

Chapter 19

Sharon gawked at the room where she was supposed to sleep. Sharing a *room* with Ada was one thing. Sharing a *bed* was a different thing altogether.

"I'm sorry, Sharon." Julia stepped forward and opened an empty dresser drawer. "I wish we had better arrangements, but Caleb assured me this would be fine—and anyway, it's all we have."

Even at home she'd had her own bed in the room she'd shared with Ruthie. How was she to sleep in a double bed with an old woman? Ada wasn't just old; she was ancient. She looked as if she might die at any moment. What if she died while Sharon was asleep in the bed?

Sharon stood as if frozen at the entrance to the room, unable to move forward.

"The bathroom is down the hall, and there's another half bath downstairs. The room before mine is where we've set up our sitting area, for reading and such." Julia turned around and clasped her hands in front of her.

Sharon almost felt sorry for her cousin's wife. Almost. But she didn't. If Julia and Caleb had said she couldn't visit, she would still be in Monroe, Indiana, tonight. If they had said no, she wouldn't be sharing a bed with an old woman she didn't even know.

"I should go down and see to that soup. We'll eat in fifteen minutes." Julia walked past her and paused outside the door. "If there's anything you need, I hope you'll ask. We want to do whatever we can to make your stay with us easier."

Sharon had to look away then, ashamed of her anger and her bitterness. She wasn't that person, but who was she? The silence had become a humming in her head, and some days it was all she could do to hear others over it, to even speak at all.

"*Danki*," she whispered.

"*Gem gschehne*." The words were passed as delicately as a dozen fresh eggs, and then Julia was gone.

Sharon walked into the room and sat on her side of the bed. The room was Plain, like her room back home. There was the single dresser, with the one emptied drawer. Six hooks had been installed on the wall next to the dresser. Someone had cleared off three of the hooks so she would have a place to hang her clothes. The only other furniture was a nightstand near Ada's side of the bed and one straight-back chair.

Sharon's side was across the room from the window. When she looked out, she could see the entire property, not that she cared to. It didn't matter what was outside her window. All that mattered was that she find a way home.

How had she ended up here? How would she endure it? And how long would she be in exile? She didn't even know these people!

It was obvious why Caleb had married Julia. She was a beautiful woman, even if she was older. Why the short courting period, though? And this house. It was huge, but they were forced to live in the upstairs rooms? None of it made any sense, which pretty much matched her life back home. All that had changed was the scene outside the window. She'd gone from a remote small town she was familiar with to a remote small town that was completely foreign.

Her mind flashed back to her dreams of the past summer—dreams of going to the city, of going away. Now all she wanted was to be back in Indiana.

She hated Wisconsin. She didn't know a thing about it, and she didn't want to learn.

What was with all the hills and forests? Why should she care?

She wanted to lie down on the bed and cover up her head, but it wasn't hers to lie down on.

It was hers and Ada's, and something told her the old woman wouldn't approve of her slipping into bed before dinner.

So she hung her three dresses on the hooks someone had cleared for her, stored her under things in the dresser drawer Julia had left open, and trudged down the hall to the bathroom. There was a small mirror hanging above the sink, but she purposely avoided glancing into it.

Why look? What difference did it make?

Instead, she splashed a little water on her face, washed her hands, and dried off with the towel draped over the hook on the wall. Making her way down the stairs, she stopped in the front room, which was full of tables.

Where were they supposed to eat? There were three large tables and two small ones—none of which had dishes or food on them.

Then she heard the sound of voices.

Sharon stared down at the floor. She would have prayed for strength, but she didn't believe God was listening. So instead she counted to ten, which was her new deal with herself. When she was overwhelmed and had to do something, she gave herself ten counts before she forced herself to put one foot in front of the other. It wasn't a great coping mechanism, but it was something. It was enough to get her feet moving toward Julia and Caleb and Ada.

"Sharon, you found us." Julia stood at the kitchen counter, ladling soup into bowls.

The kitchen was not what she had expected. There was one traditional gas stove, much like what Sharon's mother cooked on—except this one has six burners instead of four. Next to that was a double oven. She assumed it was gas as well because there was no electricity to the house. Julia and Caleb could have asked their bishop for

152 VANNETTA CHAPMAN

an exemption. Plenty of home businesses in Indiana were granted one. She supposed, because they had opted to run the café inside their home rather than in an adjacent building, they had decided against it.

There were also two large refrigerators on the adjacent wall.

Julia caught her staring and explained, "Both are new and both are gas."

"Can't have my *fraa* running back and forth to the icehouse at the same time she's cooking for customers." Caleb laughed. "It must look pretty strange to you, but we decided to trust that the Lord will bring enough customers to pay for our investment."

How much had they spent on this café, which had yet to open for business? On the far side of the kitchen was a smaller dining area, which was apparently where they were to take their meals.

Sharon sat down beside Ada. It seemed they were to be paired with each other. Caleb stood to help Julia with the tray of soup bowls. The tender look that passed between them hurt more than if Ada had picked up one of the butter knives and plunged it into Sharon's ribs.

It wasn't that it reminded her of James—not at all. It reminded her of what she no longer believed in.

Once Julia and Caleb sat, they all bowed their heads, but Sharon didn't pray. She had stopped praying while she waited in the rain on that desolate Monroe county road. Praying was for people who still had some belief.

She waited.

When she heard movement, she looked up. Caleb was reaching for fresh cornbread, Julia was passing the butter, and Ada was smiling.

"Give thanks to the Lord, for He is good."

At least that one made sense.

Ada dipped her spoon into her potato soup, swallowed, and nodded toward Julia. "My *dochder* is an excellent cook. By this time next week, her café will be full of *Englischers* asking for her recipes and promising to return with their *freinden* and family."

"From your lips to *Gotte's* ears, *mamm*."

"*Ya*, already He has heard. Just make sure Caleb has brought up plenty of potatoes from the basement."

"The potato bin is full. It was on Julia's list, and so it's done." He stuffed cornbread in his mouth as he teased his wife.

Sharon pushed her spoon back and forth in her soup bowl. She'd found at home, at first, that no one noticed she wasn't eating if she stirred her food or moved it around her plate. Somehow she thought that might be more difficult to get away with here with just the four of them sitting around a table.

"Is there something wrong with your bowl of soup?" Ada asked.

Sharon shook her head.

"Spoon broke?" Ada persisted.

"*Mamm*, maybe Sharon's merely tired."

"Too tired to eat? Humph. Food strengthens a body. Look at me." Ada lifted both of her hands into the air. "Old maybe, but I'm as healthy as you and Caleb are!"

When no one challenged her statement, she added, "My hands might ache at times. I might even use that cane Doc insisted I bring home, but the rest of me—both inside and out—is still as healthy as ever."

Somehow Sharon doubted that statement, but she wasn't going to question it. Instead of looking directly at Ada, she stared down into her bowl. She was grateful Julia had let her off the hook, though she noticed Caleb was sending her worried glances.

She could have asked to be excused, could have probably gone to bed early, but she didn't want to draw any more attention to herself than necessary. The last thing she needed was for her cousin to write home to her parents and say there had been a problem. In spite of the terrible scene at the bus station, she was hoping they would let her return soon.

So she waited out dinnertime as she pretended to nibble a piece of cornbread. The conversation hummed and buzzed around her. They spoke of details about what was left to do, talked of their neighbors' help—some *Englischers* they had become close friends with—and discussed Aaron and Lydia, who were apparently expecting their first baby. The words flowed over and around her until finally Caleb stood and stretched.

"Suppose I'll go and check on the animals one last time."

"You're not sneaking down to the river, are you?"

"In this weather? *Nein.*" He ran his hand down Julia's arm.

Sharon noticed they did that—touched each other a lot. When they saw her watching, she glanced away.

"Come spring, you might be able to catch me sneaking out for an evening of fishing, but not tonight." Caleb pulled his hat and coat from the peg in the mudroom, which was just a few feet from where they ate. "Be back soon."

Julia began carrying dishes into the kitchen, and Ada stood as if she were going to help her. That was the first time Sharon really looked at her. She wore small glasses, and her blue eyes sparkled behind them. She seemed to have a clear mind at the moment, but Sharon had been certain while they were in the buggy that she'd been disoriented. Perhaps she became confused when she was away from home.

Ada's hair was snow-white, and her skin was as wrinkled as a piece of paper that had been wadded into a ball and then smoothed back out. It reminded Sharon of the note she had attempted to write to her mother while on the long bus ride. In the end she had torn it from her tablet, wadded it up, and placed it in her purse to throw away. But in her room, before dinner, she'd smoothed it back out, carefully folded it, and placed it in the back of her Bible.

She tried not to stare at the condition of Ada's hands. They were curved as if she were holding a ball in each one, only Sharon didn't think it was something she could help. She didn't think Ada could straighten her hands.

"I'll take those," she whispered, picking up Ada's dishes as well as her own. She followed Julia into the kitchen, but not before she glanced back over her shoulder. Ada had moved to sit in her rocker in a corner of the room, pulled her Bible into her lap, and was slowly searching through the Scriptures.

Cleaning the dishes did not take long with the two of them working together. It didn't take long enough. Sharon's habit at home had been to tend to kitchen duties alone. She would stall, soaking her hands in the soapy dishwater until her skin resembled prunes and the water grew cold. After all of the dishes were washed, dried, and stacked in the cabinets—and they had a lot of dishes for nine people—she would begin to clean the counters, the stove, the table, and sometimes even the floor. She would do whatever was necessary to wait out the rest of the household. Eventually silence would settle around her, and she would know that everyone else was in bed. At that point it was safe for her to sit at the table, or stand by the window, or sometimes walk out to the barn. She would do anything to stay awake.

None of that was going to work with only four people eating the evening meal and Julia helping with the cleanup. They were finished before Caleb was back from the barn, and they all trudged upstairs together.

They passed an hour in the sitting room, where Sharon pretended to read, Julia worked on her lists, Ada again studied her Bible, and Caleb read the *Budget*. When the clock on the wall ticked over to nine, Ada stood and moved off to bed.

"I'm sure you're exhausted," Julia said. "You haven't turned a page in the last half hour, and we're probably keeping you awake. Is there anything else you need tonight?"

"*Nein*."

Panic clawed at Sharon's throat. She hadn't realized how easy it was to hide within a large family. Now what? She couldn't explain her fears to this woman she'd just met. She couldn't explain them to anyone. If someone had asked, she couldn't have said why she couldn't sleep, why the mere thought made her stomach pitch and turn. She couldn't explain it to herself. So instead she dutifully followed Ada to their room, changed her clothes, and crawled into the bed.

Which was exactly where she had longed to be two hours earlier. Except it was safe to lie down and hide in the daylight. She was able to stay awake then. Nighttime was a different matter. At night she had to fight to keep her eyes from closing.

And this evening was worse than most.

She'd been awake since four a.m., preparing for her trip. The parting with her mother had been emotional, and she had to push those memories away as she blinked, staring into the darkness. Ada's soft breathing beside her was a rhythmic lull, pulling her down, and then there was the scent of the freshly laundered sheets. Unable to resist, Sharon felt herself drifting deeper into the abyss she feared the most.

The rain continued to fall in sheets. Sharon didn't need to look down to know the Englisch *clothes she wore were thoroughly soaked. She stood shivering beneath the streetlight. Joana had answered the phone. Her best friend had promised to send help. She had told Sharon to wait exactly where she was near the crossroads signal.*

Thunder cracked more loudly than a hunting rifle, causing Sharon to jump and glance around. Had lightning hit something? Would it strike near her next?

Maybe she should move away from the streetlight, but Joana had told her to wait there. When she tried to check her phone again, it wouldn't even turn on. She should have checked to see if James had a car charger, but then James was the problem. She should have never left with him.

So many decisions to regret.

A car's lights slashed through the darkness.

Hope surged through her, but even as she stepped out onto the road, Sharon knew it could not be her father. She'd placed the call only ten minutes ago. There hadn't been enough time for Joana to reach him and for him to find a ride. She stepped back to the shoulder, but it was too late. The car slowed and then it stopped.

One middle-aged man was driving the large black car and another younger man was riding in the passenger seat. He rolled down his window and shouted for her to get in. Sharon shook her head and stepped back off the road, praying they would drive on.

The rider, who she now saw had a scar on the right side of his face, opened the door, stepped out into the rain, and motioned for her to get in the car. Sharon moved even farther into the field. Her shoes slipped in the mud as she backed away from the strangers. The man with the scar turned and said something to the person driving. She didn't hear what it was, but somehow she knew what he was going to do when he turned back toward her.

She had been considering running down the road, but she knew instinctively he would catch her there. So instead she reversed directions and ran into the field at the same moment he lurched for her, his fingers trailing down her bare arm.

Sharon stumbled through the field, through the darkness, zigzagging through the remains of the farmer's crops. She heard him at first, following her, cursing, slipping in the mud. Then all she heard was the rain, the thunder, and the thudding of her heart.

But still she didn't stop.

Running blindly in the darkness, she didn't realize he was standing in her path until she ran into him. Somehow he had circled around and found a way in front of her. Too late she tried to change directions. This time her feet slipped in the mud and she fell, hard, against the muddy ground. He caught her then, and his hands closed around her arms in a viselike grip.

Sharon struggled and kicked and fought to free herself, but she was no match for his strength. It was then she began to scream...

She woke curled in a tight ball, her hands covering her face and the sound of whimpering filling her ears. Soon enough she realized she was making the childish sounds.

She'd had the dream again. He'd caught her again.

She lay in the bed, willing her heart rate to slow and reminding herself it hadn't happened...at least the last few moments of the dream hadn't happened that way. The man with the scar had never caught her. She had run until she was so lost no one could have found her, which was part of the problem. It had taken her father and the *Englisch* driver hours of searching back and forth across the surrounding roads to locate her.

As she reached to wipe the tears from her face, she realized she wasn't alone. She remembered she was in Caleb and Julia's house, and she recognized the voice speaking.

Opening her eyes, she saw that Ada had awakened and pulled the single chair in the room closer to the bed. Her hands were on Sharon's hair, gently touching the crown of her head, and her words, as soft as the sheet on her skin, were a balm.

"The Lord is your shepherd, Sharon."

She pulled in a deep breath, closed her eyes again, and allowed Ada's words to fall over her.

"He makes you to lie down in green pastures."

Something inside of her unclenched for the first time since that night.

"He restores your soul."

She eventually fell back into a dreamless sleep, with Ada's hands lying softly on her head and the words of Psalm 23 ministering to her soul.

Chapter 20

S he's still not eating." Julia washed the sandwich plates from lunch as she looked out the kitchen window. She had wrapped Sharon's sandwich in a dishcloth. Caleb liked a midafternoon snack, so at least it wouldn't go to waste.

"Ya, but she looked like she wanted to eat. That's a step in the right direction." Caleb put his arms around his wife's waist, causing her to drop the cup she was rinsing back into the sudsy water.

Ada had gone upstairs to nap, and Sharon was outside taking down laundry from the line. The day was sunny and the temperature in the fifties. The sheets and clothes they had hung out early that morning were already dry.

She and Caleb were completely alone in the kitchen, but even so, Julia wasn't accustomed to her husband's displays of affection. She could hardly believe that perhaps he did care for her. Perhaps he hadn't married her out of pity.

"I'm worried about Sharon."

He kissed her cheek, peered out through the window, and shrugged. "She looks okay to me." Moving to the cookie platter, he snagged two and leaned against the counter.

"Except she weighs twenty pounds less than she should." Julia dried off a plate with a flourish and practically tossed it into the cabinet. "She barely speaks. And she wakes with nightmares." A cup rattled as she set it next to the plates with a bit more energy than necessasry.

"I've been warned to beware of wives when the dishes start to shake, rattle, and roll."

"Oh, you have?" Julia paused with another cup in her right hand and a dish towel in her left.

"*Ya.*"

"And who would warn you of that?"

"Can't say."

"Can I guess?"

"Probably, but that's not the point."

"What *is* the point, Caleb Zook?"

He moved closer, pulled the dish towel from her hand, and helped her store the cup more gently in the cabinet. "That you're worried about my cousin, which I appreciate. And you're trying to hurry the Lord's work, which is useless and frustrating."

Her hands free, she allowed herself to be pulled into his embrace, and when she did, Julia's tension melted like the soap bubbles in her dishwater. "You think it's the Lord's work for her to be here? You think being with us will help her?"

"It's Monday. She only arrived last Friday, but already she is smiling occasionally."

"Maybe at *mamm* when she quotes the Psalms, especially the times they make no sense."

"Which is something."

Julia sighed as she rested her head on her husband's chest, her face turned toward the window. Sharon had loaded the laundry into the basket and was carrying it toward the house. "She's a *gut* girl, Caleb. I wish I understood what is bothering her. The letter from your *mamm* didn't explain very much about what happened in Indiana."

"It explained enough. She had a bad experience with a boy, was struggling through her *rumspringa*, and her parents thought time away would be best."

Julia looked up at him. "A bad experience with a boy. What does that mean?"

"We don't know. Maybe we don't need to know. If Sharon wants to tell us more, she will. Until then, we'll be family to her." He bent his head to kiss her.

The clatter of a buggy out in front of their home broke into their tender moment.

"That should be Gabe," he said. "He offered to pick up the new menus and bring them to us."

Julia's excitement won out over her worry. They were opening the café the next day. She couldn't control if anyone would show up, but she could check off the final items on her list. Number one was inspecting the menus to be sure they had been printed correctly before storing them in the cubbyhole in the front hallway.

"I'll let him in," Caleb murmured, planting a final kiss on the top of her head before releasing her.

Sharon had made it to the back door, so Julia hurried to help her inside with the large load of laundry. They arrived at their family table at the same time as Gabe, Miriam, and little Rachel.

"Miriam, I didn't realize you were coming today!"

"I saw Grace off to school and finished my laundry early. I wanted to see the menus and the changes you have made to the house. Julia, this is amazing! I love the dining rooms."

"*Danki*. The men did most of the work, and the tables are all from your *bruder*."

"David was excited to sell them to you. Now he's busy making more for tourists who may like what they're sitting at and want to take a new table and chairs home."

Gabe set a large cardboard box on the table.

Sharon stared back and forth as if she wasn't sure what to do—stop at the table or walk upstairs to fold the laundry. Julia noticed her eyes linger on Rachel. Miriam's daughter was younger than Sharon's little sister, Ruthie, but perhaps the child still reminded her of home and better days. The letter from Caleb's mother had said Sharon would likely miss her sister the most.

"Sharon, stay with us and look." Julia patted the chair next to her.

"*Ya*, this is a big event in the Zook family!" Caleb laughed. "Tomorrow my *fraa* begins cooking all day."

Sharon glanced around as if she was looking for a way to escape. "But I was—"

Rachel ran over to Sharon and held up a small wooden horse she'd brought inside with her. Sharon had met everyone at church the day before, though Julia had not seen the girl intermingle with any of the other teens. Sharon kept to herself and didn't speak unless someone spoke to her directly.

Julia had noticed her helping with the younger children at one point, and apparently Rachel had spent some time with her then.

"The laundry will keep," Julia assured her.

Caleb cut open the tape on the top of the box and removed the packaging stuffed around their order. Everyone stared down at the menus, but Miriam was the first to speak.

"Beautiful! These are absolutely beautiful."

Julia reached in and pulled out a handful, taking one and passing the rest around. The menu listed Julia's dishes and was surrounded by Grace's artwork. The words "Plain Café" were written across the top in a simple script that looked remarkably similar to the board Wess had painted by the road. The entire page was bordered in a wavy scroll, which in the top left corner turned into a creek. Reeds grew up in front of it, and the words *Pebble Creek* were etched lightly below that. The creek symbol was repeated in the bottom right corner.

The menu was a single page, with printing on the front and back. The front had breakfast items and hours of operation. The back had lunch specials and take-out dinner items because they planned to close by six each day. This had been one of Julia's biggest worries. She wanted to offer an evening meal, but she didn't want to extend their hours into what should be family time. The idea of a take-out dinner was Caleb's and seemed like a good compromise.

Turning the menu over, Julia set it down and clapped her hands.

"It's *gut*. Don't you think?" Gabe sounded like a proud father, and he should.

Sharon stepped closer to peer over her shoulder.

"Grace drew all of these," Julia explained. She pointed to the small pictures of animals bordering the back of the menu—beaver, deer, and fox. Though the drawings were as small as a postage stamp, Grace had managed to pencil in an amazing amount of detail.

"*Ya*, and she only included animals she was certain visit Pebble Creek." Miriam ran her finger over the mouse, muskrat, and opossum. "She double-checked each animal with her father and then with her teacher, Miss Bena."

"Is that a big rat?" Sharon asked.

"Woodchuck." Caleb laughed. "Some folks call it a groundhog or a whistle-pig. Your *bruders* would know what it is."

"And they live near the creek?" Sharon's eyes widened.

"No worries." Gabe pulled out a chair and sat down. "They're more afraid of you than..."

"Actually, they're not," Miriam interrupted, "but they hibernate in the winter. Chances are you won't see one here unless you're around in the spring."

"I love being married to a former schoolmarm. She keeps me thinking."

"And reading. Did you finish that book we borrowed from the library? The one on how to modify a donkey's behavior?"

"They have a problem donkey," Caleb explained.

"I was reading it last night while I was holding Rachel."

"You both were sleeping."

"*Ya*, later. But at first I was reading to her."

Miriam shook her head and turned her attention back to the menu in her hand. "These are nicely done, Julia. They're easy to read with a nice large font."

"Jeanette helped. She googled menus—"

"She what?" Gabe pulled on his beard.

"Googled. I don't know what that is, but it's something on a computer. Anyway, she said the three biggest complaints about menus were they were often dirty—"

"Which is why we chose to laminate them." Caleb rubbed the plastic between his fingers. "Easier to clean."

"The second complaint is that it's too difficult to locate information—"

"You've certainly kept it simple," Miriam said. "No one should have problems ordering."

"And the third is that they are too hard to read because the print is often too small."

"Some restaurants want that," Caleb said. "They don't want you to find the special or know the prices."

"Not here." Julia tapped the menu. "We're customer friendly."

Rachel had been playing on the floor, but now she walked to the table and peered over the top. "*Freinds?*"

"Yes, honey. We're *freinden.*" Miriam kissed her daughter, and then she turned her attention back to the menu. "Whose idea was it to add the information about the tables and quilts?"

"Lydia's," Julia said.

"Julia's," Caleb said.

"Both?" Miriam asked, smiling.

"*Ya*, I suppose so." Julia ran her finger along the short paragraph on the bottom of the back side. "We didn't want to be obnoxious, like Amish Anthem, and we certainly didn't want to hang prices around everything on the bottom floor of our home." Julia peeked into the next room. The tables were beautiful in the afternoon sunshine pouring through the windows. They had also added a few handmade quilts from women in their district, tastefully draped over quilt stands.

"So instead we thought to add two short lines. Jeanette helped us with the wording." Caleb ran a hand over his jaw where his beard was coming in. "She's *gut* at this sort of thing."

They all studied the menu and read the lines Caleb referred to: *Dining sets and quilts may be purchased from local artisans. Please ask if you'd like more information.*

"It's a *gut* thing to do," Gabe said. "It could help other families bring in a little extra income."

"All we need now is a roomful of customers." Julia slid her menu back into the box.

"Are you worried about it?" Miriam handed her menu to Julia as Rachel attempted to climb into her lap.

"*Nein.* As *mamm* says, *Gotte* will send who we are to serve. We've done all we can, including advertising every way we can think of."

"Jeanette even posted an article about the opening on her computer. She has a blog, whatever that is." Caleb beamed at Julia as he explained, "She says it's like a newspaper, but not actually written on paper."

They stared at each other a moment, considering that. Finally Miriam asked, "Is there anything left to do?"

"A little baking."

As Julia pulled out her list, Caleb stepped closer to Gabe. "Speaking of things left to do, I could use your hand with a stall in the barn if you have a few minutes."

Caleb raised his eyebrows in a way Julia was learning to read. No doubt they would stop by and repair something in the barn, but the trip would end at Pebble Creek with a fishing pole in someone's hand.

Not that she minded.

Looking at her list, she saw that everything had been marked off except for making tomorrow's desserts and putting in tonight's dinner.

"I should take care of these clothes." Sharon picked up the laundry basket and headed upstairs. Before she left the room, though, she walked into the kitchen, fetched the cookie jar, and brought it back to Rachel.

"Is it okay?" she asked Julia.

"If Miriam doesn't mind. I should have thought of offering her something myself."

Miriam knelt down in front of her daughter and whispered the question to her. "Rachel says she would love a cookie. *Danki.*"

Sharon set the little girl up with cookies and a glass of milk, and then she made her way upstairs to the sitting room. It occurred to Julia that she had a servant's heart, but as she turned to go upstairs her shoulders slumped and it seemed she had hardly any energy at all. No wonder, between the lack of sleep and lack of food. If she could coax the girl into eating, and if the nightmares would stop, then perhaps they could help Sharon turn things around.

But in the meantime, they had a café to open.

Chapter 21

In the last several months, Caleb's life had changed radically. Stepping into the barn and doing his nightly walk-through to check on Red and Missy, it wasn't lost on him that he had been sleeping in a barn before he had married Julia. Of course, he could have found a nicer place to rent at the time, but why?

Staying in Aaron's barn had suited him fine—then. Now he couldn't imagine going back.

Aaron's barn and Aaron's cabins had been within sight of the creek. The creek had pulled him, called to him, and satisfied him in a way that few things could.

Until he'd met Julia.

Correction. He'd been acquainted with Julia for quite some time, but he'd never taken the time and effort to get to know her. Facing that shortcoming in himself honestly kept him awake some nights. If not for Ada's decree, he might still be a single man, sleeping in Aaron's barn and spending all his free time fishing on the banks of Pebble Creek. Not that he minded a free hour or two with a line in the water.

He'd found a few times to fish since the day in the garden with Julia. Like now—more often than not—he'd spent the hours thinking of his new wife. He would remember something she had done, the way the light caught her hair as she brushed it, or the sound of her voice.

When the barn door opened and she walked inside, he wondered if maybe his thoughts had pulled her from the house and straight across the yard to his side.

"Done baking?"

"*Ya.*"

"Everything ready for tomorrow?"

"I think so."

She wore a knitted shawl over her dress—something done up in a soft blue. He could just make out the color and pattern in the light of the gas lantern. Julia walked to Missy and rubbed the bay between her ears.

"The opening will be fine," he assured her. "Aaron and Lydia told me today that all of their cabins are leased the rest of the week. They promised to point hungry guests this way."

Julia nodded, pulled a strip of apple peeling from her pocket, and handed it to Missy. Caleb waited and watched as she stepped over to Red and did the same.

"You're spoiling my horse."

"*Ya?*"

"You are."

"We've talked about this before, and you admitted to feeding him treats yourself long before we were married."

Caleb thought of how to answer that without agreeing she was right.

"I think they like each other." Julia moved to the opposite wall and stood across from the horses, watching with her head cocked.

Though they were in separate stalls, they managed to *talk* to each other, or so it seemed to Caleb.

"Maybe they do."

"Maybe Missy was lonely before you and Red came to live here."

Julia turned and smiled at him, and something in Caleb's heart flipped, like a fish in a stream. "Do you have any of those apple peels for me?"

"*Nein*, but I saved you some warm apple nut bars."

"You did?"

"I'd give you a slice of apple pie, but I don't think I should cut it."

"The bars will be fine." He linked his fingers with hers and they walked out of the barn. He turned out the gas lantern when they stepped outside. The stars and moon provided enough light for them to see their way across the yard and up the porch steps.

Caleb held the door for her as they entered the mudroom.

While he stored the lantern, Julia moved into the kitchen, which smelled like heaven—or like heaven should in Caleb's opinion.

"Sharon and Ada in bed?"

"Probably not, but they're upstairs already." She poured two glasses of milk, and he carried the plate of apple bars over to their table.

"How did I manage to land such a *wunderbaar* woman, Julia Zook?" He bit into his dessert and had to close his eyes as apple, sugar, and nutmeg melted on his tongue. His life had definitely improved since his days of living in a barn.

"Land a wife? You sound as if you've caught a fish."

"*Nein*. I said it wrong, but the question was a serious one. How is it no man asked you to marry him before? You're even tempered, beautiful, and a first-rate cook."

Julia blushed, but she didn't respond right away.

He took another bite and waited.

Glancing at him, she pulled in her bottom lip. He had noticed it was something she did when she was concentrating on a thing. Finally she said, "I'm trying to decide if I should answer your question. Do you seriously want to know?"

"I suppose I do, if you want to share about that time. If you don't, I can finish off these bars and thank *Gotte* for my blessings even if I don't understand them."

She drank from her glass of milk, and glanced up at him as she set it carefully back on the table. "I was pledged to be married—once."

"He must have been a fool to lose you."

"His name was Thomas." She fiddled with her napkin as she spoke, but he could tell by her voice that no real emotion lingered in the remembering. It was more as if she were reciting a story about someone else. "I was young—nineteen. The week before we were to wed, I learned his family was planning on moving to Kentucky."

"He hadn't told you?"

"He had assumed I would go, and maybe I would have. But..."

"But he didn't ask."

She looked directly at him then. "He just took my answer for granted."

Taking another drink of her milk, she stared out the window. "I tried to explain to him my feelings about my parents and our situation. I was an only child and they needed me. Thomas, he became angry and began quoting Scripture about a how a woman's place is with her husband—"

"Scripture isn't to be used for winning fights."

"I suppose you're right."

"You know I am."

Julia picked up her napkin and folded it into a triangle. "My parents *did* need me. I was all they had. Both my *mamm* and *dat* were older when I was born—*mamm* was forty-one, which isn't young to bear a last child but is unusual for a first. By the time I was to be wed, she was sixty, and already there were signs that their health, especially my father's, was deteriorating."

"And her arthritis—"

"*Ya.* She could hardly cook or clean, though she tried." Julia met his gaze. "I broke off the wedding plans."

They sat there in the kitchen, Julia's revelation interrupted only by the small sounds of Sharon and Ada moving around in the room above them.

Finally Caleb sat back and said, "He was foolish."

Julia shrugged. "My *mamm* said it was *Gotte's wille.*"

"Did she quote a Psalm?"

"The forty-sixth. God is our refuge—"

"And strength." They finished it together, smiling.

"It's a favorite of hers, I gather."

"You gather correctly."

Picking up the empty glasses, he rinsed them and placed them in the drainer while Julia wrapped up the remaining two apple bars and placed them in a container for his lunch the next day.

"And there was no one else?" He placed his hand at her back as they started up the stairs.

"Perhaps a look or word occasionally, but none who were serious about future plans. As I grew older and *mamm's* and *dat's* health grew worse, men became less interested."

When they reached their bedroom door, he turned her toward him, tipped up her face, and kissed her lightly on the lips. "I'm a fortunate man, Julia."

He wasn't sure she believed him, but she would. He vowed then and there that one day she would.

She slipped into their bedroom. Perhaps she needed a few minutes alone, though she hadn't seemed disturbed by the retelling. He walked down to join Ada and Sharon in the sitting room and picked up the *Budget*, the same issue he'd read the night before. It was a large paper, and there were parts he would like to scan again.

He had trouble focusing, though.

His mind kept returning to Julia's story. Occasionally he'd glance over the top of the paper to Ada, who was working her way through the Psalms with an occasional stop in Proverbs, and Sharon, who was again pretending to read one of the few novels Julia kept in the house.

Several minutes later Julia joined them, and they passed a pleasant hour—the four people who made up Caleb's odd little family. He impatiently watched the clock hands move. He could hardly wait until it was a proper time for them to be alone. There were things he wanted to say to her.

Finally Ada rose and toddled off to bed.

When Julia stood and began tidying the room, an expression of panic crossed his cousin's face.

"I think I'll read a little longer," she said.

"All right." Julia paused at the door before walking across the room and enfolding the girl in a hug. "Remember we rise extra early tomorrow."

Sharon nodded and went back to staring at the book.

As he and Julia were walking down the hall to their room, Caleb heard Ada go back into the sitting room and talk softly with Sharon.

When Julia came to bed, he honestly meant to speak with her, to tell her all that was on his heart. Perhaps he shouldn't have asked about her first love, if it was love, but on the other hand he was glad he knew. He wanted to be able to heal the hurt places from her past, and how could he do that if he didn't know where they were?

He had every intention of putting those things into words, but he found it was easier to show her than it was to tell her.

Caleb discovered that in the darkness and without saying a word he could express his feelings more tenderly, more honestly, and more completely than he would ever have imagined possible.

Later, when he thought she was asleep, Julia turned onto her back and asked, "What about you?"

"Me?"

"Ya. You're even older than I am. There must have been someone else."

His laughter slid across the room as easily as leaves falling from the trees outside their window.

"That's not an answer," she teased.

"That's not a normal question when we're in bed."

"You didn't give me time to finish our conversation earlier." She snuggled up to him, her back against his chest. "What was her name?"

"Lois." He wasn't surprised that the name brought no real emotion with it. Too many years had passed. It was like pining over an old injury. At some point, you forgot which scars had come from which mishap. One day you woke and it didn't matter anymore. You were simply glad you had healed.

"How old were you?"

"How old was I?"

She elbowed him in the ribs. "You're stalling by repeating my questions."

"Ya. It's harder to realize how young I was then—and how old I am now—than it is to think about a young pup who fancied himself *in lieb* with a girl."

"So you weren't? *In lieb?*"

"Who is to say? I thought I was."

The sounds of a night bird in the tree outside their window interrupted the silence that had fallen around them. Caleb realized he could be satisfied here, with Julia. He could be content for the rest of his life.

"What happened?"

"Lois was young, probably too young, a mere eighteen." He ran his fingers through Julia's hair. It was thick and soft and felt like silk...or what he imagined silk would feel like. "We were planning to marry but hadn't made our announcement yet."

"You never did?"

He shook his head in the darkness. "She left."

"Left?" Julia flipped over on her back. "Moved away? Like...like Thomas?"

"*Nein.* Not like Thomas."

Because it seemed she wanted to know, he told her all of it. How he had counted himself so lucky to have attracted the younger girl when he was twenty-five. Now he thought his feelings for her must have been infatuation, like when one of the Amish boys saw a new horse or a new buggy and thought they had to have it. He had been that way with Lois. Only people aren't things and couldn't be had in that way.

"Where did she go?"

"She would run off sometimes with her girlfriends. They would ride in cars and such. I told myself it was because she was young and she would outgrow it before we wed. Then one night she came to see me and told me they were going to Indianapolis and wouldn't be back."

"To live in the city?"

"*Ya.* I didn't believe her. Six months later, I was still waiting, still sure she would show up and we'd pick up where we'd left off. Her friends did come back, but Lois stayed. Later I heard that she'd moved to Ohio and joined a Mennonite group there."

"She broke your heart?"

"No, Julia. She hurt my pride, and pride is a sin, *ya?*"

"I don't understand."

"I thought she would want me more than she wanted a different life. When she didn't, it left me confused about myself, but it didn't break my heart. I'm not sure how much of my heart was ever involved."

Julia thought about that a while. Finally she snuggled closer and asked, "So what did you do next?"

"I told myself I liked being alone—that being alone was better. That the fishing, hunting, and outdoor things my married *freinden* no longer had time to do, I was able to do all the time, or at least as much as I wanted. I convinced myself there would always be a chance to find another woman to share my life with."

Her breathing evened out, and he thought she was asleep when she reached up and touched his face. "You found me."

Julia's words were as gentle as the touch of her hand, as soft as her hair, as tender as her heart. They were a whisper of love.

Caleb fell asleep, thanking God for what had been and what was to come. He stepped into dreams where he and Julia walked through fields thick with tall stalks of corn, and in the distance he could make out the sunshine glinting off the waters of Pebble Creek.

Chapter 22

Sharon thought she was used to hard work. After all, she was the oldest girl in a family of seven children. Once she graduated from the eighth grade, she didn't look for a job because there was so much work to do at home. And her parents probably figured she would marry soon. While seventeen wasn't old maid status by any means, she had seen the occasional worried look pass between them. Those looks had increased when she'd begun seeing James.

Carrying yet one more armful of dirty lunch dishes into Julia's kitchen, Sharon realized she had learned several things since leaving the one-room schoolhouse in Monroe. She'd learned that sitting in a desk and learning was much easier than washing laundry for a family of nine. She'd learned that whoever came up with her favorite proverb, "Keeping a neat house is like threading beads on a string with no knot on it," must have been a woman. And she'd learned that she adored small children, especially the preschool age.

There was an *Englisch* family of three sitting in the front dining room whom she'd checked on more often than others—the impish three-year-old boy could have been the reason why. Every time she slowed at their table, he held up three fingers and declared, "Colton free."

Breakfast had been manageable, with a steady but small stream of customers.

The lunch rush was a "slam," as her brother Jonas would say. They had been nearly full since eleven thirty. The clock in the kitchen now said one fifteen, and still cars were pulling up in front of the house.

"The special is ready for table eight," Julia said, beaming even as she wiped the perspiration off of her forehead.

Opening day for Plain Café was a success by any standard, unless you counted the collapse of its two employees—three if you included Ada, who sat by the front door and welcomed customers as they entered.

Sharon hefted the plates and turned to march back into the main dining room, but her vision shifted, the room angled left and then right, and the plates teetered in her arms.

"*Was iss letz?*" Julia was beside her immediately, reaching for the plates with one hand and steadying her with the other. "Are you ill?"

"*Nein.* Only a little dizzy. I'm fine."

"You should rest. You haven't had a break all day."

Sharon shook her head. They both knew Julia couldn't wait on customers and cook.

At that moment a tap was heard on the back door and then a tall, sandy-haired boy stepped inside. He wore blue jeans and a black T-shirt with cartoon characters on the front, and even from where she stood Sharon could see that he had green eyes.

"Wess, could you take this soup and sandwich to the man sitting alone in the main dining room? It's table eight, the one nearest the window looking over the garden."

"Gotcha covered." He accepted the dishes as if he'd been carrying plates of food all his life and headed toward the elderly gentleman, who probably thought he'd been forgotten.

Sharon didn't want to know who he was.

The last thing she needed or wanted was to be around a teenage boy. Just as she felt her emotions balancing, just as Ada's voice in her

mind was becoming stronger than those of her supposed friends in
Monroe, she did not need to be around someone like him.

"I think I will take a break."

"Sure. Here, you can have this sandwich. The little girl at table
four changed her mind. And go outside—"

She never heard the rest. She fled out the back door to the barn,
to somewhere she could hide and figure out what to do.

⌒

Twenty minutes later Sharon forced herself to walk back to the
house. She couldn't leave Julia in there alone, and she would not be
run off by some *Englisch* boy. As she'd nibbled around the edges of
the sandwich, she had thought about it and ruled out any possibility
that he might be Amish and on his *rumpsringa*.

For one thing, his hair was much too long. She'd caught sight of
a ponytail as he'd left the kitchen. A ponytail on a boy! Second, he'd
said "Gotcha covered." No Amish boy could have pulled off that
slang and sounded even marginally convincing.

So why was an *Englisch* teenager helping Julia?

It didn't matter why, she decided, climbing the back porch steps
and entering the mudroom. They had four hours until closing.
She did feel better now that she'd rested and eaten a little, plus she
wanted to check on Ada. She was not going to hide because of a boy.

Julia was sitting at the table eating when she walked into the
kitchen.

"Better?"

"*Ya.*"

"*Gut.* Things have slowed a little, but only because they're lingering over dessert."

Sharon smiled. She'd never watched someone's dream come true
before. What did that feel like? From the expression on Julia's face, it
felt better than fabulous, better than anything Sharon could imagine.

"The woman at table one wants you to know your apple pie is better than her mother's." Wess placed some dirty dishes next to the sink and pulled a wad of money from his pants.

"Do I keep this or are we sharing?" His lopsided grin widened as he spoke.

Sharon walked to the kitchen cabinet and pulled out one of Julia's canning jars. Unscrewing the lid, she dumped the money from her apron pockets into it. "Tips should be shared if you're staying."

"Sure, I'll stay. That's why my mom sent me over here. To see if you needed help."

"Your mom?"

"Sharon, this is Wess. He lives next door. His parents are Jeanette and Tim. You've heard us talk about them. They have both helped us a lot since we began redoing things for the café."

Sharon didn't trust her voice to say anything, so she nodded.

"Wess, this is Caleb's cousin Sharon. She's from Indiana."

"Indiana, huh? I've never been there, but I've heard it's pretty cool."

Sharon rolled her eyes.

Indiana was not cool, but it was home. She missed it more than she would have thought possible.

The front door opened and shut, and Sharon remembered she was going to check on Ada.

"Can you stay until we close?" Julia was asking. "That's four more hours."

"Sure, but I'm going to text my mom so she'll know what's up."

What's up. Did he always speak in short slangy sentences?

It was none of her business. She checked on the tables in the front dining room and then moved to the entry hall, where Ada was still sitting, though her head was practically on her chest.

"Let me help you upstairs."

"What?" Ada looked around in confusion but relaxed when she focused on Sharon's face. "You're a *gut* girl."

"Would you like to go upstairs and lie down?"

She plucked at Sharon's sleeve. "*Nein*. Not upstairs. My rocker maybe."

"All right." Sharon waited for Ada to stand and find her cane. She didn't want her walking alone back to their eating area while she was still barely awake. She might trip and fall. She might be hurt.

So she waited until Ada had stood and tucked her right arm through hers. Her left hand clutched her cane as they slowly walked back to the rocker. The woman was nearly asleep again by the time Sharon had covered her with a lap quilt.

When she returned to the front dining room with a pot of coffee in one hand and a pitcher of water in the other, a woman at table five stopped her. "That's a very sweet thing you did, helping your grandmother."

"Oh, but she's not—"

"In this day and age, it's nice to see young people who know how to be respectful." This was said by the man sitting across from the woman. His head was bald and shiny on top, but a bit of gray fringe wrapped around the side. "Rare, unfortunately, and it's nice to see."

Sharon thought again of trying to correct them, but instead she murmured, "*Danki*" and moved on to the next table. Probably people would confuse Ada as her grandmother, possibly even Julia and Caleb as her parents. What difference did it make? She wouldn't be staying long enough for it to matter.

The afternoon was less busy than the morning, though Sharon admitted to herself it was still nice to have an extra pair of hands. Wess was able to take care of any orders that were ready when she was settling a customer's bill. And just when she thought Julia could tell him they didn't need him anymore, people started arriving and ordering food to take home.

Why hadn't they folded together some of the take-out boxes ahead of time? Instead, the pieces of cardboard sat flat and stacked neatly in a pile on the top shelf in the mudroom. Wess laughed, pulled them off the shelf without the help of a stool, and began putting them together. Julia wrapped the food in foil, and Sharon added up each order on the palm-sized calculator Caleb had purchased at the grocery.

The take-out rush lasted until exactly six p.m., when Julia joyfully flipped the sign to "Closed," Caleb stepped into the mudroom, and Wess raised his hand in a high-five gesture to all.

Julia seemed at a loss, and Caleb only raised an eyebrow. Sharon did not want to encourage Wess into thinking they were friends, but she did feel a little sorry for him, standing there holding his hand up midair, waiting. So she slapped her palm against his and ignored the grin that spread across his face.

"*Gut* day, huh?" Caleb placed his hat on the peg by the door.

"Very *gut.*" Julia tapped her fingers against the counter. "Wait until I tell you about it."

"Can you tell me while we're eating? I'm starved." Everyone groaned, and Caleb glanced around in confusion. "What did I say? I thought you liked hungry customers."

"No more customers," Wess explained, flopping in mock exhaustion onto the kitchen stool.

"Actually, I saved some of the soup and cornbread, plus we have dessert left over."

"The heavens declare the glory of God." Ada hobbled into the room. She'd been standing on the back porch staring across the fields. "What kind of soup did you make, *dochder?*"

The conversation turned to food and customers and the amount of guests they'd had. Julia pulled out her list, checked off what had already been done for the next day, and added what would still need to be finished for the morning meal.

Wess dropped the last of his tips into the jar and shook it back and forth. "Ready to count this up?"

Sharon shrugged, but in truth she was curious. She hadn't decided what she was going to do with her money yet, but she thought maybe she should give some of it to Caleb and Julia. They were letting her stay in their home for free.

She followed Wess to a table in the front dining room, and they counted out the money, dividing bills from change and adding it all together twice to be sure the total was correct. Sharon split it and pushed half across the table to him.

"No way." When he shook his head, some of his hair escaped from the rubber band holding it back. "I wasn't even here for the first part of the day."

He pulled out two of the bills and gave them back to her. "Tomorrow we'll have two tip jars. One for the morning, which you keep, and another for the afternoon, which we'll share."

"You're coming back tomorrow?"

Wess shrugged. "Why not? I don't have anything else to do. In case you haven't noticed, this town isn't exactly hopping."

Hopping. "Don't you have school?"

"Only two classes. I'm a senior this year, so I go half days—well, not even that long. I'm out by eleven."

Sharon nodded as if she understood, but to her what he'd just said didn't make any sense. She thought all *Englisch* students went to school through the twelfth grade.

Wess stood up and stuffed the money in his pockets. "At this rate, I'll be able to buy—"

But before he could finish, the front door opened and a woman walked in with two small girls. The mother was probably Julia's age but with short red hair. The girls were young. One looked to be five or six. She had brown hair pulled into two ponytails and was holding a baby doll. The other was a few years older and had red hair like her mother, which she wore in a single long braid. She was holding a small dog, who was wearing a sweater.

The second both girls saw Wess, they let out a screech and ran across the room.

≈ Chapter 23 ≈

Victoria, I told you to leave that dog on the front porch."

"I can't leave Bandit outside. He would feel terrible!"

Julia heard the voices and the commotion in the front room. She walked in as Victoria was handing a small dog over to Wess. The little pooch was about the size of a stuffed animal, with a lot of brown hair that one of the girls had tried to pull into ponytails. The sweater he was wearing said, "Beware of Dog."

"I'm sorry, Julia. I explained to them you don't have pets in your home."

"It's not a problem. I'm guessing by that sweater that..."

"Bandit." Both girls supplied his name.

"I'm guessing Bandit isn't just any pet."

"See, Mom? I told you she'd understand." Victoria scratched the small dog between the ears, and he responded with a yip.

"They wanted to walk over to see Wess at work, but we try to take Bandit for a walk every afternoon to use up some of his energy."

"Beware of dog. Is he dangerous?"

"Only in his mind," Jeanette said, with a laugh. "He thinks he's much larger than he is and quite ferocious."

Wess tried to hand the dog to Sharon, but she stepped away from him.

"Tell me you're not afraid of dogs."

"*Nein.*"

"Especially itty-bitty dogs."

"I'm not."

"Then hold him. He wants to say hi."

Both girls giggled.

"He likes you," Zoey declared.

Julia wondered if the young girl was talking about Bandit or Wess. Sharon accepted the dog, but she made the mistake of holding him up in the air in front of her. Bandit pushed his nose forward and licked her on the face.

"Oh!" She dropped Bandit back into Wess's arms.

"It's official now. You're friends for life."

Sharon shook her head and wiped at the wet spot near the right side of her mouth.

"He does that to me all the time." Zoey reached up and patted Sharon's arm. "Don't worry. His germs are good germs."

Which caused them all to laugh, even Sharon.

Julia walked the Elliots to the door, though she noticed that Sharon slipped out the back way.

"We couldn't have done it without Wess today. I don't know what I was thinking. There's no way Sharon and I can handle everything alone."

"That's wonderful." Jeanette stopped, turned, and gave her a hug. "Your first day and already the café is a success."

"I don't know about that. We'll see how many of our customers return and how the winter months go."

"One day at a time. Or in your case, maybe we should say one meal at a time. I have no doubt your customers will return and tell their friends. I'm so excited for you."

"I wanted to speak with you and Wess about his returning. We could use his help each afternoon."

As they all filed out onto the porch, Jeanette looked up at her son. "Are you interested in part-time employment?"

"Sure. I don't have much else to do," Wess said, tugging at his ponytail.

There was a story about his hairstyle, Julia was sure. Sooner or later he would tell them. Even as he answered his mother, he was glancing back through the open door, looking for Sharon. Jeanette and Julia's eyes met, and they shared a smile.

While Julia didn't want Sharon to be involved with another boy, especially an *Englisch* boy, the young girl could use some friends her age.

"As long as your grades don't suffer, it sounds like a good arrangement to me."

"Mom. Seriously? Have my grades ever suffered?"

"There was the one time you became obsessed with that video game and you—"

"I was twelve years old, and you're still bringing that up!"

"Just saying..."

"Just saying," both girls echoed.

Wess set Bandit on the ground and handed his leash to Victoria. The leash was black leather with shiny jeweled decorations. Julia knew the Elliotts were embracing the simple life. Tim had been farming their way for more than a year. Jeanette had shared with her that she'd begun sewing the girls' clothes, and they were attending church again for the first time in years. She was also working with the children to cut back on television and computer time.

Simple things, which often seemed difficult for *Englischers*.

The Elliotts were adjusting well.

As they walked home next door, Bandit's fancy leash caught and reflected the last of the day's light. Everyone was apparently on board with a simpler lifestyle except the dog.

⌒

Dinner was good, as usual.

Caleb was tired from his day of loading and unloading orders.

He'd arranged to cut his workdays back to three days a week—Tuesday, Thursday, and Friday. That way he could help around the café and also tend to things on the property the other days of the week. His boss had been willing to consider the new arrangement. Caleb had been working there a year, he was a good employee, and he had agreed to try to deliver five days of orders in three.

It had worked out, but he and Red were exhausted.

There had been no time to stop and chat during his deliveries, and he'd actually eaten the lunch Julia had packed while he was driving. In the old days he'd often take an hour off to sit by Pebble Creek. Those days were over now. The upside was that tomorrow he would be home.

Looking around the table, he was thankful his boss had agreed to the new hours. His family looked as if they might fall asleep in their soup.

"Tell me about your day. Which part was busiest? What part was slow? And did you have any difficult customers?"

At first Julia was the only one who spoke, her eyes sparkling and energy returning to her voice as she relived the day's events. He could tell by listening to the details how much the opening of the café had meant to her. Her enthusiasm pulled on his heart and caused him to care for her even more than he had. It was a thing that would have been hard to explain. He wanted to do whatever was necessary to give her another day just like today, to give her a whole string of them.

Soon Ada joined in, describing an old *Englisch* couple who sat in the front room and didn't speak to each other at all—until the man had reached across the table and helped himself to something on the woman's plate. She had feared there was going to be a fight. Sharon started laughing then and told about the children. She'd thought they would all be in school, but there were plenty of younger children brought by their parents and grandparents.

"A successful day," Caleb declared.

Julia sighed as she pushed her plate away and pulled out her list. "We might have had a little too much success. I thought I would get more of the cooking done for tomorrow. Now it's late, and I still need to make desserts, sandwich spread, and two vegetable casseroles."

Ada yawned and Sharon slumped in her chair.

"It can't be so bad."

"Maybe we could get up early," Sharon suggested.

"*Nein*. We're already getting up early to put the breakfast casseroles in. Tomorrow will be better. I'll be more organized and work on the next day's meals whenever I have a free moment."

"How are you going to do that?" Caleb asked.

"I won't need to help Sharon because Wess will be here."

"Wess was here today," Sharon pointed out.

"True, but he didn't come over until Jeanette saw all the cars. Tomorrow he'll get here as soon as his classes are out."

"And I'll be faster at making change." Sharon stood. "Which reminds me that I want to make sure we have plenty of everything we need in the cash box."

"I can do that," Ada said. "I might be old, but I can still count dimes and quarters."

The extra activity in the house seemed to have invigorated Julia's mother. Although she'd apparently needed to rest a few times, her color was good, her eyes sparkled, and her hands looked better than Caleb had ever seen them. They were curved but not cramped.

"And I can help with the cooking." Caleb put his hands on his hips when everyone stared at him. "Are you saying a man can't cook? Just tell me what to do."

Julia started laughing, but she agreed it was a plan.

"I can wash up the dishes while you two are cooking." Sharon started up out of her chair, but she reached for the table when she stumbled.

Julia was at her side immediately, easing her back into the chair. "Are you dizzy again?"

"Possibly a little, but it's nothing."

"I want you upstairs resting."

"But—"

"*Nein.* Upstairs. We need you tomorrow, and it has been a long day."

Instead of arguing, Sharon ducked her head, stood slowly, and made her way out of the kitchen and up the stairs.

Caleb helped carry the dishes to the sink. He didn't bring the subject of Sharon up until he heard water running upstairs. "What do you think is wrong?"

"I'm not sure. She didn't eat."

"She never eats, and she barely sleeps," Ada said. She'd retrieved the cash box and was checking the ones, fives, tens, and twenties. They had decided they would start each day with two hundred dollars in the cash box and keep the rest of the money upstairs, ready to be deposited in the bank at the end of the week.

Caleb rolled up his sleeves and began running dishwater. "Has she talked to either of you about what happened in Monroe?"

Both women shook their head.

"She hasn't said a word to me either, but she seems to like it here."

"Liking it is one thing." Julia set her ingredients on the counter—bologna, onions, cheese, and pickles, and then she washed her hands at the sink. "But a body has to have food and rest. I'm worried about her."

"*Gotte* makes His people strong." Ada broke open a roll of quarters and dropped them into the appropriate compartment.

"Ada's right. *Gotte* will make Sharon strong. We need to give her time."

Julia began measuring and chopping the meat, cheese, and onions. The ingredients quickly filled up the large ceramic bowl as she worked. She added mustard and mayonnaise, put her hands in the bowl and began to mix the spread together. Finally she admitted, "I still worry."

Ada cracked open a roll of pennies. "God gives His people peace."

"*Ya*, I know, *mamm*, but maybe we should do something."

"Keep praying," Ada said. "Pray and cook and be there for her. Sharon's a *gut* girl. She'll be fine."

"I suppose." Julia added pickles to her mixture.

A Wedding for Julia

"Are you making Guey Louie sandwiches?" Caleb asked. His stomach was full, but maybe not completely full.

"*Ya.* Wednesday is Guey Louie day or vegetable soup. Didn't you read the menu?" She pulled out four packages of buns, filled them with the mixture, and wrapped them in foil.

"I read the menu, but I didn't pay attention to it so much. Maybe you should let me try one of those when they come out of the oven."

"Then I'll only have thirty-one."

"Thirty-one is a *gut* number."

"You already ate."

"But I worked extra hard today."

"We still have to make Sunbonnet cake."

"You're not going to let me cut a piece of that cake tonight." Caleb's hands were becoming wrinkled in the dishwater. He glanced down and realized his skin looked like prunes. He turned his attention back to the stack of dirty dishes, which seemed to be growing.

"I was going to make two batches of batter—one to use for the cake and the other to make cupcakes. It seems cupcakes are a very popular item now."

"And you'd let me eat a cupcake?"

"You can't have a cupcake and a Guey Louie. You'll be sick." Julia shook her head at him, but she was also smiling.

He was learning to recognize his wife's mannerisms. He already knew that when she smiled with her ducked head down, she was enjoying their conversation.

"I suppose the sandwich could wait until tomorrow."

"It probably should. You know, living inside a café could be dangerous. You don't want to become like some old Amish men who need suspenders to keep their pants up. You might want to watch your waistline."

Caleb had grown up in a family full of rowdy boys. He'd helped wash dishes a time or two. So it was a natural reaction for him to put his hands into the last of the soap suds, catch a handful, and flick them at his wife.

She stared down at the front of her apron as if he'd thrown some of Missy's dropping on her, but the shock gave way to amusement, and the amusement was replaced by a look he'd seen from his brothers more than once. It was the I'll-get-you-back-for-that expression.

He continued to clean while she cooked, and the kitchen was soon filled with delicious smells.

Ada eventually closed the cash box, said good night, and toddled upstairs.

Caleb waited until he was sure they were alone before he stepped behind Julia and slipped his arms around her waist. "Have I told you how beautiful you look in that apron?"

"You're lucky this apron is dry now."

He nuzzled her neck. "*Ya*. I shouldn't have splashed you. For a minute there I thought you were one of my *bruders* back at home. We always played around."

She turned in his arms and gazed up at him with her pretty brown eyes. "Are you saying I look like your *bruders?*"

"*Nein*. They're even uglier than I am."

"You're not ugly," she whispered. Standing on her tiptoes, she kissed him softly on the lips.

He reached to lengthen the kiss but she slipped out of his arms like a fish slipping off the line.

"Cake's ready," she said with a smile, a mischievous look in her eyes.

Hmm. Somehow he thought Julia Beechy—correction, Julia Zook—realized how crazy she made him. At the moment he would take her over an entire Sunbonnet cake or a tray of Guey Louie sandwiches. But because she was already moving toward the table with the cupcakes, he opened the refrigerator, grabbed the milk and two glasses, and joined her.

Suddenly he didn't feel tired at all.

Maybe after he'd helped her frost the cupcakes, they would have a small sample for their dessert. Maybe when her work was done, he could talk his wife into taking a nighttime stroll down to the river.

$\approx$ Chapter 24 $\approx$

Caleb spent all day Wednesday working on the bridge that would connect their property to Aaron's cabins. The sky was overcast, but the temperatures weren't cold. It was good weather in which to do the work. Tim showed up bright and early to help. He brought the designs he'd been working on. Caleb chose the most simple one, which was for a bridge three feet wide, using split logs and having two handrails.

"Safe and stable. Have you chosen a spot?"

"Ya. Narrowest point, like you said. Let me show you."

They hadn't had much rain, so the water level in Pebble Creek was low—maybe only a foot and a half deep. Caleb donned his rain boots and slogged across the water, holding on to one end of Tim's tape measure.

"Fourteen feet," Tim called out.

Caleb nodded and headed back. He only paused once to watch a fish dash downstream.

"We'll add a six foot overhang—three on each side."

"Makes for twenty feet. David's delivering wood midmorning."

"We have time to go to town then and pick up supplies."

By the time they had returned, David was there waiting. He

insisted on staying to help. "I've built a lot of things, but I've never put together a bridge."

They had been sawing and hammering for less than thirty minutes when Aaron and Seth showed up.

"Sounds like you need help over there," Aaron said, standing on the opposite bank.

A corner of cabin eight's roof was just visible over his shoulder. Caleb remembered the cabin well—it was the one farthest from the office and the barn. The path between the cabins curved back toward the river, so that cabins nine and ten were actually closer to the office. He'd had to walk the entire circle, checking each building before bed when he'd lived in the little room in the barn. That seemed like another lifetime now.

"*Ya*. Sounds like you need our help badly." Seth squatted down and stared across at them.

No doubt the boy would rather do anything than yard work. Boy? He was to marry in another week.

"We could use some help," Caleb admitted. "If you don't mind getting your feet wet."

"I'm way ahead of you." Aaron held up two pairs of rain boots.

With the five of them working, the bridge took shape quickly. David used a handsaw to cut all of the split oak into thirty-six-inch lengths. Caleb and Seth dug six-foot trenches parallel to the creek on each side—wide enough and deep enough to hold the footings for the bridge.

Aaron notched the footings with an ax. The ends of the logs, which were not split, went into the notches and spanned the creek.

"I can't believe you were able to deliver these." Caleb had fallen asleep each night thinking of how they would do this, and now it was all taking shape in front of his eyes.

David grunted as he picked up one end of a log. "Not so hard with the trailer we use for hay and my two best horses."

"That too heavy for you, *dat*?" Seth waded back across and shouldered the other end of the log.

"I'll let you know when something's too heavy for me, son."

"Just checking."

"I appreciate that."

The grin that passed between them assured Caleb they were good-naturedly harassing each other. Then he realized that they were sharing their passions. Seth loved being outdoors. It was why he'd stayed with the job at the cabins for so long. And David loved working with wood, building all manner of things he sold in a shop next to his house. Caleb was guessing it was rare for those two interests to cross, but today they had.

Tim wanted to use a drill, bolts, and nails to attach the twenty-foot logs to the footings on each bank, but Caleb, Aaron, and David all shook their heads. They showed him the Amish way, using wooden pegs.

"For a bridge?"

"They will hold a house together," Caleb reminded him.

"And a barn," Aaron said.

"They will hold this bridge longer than nails will." David set to work as everyone else began laying out the three-foot split logs.

They had stopped for lunch, but they were making good progress and didn't linger over the delicious food Sharon brought down. Tim seemed surprised that they could finish in one day, and Jeanette had shown up once to take photos of the structure in progress—waiting until the Amish men were out of the picture to snap her pictures. She planned to use them for another blog post.

What they were doing didn't seem so different from any of the barn raisings Caleb had participated in. Fewer workers, smaller work space, same result.

As the day's light began to fade, the men gathered up their tools. Aaron and Seth walked across the bridge as they headed back to the other side of the creek.

David cocked his head and shifted his tool belt from his left hand to his right. "You can ride home with me, son."

"Can't. Sorry, *dat*."

Seth had stopped in the middle of the bridge, and he jumped up and down a few times, testing the structure. It was sturdy, as Caleb knew it would be.

"I left my rig at the cabins," he explained. Then he turned and followed Aaron across the water and around the bend in the path, out of sight.

Tim turned to Caleb and asked, "When are you off again?"

"Saturday."

"We can put the handrails on then."

"Sounds *gut*."

"I can be here for a few hours Saturday morning," David said. "In the afternoon I promised to take the kids to town to give Anna a few hours alone."

"I appreciate any help you can give me, but you be sure to follow through on your promise to your wife. With six children, I imagine she can use a break."

"Soon to be five. She's having a hard time with Seth leaving."

"He's leaving?" Tim asked.

"Not leaving. He's marrying," Caleb explained. "He'll still be in Pebble Creek."

"*Ya*, but Aaron's been able to buy more land adjacent to where he lives, and there's an old house on it. He offered free rent to Seth if he'll help with the harvest each year. So he and Clara will live there to begin with, which is a real blessing. Clara will be able to lend a hand with her *dat*—"

"How is Menno?" Caleb asked.

"Some days are bad. Others are better."

"I know both Lydia and Clara are a help to their *mamm*."

"Sure. And Clara will be able to ride into work with Lydia and Aaron. It works out well." David stopped next to his buggy. "But it isn't what Anna imagined. She thought Seth would bring his bride home. Sort of like I thought my oldest would follow me into woodwork."

"He did some fine work today," Tim pointed out. "We all did."

They spent another moment slapping each other on the back and brushing off Caleb's thanks. Their words echoed in his ears and in his heart as he climbed the steps of his home. The last of the day's customers were leaving, and Caleb knew the bridge they were building would be worth the effort.

Julia was amazed that they managed to finish the footbridge on Saturday. She could remember dozens of recipes without consulting her cookbooks, but she couldn't fathom building a bridge over a creek in just two days.

Sunday morning, after they'd had breakfast and rested, they had their Bible study in the sitting room. There was no church service that day, but Caleb, Julia, Ada, and Sharon were to attend a lunch social. They gathered their things together and prepared to spend an afternoon out in the fall sunshine. The luncheon happened to be at the cabins, which meant it was the perfect opportunity to try out the bridge.

Julia clutched her casserole dish and stared at the wooden structure. She'd been meaning to find time to walk down to the creek and peek at it, but it seemed each day was busier than the one before it. Now all she could do was gawk and swivel her head from Caleb to the bridge and back again.

"Do you like it?"

"She loves it," Ada said. "I've only seen that look on her face once before. It was when her *dat* made a stool for her so she could stand on it and cook. She was beside herself with happiness. Same look."

Ada raised her cane and thumped it against the first step. "Sounds solid."

"*Ya*, it is. Seth jumped up and down in the middle to test it. Nothing moved at all."

Finding her voice, Julia turned to her husband. "It's beautiful. *Danki.*" She closed her eyes, not wanting to cry and ruin the moment or the morning.

Caleb touched her shoulder and whispered, "*Gem gschehne,*" and then he moved forward to help Ada step up on the bridge.

But before he reached her side, Sharon was next to his mother-in-law. "One hand on the ledge and one on your cane, Ada. I'll walk close beside you in case you need help."

"It's a nice view from here. Isn't it? Wonderful are His works. My soul knows it very well."

"*Ya,* I know that one. My *mamm* used to say the first part of that verse every time a *boppli* was born in our district."

Ada smiled and supplied the words. "We are fearfully and wonderfully made."

As they walked on across the bridge, Caleb moved back beside Julia.

"Ada and Sharon seem *gut* for each other." He shifted the bag of supplies to his right arm and with his left reached for her hand.

"And you're *gut* for me, Caleb Zook." Julia was surprised she'd found the courage to say the words. Many things she did surprised her lately, like when she'd twirled in his arms and kissed him the other night. She was not accustomed to being so open with her emotions, but there was something about being around Caleb, something about his care that was making her stronger and bolder.

"I am?"

"*Ya.*"

"You're just saying this because you like the bridge."

They paused in the middle and surveyed Pebble Creek. Some of the trees still held their leaves, but most had dropped them to the bank, which was now thick with colors of red and gold and brown. The water was still low, as there hadn't been any rain, but Pebble Creek rushed on. Fish darted in and out of shadows. From the brush, a fawn stepped out, saw them, and darted back into the safety of some nearby cover.

"I do like the bridge, very much, but I'm saying it because it's true."

They turned and continued on their way.

"Aaron is going to put a sign here reminding guests from his side what days and times the café is open and asking them not to cross when it's closed."

"We make a good team, the four of us."

"We do."

"I'm excited about Lydia's *boppli*."

Her husband squeezed her hand, and she realized she might have made him uncomfortable. "I'm not saying that I'm envious, Caleb. I don't know if we're to have children. We have so much already that it's hard to imagine *Gotte* blessing us with more."

"I'm a content man, either way."

They followed Ada and Sharon past cabin eight and on toward the picnic area. Julia had been worried about Ada walking so far, but Caleb had assured her someone would give her a ride home if she needed one. At the moment she was hobbling down the trail at an impressive pace.

Julia decided Caleb was probably right about Sharon being good for Ada. There was no doubt Ada was helping Sharon to improve both physically and emotionally. She hadn't been awakened by Sharon's nightmares the last three nights. Of course, it could be that the girl was too tired to wake in the middle of the night, but Julia had a feeling it had more to do with Ada's presence, her prayers, and her influence on the young woman.

Julia could see that a fair-sized group had gathered at the picnic tables already—Lydia and all of her family, along with David and all of his family. They had also invited the Elliotts, and she hoped they would stop by on their way home from their church service in town.

Though guests were at the cabins, they kept to themselves or walked down by the river. The picnic tables were a good meeting place for the Amish families, and Lydia had insisted their guests wouldn't mind.

"Ella and Menno came," Julia said softly.

"He must be feeling better."

"Do you know how long he has had farmer's lung?"

"Aaron said several years, since before Lydia finished school."

And then they were in the midst of everyone and there was no chance to talk privately.

Lydia managed to waddle around and push casserole dishes into a straight line, but that was the most anyone would let her do.

"I'm pregnant, not sick," she muttered.

"Yes, *fraa*, but we don't want you tumbling into the water." Aaron's words were delivered with a small grin.

Julia noticed that through the prayer and during the meal, Aaron often glanced up to check on Lydia. Even when the men went off to discuss whatever men discussed, he turned and looked for her—as if he needed to convince himself she was still okay.

"Aaron seems a little nervous about the baby."

"We had false labor the other night," Lydia explained. "I've had trouble shaking him since."

Ella was holding Anna's baby. "Soon you will both be holding a precious *boppli* like this one. It's natural for a father to worry, especially with a first child."

"David acted like a cat before a storm with each of ours." Anna reached down and ran her hand across Pumpkin's yellow fur. "Where did you get this kitty?"

"He adopted us back when Aaron first came to the cabins. Now he's a mascot of sorts. Returning guests come in and speak to him before they speak to us."

"I never could abide pets in the house." Anna shook her head as if the idea was beyond her. "But I don't mind a cat around the place sitting on the porch and sleeping in the yard. They're good mousers."

"Pumpkin caught a mouse last week and left it on the mat in front of the office. Not exactly what I want to see when I show up for work."

"The Elliotts have a little dog," Julia said. "You should see him. He wears—"

At that moment a car drove into the parking lot and the Elliotts spilled out.

"Speaking of the Bandit," Sharon said, which was the first thing she'd said since they had arrived.

"They must have gone home to change." Julia rose and began to wave so Jeanette would see where they were sitting. "I hope the dog doesn't bother anyone."

"Come one and come all," Ella said.

Tim walked toward the men, while Jeanette and the girls joined the women.

Most of the teenagers had gone off to the barn. Clara hadn't, because she was talking wedding plans. Sharon hadn't, either. She didn't seem to be talking much at all and had refused an invitation to play volleyball.

Wess motioned for her to walk with him to the barn, but Sharon shook her head. Julia supposed she simply wasn't ready to fall into a new group of teens yet, or maybe she was hesitant to make friends she might have to leave in a few weeks.

Victoria and Zoey spied Sharon, though, and came running toward her.

"My doll has a new dress. Do you like it?" Zoey plopped the baby doll into Sharon's lap.

"And Bandit has a new collar. It even has his name on it." Victoria picked up the little dog and traced the letters with her finger.

It seemed to Julia that Sharon looked a bit overwhelmed, but instead of shooing the girls away, she allowed Zoey to crawl up in her lap and leaned forward to study the lettering on Bandit's collar.

Pumpkin took one look at the dog, blinked, stretched, and lazily walked away.

"Sorry we're late," Jeanette said. "They were having a potluck at church. We stayed to eat, but the girls insisted we leave before dessert so they wouldn't miss seeing Sharon. I brought snickerdoodles. Do you think anyone will eat them? Or are you all full already?"

"We have men and children. Your plate will be empty when you take it home." Lydia scooted down on the bench to make room for Jeanette, who sat beside her.

"A hen fest. This is just what I needed."

And a hen fest it was. They talked of laundry and cooking, wondered when the first real cold snap would come, hashed out all the details of Clara's wedding, and made Lydia go over every item she had for the baby.

At some point Victoria and Zoey tugged on Sharon's arms until she stood and followed them down the path that led to the river.

Clara left soon after that to join the volleyball game.

Julia tried to keep her eye on Sharon to see if she were interacting with the other teenagers, but she only saw her twice. One time she was alone with the Elliott girls, and another time she was surrounded by all of the young children, apparently directing a game of duck-duck-goose.

She tried to watch for Caleb, but then their conversation turned to men and how hard it was to steal a private moment in a houseful of children. Julia's cheeks warmed, and though she didn't make eye contact with anyone, they were soon questioning her about her first week of marriage. Ada dozed in the shade of the maple tree, but she had a smile on her face.

Something in Julia's heart began to believe that perhaps everything would be all right after all.

Bishop Atlee had said there might be days where she and Caleb would have doubts because their marriage had begun a little unconventionally. He had called it a "strange and *wunderbaar* beginning." Sitting with her friends and family and sharing a Sunday afternoon, Julia felt a peace settle into her heart. It was difficult to imagine doubting their decision to marry, and she couldn't begin to imagine doubting Caleb's love for her.

Chapter 25

On Mondays the café was closed, same as the cabins. Sharon was relieved to have the extra day of rest and time to help with the household chores, but she was also worried. Too much free time wasn't good. With too much free time her mind drifted back and dwelled on things that had happened at home.

So she was relieved when Julia asked her to search for any remaining elderberries in the bushes by the creek. Most had been harvested already, but some could usually be found that had ripened late. The day was sunny, though there was a hint of coolness in the air. Sharon eagerly pulled on her wrap and headed out the back door.

She liked to stay busy. Busy was better.

Besides, she sensed Julia and Caleb would like an hour alone. Ada was napping, and it wasn't difficult to pick up on the looks passing between them. What was it like to have that sort of romance when you were so old? Maybe it was because they were recently married. Or maybe it was that they truly were in love. Did she even believe in such a thing?

Her thoughts traveled down that path—thinking of married couples she knew who seemed happy, like Julia and Caleb, Miriam and Gabe, and Lydia and Aaron. Lydia was now so close to the delivery date of her baby that she looked terribly uncomfortable and shifted from side to side when she walked. Still, Aaron's eyes filled with adoration whenever he glanced her way.

She'd also watched Lydia's parents at the picnic the day before. Menno was having a good day, or so everyone said, but his good days seemed pretty poor to Sharon. Ella watched over him like a mama cat over a newborn kitten. For one moment, when he'd gone off with the men, Sharon had thought Ella might follow. Was that the kind of love a woman and man shared? Did it include a protective sort of love? She had thought about men protecting women by providing for their needs. Men planted and cleared the fields. They cut and brought in the wood. But she'd never thought to really consider that time in life when a woman might need to take care of a man.

What she had felt for James was nothing like that, and she didn't think he'd felt anything for her.

Sharon walked the path along the creek, past the new bridge, and past the fishing spot Caleb loved. She found the elderberry bushes on the edge of a small clearing, exactly as Julia had described. Setting her pail down, she spied the dark berries that had yet to be harvested in the middle toward the back of the clump of bushes.

She craned her head back. The bushes themselves were quite tall—easily ten to twelve feet in places. As they had grown up, their branches had lengthened over the years and become heavy until they draped all the way to the ground. If she crawled underneath, she could probably stand up inside the circle of bushes and reach the ripe clusters of berries.

She'd certainly soil her dress in the process, but it was an old one—the one she'd brought specifically for cleaning day. Dropping to her knees, she pushed the pail in front of her and inched under the bush. Once inside, she found that the group of bushes acted much like a willow tree. The ground was smooth underneath, and the long branches formed a canopy she could see through. She could also stand up. Her head popped out through some of the lower branches when she did.

Pulling her *kapp* back into place, she began gathering the nearly black berries and dropping them into her pail. They would make a fine dessert filling. There was enough for several pies.

She'd filled more than half of her pail when she heard voices. Company was the last thing she wanted, but there wasn't a quick exit. Maybe if she held perfectly still, whoever it was wouldn't see her.

Who would be on their property anyway? The cabins were closed today. This should be her time alone.

Then Wess stepped into the clearing, and Sharon felt her pulse trip. Following close behind him were Victoria, Zoey, and Bandit. The dog was sniffing everything in his path. Both girls were consumed by a fit of giggles.

"Stop!" Zoey screamed as she danced away from her big brother. "No tickling!"

"I'm not tickling. That was a zche-zche bird."

"Uh-uh." Victoria declared. "There's no such thing."

"What?"

"Mom showed us how to look it up."

"You're believing a computer over—" Wess stopped midsentence. He froze in place as he stared into the bushes. "Look at what I found."

"A zche-zche bird?" Victoria grabbed his hand and attempted to pull him farther along the trail. "Come on. You make that up all the time so you can tickle us."

"I'm not making this up." Wess's grin spread. "Look in those bushes, girls."

Sharon wanted to disappear. She wanted to sit on the ground underneath the elderberries and hide, but then Bandit noticed her and began to bark. Zoey turned around to see why Bandit was excited, spotted her, and began to hop from foot to foot.

"Sharon! How did you get in there?"

Before she could offer an explanation, they were all crawling under the bushes to join her. She ducked down to speak to the girls and give Bandit a pat on his head, which earned her a sloppy lick on the back of her hand. Sun danced in through the branches, marking a quilted pattern of light and dark on the smooth dirt.

"This is so cool!" Zoey was holding her doll, and she danced it around on the ground.

It was easier for Sharon to sit on the ground than bend over, not that she welcomed the interruption, but she wanted to speak with the girls. They were quite excited with the hidden area and with finding her, throwing their arms around her neck before bounding off.

"We could play here. It's like a perfect little hidden house." Victoria's voice took on a reverent tone. "It's like the secret garden in the book Mom was reading to us."

"Probably your mom wouldn't want you to be so dirty," Sharon reminded them. Bandit lay on the ground beside her, his head resting on his paws.

Wess was standing straight up, looking out over the top of the elderberry bushes. All she could see of him was his legs. She could, however, hear his voice loud and clear.

"Hey, girls. Want to try some of these berries?"

"*Nein.* Wess—" Sharon scrambled to her feet, but she was too late. She heard him coughing and sputtering, and then he crumpled to the ground, holding his throat as if he were choking. Bandit jumped on him and began licking his hands, ears, and face.

"Did the zche-zche bird get you?" Victoria asked.

"Maybe you need to hold this." Zoey tried tucking her doll into his hands, which were still clutching his throat. He smiled at his little sister as he took it from her.

Both girls began a game of running in and out of the branches—from sunlight to shadow, flitting between the two like fall butterflies.

"Don't eat the berries," Sharon called after them.

"We won't," Victoria promised.

"We ated lunch already," Zoey assured her with a smile before darting back out onto the path.

"Why didn't you tell me?" Wess stared up at her with accusation and maybe amusement in his eyes.

"What?"

"Not to eat the berries."

"You didn't ask." Sharon sat down beside him, and Bandit crawled into her lap.

Wess was trying to wipe his tongue on his shirtsleeve—a pretty funny sight. She would have offered him water if she had any. As it was, all she could do was watch and try not to laugh.

"Why are you even picking them? They're terrible. Really awful. You could bottle that stuff and punish kids with it."

"Elderberries are *wunderbaar* when you bake them with sugar."

"I doubt it. My taste buds are permanently scarred." Wess shook his head, causing his ponytail to jump back and forth across his back.

"Try some of Julia's pie tomorrow. You'll feel differently."

Wess gave her a look that said *"I'm willing to wait and see, but I don't think so."* She recognized it from working with him for an entire week. It seemed as though she'd known him a lot longer. His grin, his eyes, and even his teasing were familiar now.

"Why are the girls out of school early?"

"Parent-teacher conferences. Both of theirs were right after lunch, so here we are, giving my mom some time to focus on her work."

"Speaking of work, I need to finish what Julia sent me here to do." Sharon removed the dog from her lap and popped up to resume pulling at the berries and dropping them in the pail.

Wess stood and stretched his arm past her to the darkest berries out of her reach. "I'll help as long as I don't have to eat them."

They had filled the pail to full within five minutes. By the time they both crawled out from under the branches of the bush, the girls were drawing hopscotch squares into the dirt path with a stick.

"We need Bandit with us. He loves hopscotch." Zoey picked up the dog's leash and then she took the doll from Wess and shoved it into Sharon's hands before racing off again.

"Ha!" Wess said. "You have doll duty."

Sharon rolled her eyes. As if it was a problem to hold the small toy. Jeanette had knitted a blue sweater for the doll that matched Zoey's, and Zoey had smeared pink, glittery lipstick on the doll's mouth.

"They never used to do that." Wess had sat down on a fallen tree and was studying his sisters.

Sharon glanced down the path to her right. She could excuse herself and head back to the house, but something in his voice caused her to turn, walk to the fallen tree, and sit beside him. "Do what?"

"Play and laugh. Before we moved here, I don't remember them laughing much, and playing was something they did in front of the TV or in their bedroom."

"You lived in the city?"

"Yeah. Chicago."

Sharon didn't respond. She didn't know what to say. She'd never been to anywhere bigger than the outskirts of Indianapolis, but she'd heard about Chicago. She knew it was large with tall buildings, traffic jams, and a subway system.

"My parents took a chance when they moved here, but I'm glad they did."

"Why was it a chance?"

Wess shrugged. "Jobs, for one thing. Look at my dad. He's trying to be a farmer, but he doesn't know how to do that."

"He was an engineer before, right?"

"Yeah. That was part of the problem."

Zoey and Victoria threw their place markers, then hopped and skipped—one, two, three, four. Zoey's marker, a small rock, landed in the dirt with a tiny thud in front of Victoria's plastic bracelet. She held her arms out to her side and hopped on her right foot. Bandit ran along beside her.

"Does your father enjoy farming?"

"I suppose. Some days, when he hitches things up right. You should hear him holler when he does it wrong." Wess hung his head between his knees, and Sharon knew he was smiling. "He might not be a good farmer, but he's better now. He laughs sometimes, and he's there for my mom and me and the girls. He's trying."

Wess looked at her then, right at her, his green eyes searching. "That counts for something. You know?"

"You said he's better. Was he sick before?"

"Kind of."

"Country air sometimes helps people. That might sound like a folk remedy, but often we see people whose health improves when they move away from the city. The air is cleaner and—"

Wess laughed out loud then. "I don't know if it's the country air. It might be the country work. In the city he couldn't sleep. He'd pace the house like a caged tiger. Now, some nights, he's snoring in his chair before Victoria and Zoey are in bed."

The girls tired of their hopscotch game and ran back to their brother's side.

"You promised to take us to the bridge, Wess." Victoria jiggled the plastic bracelet back onto her arm, shaking her head and causing her red ponytail to swing back and forth. Sharon could read the bracelet now. It said "Race 4 a Cure."

"What about your game?" he asked.

"We're done, and we want to walk across the bridge. You promised." Victoria grabbed his hand and pulled with all her might.

"And my baby wants to see it." Zoey claimed the doll from Sharon's lap. "I already told her we would. Victoria, you hold Bandit's leash. I'm tired."

"Uh-uh. Wess, you hold it."

Wess stood, took the leash, and reached for Sharon's hand. "Go with us?"

When she hesitated, he added, "It's on your way. Besides, it'll make the girls happy."

He'd figured her out already. Victoria and Zoey were a weakness. She liked their laughter. They were easy to please, and Zoey reminded her of Ruthie.

"All right." She accepted his hand and allowed him to pull her from where she'd sat on the fallen tree.

With a squeal of delight, the girls took off running down the path in the direction of the bridge.

"Don't run too far ahead," Wess called out. He released her hand and picked up the pail of berries.

They walked a minute before she returned to the conversation about his parents. "Does your dad miss being an engineer?"

"I don't think so. It...well, it was kind of the problem. Or maybe he was the problem. I'm not really sure. All I know is he was never home, and when he was he was on the phone. He worked for a big firm that was never satisfied, no matter how many hours he put in."

Sharon thought of her parents and of how badly she had treated them. Though they might not understand her, there was no question they had been there for her every single day. Her dad had been at the supper table every night.

"I think maybe he started taking something to deal with the pressure. I don't know what for sure. I tried googling it—maybe oxycotin or hydrocodone. They're the most common stuff adults abuse."

Sharon remained silent. She had no idea what she should say.

"I had a kid at school try to sell me both of those once."

"Drugs? Here?" Her voice squeaked, and both girls turned around to look at them before facing forward again, putting their heads together and whispering.

"No, that was back in Chicago. Here the kids only seem to have beer and pot. Or maybe I've just made it clear I'm not interested, so they don't offer."

Sharon thought about that as their feet crunched leaves and the fall sunshine fell on her shoulders. *Englisch* schools were different than Amish schools, but some things were the same everywhere. She thought of James buying beer illegally and how all her friends had been angry at her for telling the clerk and her parents, who told his parents.

Some pressures were the same no matter where you were. No matter who you were.

"How has your mom liked the move?"

"I think..." Wess switched the bucket of berries to the hand that held Bandit's leash and ran his free hand over the top of his head and down his ponytail. "I think she was afraid it wouldn't last. Afraid to believe things were better. But now she seems good with it. She can do her work anywhere."

"So Chicago was a bad place to live?"

"Well, there were more pizza places there." Wess whistled sharply as the girls reached the bridge. They both stopped and then sat down on the bottom step to wait for him. "I don't know if I'd say Chicago was bad, but this is a whole lot better. At least it is for our family."

Zoey and Victoria were picking some pebbles up from the ground. As Sharon and Wess came closer, both girls stood up and stuffed the pebbles into their pockets.

"What about for you?" she asked. "Is it better for you?"

"I don't know."

"Will you stay after you graduate?"

Wess shrugged, and then he tilted his head and smiled at her. "We're kind of too young to know where we want to be or what we want to do, don't you think? I sure haven't figured it out."

He handed the pail back to her, wound Bandit's leash up on his wrist, and then took both of his sisters' hands as they walked up onto the bridge. Sharon wanted to walk away, to walk to the house, which she could now see from where she stood.

But she heard Zoey and Victoria talking about the fish and the water and the view.

She thought of Wess admitting he didn't know yet.

There were a lot of things she didn't know. It was nice to be with someone who could admit to not having all the answers. Someone who was okay with that.

Wess made her feel almost normal.

So instead of turning toward the house, she walked up on the bridge and joined the Elliott kids, who were throwing tiny rocks down into Pebble Creek.

∽ Chapter 26 ∽

J ulia was pleased. By the end of the café's third week, they had
found a nice rhythm. Sharon handled the morning guests easily. Wess arrived in time to help with the lunch rush. Two days
a week, he took off at three to help with his sisters. One day a week,
Julia insisted that Sharon take off at three and find something else
to do besides work.

Ada continued to improve—at least cognitively. She no longer
stared blankly ahead as if lost in another time. The Psalms she chose
to quote were more appropriate, and she even laughed occasionally.
The added stimulus of so many people perked her up, like Julia's garden after a nice soaking spring rain. Her mother still walked slowly,
with her hand holding the cane, and those hands were often still
curled in discomfort from the arthritis. Overall, though, Julia worried less that her mother would immediately follow her father and
leave her alone.

Though there was no danger of her being by herself anymore. Not
since her mother's decree. Not since she had married Caleb and her
life had expanded in more ways than she could have ever imagined.
As she placed two loaves of bread into the oven, she glanced over at
Ada, sitting in her rocker and watching the birds outside the window on the feeder.

The café was quiet. Two in the afternoon was their slowest time. Sharon was dusting windowsills, and Wess was assembling take-out boxes in the mudroom. Caleb was in the barn, patching worn spots in the roof before the winter snows began. His boss had asked him to work one Saturday a month. They had agreed that on those weeks he would take Friday off instead. This was the week he switched days.

Julia walked across the room and squatted down in front of her mother's chair. "*Mamm?*"

"*Ya?*" Ada shifted her gaze from the birds to Julia.

"*Danki.*"

Ada reached forward to cup her daughter's face in a trembling hand. "For what, dear?"

"Everything. For making all this possible. For seeing what I couldn't see."

She expected one of the Psalms, perhaps the hundred and eighteenth. Instead, her mother leaned forward, kissed her on the forehead, and said, "*Gem gschehne.*" Then she patted her hand and went back to watching the scene outside the window.

Julia stood, straightened her apron, and returned to the kitchen. After checking on her bread, she decided she had enough time to walk down the lane to pick up their mail. The errand usually took her ten minutes, there and back, and it helped to clear her head when she'd been in the kitchen cooking all day.

She passed one car of customers, which she knew Sharon could handle. As a young girl, she would run down to the mailbox, open it, and pop her hand inside, but one day that had earned her a sting from a wasp's nest that had set up shop in the back of the box.

Now she always looked first, though she knew there would be no wasps or bees this time of year.

She found two letters. Both letters bore postmarks from Monroe, Indiana. One was to Sharon from her mother, and the other was to Julia from Caleb's mother. She had replied to Betsy's first letter the day after their wedding and had received a reply the next Friday. Apparently Betsy wrote her letters on Wednesdays.

Julia had never received much mail before, and she found she liked it. As she read Betsy's letters, she felt as though she were visiting Indiana and sitting in the home Caleb had grown up in. Maybe one day they could visit, but until then the letters were a nice substitute.

There was still only the one car of customers, and Sharon had already served them.

Julia probably had another ten minutes or so before the late afternoon group started trickling in. She walked through the house and handed Sharon's letter to her. The girl simply stuffed it into her apron pocket.

"Would you like to read it?"

"*Nein*. Tonight is soon enough."

"I think I'll step out on the back porch, then. Call me if you need me." Julia took a glass of water and a gingersnap cookie with her. She sat in the old rocker, the rocker she could remember sitting in with her father, and slit the letter open.

> *Dearest Julia,*
>
> *I am happy to hear the café is doing so well. I can picture the bridge crossing your small creek. It's a lovely thing to think of your place connected to Aaron's. I wish you could have known Caleb and Aaron when they were growing up. They were always finding something to do outside with birds or snakes or fish. Caleb was much older, of course. Aaron was like a baby bruder and often tagged along. Ask Caleb to tell you about the scar on his right hand, and what Aaron had to do with it.*

Julia glanced out toward the barn where Caleb was working. She knew the scar Betsy was talking about. It was between Caleb's forefinger and thumb and looked like a puncture wound.

> *I know it might seem too early to speak of such things, but we are praying that if it's Gotte's wille, you and Caleb will have a full and complete family. There is no joy like that of carrying an infant, of holding it in your arms, and of one day knowing he or she has married the person Gotte intended them to wed. We also*

*pray that Sharon is doing well. It's gut to hear she likes working
in the café.*

> *All my love to you both,*
> *Betsy*

Julia stared toward the barn before rereading the last paragraph
again. Hadn't Caleb told them her age? Hadn't he warned them that
children probably wouldn't be in their future? Or had he left it for
her to do so?

There is no joy like that of carrying an infant, of holding it in your arms...

Julia understood what Betsy was saying. She had never thought
such a future was for her. It had been years since she had dared to
hope. Images from the last few weeks flipped through her mind.
Lydia placing her hands on her stomach. Ella holding Anna's baby.
Miriam handing Rachel to Gabe.

She knew. She understood what she had missed. Did Caleb?
How important was it to him that they have children?

Slowly she folded the letter and slipped it back into the envelope.
She placed the letter into her pocket, stood, and went back to work.

$\approx$

Caleb looked down at his dinner and tried not to grimace—
chicken casserole again. Julia was a wonderful cook, and she was
also careful with their money. She threw everything that was left
from the week into Friday's chicken casserole, and it was tasty. Probably he was only tired, and that was why he was wishing for a piece of
fish. He'd actually caught sight of a few fish swimming downstream
while he'd worked on the roof of the barn.

As he reached for fresh bread and slathered it with butter, he
reminded himself that less than a month ago he'd been living in a
barn, mostly eating things out of a can or whatever Lydia brought
him from her family meals.

There were those afternoons, though, when he'd finished early at the grocery and headed straight to the creek. One or two fish had been plenty, and often he'd cooked them outside over the little pit fire Aaron had set up near the picnic tables.

"Something wrong with the casserole?" Julia asked.

"*Nein*. It's *gut*." Caleb shoveled a big forkful into his mouth and followed it with a large bite of bread. She had worked all day too. He was being ungrateful to wish for the old days—to wish for something different than what everyone else who had walked into their house—correction, their café—had been served.

"The customers certainly liked it," Ada said, scooping some into her spoon. Forks had become too difficult for her to handle.

"*Ya*, well, they probably don't have it every Friday." Caleb's voice was quiet and low, and he meant his response as a sort of joke. He'd spent very little time around women, not counting the last three weeks. Men tended to say what was on their mind and laugh about it later. One look at Julia's face told him there wouldn't be any laughing.

"I didn't mean that the way it sounded."

"Of course you did. That's why you said it."

"*Nein*. I was trying to be funny because I'm tired. Your cooking is *gut*, Julia."

"The best cooking can grow old when you eat it time and again." She stood, pushing away the plate she'd barely touched.

Sharon glanced from one to the other, not saying a word.

Ada piped up with, "Think before you speak, but don't speak all you think."

It was the first time Caleb had heard her spout a proverb, at least he thought that was what it was. Best to keep eating. That would show Julia he hadn't meant what he said.

But she didn't return to the table. Instead, she worked in the kitchen, and when he carried his empty plate in and tried to help with the dishes, she only shook her head and turned away.

So he went upstairs. He tried to read the paper, but he couldn't focus on the printed words. What he needed was a hot bath to help with the aches, and why was he so sore? It wasn't as if he were an old man. Somehow the roof work had been harder than he'd expected, even without the fall. It still embarrassed him to think of how foolish he'd been. He knew how to properly set a ladder so it was safe.

He soaked in the bath, practically dozing, until the water became cold. When he walked out into the hall, he was surprised to see the light out in the sitting room.

Maybe everyone was as tired as he was.

And they all had a long day ahead of them beginning early the next morning. Caleb was certainly looking forward to Sunday, a day of rest.

He was relieved to see a light on in his bedroom. Perhaps Julia was still awake. He wanted to apologize for his earlier remark. Plainly he'd hurt her feelings, and that had not been his intention.

Unfortunately, he wasn't going to have the opportunity to clear his conscience. His wife was in bed with her eyes closed and the covers pulled up to her chin. At least she'd left the bedside lamp on for him—a small gas lantern that sent shadows leaping across the ceiling. As quietly as possible, he pulled back the covers and climbed into bed.

"What happened?" Julia's voice landed somewhere between disbelief and accusation.

For a split-second Caleb thought she was still referring to his ill-timed dinner comment, but then he saw her staring at his left arm, which was already turning purple and blue.

"Oh, ya. That." He ran his right hand over the bruise. "I fell off the roof of the barn."

"You what?" She popped up in bed, the covers falling forward and her long brown hair spilling around her shoulders.

He realized again how much he'd grown to care for her, how fortunate he was to be married to this amazing, beautiful woman. He reached up to touch her, but she pushed his hand away.

"Caleb, what do you mean you fell off the barn? Your arm. It's hurt. Weren't you going to tell me?"

"What's to tell?" He shrugged and lay back against the pillow. "I was climbing on the ladder and didn't have it positioned securely. It tossed me on the ground like a horse will toss a rider."

"That's it?"

"Pretty much."

"Why didn't you call for me?"

Caleb used the thumb and middle finger of his right hand to rub his temples. "What could you have done? I would still be on the ground and the roof would still need patching."

"Did you ever think that maybe you should go to the doctor?"

Caleb studied the pattern of light on the ceiling. "*Ya*, when I first landed, but then I stood up and nothing seemed broken. So I went back to work."

"Your arm is purple."

Holding it out in front of him, he flexed his forearm back and forth. "True, but it's not broken."

"Maybe something else is wrong. Maybe you have a blood clot or... or...I don't know what. That's what the doctor is for. I know Doc Hanson would have fit you into his schedule if you—"

"There was no need, Julia. I appreciate your concern, but it's only a bruise." Caleb reached for the lantern and turned it off. Darkness blanketed the room, effectively ending their conversation.

He could feel her staring at him, and he was aware she was still sitting up in bed.

One part of him wished he could think of something to say to her, something to settle her emotions, but his batting average wasn't so great in that area tonight. Probably best if he let her rest.

So he rolled on to his right, away from her, so as not to lie on the bruised side. It was better that she didn't know the bruises continued down his hip and leg. They would fade soon enough. Like a spat at dinner, most things took care of themselves given a little time.

At least, that was his reasoning as he drifted off to sleep.

～ Chapter 27 ～

The day had gone very well, or perhaps Sharon had discovered a pace that wasn't too hurried but still met the needs of their customers.

Which was one thing they had plenty of—customers in every size, age, and color. The weekday morning customers were regulars now. Folks who worked outside an office, started early, and were able to take a break around ten. They chose to stop at the Plain Café for a bite to eat and to work on their computers. Sharon grew used to seeing lone customers sitting at tables with food and coffee to the side and laptop computers at the ready.

She didn't actually understand how the computers could work on the Internet in their home, but then a customer explained to her that he had 3G, which allowed him to go online. Computers still made no sense to her, but she assumed they worked off the same principle as a cell phone. Because she didn't need either one, it didn't really matter as long as the food orders came out quickly and the coffee stayed hot.

It did surprise a few of their computer customers the first time they asked where the electrical outlets were so they could charge one of their devices. When Sharon explained they had no electricity, they would glance around and then blink once or twice as if seeing the room, the furnishings, and her for the first time. Then they would nod and mumble, "Of course. Thank you anyway."

Weekends they tended to have guests she'd never met before.

Not all of their customers were pleasant, but those few who were rude had always been in the lunch crowd.

One middle-aged woman Sharon had served a few hours earlier had earned the ribbon for least reasonable. She wanted the Cinnamon Flop cake for dessert, which they had sold out of. Thin, pale, and dressed in a business suit even though it was Saturday, she pursed her red lips, tapped a brightly painted red nail on the menu, and said, "Cinnamon Flop cake. It's listed right here."

"Yes, but we've sold our last piece."

"Unacceptable."

"We have oatmeal cake or caramel pudding."

"I didn't ask for oatmeal cake or caramel pudding." The woman lowered her chin and stared at Sharon as if she were daft. "There's no use talking to you is there? Where is the owner?"

At that point all of the other customers in the front dining room were staring and listening. Sharon didn't want to bother Julia, but she also wanted everyone else to go back to enjoying their meal. She was willing to bet her only pair of knitting needles that the woman didn't even want the cinnamon cake. She'd probably heard Sharon tell the family at table three that they were out and then decided to make a scene.

Keeping her tone polite but firm, Sharon explained, "The owner makes all of our desserts fresh, including the Cinnamon Flop cake. She couldn't have more available before Tuesday at the very—"

"Did I hear my name?" Julia appeared at her side, smelling of chicken and dumplings and fresh bread.

Sharon didn't know how she managed, but somehow the work in the kitchen only made her look more beautiful. It must be because she was so happy doing what she'd always dreamed of. At least, that's what Julia had said earlier in the week as they had all sat upstairs and read.

"I want Cinnamon Flop cake." The woman stabbed the menu with her nail. "And this girl won't bring it to me."

Julia turned to Sharon, rewarding her with a smile and a touch on the shoulder. "Could you check on the trays of cornbread I have baking? I believe they might be ready."

Sharon nodded and turned to go, but as she walked away she heard Julia explain that they weren't a fast-food chain; that cakes weren't lined up in the freezer; and that, in fact, they didn't own a freezer, though they did have an icehouse.

"We value every customer's business, but if you'd rather dine at one of those other fast-food establishments, your meal with us today will be free and I can provide directions to town."

Sharon couldn't help peeking out through the kitchen doorway. The thin woman's face had taken on a pink tinge, and she'd pulled her hands into her lap. Finally she said, "I don't think I want dessert today. I'll just have more coffee."

"Excellent. Sharon will be happy to bring you some. She's a very *gut* waitress, *ya?*"

The woman nodded once, a curt move of her head.

Julia turned to speak to the couple at the next table, and Sharon ducked back into the kitchen.

She couldn't believe what she'd just witnessed. Julia had stood up for her. She had praised her work and the other customers in the room had all nodded in agreement.

Some of the shame she had been carrying fell away in that moment as she stood near the big black oven, opened the door, and pulled out the cornbread. She placed the trays on the cooling rack, breathing in the scent of cornmeal and the rich goodness of the butter Julia had brushed on top. When she turned to go back into the front dining room, she nearly bumped into Ada, who stopped in front of her, put both hands on her cheeks, and patted them once, twice, and then three times. After that she toddled off to her chair in the corner of their dining room.

Wess tried to catch her attention from the hall, holding up his

hands in a "What?" gesture. Sharon shook her head and turned back
to care for the customers at her tables. She and Julia and Wess and
Ada were an odd group, a family almost, but they had learned how
to cover for one another in a very short time.

Maybe that was why Sharon agreed to go to the Elliott home for
dinner that evening. Possibly her resolve to remain distant weakened
when Zoey and Victoria began to beg.

"Please, Sharon. You haven't even seen our room yet."

How could she say no to those faces? They were scrunched up in
such concern, as if she might disappear tomorrow without first walking the five minutes across the field to their house.

Wess was amused by the entire thing.

"Hard to say no to, aren't they?"

"I imagine you find a way."

"Sure, but I've had time to grow used to the pleading look."

Sharon laughed as they all made their way past Julia's garden and
down the path that led around the backside of the Elliotts' horse
pasture.

"All of this was once Julia's?" she asked.

"That's what I hear. She sold it to my folks. The house we live in
was already built."

Sharon could see it now, a one-story frame home. They were
approaching the side of the house and headed toward the back
door, but she could just make out the corner of a wraparound porch
stretching across the front and no doubt continuing around the far
side. "It's a *grossdaddi* house."

"What did you call it?"

"A *grossdaddi* house."

"What is that?"

"Where our *grossdaddi*—"

Wess gave her the look.

"Where our grandparents live when the child who has stayed home marries and has children."

"Gramps and Grandma get pushed out?"

"Not pushed out." Sharon shook her head, causing her *kapp* strings to twirl. "A *grossdaddi* house is smaller with less upkeep. It's close enough to the son so that the *daadi* and *mammi* can have help if they need it, but far enough away to allow for privacy."

"Like an on-site nursing home."

"Yes. Sort of like that. Very few Amish go to nursing homes. Because of our large families, it's rarely necessary."

Both girls had run ahead and stood waiting impatiently at the back door. Wess tugged on Sharon's hand as they climbed the wooden porch steps. "Welcome to the *grossdaddi* house, then."

It was an Amish home, and it wasn't.

She would have known if she'd walked in blindfolded and then had the blindfold removed that she was standing in what had once been an Amish house. She could see the giant black stove that sat between the sitting room and kitchen to keep the family areas warm. One look at the cabinetry, and she knew the woodwork was done by an Amish person—no veneer, solid wood.

She wasn't sure how she knew such things, but she did.

There also hadn't been any electricity in the house. This was a problem when *Englischers* purchased Amish homes. They hired someone to come in and wire the house, but it never looked quite the same. For instance, the Elliott's didn't have lights on the ceilings. They had opted for lamps instead. Little things, but Sharon could tell. Not that she'd been in a lot of *Englisch* homes, but she'd helped to clean a few back in Monroe when she'd needed extra money for Christmas.

This was not an *Englisch* home, at least not naturally. It was a *grossdaddi* house. But it was no longer Amish, either. There were definite changes other than the electricity.

For one thing, Bandit met them at the back door, full of energy and wanting attention. Sharon had never known an Amish family who kept pets inside the house, though she knew plenty that had barn cats and dogs for hunting and to help with the livestock such as sheep. She'd heard *Englischers* say Amish weren't attached to their pets, which couldn't be further from the truth. Her youngest *bruder* had hidden in the hayloft and cried for hours when their dog Gus had died of old age. Her *mamm* still hadn't been ready to get a new one a year later when Sharon had left. They had all loved that dog, even though he was only a mutt.

"What kind of dog is Bandit?" She asked Wess as he picked up the little dog and scratched it behind the ears.

"Half Jack Russell terrier, half poodle."

"That explains the curly hair."

"Yup. He's smart, has lots of energy, and looks a little crazy. Plus he's the prince of the family." Wess set Bandit on the floor, and the pooch took off in search of the girls.

Music played in the living room. It was set on a low volume but seemed to carry through the different rooms of the house.

"My dad installed remote speakers," Wess explained. "Mom loves jazz, especially if she is working or cooking or cleaning."

There was no doubt Jeanette was happy to see her. "Sharon, I'm so glad you came. You must need a rest after a long day of working."

"You never tell me I need a rest." Wess held out his hands, palms up. Sharon was learning he liked to express himself with his body language.

"You don't need rest. You have boundless energy and probably sleep in three hours later than Sharon does."

Sharon glanced from son to mother and back to son again. She'd never noticed the resemblance because Jeanette had red hair and Wess had sandy hair like his father's must have been at one time. When Wess and Jeanette stood next to each other, though, she saw the resemblance in their noses, their eyes, and even the way their mouths seemed to laugh with what they were about to say.

"True?" Wess asked.

"Maybe. I get up at four thirty."

"Oh! No. Do not tell me that. It's still night at four thirty." He dodged his mother's push.

"I don't want to hear any complaining on Monday at seven when your alarm beeps."

"Shaaa-ron. You said you'd see our room." Victoria grabbed one hand and Zoey laced her fingers through the other.

They were pulling her across the living room and down the hall when Tim stepped out of what must have been the master bedroom. She'd seen him several times at Julia's, but not in the last few days. Not since Wess had shared about their troubles in Chicago.

He smiled and ran a hand over his head—which was bald and shiny, even in the semidarkness of the hall. "Sharon. It's great to see you."

"You too, Mr. Elliott."

"It seems my girls have captured you."

"Daddy, she promised." Victoria flopped her head to the side.

"Uh-huh. Well, if you become lost in the piles of toys, holler. We'll send help."

He didn't seem stressed. In fact, he seemed like most every other father she'd known, only in *Englisch* clothes. He watched his girls drag her away, a look in his eyes that said he was relieved to have a few moments of rest and also he knew their young ages wouldn't last. It seemed to Sharon that parents had so much to balance—devotion, exhaustion, and the future.

She thought of Caleb and Julia's spat the night before. It really wasn't a surprise. They were both working so hard, and they barely knew each other. What Caleb had said had sounded like something one of her brothers might have said, though he'd have been given kitchen chores for rudeness. Sharon didn't think anyone would be giving Caleb kitchen duty. In fact, she'd heard him offer to help and Julia had turned him down.

Probably because her feelings were still hurt. Were adults that much different than teenagers? Did she want to be married and have a houseful of babies? Because Amish didn't stop with two or three.

Wess's words came back to her. *"We're kind of too young to know where we want to be or what we want to do."*

Sharon loved children, but she was only seventeen. She wasn't sure when she'd be ready to have her own. Maybe it was okay that she didn't know. Maybe Wess was right.

"Do you like it?" Victoria let go of her hand and fell onto a purple beanbag chair.

"Do you want to play?" Zoey pulled her toward a corner of the room that was full of dolls.

Sharon had never seen so many, except maybe when she had shopped in a store.

"We can play with them. Which one do you like best?"

"She's too old for that, Zoey."

"Uh-uh."

"Is too."

"Is not. Tell her you're not, Sharon." Zoey tugged on her hand until she knelt on the floor next to her and the dolls.

"I haven't played with a *boppli* in a while. My little *schweschder*, Rachel, likes to play with her dolls. They're a little different from yours."

"What's a *schweschder*?" Victoria sat down beside them.

"What's a *boppli*?" Zoey asked.

"A *schweschder* is a sister, and *boppli* can mean baby or doll."

"You have a sister?" Zoey fell over onto the pile of dolls, giggling.

Victoria picked up one of her sister's dolls and studied it. "What did you mean that her dolls are different?"

So Sharon explained that Ruthie's dolls were Plain, with clothes made in an Amish fashion and with no face.

Zoey's voice dropped to a hushed whisper. "They have no face?"

"Think of it as a coloring page you haven't colored yet. Instead, you imagine what her face would look like."

Zoey thought about that a minute. "I like to color," she declared, and then she threw her arms around Sharon's neck, nearly pushing her over backward.

"I like coloring and I like you!" After a quick hug, she was off, digging through the pile of dolls and finding three that would do for Sharon.

Victoria went to her side of the room and pulled two dolls off of a shelf. Apparently she was too old to play with dolls on a regular basis but not quite ready to give them up yet. For the next few minutes, they changed clothing, combed hair, and set out tea things at a tiny table. Sharon noticed that Zoey's favorite doll, the one with the sweater like hers, remained in her pocket. She seemed to be exempt from the mass of toys on the floor. She was special.

"Tell me they are not making you serve tea to dolls." Wess's voice in her ear caused her to jump, nearly knocking over a doll in a chair.

"You've been serving folks all day, and now you have to wait on dolls. That is totally not fair." Wess held out a hand, which she accepted, and he helped her to her feet.

"Where are you taking her?" Victoria glanced up, a doll in both hands.

Zoey gestured to the tea party in progress. "Yeah, Sharon can't go. We're not done. No one's had their tea yet."

"You're done now. Time for dinner, my little minions."

Chapter 28

Julia realized she had overreacted the night before.

And she even understood how Caleb could be tired of eating the same meals every day. The menu was predictable. The menu was...well, it was printed and laminated.

Food was for nutrition, but it could still be interesting. She had longed to open a café because she enjoyed cooking. What good was that if she made all of Pebble Creek happy but frustrated her own family? She was a little weary of eating the same things herself if she thought about it. She'd just been too busy and excited and tired to focus on the problem.

Caleb's comment had surprised her, but wouldn't she rather he be honest? She shouldn't fault a man for that. Well, she could. However, Caleb had admitted several times that he was clumsy with words, and he had tried to apologize.

As for the bruises she'd seen the night before, she didn't even want to think about those. She needed to talk to him about why they had frightened her. His health was important to both of them. That was a hard thing for her to admit. She was finding there were many things she didn't like to admit. It was easier to make lists and mix casseroles and serve strangers.

Maybe she should talk to him about his mother's letter. Her

stomach turned once, like the special pork chops she was sautéing, and then it flipped and settled back down. She wasn't ready to talk about the letter or babies. One problem at a time.

Sharon had agreed to eat at the Elliotts', which completely surprised Julia. She wasn't sure if Zoey and Victoria were winning Sharon's heart or if Wess was. A budding romance between Sharon and Wess could be another problem, but not one she had to solve tonight. She should talk to Caleb about it, maybe tomorrow. She had an urge to start a list, just in case she forgot something.

That was ridiculous, though. Who made a list of their problems?

Ada had opted to eat leftovers earlier, and she was now reading upstairs. Maybe her mother had realized she needed a little time alone with her husband, or maybe the week had worn her out.

She heard the stamping of boots at the back door, and then Caleb walked into the kitchen.

"Where is everyone?"

"*Mamm* is upstairs. Sharon's next door."

"So we're all alone?"

"*Ya.*" She glanced back at him and smiled tentatively. She had been rude the night before. Should she apologize for that now?

Caleb walked behind her, stepped close, and craned his neck over her shoulder. "Smells *gut.*"

"It does?"

"I haven't had pork chops in a long time."

"They'll be ready in ten minutes. I only need to make the gravy."

"Gravy too?" The smile on his face reminded her of a young boy, which reminded her of the letter from Betsy and the scar on his hand. She'd meant to ask him about it.

"I can clean up in ten minutes."

They ate sitting next to each other with the last of the day's light playing outside the window.

Caleb told her about his week. One order of groceries had been filled incorrectly, causing him to make a trip twice. Red had shied away from a truck, nearly tossing them both into a ditch. He'd spent twenty minutes calming the horse down, and that had made him arrive home later than he would have liked to. The highlight of his delivery days had been the large buck he'd seen standing at the side of the road, just watching and waiting.

She asked about Lydia, but there had been no change.

"Aaron says her last visit with the midwife went fine."

"That's *gut*."

"Not that I know much about midwives."

Julia thought of the letter, tucked safely in her drawer upstairs, but she still wasn't ready to discuss babies and her hopes and fears. So instead she reached out and touched his right hand, between the thumb and forefinger, on the scar.

"I'm supposed to ask you about this."

"*Ya?*" Caleb sat back, claiming her hand and running his fingers along her palm.

A light shiver ran up both of Julia's arms. Would she always feel this way when he touched her?

"Your *mamm* wrote again. She said Aaron had something to do with it."

"He did." Caleb laughed. "I was *freinden* with Matt, Aaron's older cousin. We'd been in school together and continued to spend time with one another as we grew older. The night of the accident we had been out of school for several years. We both worked on our *daed*'s farm all day and would sneak away to fish and hunt any time we could, though it sounds strange to say grown men were sneaking out at night. But you know how farm work is—there's always something else to be done. So twice a week we would slip away to one of our favorite fishing spots. Aaron had just started school that year. He was a little runt of a kid who insisted on following us around, especially on weekends when he stayed at his *aenti*'s house."

Julia tried to picture Aaron small and skinny, maybe the same size as Zoey.

"One night we were out fishing at this pond. It wasn't our pond, and we probably shouldn't have been fishing on it. But the old guy who owned it was a member in our district. He didn't seem to mind. At least he never said so."

"Did he know you were there?"

"Hard to say. We usually sneaked in the back of his property."

"Why?"

"If you sneaked in the front, he'd put you to work. He claimed boys took too much time off, and he'd set you to helping in his field or his barn. We never dared say no for fear he would tell our parents we weren't at school."

"You skipped school?"

"Only once or twice. And only on days that nothing was really happening."

Julia rolled her eyes. He'd feel differently if it were his son ditching class. The thought popped into her mind before she had time to squash it.

"We were too old to be told on by this point, but still we'd fish at his place occasionally, always at night. Less chance of getting caught that way."

"I'm shocked."

"We'd always leave him some of the fish on his back porch in his icebox. I think we were doing him a favor." Caleb scrubbed a hand across his jaw. His beard had come in nice and full, completely brown, unlike the hair on his head, which had a peppering of gray.

"The night *mamm* wanted me to tell you about, Matt and I had been fishing maybe twenty minutes when we heard something behind us. I thought it was a wild dog, but *nein*—it was Aaron."

"He'd followed you."

"Exactly. He was no taller than my waist, but he'd followed us and hid until it was too late for us to send him back. So we let him stay. And he whined so much we finally let him fish. Only thing was, he couldn't cast so well yet."

Julia pulled in her breath. "A fishhook?"

"Right through my hand. I reached out to swat it away. The thing was headed straight toward Matt's head. Instead of dropping the tip of his rod, Aaron jerked on it, and pulled the hook right through the flesh of my hand."

Julia traced the scar with her index finger. She thought of the bruises she'd seen the night before, and she knew the answer to her next question before she even asked it.

"Did you go to the doctor?"

"*Nein.* Then we would have had to explain what we were doing, and why we were acting like schoolboys. Matt cut the hook with a pair of pliers we kept in the tackle box, and then he pushed it out. The incident completely ruined our fishing as my hand wouldn't stop bleeding, so we had to leave. When I got home I found the basket of medical supplies my *mamm* kept—"

"Tell me this wasn't an everyday occurrence."

"Not exactly, but it wasn't rare, either. With six boys medical supplies were always coming in handy. I poured some of the bubbly stuff on it—"

"Hydrogen peroxide."

"Right. Then I slapped some cream from a tube over that and bandaged it up."

"Did you even think you might need a tetanus shot?"

"I had one the year before. *Mamm* made sure she kept our shots up to date, especially the tetanus shot."

Julia closed her eyes. Maybe there was a reason Betsy had told her to ask about the scar. Possibly Betsy had guessed there were things about Caleb she needed to understand.

Caleb leaned forward. With his fingertips he traced a path from her eye to the tip of her chin. "It's only a scar. Everything healed fine."

He kissed her softly. Instead of pulling away, she scooted closer. Caleb's hand went to her *kapp*, releasing the pins which held it, and then he worked his fingers through her braid.

Closing her eyes, Julia allowed her tension and her worries to melt away. She nearly groaned when Caleb began massaging her scalp, then her neck, and finally her shoulders.

"We can soak the dishes." He nibbled on her ear.

"I made dessert."

"It'll be perfect for breakfast."

How could she argue? Suddenly washing dishes didn't seem to matter, and there were only the two plates. They would keep, but moments like this? Something told her they might be rare. So she followed Caleb to the kitchen, placed her dish into the sink, and added soap as he ran enough water to cover them.

He turned and kissed her once more, and then he reached to turn out the gaslight.

"Leave it for Sharon," she whispered.

"*Gut* idea."

Caleb led her upstairs to their room, to the one place she could put aside every single thing on her list and just be. She didn't protest when he helped remove the few remaining hairpins. In the darkness, he rubbed away the knots in her shoulders and left a trail of kisses as he brushed her hair away from the back of her neck.

Julia felt like her garden—tenderly cared for.

She realized she might not understand all of Caleb's past. She certainly didn't know their future and whether it would or would not include children. But she couldn't doubt his feelings for her as he joined her in the big bed under the double wedding ring quilt.

⌒ Chapter 29 ⌒

Dinner had been the same and also very different from what Sharon was used to. With the three Elliott kids, herself, and Tim and Jeanette, the table was more crowded than at Julia's. It was more like home.

Many people thought the Amish ate quietly with no one speaking, but at Sharon's house mealtimes had always been rather busy affairs. It was a time when everyone caught up on the news of the day. Sheer numbers guaranteed a small degree of chaos. After all, with seven children there was bound to be a certain amount of jostling for the last biscuit, the occasional frog sneaked into the house by way of someone's pocket, and once in a while a tense situation because one or the other of them had managed to find themselves in trouble.

The Elliotts' dinner table was similar as far as the chaos factor, but it was different in other ways. Soft music continued to play from the living room. The girls each wanted a special place for their dolls at the table, but Jeanette convinced them that all of the baby dolls were full from their late afternoon tea. Tim blessed the food with a short, simple, and verbal grace. Amish prayers were always silent. Then there was Wess, glancing at her every few moments, offering to refill her glass of water, and touching her hand when he asked her to pass the basket of bread.

Conversations started and stopped before bouncing from one topic to another. Sharon finally learned the story behind Wess's long hair, which oddly enough was connected to Victoria's bracelet.

The older Elliott girl was sitting on Sharon's left, and Wess was sitting on her right. Each time Sharon passed Victoria a dish, she noticed the plastic bracelet on her arm and the words "Race 4 a Cure."

"Tell me about your bracelet, Victoria."

The young girl pushed a forkful of spaghetti into her mouth and said, "It's—"

"Chew and swallow first." Jeanette delivered the reminder with a smile, and Victoria moved her head left, right, and left again as she followed her mother's directions.

"It's for my Aunt Noreen. She has cancer, so we're racing for her." Victoria smiled and popped another forkful of spaghetti into her mouth.

"My sister," Jeanette explained.

"I'm sorry."

"It's not your fault, and actually she's in remission. The treatments have worked very well."

"That's why Wess is growing hair like a girl," Zoey explained, giggling when he sent her a warning look. "It *is* like a girl. You have a ponytail."

Sharon glanced at Wess, but he only shrugged.

"The program is called Locks of Love." Jeanette sat back and sipped her iced tea. "Have you heard of it?"

"*Nein.*"

"They make custom wigs and hairpieces for children who have lost their own hair due to various diseases."

"Like cancer."

"Yes, or the radiation therapy and chemotherapy that accompanies cancer."

"There are other reasons too, though." Wess set his fork down and reached for more bread. "When we visited Aunt Noreen at the hospital, she took us to the children's ward."

"Noreen is a nurse," Jeanette added, rising to fill the girls' glasses with more milk.

"We were worried about her hair." Wess's hand traveled the length of his ponytail. "She took us to the children's ward to see the kids. Some had lost their hair from burns, trauma, and even genetic problems. There were all sorts of reasons."

"Aunt Noreen wears a wig! She has different ones and some are different colors." Victoria pulled her red braid to the front and stared at it, as if she were trying to imagine it being a different color.

"So that's why you're growing your hair." Sharon stared at him, no longer pretending to stir her food.

"Sure is. It has to be ten inches from where you cut it. Mine should be ready by spring."

Silence settled around the table, broken by Tim rubbing the top of his bald head. "I'm thinking about growing mine, but it will probably take longer than six months."

Zoey slid down in her chair laughing, followed by Victoria. Soon they all had joined in, even Tim...and even Sharon.

The conversation made her feel comfortable, but eating was somewhat trickier. Sharon did what she always did. She took the three bites she allowed herself, carefully taken at the beginning, middle, and end of the meal. For the rest of the time, she scooted her food around on her plate and hoped no one would notice. It seemed she had been successful, until Wess was walking her home.

The night was cool enough that she was glad she'd brought her wrap, but not so cold that they hurried. A light breeze stirred the bare branches of the trees. Stars shone brightly above them. If she listened closely, she could hear Pebble Creek behind them, carrying on oblivious to the darkness.

"When did you stop eating?" Wess walked beside her, close enough that their shoulders were touching. His voice held no accusation, but behind the question was a statement, or perhaps several statements.

I care.

You matter to me.

I'm worried.

He had noticed.

Maybe he had noticed long ago, as they worked together every day. She should have known she couldn't fool him by using her fork to stir Jeanette's spaghetti around on her plate. Parents were busy and often didn't notice things, but Wess? He was someone who paid attention.

"Before I came here, I guess. When...when it happened."

She had told him there had been trouble at home, but she'd never gone into the details.

"Do you want to talk about it?"

Sharon shrugged her shoulders, and then she realized he probably couldn't see that. Maybe he felt it, though. They were walking that close. "There's not a lot to tell. I messed up."

"All alone? By yourself?"

"It only takes one person to foul up a thing. One person not thinking." Her voice was so low he had to bend closer to her in order to hear.

"Sometimes," Wess agreed. "Other times it takes a group not thinking, or it takes one person not thinking and another person being purposely hurtful."

"I don't know."

The story slipped out of her as they walked between the two homes. Maybe it was the cold, crisp air, which reminded her of winter's coming and that summer and fall were behind her now. Maybe it was the darkness that allowed her to speak of those days without Wess seeing the expression on her face. Whatever the reason, she told him about James and how she had been foolish enough to believe he was "the one." She spoke about his old truck, his blue eyes, and how he always managed to say the right thing—the thing that would convince her to disobey her parents one more time.

She didn't notice she was shaking until Wess put his arm around her and pulled her toward the far side of Caleb's barn. "Let's move out of the breeze."

They sat on the ground, their backs against the barn, and she told him about that night and James's drinking. She described the convenience store and the clerk who had looked at her with such a blank expression. Her throat felt thick as she talked about walking for hours, the intensity of the storm, and how she finally broke down and called her friend. When she reached the part about the car that stopped and the man with the scar on the left side of his face— the man who had chased her through the field—Wess picked up her hand and held it gently between both of his.

He didn't interrupt her, though. He let her keep talking.

So she told him about her dad finding her—finally. How ashamed she'd felt, standing in the rain, soaked to the skin and wearing *Englisch* clothes. She had been exhausted and terrified from running. Her dad had asked the driver to take them home, where her mother had wrapped her in a quilt, helped her upstairs, and run a hot bath for her. She'd talked to her mother the entire time, crying and trying to explain. After her brothers had left for school, both of her parents had sat with her at the table, given her a meal, and insisted she tell the full story again, this time with the bishop in attendance.

"I couldn't swallow a thing. We were sitting there, in our kitchen, and my *mamm* had put a late breakfast on the table. Our bishop, he's a *gut* man, but I wasn't ready to talk about it again. I definitely couldn't eat, though my *mamm* kept pushing dishes toward me, even spooning food onto my plate."

Sharon stared out into the darkness, but she could only see stars— a million stars twinkling in the night. "Suddenly, I realized I couldn't control any of it. I couldn't control what the bishop would say or do, or if he would decide I deserved punishment for my part in what happened. I couldn't control what James would say, and I was sure he would deny my story. I couldn't even control what my parents thought. The disappointment in their eyes—it was worse than any reprimand."

Sharon stopped talking, her mind reliving that time in their home in Indiana. The memory was broken when she heard the horses in the barn behind them. Missy called out in her stall. She heard Red answer. The familiar sounds brought her back. They helped her to finish what she needed to say.

"I knew then that there was only one thing I could control."

"What you ate."

"It sounds silly now, but it's important..." The words stuck in her throat. She licked her lips, stared out at the darkness, and finally looked down at her hand in Wess's, though it was too dark to actually see. "It's important to have control over something in your life, ya?"

Instead of answering that question, he rubbed his thumb over the back of her hand. "So what happened? With your parents and the bishop and James?"

"The bishop said no formal confession was necessary because I wasn't a member of our church yet. But he needed to meet with James's parents, and he was concerned about the man who...who chased...who chased me."

"You had to go to the police station and give a statement."

Sharon nodded her head. "The police were quite polite. There had been two other instances, and they were able to show me photographs. I could pick out the one, the one with the scar, but not the driver. I don't know if they have caught them yet."

"And James?"

"He denied it all to his parents. To our *freinden*, he planted the rumor that I was jealous over one of the other girls. He claimed that was why I had turned him in to the store clerk and refused to ride home. He said the beer was for a *freind* and he hadn't had any of it."

"Your word against his."

"And his was backed up by several other boys." Sharon's mind ran over the days that followed that night, like a tongue seeking out a sore spot on the gum. She'd replayed it in her mind so often. Revisited James's hurtful lies too many times. To her surprise she found she didn't feel any real pain thinking on it all now.

It seemed like another lifetime. That girl, who had run and stumbled and run some more, seemed like another person.

"Why did you come here?"

"There was a scene with one of the girls when we met for church. *Rumspringa* is a time of freedom, and we're not supposed to—"

"Rat on each other?"

Sharon laughed softly. "An odd expression, but *ya*, I suppose so."

"But you didn't rat on James. You tried to keep him safe, and then you tried to keep yourself safe, and finally you only answered questions you had to answer."

"You and I see it that way."

"Because we're right." Wess stood, reached for both of her hands, and pulled her to her feet. "You did the smart thing that night and the nights that followed. You were really brave, Sharon."

"I don't know. A brave person wouldn't be haunted by what happened. A brave person would be able to move past it, to sleep and function normally. I couldn't do any of those things. It's part of the reason my parents sent me away."

"There was something more?"

"The fight at church."

"Uh-huh."

"I believe they were also worried I might be persuaded by James again."

"That wouldn't have happened."

"And I'd begun having terrible nightmares. I'd wake screaming, and I shared a room with my little *schweschder*. They wanted me to see a doctor, but I refused. My solution was easier...to stay awake."

"Do you still have them? The nightmares?"

"*Nein*." Sharon couldn't have stopped the smile spreading across her face. "Ada and her prayers and her Psalms seem to have taken care of them."

"That's good." Wess started to speak, stopped himself, and then pushed on. "I can imagine how scared your mom was. She had to know about your not eating."

"She did."

"Moms always notice. Sometimes they don't speak up about it, at least not right away, but they always notice."

He walked her to the back door of Julia's house. A gaslight softly lit the kitchen. Julia and Caleb and Ada had already moved upstairs. Maybe they were in the sitting room, reading and growing drowsy, or maybe they had already gone to bed. It had been a long week for everyone.

"You were right about James and what you did, but you're wrong about the other thing." Wess stopped at the back porch.

Sharon had already moved up onto the bottom step. When she turned around, they were exactly the same height—standing eye to eye. She could just make out his expression in the dim light offered by the lantern in the kitchen.

"I'm wrong?"

"About the control thing."

"I—"

He put a finger to her lips and then kissed her. "You're one of the smartest, hardest working people I know. You control your present and your future, Sharon, not just what you eat."

"Yes, but—"

He kissed her again. "You control your thoughts and what you choose to believe about yourself and others. I'd be happy to give you an opinion about that loser James, but you control how you see that situation. No one else does."

She wanted to argue, but she knew if she spoke he would kiss her once more. Did she want him to kiss her again?

"And you control what happens next in your life."

"But *Gotte* has set a path—"

"Yeah. Maybe He's set several paths." She must have looked surprised because he laughed and touched her face. "I listen at church too."

"You go to church?"

"Sure. It might not last three hours like your Amish services, but I think it still counts."

She smiled and stared down at the porch. His teasing helped. He didn't treat her as if she were made of glass, as if she might break at any second. Standing there with her arms wrapped tightly around her waist, his words helped her to believe in herself and believe everything could be all right.

"Remember, you are the one who decides what happens next in your life." His voice was softer now, nearly a caress.

When she remained silent, he pulled her arm away from her waist, ran his hand down the length of it and circled her wrist with his thumb and forefinger. She had lost so much weight since that night. She'd stopped checking her reflection in the mirror long ago, not wanting to see the dark circles and haunted eyes of the girl in the reflection.

"You also decide when it's time to start taking care of yourself again, because what you put in your mouth goes a long way to deciding how you feel each day." He kissed her once more, just a brush of his lips, before he turned and walked out into the night.

⟿ Chapter 30 ⟿

Julia stood in Elizabeth Troyer's kitchen, holding a plate of sliced ham and unsure what to do. The morning service had gone well, though there was an air of tenseness. She hadn't been able to put her finger on what was wrong. She'd been focused on her mother, who wasn't having her best day. Ada woke thinking she was back in Pennsylvania, and no amount of conversation could convince her otherwise.

It looked as if they would need to see Doc Hanson the next day. Julia's heart twisted. Her mother had been doing so well, but now it was as if they had taken two giant steps backward. Maybe she should have picked up earlier on something being wrong. Perhaps Ada's going to bed early the last few nights had been a sign. Julia had been too preoccupied with her own problems, her and Caleb's relationship. She should have paid more attention to her mother.

At the end of the service, Bishop Atlee had asked for special prayers and support for Nathan Glick's sister, Frannie. He didn't say anything else. Julia knew the Drakes. She'd gone to church with Nathan and Susan all her life, though they were a good ten years older than her. She had never met Frannie, who now stood at the back of the kitchen crying.

"I'll help you with that plate," Elizabeth said. "Could you bring the macaroni casseroles out?"

They were eating outside again, which was odd for the first Sunday in November. The day had dawned unseasonably warm.

"Why is she crying?" Julia walked close and kept her voice low. She wasn't gossiping. She was genuinely concerned.

"I guess you haven't heard."

"*Nein.*"

"Her husband left."

"Left? Left where?"

"Just left. They live in the northern part of the state, and she's been trying to make it on her own the last few months. Her district has been helping, but with the children it's been hard. Last week she allowed the deed to their farm to default to the bank."

They set the dishes on the picnic table and walked back to the kitchen.

"But her district would help with the payments."

"Seems her husband didn't tell anyone how far behind they were. Her bishop offered to hold an auction to help with expenses, but Frannie says she can't run the farm alone. She has four children to raise, so they've come to stay with Nathan and Susan."

Julia picked up a plate of cold chicken, and Elizabeth grabbed two baskets of rolls. They headed back outside again. Frannie was no longer in the kitchen. One of the other women said she was lying down in a back bedroom.

"Why did he leave?"

"She hasn't said. Maybe financial pressure. Maybe something else."

"He could come back."

"It's possible." Elizabeth shrugged her shoulders.

Julia realized Elizabeth probably understood Frannie's predicament better than most. She'd been a widow for two years now. Options for Amish widows were few. They could remarry or they could depend on the charity of the church. It was rare that they had the means to be financially independent. Frannie's options would be even less. She would not be allowed to remarry.

The meal continued as normal, but everything seemed a little off to Julia. The women took turns sitting with Frannie. Lydia hadn't attended church because the midwife had put her on bed rest. Aaron had come to church but left as soon as the service was over. The men continued to talk about the weather. Julia didn't pay much attention to their conversation, though she heard "setting records," "nineteen eleven," and "extremes."

Those things meant nothing to her. Perhaps they were worried about the livestock.

She needed to think about Ada, who was still somewhat dazed and was only picking at her food. How could she have gone downhill so quickly?

When she asked Caleb if they could go home early, he readily agreed. Sharon helped to gather their things, and Julia guided Ada to the buggy. But even as Red trotted down the two-lane road, her mind was traveling in circles—from Elizabeth to Frannie to her mother.

Why was life so difficult? She suddenly felt vulnerable, more than she ever had.

Glancing left, she peeked at Caleb. He was studying the road, probably still worried about the weather.

What would she do if he died? Wouldn't she be in the same situation she'd been in before she married him? She'd be able to keep her home, but only if she could afford to pay the taxes and upkeep. And what if he left—not that he would do such a thing—but what if he did? How would she cope? She didn't have a brother to live with. She didn't want to go anywhere.

She remained distracted the rest of the day. If Caleb noticed, he didn't say anything. Ada seemed to grow worse, her fever rising by the time they readied for bed.

"What do you think it is?" Sharon asked.

"I'm not sure. Would you mind sleeping on the couch in the sitting room? I'd like to stay in here with her."

"I'll sit up with her." Sharon chewed on her thumbnail. They were both standing beside Ada's bed. She was asleep, though her hand moved restlessly on top of the quilt.

"*Nein*. You rest, and if I need a break I'll come and wake you."

But she didn't wake Sharon, and she barely spoke to Caleb when he came in to tell her good night.

⤍

The next morning Ada's fever had vanished, but she was still disoriented. Julia took her to see Doc Hanson.

"It's normal with a urinary tract infection, Julia. She has mild dementia anyway, and the infection makes that worse."

"Should I have done something different?"

"No. You did exactly the right thing by bringing her in to see me. I'm giving her a strong antibiotic, and you should see improvement in the next twenty-four to forty-eight hours."

Thumping her cane against the floor, Ada demanded that someone tell her where her quilting supplies had disappeared to. It hurt Julia's heart, but she understood it was part of the dementia. Ada was remembering better days.

Doc Hanson smiled.

Julia looped her arm through Ada's. "We'll find your things, *mamm*. No need to worry."

By noon Monday they had finished at the doctor's office, picked up Ada's prescription, and were riding home. Julia should have felt better, but she didn't. The week had started off on the wrong foot, and the weather was making her *narrisch*. Even Missy seemed skittish, tossing her head and pulling left when traffic approached them—pulling into the oncoming lane. It took all of Julia's concentration to get them safely home.

Once she tucked her mother into bed, she had half the day left—half the time to complete all of the items on her list because tomorrow the café would be open again.

Her dream had come true, though, and complaining about it

would help no one. So she trudged downstairs, opened the windows to cool the rooms, and set to work.

≈

Caleb didn't know what to make of the unseasonable temperatures.

He'd seen strange weather before. He was from Indiana, after all. They had their share of tornadoes, droughts, and even the occasional flood. God was in control of the seasons, not man, so he'd never paid it much attention.

But sixty degrees the first week in November was unusual. It made him itchy. And it made his animals nervous.

Tim had stopped by earlier in the morning. Jeanette had been on the Internet and checked—the average high temperature for this time of year ranged between forty-five and fifty-five. Not so far off. Not really.

So why were they all acting as if boulders were going to fall from the sky?

He'd told Tim not to worry, and he'd gone back to repairing his barn. Winter would arrive. It was only a matter of time, and when it did, it would probably be a good one. That was it, he realized as he stared out across Julia's garden.

They were no doubt in for one very long, very cold winter.

He'd seen it before, and he should have recognized the signs all around him—warm weather, unsettled animals, and people on edge. Winter was coming. He didn't need a computer to tell him that.

So he spent a few extra hours in the barn, making sure things were as tight and snug as he could make them.

When he went inside for dinner, it took only one glance to see how tired Julia was. She looked ready to fall asleep in her chair.

"Is Ada any better?"

"I think so. She's sleeping well. Not..." Julia moved her hand back and forth across the top of the table, mimicking Ada's earlier agitations.

"That's *gut*. Hanson, he's a fine doctor. Everyone says so."

Julia attempted a smile but didn't say anything. She was exhausted. They all were.

He should talk to her about hiring more help in the café, but they didn't actually know how much money they were clearing yet. Wait another week, maybe two, and then they could sit down and look at the finances.

"Where's Sharon?"

"Sitting upstairs with her. They both had some soup earlier."

The rest of the meal passed in silence. Caleb wondered if anything else was wrong. He couldn't imagine what. Ada was on the mend. Sharon seemed to be doing better. The little spat they'd had last week was behind them.

"Is there anything I can do to help get ready for tomorrow?"

"*Nein.*"

"You look as though you feel bad. Is something wrong?"

She glanced at him sharply but shook her head. "I just...my head is hurting. That's all."

He'd never known her to complain of a headache before. Probably it was the weather.

"I'll do the dishes. Go lie down." When she protested, he insisted. "You were up all night with your mother, Julia. I can clean up a couple of bowls."

So she nodded and dragged herself up the stairs—it was the only word for it. He could hear her pulling one foot behind the other. *Clomp. Clomp. Clomp.* As if her shoes or her feet or her entire legs were too heavy to pick up and move to the next step.

The weather would cool. The first snow would fall, and they would all feel better. It was only a matter of time.

After Caleb finished the dishes he went upstairs. No one was in the sitting room, and there was no light on under his door. Caleb thought of going in to check on Julia, but he didn't want to wake her. So instead he pulled out a pillow and blanket from the closet, made a comfortable bed on the couch, and within five minutes was asleep.

Chapter 31

Sharon didn't change her eating habits immediately after her conversation with Wess. She'd gone upstairs, found everyone in bed, and pretended to read awhile. Actually, she'd sat and thought about what he'd said. Then she had gone to bed—same as always. She did not have nightmares. The terrible dreams of being chased as she ran through the rain seemed to be in the past.

The next morning they had realized how sick Ada was.

And Monday she'd done the laundry while Julia took Ada to the doctor. It wasn't until Monday afternoon as she was washing dishes that she made up her mind she would like to go to town. She talked to Julia about it. They decided that Mattie, one of the girls in their district, could come in and cover the Wednesday morning shift.

"Are you sure?"

"Absolutely. Mattie has asked if I would give her a try. Wednesday morning will be a perfect chance for her to see if she likes it—"

"And if she's any *gut*," Caleb pointed out.

"That too, though I suspect we can teach her what she needs to know."

Sharon didn't know much about Mattie. Miriam had once mentioned she'd had problems with a boy a year or so ago. He was living in another town now and his name was Jerry Beiler. He was the bishop's nephew, the bishop for the other side of Pebble Creek, which all meant nothing to her. They were a family from the east side of Pebble Creek. She'd barely learned the names of the people on their side—the west side.

Mattie would either work out or she wouldn't. If she did, then they would have someone to help on extra busy days or when Sharon or Wess needed time off.

Caleb was off on Wednesday, and he said he didn't mind taking her to town. He needed to pick up some supplies anyway. The ride along the two-lane road was pleasant, and she found herself feeling excited as she checked her purse one last time to be sure she'd placed part of her earnings in there. She'd spent very little of the money she'd made. The fall communion service had already occurred when she arrived, so she'd missed the offering. Instead, she set a portion of her tips aside for the spring offering. Whether she was home or still staying with Caleb and Julia by then, she wanted to be able to do her part.

The only other money she had spent out of her earnings had been to purchase candy for Victoria and Zoey. One of the guests at their restaurant delivered candy to stores in town, and he'd been happy to sell her a few chocolate bars from his sample case. The girls had clapped and squealed. Wess had joined them as his sisters were sitting next to Sharon on the porch swing, hands sticky from the sweet treat. He had rolled his eyes.

"I checked with your *mamm* first."

"They're still spoiled rotten!" But Wess's smile spoke louder than his words did.

Because she worked five days a week, her envelope of money was growing. She'd even tried to pay Caleb and Julia for her room and board, but they had refused.

"You're more than earning your keep, Sharon."

The words left a warm glow inside her. Or maybe it was the way Julia had smiled when she'd said them.

Julia seemed preoccupied this week, still worried about something. Ada was improving with the medicine, so Sharon wasn't sure what the problem was, but then adults had a lot more to worry about than teens did.

Her growing amount of money was her biggest worry at the moment. Christmas presents would need to be bought, depending on where she was living at the end of December. She should purchase some crocheting supplies today. Maybe she would look if she had time. She could crochet, knit, and quilt, but by far her crocheting skills were best. Those projects seemed to be finished much more quickly than others.

Would she be home for Christmas? Or would she still be here in Wisconsin? She had wanted to talk to her parents about it, but what would she say? What had changed? She hadn't had the courage to call them, and anyway her parents didn't like talking on the phone. She'd not even picked up a cell phone since the incident in Monroe. Aaron had a phone at the cabins for business, and she knew he would have been happy to let her use it. But what would she say if she called home? What would they say to her?

Her mother had written several times, but Sharon hadn't answered yet. She meant to, and then in the evenings she always decided to put it off until the next day.

She and Caleb arrived in town, and he parked the buggy next to the feed store.

"Need help finding anything?"

"*Nein.*"

"Will an hour be long enough for you?"

"An hour will be fine, Caleb. Thank you."

She turned away from the buggy and started down the street. The day was unseasonably warm, and she didn't need her coat or even a wrap. Down the road, she could see Amish Anthem, the tallest building in town, but she didn't think what she was looking for would be there.

She passed the city offices, a small café with checkered curtains, and a gas station. She saw the grocery in the distance and realized she was nearing the end of the two blocks which made up the downtown area.

Perhaps she would need to try Amish Anthem after all.

Looking left and right, she prepared to cross the street, and that was when she saw it—The Book Nook.

Maybe they would have what she needed.

A bell chimed as she pushed the door open. A large fluffy dog was lying on a rug in front of the register, but she stood at the sound of the bell, stretched, and then padded over and placed her cold black nose against Sharon's hand.

"Dixie won't bite, dear. She loves customers."

Dixie was obviously a mixed breed. Sharon didn't know a lot about dogs, but this one seemed to have a little German shepherd, some Labrador, and possibly poodle in her family tree. The result was big, curly, and gentle. Brown hair flopped over dark eyes that gazed up at her expectantly.

"Hi, Dixie." Sharon patted the dog on her head and received a look of complete adoration for her trouble.

"What can I help you with today?" The owner was a small *Englisch* woman with graying hair, half glasses, and kind eyes.

Sharon described what she was looking for.

Tapping a neatly trimmed nail against the counter, Mrs. Shepard— Sharon could see her name tag now—didn't answer right away. Then she smiled and pointed to the far side of the store. "Last aisle, at the end but at the top. Would you like me to show you?"

"*Nein.* I can find it myself."

"Let me know if you need anything else."

Because she was alone, except for Dixie, she was able to take her time and pick out exactly what she wanted. On her way back to the counter, she spied some stationary—simple but a pretty lavender, and lined, which was unusual. She preferred lined paper, as her hand-writing tended to angle when she wrote until it looked as if her sentences were drooping off the page.

"I love this paper," Mrs. Shepard said. "It's a shame people don't write letters as much as they used to. At least *Englisch* people don't."

Sharon smiled at the store owner's use of the term. Apparently she had grown used to having both Amish and *Englisch* customers. "Yet *Englischers* have e-mail and such, which is much faster, *ya?*"

"Faster, but not as permanent." Mrs. Shepard handed over her change. "Stop by and see Dixie and me again. Maybe by the time you do, we'll have winter weather like we should."

"That would be nice. I've never been in Wisconsin in the winter."

"We have lots of snow, and it's usually quite cold."

"Sounds *wunderbaar*." Sharon patted the dog one last time and had made it to the door when she remembered to ask about yarn.

"One block over, behind us. The Yarn Shop—it's a small yellow house. You can't miss it."

She didn't miss it. In fact, she could have spent her entire hour there among the yarns and patterns. She didn't need a pattern, though, and she knew Julia and Ada had a basket of crochet hooks. So she settled for buying a lovely teal-and-purple variegated yarn— three skeins of it, enough for a shawl.

It wouldn't make up for the things she had said to her mother, but it would be a start.

When she arrived back at the café, the lunch crowd was in full swing. She ran upstairs, dropped her two packages on her bed, and headed back down to the kitchen.

"How do you manage all day?" Mattie asked, her brown eyes wide and her cheeks flushed. "I'm exhausted."

"You did very well, Mattie." Julia slipped piping hot cornbread on a plate along with a bowl of potato soup and handed it to Sharon. "Table four, Sharon. Glad to have you back."

"I'll say. I'm ready for a nap after this morning!" Mattie sank onto a stool and reached for her glass of water.

"You should have seen me the first day. I—"

"You were tired?" Wess arrived with a tray of dirty dishes. "Hmm. I thought you were the Energizer Bunny."

Mattie, Julia, and Sharon all stared at him, but Mattie was the one to ask, "Who?"

Sharon liked the laughter that followed as she carried table four's food into the next room. It was as if they were a team, and they worked together pretty well.

On her break later that afternoon, she ran up to her room, picked up one of her packages, sat in the chair by the window, opened the journal, and began to write.

The idea to use a journal had come to her the evening Wess had kissed her, after he had reminded her she was in control of her choices.

But it was easy to forget that late at night when she was trying to fall asleep. Or early in the morning when she didn't think she had the energy to begin the day's work. She had been puzzling over it as she'd carried dishes in to wash the day before when Julia had pulled out her list and added another item to it. Julia and her lists. They all teased her about them, but everyone had also admitted that her lists and her organization kept the café running.

If lists could work for Julia, maybe they could also work for her. And wasn't the book of Psalms, which Ada was so fond of, simply a list? A list of what God had done in the psalmists' lives.

Sharon ran her hand over the front of the journal. It was a soft green, which reminded her of spring. The thought of spring always lifted her heart. It gave her hope, as if the horrors of this fall would not last forever. Perhaps they would die with winter, and she could begin again.

The journal was fastened shut by an elastic band sewn into the back cover and looped over the front. Sharon slipped her hand under the elastic, opened the cover, and turned to the front page—lined and blank.

But she couldn't write on it. The first page seemed too vulnerable, too exposed. What if someone found it? What if they read her thoughts?

She settled for penning her name on the third line. Then she turned to the next page, put the date at the top, and began to write. She listed all the choices she had made that day. The decisions she had made.

All were small things—which dress to wear, to surprise Julia by rising early and having their breakfast on the table, to ride with Caleb into town. Nothing earth shattering. When she was finished, her words hadn't filled even half of the page.

You control your thoughts and what you choose to believe about yourself and others.

She skipped a line and began writing again.

When she had reached the bottom, she placed the cap back on the pen and read what she'd written, what was below the skipped line, what she chose to believe about others and herself.

Julia and Caleb love me.

Ada is a gift from Gotte.

Zoey and Victoria are a joy.

Bandit makes me smile.

Wess is special.

Gotte has taken care of me.

Closing the journal, she pulled the elastic band around the top and across the front and tucked her pen into the spiral binding.

Maybe it was a small step, but it was a step. She sensed that as surely as she sensed a storm was coming soon, one that would relieve them of the heat and return the winter weather they should be having.

Maybe writing her list each day would help her step onto the path she should be traveling down. Tucking the journal in her drawer, she hurried downstairs. Her lunch break was over, and she hadn't eaten, which wasn't a problem. She could sneak in a snack between customers. If there was one thing she was sure of, it was that Julia was always happy to see her eat.

Later that night she helped with the dinner dishes. It had been a long day, and she was looking forward to sitting upstairs. Maybe she would even go to bed early. Her stomach felt uncomfortably full, which was probably why she was so tired. For the first time since that night in Indiana, she hadn't counted her bites. She wouldn't allow herself to, though it was going to be a difficult habit to break. Not that she had exactly cleaned her plate, but she had eaten more than usual. Caleb and Julia had certainly been smiling about something. Though it might have nothing to do with her, Caleb had said, "Maybe Sharon wants dessert tonight."

But she couldn't have fit dessert into her stomach no matter how hard she might have tried. Small steps, she reminded herself. Keep moving in the right direction, and small steps were fine.

They did the dishes and were upstairs within an hour, each taking their turn in the bathroom.

Things seemed almost normal. Ada thumbed through the Psalms. Caleb read the *Budget*. Julia worked on her lists. She still seemed worried. Preoccupied, really. She kept chewing on the end of her pen before scratching something off and writing another thing down on the paper. Sharon pulled her book off the shelf, the same one she'd been pretending to read since the day she'd arrived. Staring at the page, she kept thinking of the teal-and-purple yarn. She could probably finish the shawl in a few weeks, and then she could go back and buy the blue-and-yellow—a nice blend that Ruthie would love.

Excusing herself, she went to her room and retrieved a skein. Julia kept her crochet hooks and knitting needles in a basket on the same shelf as the books. When she walked back into the room with the yarn, Julia smiled and nodded toward the basket. Sharon selected a size J hook, which would work nicely for the pattern she had in mind.

She was surprised when Julia put down her list, walked over to a sewing basket, and picked up a quilt top. She'd never seen Julia sew except to darn a few things. Moving back to the couch, she sat beside Caleb, threaded the needle, and began to stitch a border strip around the top.

Sharon watched Julia and thought of her mother. She'd received a letter each week from her. Julia always wrote back to her. She knew this because Julia would read the return letters out loud to her and asked if she wanted to add anything. Sharon didn't know what to say to her mother, though.

The lavender paper sat in her room, waiting for her to use, but she didn't know how to begin the conversation she needed to have with her parents. So instead she began to crochet. She allowed the hook and the yarn to sooth the worries in her heart. She allowed the rhythm of the crocheting to calm her anxiousness.

When Ada tapped her Bible and began to read, Sharon found herself listening, really listening, rather than merely tolerating her.

"'I will both lie down in peace, and sleep...'"

Caleb folded his paper and placed his arm around Julia.

"'For You alone, O Lord...'"

Julia lowered her sewing and smiled over the top of it at Sharon.

"'You alone, O Lord, make me dwell in safety.'"

At the last words, Julia glanced down and something crossed her face—a shadow maybe or it could have been she was having a stomachache.

Soon after that Ada said good night. Julia sewed another ten minutes and excused herself. Caleb folded his paper and followed.

But Sharon wasn't ready for bed. She wanted to crochet just one more row. She wanted to think about the things she had to say to her mother and how she would ask for her forgiveness.

~ Chapter 32 ~

J ulia pulled away from Caleb, stood, and walked to the window. The night was so warm they had opened it, but no breeze stirred her gown as she stared out into the darkness.

The week had been exhausting, beginning on Sunday by learning about Frannie's tragic situation. The woman had even come into the restaurant yesterday, brought in by Susan while the children were in school. Seeing her had driven the panic deeper into Julia's heart. Seeing her had been like holding a mirror up to what might be her future.

She'd tried to talk to Ada about it yesterday. Her mother was on the mend but noticeably weaker than before. She had again joined the family downstairs, but she was no longer able to sit in the front hall and greet visitors.

"*Were you ever afraid?*" Julia asked.

"*Of what?*"

"*That dat might leave or die?*"

"*He did die.*"

"*But—*"

"*Julia, be strong and take heart. Hope in the Lord.*"

When Julia had only stared down at the floor, her mother had added, "And talk to Caleb. Tell him what has frightened you."

Now Caleb was waiting, wanting to know why she'd become so silent and why she pulled away from him when he tried to hold her.

How could she find the words to explain her deepest fears? And even if she had the words, the right words, did she have the courage to share them?

"Tell me what's wrong, Julia. Maybe I can help."

"You can't!" The statement leapt from her—too harsh, too absolute.

"How do you know that? You haven't even given me a chance."

He was beside her now, standing so close she could smell the soap he'd used earlier when bathing. It was all she could do not to turn and bury herself in his arms. Would that make things better or worse?

"Julia, what are you afraid of?"

"What am I not afraid of? That *mamm* will die. That the café will be a failure. That it will be such a success I won't be able to rise to the challenge. That we won't have children. That you will leave!" She pressed her fingers to her lips, wishing with all her heart she could pull the confessions back, especially the last one.

Why hadn't he simply let it go? Why did he always have to push? Always need to talk things out? Why couldn't he let her carry her fears and burdens alone?

"Why would I leave?" He hadn't moved, but she could feel the tenseness in his body. How was it that she knew him so well after so short a time?

"Some men do—"

"We're Amish, Julia. Our commitment is sacred and for life. Together we—"

"Some Amish men do." She turned on him now, though she couldn't see him clearly in the darkness of their room. "Some Amish men do, Caleb. They leave. They just disappear. Do you realize what has happened to Frannie? What happens to women who are abandoned? We are left in limbo—unable to marry, no longer single. We're left to provide for ourselves or depend on the charity of others."

"I am *not* one of those men." His voice was almost a growl.

She knew she had pushed too far, understood that these fears, the ones that woke her in the middle of the night, were things she should wrestle with alone. She shouldn't have admitted them to anyone, especially not her husband.

"How do I know that?"

"How can you not?" He reached for her then, but she stepped away.

"I don't even know you."

"You do." He turned, walked to his side of the bed, and picked up his pillow. "You do know me. Maybe what frightens you is that you know you can depend on me. You know how much I care."

Without another word, he walked out of their room and shut the door quietly behind him.

Julia thought she would cry all night, but exhaustion won. She woke at her normal time, well before dawn. The day was already feeling warm. Regardless of what had happened between her and Caleb the night before, there would be people to feed.

She dressed, stopped by the bathroom, and peeked into the sitting room. Caleb was already gone. His pillow was still on the couch, placed on top of a neatly folded sheet. It wasn't his Saturday to work at the grocery, so he must be in the barn.

Why did she doubt him? He was a good man and a tender husband. He'd done nothing to warrant her distrust. Maybe she was having typical newlywed jitters. Perhaps she should have talked to Miriam or Lydia about it, but there had been no time.

She made her way to the kitchen and began preparing the dishes they would be offering on the lunch menu. It was the second Saturday in November, and with the unseasonably warm weather she expected they would have plenty of customers. Why didn't that thought make her as happy as she had imagined it would only two months ago?

Peeking into the next room, she ticked off each item on her morning checklist—the list she no longer needed to see. Each table was properly cleaned, and a single fresh flower had already been placed in each vase for a centerpiece. Sharon must have been in the garden early. She was a *gut* girl, and Julia realized with a start that she would miss her if she decided to go home at Thanksgiving. A part of her hoped Sharon would stay with them. There were plenty of girls in Pebble Creek to hire for help, but they weren't family.

Family. The word sent an ache through her heart.

Where was Caleb? And what could she say to him to bridge the distance that had grown between them over the last week? It was unnatural and wrong. She needed to trust what she couldn't control to the Lord. Her mother was right about that.

Her cane tapping against the floor, Ada hobbled into the room as if thoughts of her could produce her presence.

"*Gudemariye, dochder.*"

"And you, *mamm.*"

"Whatever you're cooking smells *wunderbaar.*"

"Indeed it does."

Caleb's voice sent her stomach tumbling. She missed him—missed everything about him. More than anything she wanted to walk into his arms and feel his kiss, hear him murmur her name, see the teasing look in his eyes.

But she couldn't do any of that, not with Ada in the room and Sharon somewhere close. So instead she managed a smile and said, "I've made your breakfast. It's ready and set on the table."

"*Danki.*" Caleb walked across the room. He stopped behind her, reached over her head, and withdrew a glass from the cabinet.

"There's *kaffi* and juice on the table." She did not want to talk about breakfast beverages. She longed to turn in his arms and bury herself in the smell and comfort of him, but Ada was watching them as if they were two kittens determined to chase a ball of yarn around the room.

"*Ya,* and I'll drink them both. It's so warm, though, some water would be *gut* first."

Sharon joined them, washing her hands at the sink. "It was warm when I cut the flowers, and the sun was barely up."

"You're up early every day now. What would your parents think?" Caleb laughed as he finished the water and rinsed the glass.

Julia appreciated the fact that he didn't allow the tension which existed between them to affect the way he interacted with the rest of the family. She joined them at the table, and they all bowed their heads to give thanks. Julia marveled at how different it was, praying within this circle. She'd always believed God heard her, but knowing that Ada, Caleb, and Sharon were offering up their thanks and concerns at the same time soothed her heart. Perhaps everything would turn out well after all.

Caleb reached for the bacon. Sharon poured some juice. Ada stared out the window at the warm November day. "I remember when we moved here. That was before you were born, Julia."

Sharon snickered, and Caleb raised his gaze from his plate with so many emotions behind his eyes that Julia had to look away.

"So long ago, *mamm*." Julia played along, grateful to see Sharon in such a fine mood this morning. "It's amazing you can remember something from way back then."

"*Ya.*" Ada's eyes clouded in that way when she wasn't completely with them, and her voice took on a softer quality. "It doesn't seem so long ago. I was hoping for a *boppli*, but we hadn't been blessed yet. We moved to Wisconsin in nineteen seventy. Even then there were a few old-timers in our district. They remembered that day. One woman was ninety-four. She lived close. Her name was Priscilla, and she taught me so much about quilting..."

Ada raised her cup of *kaffi* to her lips, her hand shaking slightly. "She taught me about quilting and about life. She was the one who told me about that day."

Sharon had scooped a spoonful of eggs onto her plate and reached for a biscuit, which she was covering with butter and jam. "What day, Ada?"

"The day of destruction." Ada set her cup into its saucer with something of a clatter. It landed off center, tilted, and nearly spilled its contents.

Caleb reached out and caught it in time.

"*Danki*, Caleb."

"*Gem gschehne.*"

The old words. Spoken so early in the morning, they sounded like blessings, and they brought tears to Julia's eyes. Why was she so emotional? She had much left to do before they opened, but suddenly she only wanted to preserve this moment—to reach out and hold on to it, to embrace each person at the table.

Ada picked up her fork and began tearing her biscuit into pieces.

"Why was it called a day of destruction? And when was it?" Sharon opened her mouth wide and took a giant bite of the buttermilk biscuit covered with blackberry preserves.

Caleb caught Julia watching her eat, and they shared a smile—shared that small victory.

"Because it was," Ada said, still focused on working the fork into her biscuit. "The weather was warm, like today."

She glanced toward the calendar on the wall in the kitchen, squinted, and said. "Perhaps this old world knows. It was the eleventh of November, nineteen eleven."

"*Ya*, but the eleventh hasn't arrived yet, Ada. You girls have nothing to fear today—or any day for that matter." Caleb wiped his mouth with his napkin and refilled his *kaffi* mug.

"Do you know what she's talking about?" Julia reached for the tie of her prayer *kapp* and ran her fingers down the length of it.

"Sure." Caleb sat back and studied the scene outside their window. "Folks were talking about it at the grocery earlier this week and even over at the cabins."

"I heard something at the church luncheon," Sharon said.

"It was a terrible day. Priscilla said she thought it might be the end-times—first the heat, followed by the tornadoes, and then the blizzard. So much death and so many things destroyed." Ada glanced from Julia to Sharon to Caleb. "Many wondered if it was the day of the Lord's wrath."

"It was a day of unusual weather, that's the truth. And the forecast does call for colder weather according to Tim. He came by yesterday. You all should be fine for today, though I expect you'll be hot in this house even with the windows open." He stood and carried his dishes to the sink.

Julia followed him, needing to be next to him if only for a moment. Something in her mother's voice had felt like a premonition, or maybe a vision from God, and it had unsettled her.

She whispered, "I want to say I'm sorry about—"

He ducked his head and brushed his lips against hers.

They both placed their dishes in the sink as Sharon walked up.

"Are you sure you don't need me to stay around?" Caleb stood close beside his wife. His arm brushed against hers, and his voice in her ear, soft and filled with tenderness, made her heart lift and soar. Perhaps tonight it would be like it had been before. Perhaps tonight she could cross the distance she had created between them.

"Aaron is expecting you, *ya?*" She turned so that she was standing even closer, standing against him.

Sharon stepped out of the room. "Guests are coming," she announced.

Caleb reached out and touched her face, ran his fingers down under her chin, and kissed her again on the lips. "I told him I'd be there after breakfast."

"Then go." She reached up and combed her fingers through the bangs which were again growing long. "If you make it back early, maybe we'll have time to give you a haircut."

"You're saying I look shaggy?"

"You do." Ada bustled past them. "Even these old eyes can see as much."

"Hmm." Caleb's eyebrows shot up and then back down. "I'll see if I can't finish my work early then. You finish your lunch crowd by four?"

She nodded. She wanted to reach up and kiss him again. More than anything, she wanted to apologize thoroughly, but she knew now wasn't the time.

"I'll be home by three thirty so I can help you clean up." Whistling, he snagged his hat off the hook by the back door and headed out into the fall morning.

When he opened the door, a draft of too-warm air filled the room.

Day of destruction, indeed.

Julia would welcome the cold front, but she suspected that by spring they would remember this morning fondly.

⌒

Caleb and Aaron had worked all afternoon adding an extension to the front porch that ran the length of the cabins' office. It had become quite the meeting place for guests morning and afternoon, and Lydia had wanted it wrapped around the side of the building. The men had been able to keep tabs on the coming and goings of guests while completing the work.

"We should have done this in the spring when it was cooler," Aaron muttered as they hammered the final boards in place.

"No one could have guessed we'd reach seventy-three degrees in November." Caleb guzzled water from the plastic jug he'd brought. When he finished, he wiped the back of his arm across his mouth. "We might have broken the record high."

"I don't care about records. I'm ready for things to return to normal. Our baby's due any day, and this hot weather is making Lydia *narrisch*."

"She'll be happy with the porch. It looks nice. There will be room for half a dozen more rockers."

Aaron's smile was slow but genuine. "I don't expect Lydia will be making it over here to rock until after the *boppli* is born. I'm glad she promised to stay home today—simply walking is hard enough."

"You can describe the work we've done to her. With the view of

Pebble Creek and the woods, this will be a perfect spot for an afternoon rest."

"Clara can tell David to bring the chairs over next week." Aaron
studied the sky, which was darkening at an alarming rate. "It looks
like we finished just in time. Tim's storm is nearly here. He's been
talking about it for two days. The man has adapted to the Plain life
well, but he does enjoy researching local history on his computer."

"He's not the only one. Ada mentioned the nineteen-eleven
storm this morning. I need to get her and Tim together. They would
have a fine time—"

But he never finished the thought because the wind suddenly
picked up, coming out of the north and dropping the temperature
instantly.

Aaron grinned. "Time to put up the tools for the day. Help me
close the office?"

Together they went through the main room, shutting windows
and locking the front door. It took some effort to push the door
closed with the wind blowing in alarming gusts. As Caleb gathered
his tools and placed them into his toolbox, Aaron went to speak
with a man and woman from cabin two who were worried about
the weather.

Caleb checked to make sure nothing was left on the ground. It
wouldn't do to leave a hammer or screwdriver outside during a storm.
The wind might pick it up and strike someone or something, causing
real damage. He had to hold his hat down with one hand and bend
his body against the wind to cover the short distance between the picnic tables—where he picked up a rake someone had left outside—to
the front of the building where everyone was gathering.

By the time he'd joined Aaron at the front door, guests from cabins three and four were standing on the porch looking out at the
wind, which was sending pots of flowers, a birdhouse, and even a
folding chair scurrying across the lawn. A few people were pressed
up against the wall to stay out of the wind, but most seemed to want
a better view of what was happening.

"The temperature has already dropped ten degrees in the last fifteen minutes, and there are reports of possible tornadoes." The *Englischer* who was speaking was holding a phone in his hand and swiping through screens as he talked. From what Sharon had explained to Caleb, the phone was a type of handheld computer.

"Do you want the horses in or out?" Caleb asked.

"That barn is solid, especially the portion banked against the hillside. Outside, they could be hit by debris."

"Outside they have a chance to run from whatever's coming." Caleb's heart was racing. He realized they were taking a giant chance either way. If a tornado did hit where they were standing, they would have more to worry about than the welfare of the horses. Perhaps they should put the people and the horses—

"Guide them to the back stalls. They won't be able to hear as much there. It should calm them. Our property is relatively small, and I'm afraid they'd run out into the road. We're going to have to trust their instincts."

Caleb didn't bother answering. He was already running toward the horses that had been left grazing in a pen next to the barn. How had the weather turned so quickly? How had they not noticed while they were working? It didn't seem likely it could have happened as quickly as the *Englischer* had suggested.

He knew he could count on Tim and Jeanette to warn Julia, Sharon, and Ada. The basement under their home would be a safe place to wait out the storm. God would protect them. Even as the wind whipped the hat from his head and sent it flying toward the river, he prayed, *Please*, Gotte, *protect my family*.

The horses stomped and tossed their heads, but they allowed him to lead them into the back stalls of the barn. He fought the barn door, throwing all of his weight against it and finally latching it shut before running back to the front porch. By the time he reached the bottom step, more than thirty people huddled under the roof overhang and inside the small office building, which Aaron had unlocked.

The rain started falling in sheets, and he could tell the temperature had dropped even more. In addition, it had grown dark—nearly as dark as night, though it was still early afternoon.

Most of the cabin guests were on their phones.

Snippets of conversations washed over Caleb, but he wasn't actually hearing the words. He was thinking instead of what Ada had said a few hours earlier. Her words echoed in his mind, striking against his heart like the pieces of hail which now pounded against the roof over their heads—*"It was a terrible day. Priscilla said she thought it might be the end-times—first the heat, followed by the tornadoes, and then the blizzard. So much death and so many things destroyed."*

The cat who had adopted the cabins, Pumpkin, rubbed against his legs. He bent to pick up the orange tom. When he did, a flash of lightning streaked across the sky and he saw the funnel.

It was still a long way off, but it was barreling straight toward them.

Chapter 33

J ulia had been working in the kitchen, making extra amounts of everything on the menu. They had suspected the day might be busy, and they were right. She occasionally glanced out the window over the sink or past the countertop into the breakfast room and larger dining area. What had once been their sitting room had a wall lined with windows. She wasn't completely oblivious to what was going on outside.

An hour before she'd been called to a table in the front dining room to accept a woman's compliments—the apple-cinnamon pie was apparently the best she'd ever had. While walking back to the kitchen, Julia had heard several guests commenting about the unusual heat. Most were making predictions that the weather could turn nasty.

It was always a possibility. She'd been born and raised in Wisconsin, in this very house. Their worst weather was by and large in the depths of winter. When they had opened the café, she'd worried about how light the crowds could become once the snow and cold temperatures set in. Today, she found herself thinking of such problems fondly.

Somehow Julia had managed to take any worries over the weather and push them to the back of her mind. She focused on feeding everyone and surviving the lunch crowd. She counted the moments until Caleb would be home at three thirty. They could discuss the weather together and what, if anything, should be done.

Ada had gone upstairs for a nap around one o'clock. She had seemed more disoriented than usual. It pained Julia to see her that way, but she was learning there would be good days and bad ones. Apparently today landed squarely in the worse-than-usual column.

All of those thoughts were colliding in her mind as she frosted an additional Lazy Daisy oatmeal cake. She'd baked three the night before, but the last was nearly gone. Surely one more would see them through the rest of the afternoon. That was her final normal thought when she glanced up and saw Sharon standing in the doorway of the kitchen.

Her face was as white as the *kapp* covering her perfectly braided hair. It was her eyes, brown, wide, and as frightened as a doe's, that caused Julia to drop the bowl of frosting into the sink.

What had happened? Why was Sharon standing there looking as if the sky had fallen? Looking more lost than the first night she'd appeared on their doorstep—

Unless something terrible had happened. Unless something had happened to one of their guests or to Ada.

"*Was iss letz?*"

Once Sharon began speaking, a part of Julia's mind keyed in on the conversations going on in the next room and the fact that most of her customers were now standing at the windows, staring out at the weather.

"It's the storm. They say it's coming." Sharon's eyes widened even more, and she clasped her hands in front of her. She glanced back over her shoulder, as if whatever she feared might follow her into the room.

Wess stepped closer. Julia hadn't even noticed he was there until he put his arm around Sharon's shoulder to try to still her shaking.

"Wess, you went home an hour ago. Why are you—"

"My family's on their way."

"Here?" Julia wiped her hands on her apron as she moved across the room to peer out the window.

"They sent me over first to warn you. Everyone needs—" He too glanced over his shoulder. "Everyone needs to get into the basement. Dad said to hurry."

Julia saw it all then, saw it in an instant as clearly as she could see a recipe coming together. As understanding dawned on her, a memory from her past surged forward. She'd been a young girl, still clutching a baby doll. Her father had grabbed her hand and told her mother to run.

A shiver snaked down her spine.

The sky outside had grown unnaturally dark. Wind from the north was blowing the trees so hard they were bent nearly to the ground, and the temperature in the kitchen had dropped. When had it become so cold?

A baby cried out from the front dining area.

How many customers remained? Fifteen? Twenty? How many would the basement hold? Her mind blanked. Suddenly she couldn't picture it.

She glanced past Sharon and Wess to the people gathered at the windows. They would have to fit. They had no other option.

"Wess, go with Sharon and help Ada down the stairs. Carry her if you must."

Flipping off the burners to her gas stove, her heart racing as if she had run from Tim and Jeanette's house, she rushed into the main dining area.

"We're under a tornado warning," an *Englischer* declared, frowning as he stared down at his telephone.

A middle-aged woman sitting near a window was holding hands with an older woman. "My daughter just texted me that one has already hit a town south of here."

"We need to leave." A younger woman, the one with the baby who had been crying, began gathering up her things.

"Leaving would be a mistake." Julia stepped forward and forced her voice to sound calm. "Driving during a storm like this is very dangerous."

"How can you know anything about a storm like this? The news is reporting that the temperature has dropped nearly twenty degrees in the last forty minutes." The same man who had told of the tornado warning was still staring at his phone. His frown had deepened to a scowl. Everyone in the room quieted as he read from a news page.

"The national weather service is declaring an imminent emergency. An arctic front has slammed into the warm humid air system this area has been under." He glanced back up at Julia. "You can't know what to do. There's never been a storm like this."

"Actually, there has been. The year was nineteen eleven." Ada limped into the room. Her prayer *kapp* was askew, revealing wispy white hair that showed her age in a way Julia hadn't yet come to terms with. In spite of her disheveled appearance, her eyes were clearer than they had been all day. "And my *dochder* is right. Driving now would be dangerous. We need to all go to the basement before we feel the storm's full wrath. The Lord will keep us from all harm."

At that moment a tree cracked and splintered. Several people screamed and jumped away from the large windows. The tree fell next to the house, its branches crashing into one of the panes and scattering glass throughout the room.

"What is she talking about?" asked the middle-aged woman who had seconds earlier been sitting near the window that had just shattered.

"A storm happened long ago. It was much like this one." Julia shook her head. "There's no time to explain. Go out the back door and to your left. Keep your left hand on the house and within ten paces you'll bump into two steps and a door which opens down to the basement. It's latched on the outside, so two men should lead the group—unlatching and opening it in this wind will be difficult. More stairs lead down. Everyone be careful and stay together."

Ada moved to sit in one of the chairs, but Julia stopped her. "We need to go now, *mamm*." The teenagers were at her side before she could call out for their help.

"We've got her," Wess said.

"What about your parents?"

"They just pulled up out front."

Julia turned to run to the door to check on them, but the baby began crying again. Its wails were barely discernible over the howling of the storm. Grabbing a quilt off of a stand positioned against the wall, she wrapped it around the infant, who looked to be only a few months old.

"Thank you," the young mother said. "I'm so afraid, and my husband didn't come because of business. I came with my sister instead."

"We'll help you. Hold your *boppli* tight. I'll walk on one side of you and your sister—"

"Khloe."

Julia smiled at the other woman, who had long black hair and seemed almost paralyzed by all that was happening. "Khloe will stand on the other side, nice and close. Right, Khloe?"

Moving next to her sister, Khloe nodded, and they started toward the back porch.

As they moved, Julia prayed that everyone was out of the house, that Caleb had found a safe haven at the cabins, and that the storm would move over them quickly. She prayed that this day would not be like her mother's long-remembered day of destruction.

She'd made it to the back door when Tim and Jeanette caught up with them, their two younger girls and Bandit huddled between them.

"Hurry, Julia." Tim's face said all she needed to know. They had run out of time. Still, she paused at the back door. Would her home be standing when they emerged from the basement?

"Don't look back. Just go!" The words were practically torn from Tim's mouth as the front door of her home was ripped off its hinges. The last thing she saw was it slamming into the Elliots' car, straight through the windshield.

Had that happened? How could that have happened?

Jeanette had moved in front of their group and was now holding their youngest girl in her arms. Zoey clutched Bandit to her chest and buried her face in his fur.

"Put your hands on my shoulders and don't let go!" Jeanette was screaming to two of the guests, but the words could barely be heard over the noise of a train screaming in Julia's ears.

She glanced down at her feet. Though she remained inside the house, the floor of her home was now ankle deep in leaves.

Tim thrust Victoria into Julia's arms. She staggered under the sudden weight of the ten-year-old. Then a hand was pushing her out the back door.

With one arm, she clutched Victoria to her, and with the other she encircled the shoulders of the young mother, the woman whose name she didn't know. Together they stumbled into the afternoon that had become total darkness, in the direction Julia knew would lead to safety. Slamming her knee into the basement door, she nearly fell, but Tim was behind her, pulling her back to her feet. Before she could regain her balance another force, a stronger one, picked her up, then pitched her back down again—down and into the hole.

Her feet never touched the steps.

Julia did her best to fall to the side, to not land on Victoria or the mother holding the infant.

Behind her she was aware that Tim and someone else was struggling with the door. That was why he'd given her his child. He had known he would need to stay out in the storm. He'd known he might not make it into the basement.

Tim and the man who had stayed at the opening to the basement were screaming for help. Wess and the man with the phone rushed past her. She could just make out their figures in the cracks of lightning that were now almost constant.

Victoria's arms were locked around her neck, and she was aware the child was sobbing, but her attention was focused on the door at the top of the stairs.

Still it wouldn't close. Why? What was wrong? Had the wind broken it? Would they all be pulled out of their only safe haven?

Bandit barked as if all of their lives depended on him.

Tim shouted, his voice reminding Julia of her father the one time she'd seen him angry—angry with a force he couldn't battle. Angry with a storm that threatened his family.

"On three!"

The wind tore the first two numbers, but when he shouted "three" again there was a thump. They were suddenly shrouded in darkness and silence.

Then she heard a sound she'd only heard twice before, and it knocked loose a memory she'd buried somewhere in the deep recesses of her heart.

It was the sound of a bar sliding through a lock.

~ Chapter 34 ~

Caleb moved through the darkness to Aaron's side.
Some part of his mind registered the sounds around him—people praying, some weeping, the horses stomping and making a noise he'd never heard before. Pumpkin yowling as if he could save them with the intensity of his cries. Over and above all that was the storm, unleashing a fury he could never have imagined. He couldn't imagine it still, and yet it was wreaking destruction around them.

"We need to make sure everyone is here," Caleb said.

"What does it matter? No one could—"

"We need to make sure."

He had his arm across Aaron's back and felt his shoulders slump. In that moment he knew that his friend was struggling with the same emotions, the same fears, he was. "Lydia is in *Gotte*'s hands. We need to care for these who are here. Let's be sure."

"All right."

"Flashlights?"

"Near the front if you can find them in the dark."

"You can use my phone." A hand reached forward from the darkness and handed Caleb a cell phone. The hand was shaking, but the voice persisted. "There's no cell service, but the flashlight app works."

The teenage boy pushed a button, and a bright beam of light emitted from the device.

"*Danki*. Do you have something to write with?"

"Nah."

"I do." An older woman with short spiky hair handed him a pen.

"We'll need two." He had to shout to be heard over the rain and hail.

She fumbled around in her purse until she found another, which she gave to Caleb.

"I don't have a fancy phone, but I have a small flashlight I keep with me." An older man with a short-cropped gray beard handed over his device.

"This will help, and we'll return your items to all of you once the storm has passed."

"If it passes—" the teenager said loudly.

"All things pass, son." Caleb turned toward Aaron. "You take the right side. I'll take the left. Ask their cabin number and if everyone in their party is here. We'll meet at the back wall."

He didn't tell him to hurry. There was no need. The screaming sound from the front of the barn was all the warning they needed.

If anyone was missing, he didn't know how they would go and look, but it was better that they do something. As he made his way down the last three stalls, where the *Englischers* were huddled, he reminded everyone that they were in the safest possible place, that the barn had stood for more than a hundred years, and that *Gotte* would protect them.

A few of the women were weeping and some of the children wouldn't raise their heads to look at him, but the men seemed like a solid group. The fact that he and Aaron were checking to see that all the guests were present and accounted for had a calming effect on everyone.

Caleb reached the back wall as Aaron was speaking to a couple huddled together.

"What's wrong with them?"

"The man was hit in the head with some flying debris. He doesn't seem to have a concussion—he's aware of where he is and what has happened—but he's bleeding more than I'm comfortable with."

"One of the women on my side has medical training. I'll go ask if she can help."

Caleb made his way back down his side until he found the woman, who was middle-aged with red hair. She followed him to the wounded man, but he didn't stay to hear her assessment. If anyone was still outside, the window of opportunity to fetch them was quickly closing.

"Cabin numbers?" he asked Aaron.

Aaron ran down his list.

"And everyone was accounted for?"

"*Ya.* Only minor injuries except for the one."

"Then we're all here." Caleb felt one of a dozen burdens lifted off of his shoulders. These weren't his cabins, but somehow it felt as if these people were his responsibility until the storm passed.

Why was that?

Aaron was the owner. After deciding to marry Lydia and settle down in Wisconsin, he had purchased the property from his Aunt Elizabeth. He'd always been levelheaded and able to handle whatever came his way. Suddenly, though, in the light of the *Englischer's* phone, Caleb realized Aaron was only twenty-four-years old. The naked fear on his face reminded Caleb of Aaron's youth and of the young boy who used to follow him around.

In recent weeks Caleb had suspected he'd followed his best friend's cousin here because God intended for him to meet and care for Julia. Maybe there was another reason, though. God was all-knowing.

Nothing surprised Him—not even the wrath of a once-in-a-century storm. And perhaps, just maybe, God had placed him here, in this barn, to help his young friend at this moment.

He put a hand on Aaron's shoulder. "*Gotte* will see us through this. He will command His angels concerning us to guard us in all our ways." The words should have come from Ada, but as they surged into Caleb's heart, he knew the truth of them. Even as the structure over the front portion of the barn creaked and groaned, any remaining fear he felt vanished.

The promise from the Psalms had barely left his mouth when the front portion of the barn began to shake.

"It's coming down," someone screamed.

The horses panicked and attempted to knock down the walls to their stalls.

Caleb tried to holler out for everyone to move toward the back wall, but he couldn't hear anything except for a loud roaring. So he pushed Aaron to the ground, up against the earthen wall, and he ran in the opposite direction, the direction his body did not want to go— toward the front of the barn.

He made it to the third stall, where he'd first begun counting guests. Most were now standing, watching in horror as the large doors of the barn were torn off and tossed high into the air. As lightning continued to pulse across the sky, he had a brief glimpse of the scene outside. One cabin flew through the air. An *Englischer*'s car slapped against the front of the barn.

"Get back. Everyone move back!" Though he was screaming, the black funnel at the door of the barn seemed to tear his voice away. He turned from the sight of it and began pushing people toward the back wall.

He heard them stumbling forward in the darkness and then a giant, ripping sound filled the air.

Someone shouted, "It's not going to hold."

Pumpkin shot past him in the darkness.

Caleb clapped his hands over his ears, sure his eardrums were going to burst. He fell forward in what he hoped was the right direction—toward the earthen wall the back of the barn had been built against. He could no longer hear the horses or the people around him. He also couldn't see. Somewhere in the last few moments he'd either dropped the phone with the flashlight or it had been ripped from his hands.

They were now in total darkness.

And still the monster outside the front of the barn kept advancing. He was aware of creaking and groaning as the structure fought to remain standing. When the front portion collapsed, he feared they would all be buried alive.

Throwing himself over the two people closest to him, he covered his own head with his arms and waited for the blow to come. His heart ached as he realized he would never again hold Julia in his arms, never hear the Psalms fall from Ada's lips, never see Sharon grow into the young woman God intended her to be.

"The Lord is near to all who call on Him."

Was it Ada's voice or King David's he heard? He didn't know and it didn't matter.

He called, he prayed, and he cried out from the depths of his heart as Aaron's barn fell down around them.

The prayers were still echoing in his heart when they were shrouded in complete and total silence.

Chapter 35

Sharon sat on the floor of the basement, pressed between Ada and Jeanette.

The small windows at the top of the walls did not let in much light, but the lightning still occasionally flashed. Between that and the cell phones used by their guests, she was able to keep an eye on Julia's movements.

Apparently the phones weren't good for much beyond providing light. She caught snippets of "Still no service" and "Why won't it work?" but she suspected it would be some time before any type of phone service was operational again. Storms in Wisconsin were no doubt similar to those in Indiana. They came swiftly and landed hard. This storm was unlike anything Sharon had ever experienced. No doubt it had destroyed more than power and phone lines.

At least the terrible noise had stopped, the sound she thought would be the last thing she would ever hear. The last thing any of them would ever hear.

"Are you sure you're okay, Ada?" Sharon squeezed the old woman's hand again. She was literally skin and bones. It seemed a miracle that she'd survived—that they had all survived.

"You have been my God from the moment I was born," Ada whispered.

"Is she all right?" The man who had read the weather predictions scooted across the floor toward them. "My name's Brad. Is this your grandmother?"

"*Nein*, but she...she is family." What was Ada to her? Someone special. Someone she needed in her life.

"She seems disoriented." Brad pushed a button on his phone and held the light up to Ada.

When Sharon saw the large lump on Ada's head, she flinched. Was Ada all right? She was fragile and shouldn't be out in this cold. She certainly shouldn't be sitting on the basement floor, and now she had somehow taken a bump on the head. Was she hurt anywhere else?

She needed to be in her bed. She needed a doctor. How long would they be down here?

"It could be that she has a slight concussion. They can cause someone to talk out of their head a bit."

Ada patted her hand, and Sharon smiled. "She's only quoting the Psalms. It's...well, it's what she does."

Brad shared their smile. "We could all use more of the Scriptures, especially today. I'll ask your mother if there's any water down here. We'll try to make a compress to put over that lump."

He was gone before Sharon could correct him about Julia being her mother. She had a mother back in Indiana—one she hadn't treated very well. Would she live to remedy that?

So many regrets.

She hadn't appreciated her family. She hadn't appreciated her life. What if she were to lose both now, have them ripped away from her by some stupid tornado?

Tears tracked down her face, but she didn't bother wiping them away. Others around her were crying. It was nothing to be ashamed of. Fear was nothing to hide.

Even Bandit was frightened, shaking so hard that the collar he wore shimmered in the beam of the *Englischer*'s flashlight. The little dog had fallen silent as soon as the door was slammed shut, but he seemed to understand the danger they all were in. He would raise his eyes occasionally and look toward the stairs before dropping his head to his paws—all the time trembling as if he were standing outside in the storm.

Zoey crawled into her lap. "I'm scared, Sharon."

"You are?"

"Yes, and I dropped my doll when we were running from the car. I want her back. I want my doll." Wess's little sister began crying in earnest.

"I'll help you look for her as soon as we can go outside."

In another streak of lightning, Sharon saw Zoey raise the hem of her purple blouse and wipe her nose on it. "What if we can't find her?"

"I suppose that would make me sad, like you're sad. Many things are lost in a storm, Zoey." The little girl sat up straighter in Sharon's lap, clearly not expecting this line of reasoning. She found one of Sharon's *kapp* strings and ran her fingers from top to bottom, repeating the motion while she thought about never seeing her doll again.

"What then? What if we can't find her?"

"I could make you another."

Zoey put both of her hands on Sharon's face and pressed their foreheads together. "A Plain doll?"

"*Ya*. That's the only kind I know how to make."

Throwing her arms around Sharon's neck, she squeezed as tight as her little arms would allow. "*Danki*," she whispered.

"*Gem gschehne*."

Julia came to them at that moment with Brad at her side.

"*Mamm*, Brad said you're hurt."

"*Nein*. The Lord upholds all who fall."

"I know He does."

Brad again focused the light from his phone on Ada's head. When he did, it also bathed Julia's arm, and Sharon thought she might faint. The entire left sleeve of Julia's dress was soaked in blood. Though she'd found some clean cloths and wrapped it, the wound was still bleeding.

"Julia, you need to—"

"Let's help Ada, Sharon." Julia's eyes transmitted what she wasn't willing to say in front of her mother. "I don't have ice, but I was able to wet this hand towel. Could you hold it against her head?"

Sharon shifted Zoey to the spot where she'd been sitting and Bandit jumped into the little girl's lap.

"I have her," Jeanette whispered, collecting her daughter and the dog. Victoria was pressed close to her side as if she was afraid she'd be pulled away at any moment. "Help Julia."

Kneeling close to Ada, Sharon accepted the wet hand towel Julia was holding.

"*Mamm*, can you rest back against the wall?"

Ada glanced left and then right as if the room were only now coming into focus.

"Take my jacket," Brad said, shrugging out of his sports coat.

Julia placed a hand on his arm. "Thank you—"

"You're welcome." Smiling reassuringly at her, he rolled it into a makeshift pillow and placed it behind Ada's head.

Sharon was relieved when Ada closed her eyes and allowed her to place the wet towel against the bump.

"Don't let her sleep," Julia cautioned. "Keep her talking every few minutes. *Mamm*, do you hurt anywhere else?"

"*Nein*." Ada's hand came out, waving her away with a flutter. "I need to go and tend to others who are injured."

Others were hurt? How many? How badly? Sharon closed her eyes and breathed a prayer of forgiveness. She'd been sitting there, wallowing in her regrets and fears, and not even thinking to check if others had been hurt.

Someone found candles and lit them. A soft light filled the basement—not enough to read by, but enough to chase away the darkness and push back the horrors happening outside their door.

Several men came back from the basement door, shaking their heads.

"Jammed up good," one said. "Something's blocking it from the outside."

"We could try to climb out." Jeanette glanced up at the long row of windows running the length of one wall. By some miracle they hadn't shattered, but they were also blocked by tree limbs.

"Let's wait," Tim said. "People will come—neighbors and first responders. Until then, the safest thing would be for us to be patient."

He didn't add what they all knew. The temperature outside was dropping and was probably already below freezing. How had that happened? Sharon felt dizzy thinking of all that had occurred in just a few minutes—first the warmness of the day and then plummeting temperatures followed by torrential rains and the tornado. The thought of going outside made her shiver.

At least in the basement they had shelter. Outside, rain and hail continued to pound against the windows. Who knew what was left of their home, of their lives.

Tears stung her eyes, and she tried to think of what to say. She was supposed to keep Ada talking.

"Let me help you with Ada," Wess said, appearing at her side. Bandit immediately jumped up and began licking Wess's hand. He scratched the dog between his ears and whispered something to him. Immediately Bandit found Zoey and climbed in her lap.

"Let me help," Wess repeated.

That was his way, Sharon realized. He always seemed to appear when she needed him. And wasn't that what friends did? He'd been trying to tell her that since she'd arrived, but she'd been too afraid to believe him. That was a different kind of fear—a fear that someone could hurt her the way James had, with his truck and his blue eyes and his lies. She knew now that people could only hurt you if you let them.

No one made her ride in his pickup. No one forced her to stare into his blue eyes. And she certainly didn't have to believe his pathetic lies.

But life was too hard, too unpredictable to handle alone. She needed others. She needed Wess.

"Maybe Ada can explain to me how to read through the Psalms. I keep trying, but my attention shifts."

Ada opened one eye and studied him.

"You're a *gut* boy. You both are *gut* children." She reached out and covered their hands with hers. "I remember being young and wanting to do what was right."

Sharon and Wess shared a smile. It was hard to imagine Ada ever doing anything that was wrong. Had she rebelled at one time? Had she struggled with regrets?

"Julia's handing out bottled water." Wess took the cloth from her hand. "I'll hold this. Why don't you fetch Ada a bottle?"

Sharon stood and hurried toward the back of the basement. It felt good to stretch her legs, and seeing the others did much to alleviate the terrible things she was imagining as she had sat holding Zoey.

The woman with the baby was sitting in a corner, her sister positioned in front of her with the quilt Julia had grabbed around them both. Sharon couldn't help smiling as they adjusted the quilt and she saw the mother move the babe from one breast to the other. Tornadoes might strike and darkness could fall, but a mother's love? Nothing changed that.

The first thing she was going to do when she left this room was write her mother and her dad a long letter. And come Thanksgiving she was going home. She didn't know if she would stay, didn't know what God wanted her to do yet, but she knew there were some things she needed to put right.

Returning to Wess's side with three bottles of water, she was surprised that several people had scooted closer, and Ada was speaking in a soft steady voice. This time it wasn't the Psalms, but instead she told of what had happened before.

"My babe was born in this house, you know."

"Julia?" Wess asked.

"*Ya.* She was our only child. *Gotte* blessed us with her. Twice we had to take refuge in this room."

"What happened?" Victoria crept forward on her knees. Her hair, usually in a straight neat braid, had pulled loose and was tangled around her face, which was smeared with dirt and tears. "Did anyone die?"

"The first time, in nineteen hundred and eighty-four, the Lord took twelve souls home, but not from here in Cashton. We thought He would. Yes, we thought He would." Ada reached for her prayer *kapp* and seemed confused when she didn't find it there. It had been knocked loose in the trip from the house to the basement.

Reaching forward, Sharon placed an open bottle of water in Ada's thin, wrinkled hand. Ada glanced at it, took a small sip, and continued with her story.

"I remember that July day as if it were only yesterday. One moment the wind was whispering through the cornfield, the next—" Her hand came out to indicate something being wiped away. "Jonathan, my husband, grabbed Julia and told me to run. I was in this very room, already down the stairs. I can still hear the sound of that black cloud, coming out of the sky, as it reached for my family."

She laughed, and the sound seemed so completely out of place that Sharon glanced around uneasily. The group around Ada had grown. It seemed everyone in the basement was caught up in the story. Even Bandit was watching her, and Julia had stopped to rest on an upended crate. She was looking at her mother with such love that Sharon once again felt a hand press heavily against her heart.

How she missed her family. How she prayed she would live to see them again.

"The door to the outside wouldn't shut, much like today. Jonathan, he was a quiet man. He still is, I suspect, if we keep our present ways in heaven. He came down those stairs holding Julia." Ada looked up and around the group until she found her daughter. "The force of the tornado was pulling them back outside, but he screamed— actually screamed and threw her at me."

No one moved or spoke, but Bandit whimpered.

"Do you remember, Julia?"

"Yes. I remember you catching me, and *dat*...I remember him struggling with the door."

"I fell backward with you, fell to the ground. I was so afraid I'd hurt you. When I looked up, he'd yanked the door shut and thrown the bolt. I don't know how he did it. Never knew how—"

"I remember him screaming." Julia's expression had taken on a far-away look, and Sharon realized she wasn't seeing them anymore or this cold November afternoon. She was seeing a July day when she was a small girl.

Chapter 36

J ulia could hardly feel the fingers of her left arm.

She was aware she'd lost a good deal of blood, but she didn't think rewrapping the wound was a good idea. When she'd landed at the bottom of the stairs, thrown there by the force of the tornado, she'd crashed into several of the jars of canned preserves that had fallen onto the floor. The glass had carved a jagged wound from her shoulder to her elbow.

At first she'd been consumed by the fear that she'd hurt Victoria, or that Victoria had also been cut. It had taken a few moments to realize just how much blood was streaming down her arm as the men had struggled with the door and slammed the bolt shut.

Staggering to her feet, she'd pushed Victoria into Jeanette's hands and headed to the back of the basement where she knew old clean rags and towels were kept next to the washing machine.

The woman who had complimented her apple-cinnamon pie, Frances, had been there with her back pressed against the wall. She hadn't even hesitated. While her friend Terra had held up a small flashlight she'd fished from her purse, Frances had pulled the pieces of glass free and bound the wound with some of the cloths.

"You'll need stitches soon," she'd cautioned. Frances was older, her skin a warm brown from days in the sun or possibly from her ethnic heritage. She was also as thin as a willow; whereas Terra was more solidly built. Both women seemed unharmed but rattled by what they had been through.

Julia wasn't sure about the stitches. She'd never had stitches before and hoped the bleeding would stop soon on its own. "*Danki*, for your help. We should check on the others."

They moved in a sort of circle around the room. Frances and Terra worked their way around the right side of the basement while Julia had moved around the left. The makeshift bandage had staunched the bleeding of her wound at first.

Staring across the candlelit basement into her mother's eyes, Julia knew she would need to seek Frances out again soon. The wrapping was too wet, the bleeding increasing. But for now, she was caught up in her mother's memories, and it felt so good to sit and rest.

"He was angry," Ada said. "Your *dat* was always a peaceful man, but he was young then and not yet given over to *gelassenheit*."

Inquiring eyes turned to her, but Julia didn't know how to explain such a cornerstone of their faith, of their lives. So instead she shrugged. "I was young and afraid he was angry with me."

She glanced at the stairs, as if she might see her father walking down them, walking toward her as he had that evening.

"I remember flying through the air, into your arms, just before he screamed. Then there was the noise like a train. It was similar to what we all heard earlier."

"A tornado hit here before?" Wess asked.

"*Nein*." Ada turned the bottle of water in her hands. "He shields all who take refuge in Him."

Julia noticed a few people look to each other in confusion, but she could no more explain Ada and her Psalms to them than she could explain *gelassenheit*.

"You can see the historical clippings at the library. The tornado skirted our area that July day—hovering, it seemed—and then moving past. *Dat* slammed the lock shut and came down the stairs, not saying a word. When he put his arms around us, I knew." Julia closed her eyes, remembering the touch and smell of her father, remembering his presence.

She had felt his loss almost daily since that cold March morning when she'd stood at his graveside next to her mother. Somehow though, sitting in the basement with blood running down her arm and the world above in chaos, she no longer missed her father.

How could she miss him when his presence was so strong? How could she miss what wasn't gone?

"What did you know?" Victoria asked.

Julia opened her eyes, reached forward, and tucked the girl's hair behind her ears. "I knew he wasn't angry with me, but with the storm—with what he couldn't control. And I knew I was safe in my father's arms."

A silence settled over the room as the truth of Julia's words sank into their hearts.

"You said you sheltered here two times." Brad glanced back toward the windows. "The first time there was a tornado—"

"*Ya*, that one only skirted the area." Ada took another sip of water. "St. Croix and Dunn took a direct hit."

"And the second time?"

Julia answered. "I was nine and remember those details better. We all sheltered, *dat* threw the bolt as before, but the tornado didn't appear here in Pebble Creek."

"One soul was called home—in Waukesha." Ada's voice was low, and her eyes were closed.

"Should we get her up and try to walk her around a little?" Sharon asked.

Julia looked to Frances, who shook her head.

"Let her rest for fifteen minutes. Then wake her and be sure she can answer questions such as her name, who you are, and where she lives. Keep doing that every quarter hour."

Julia stood and motioned for some of the adults to follow her into a corner by the stairwell.

"Your arm looks bad, Julia." Tim was the first to speak.

"I'll have Frances look at it again in a minute. I thought we should speak of our situation. We have enough food and water to make it several days."

"Days?" Brad's eyes bulged. "You think we might be down here for days?"

"Listen to the storm." Julia watched their faces as understanding dawned on each one. The wind continued to howl outside their sanctuary, but now there was a muted heaviness to it. "The rain turned to snow half an hour ago. We can't go out by the stairs because the door won't open. The windows are blocked by fallen limbs and possibly other debris as well."

"I'm not sure staying here is the wisest course." Brad shook his head.

"Outside in a blizzard at night would be worse. It's completely dark out there now. I don't know why. It's too early for evening, but I can't even make out the limbs outside the window anymore." Tim glanced around at their group. "Let's set up a makeshift bathroom in the corner. Brad and I can hang a curtain around it."

"Frances and I can find food to distribute." Julia moved to the shelves against the wall.

"I can help with that." Terra moved forward. "Let Frances see to your arm now."

"I'll help as well." Jeanette had left her children and Bandit with Wess and Sharon.

Julia nodded. She was feeling lightheaded suddenly and reached out to rest her good arm against the wall nearest her. "Look along those shelves. There's plenty to eat that wasn't broken.

Tim ran his hand up and over the top of his head. "After we see to the bathroom, we'll search for items to make pallets for sleeping. It would be better to keep folks off the cold floor as much as possible."

"We should remind people to only check their phones periodically." Brad scrubbed a hand over his face. "Best to save the batteries."

"Agreed." Tim reached out and stopped Julia as she moved away. "Caleb's all right. He would have sheltered in the barn."

She couldn't speak past the lump in her throat, so she only nodded.

"And at first light, I'll prove it to you. Whatever I have to climb through, I will find a way out of here."

~

Caleb crouched in the semidarkness at the back of the barn. The few gas lanterns he'd found cast a comforting glow throughout the half of the barn they were huddled in—the half that hadn't been crushed by the tornado. The front half was now impassable. No one was leaving in that direction.

The front entrance to the barn simply didn't exist anymore. It was a mass of wreckage—lumber, trees, and debris. Fortunately, the rubble had at least sealed out the storm on that end.

And while they should be able to go out through the back, a snow bank was fast building up against the loading bay doors. Every hour he faced the blizzard with two other men and shoveled the accumulating drift away from their only exit. They hadn't dared to travel far from those loading doors, though. The temperature had dropped below zero, the wind was howling, and snow was still falling at a dangerous rate.

No one's cell phone was working.

As much as it pained him, they had all agreed it was best to stay put until morning. To go outside into the storm, especially after the damage the tornado had caused, would only invite more injuries.

He had to trust that Julia, Ada, and Sharon were safe.

What help would he be to them if he survived the tornado only to become lost and freeze to death in the blizzard? No. It was best to wait and pray and help those who were trapped with him.

At the moment he had his hands full calming Aaron, who sat propped up against one of the horse stalls.

"You're sure it's broken? Because I think I can walk on it. I can at least ride if you'll help me up on Patches. If you'll saddle him, I could take—"

"You know as well as I do the gelding won't make it half a mile in this storm." Caleb understood his friend would walk home if that were the only way to check on his family. From the expression on his face, he knew Aaron would like to try, but he also knew that leaving tonight just wasn't possible.

Brenda Stiles, an older black woman with short hair, shook her head and pointed a finger at his leg. "Trust me. It's broken. I've splinted it, but you won't be able to walk on it until you see a physician and have it set properly. Even then you'll need to use crutches until it heals."

Aaron made a sound which resembled a growl.

Brenda looked unfazed. "I'm used to working with babies. It's been a while since I had a full-sized patient who could argue with me."

"We're grateful to have a doctor here," Caleb said. "*Gotte* sent you to us."

"I thought He was sending me on vacation, but maybe you're right." Brenda shook her head. "It's amazing we don't have more injuries. I think that tornado was an F3. Maybe an F4."

Aaron struggled to sit up straighter. "I have to go home. My wife is expecting our first *boppli*. I've heard that things like big storms can cause women to go into labor."

"Is she alone?" Brenda asked.

"*Nein*. Her mother will be with her, but—"

"And has her mother ever attended a birth before?"

"Yes, of course, but—"

"Don't Amish often give birth at home?"

"Lydia was planning to have her child at home," Caleb explained. "Not in the basement, but at home. And her *mamm*, Ella, has assisted in several births just since I have been here."

"Is she near term?"

"Yes. That's why she wasn't here at the cabins today." Aaron sank against the stall's wall, defeated.

"I know you want to be with her." Caleb rubbed his hand over the top of his head and through his hair, and came away with leaves.

"You don't even know that the babe is coming, but if it is, then this is the day the Lord appointed, Aaron. Don't you think I want to be with Julia? She's only across Pebble Creek—"

"Which is probably raging now."

"No doubt. We must trust in *Gotte*. If our faith can't see us through tonight, if it can't see us through the worst of times, then what *gut* is it?"

Aaron pulled at his beard, but he finally nodded and accepted the cup of water handed to him by one of the guests. Fortunately, most of the supplies in the barn had been stored against the back wall in case of just such an emergency. They had blankets, a few lanterns, some food, and plenty of water.

Caleb turned back to Brenda. "How's the little girl with the hurt foot?"

"Her name is Darby, and she'll need a tetanus shot, but she'll be okay. Most fatalities during a tornado are caused by flying debris."

Aaron stared at her. "Are you sure you haven't been hit by something, Doc? Maybe it rustled around the facts in your head a bit. I always thought it was the getting sucked up in the air and slammed back down that did you in."

Brenda patted his arm. "It happens, yes. But debris is more likely to harm people. You two did a good thing moving everyone in here. I was just driving up in my car when I saw the group running toward the barn. It was a smart thing to do."

Shaking his head, Aaron stared down at the barn floor.

"She's fine," Caleb assured him. "Your house has a cellar, as does Ella and Menno's. If the homes are gone we will rebuild, but your family is safe underground."

When Brenda glanced from one to the other, Caleb explained, "His wife's family lives next door, and his father-in-law has been very ill. I'm sure they would have gathered together as soon as the weather changed."

"Ah. Then we'll pray for all of their safety. If your wife is as practical as you are, I'm sure she headed downstairs early."

It was the first thing anyone had said that caused Aaron to smile. "Lydia's as sensible as they come. When we first met, she was in charge of these cabins."

Brenda looked surprised. "An Amish businesswoman? Now there's someone I'd like to meet."

"She would have checked you into your cabin, but I insisted she stay home today."

"And maybe that was a *gut* thing too. At your home she's in the safety and warmth of a basement rather than this smelly barn." Caleb stood and stretched. "Think I'll make the rounds and check on everyone again."

As he walked past the horse stalls, which miraculously had remained intact, he couldn't help feeling a pull toward Aaron's gelding. The horse might make it through the storm, not with the younger man riding, but if he were to take it out. He might be able to make it down the road to check on Julia.

First he needed to check the weather. He needed to see if the snow had let up any.

He walked to the end of the barn, which wasn't that far now that the front portion had collapsed. Two of the *Englischers* waited near the bay doors. One was Rupert and another was Eddie—Caleb was having the hardest time telling them apart. It seemed all *Englischers* looked the same, though he knew that wasn't true. Probably he was just tired.

He didn't mention his hopes to ride home as they pushed against the doors to open them. Which turned out to be a good thing, because his hopes faded more quickly than water passed through his fingers when he reached a hand down into Pebble Creek.

At first it seemed perhaps something had fallen in front of the doors.

"It's only been thirty minutes," Rupert muttered. Or was it Eddie?

"Might need to change our snow patrols to every twenty minutes, Eddie." Rupert stopped pushing and dropped to his knees. He was a big man, with a large stomach, but Caleb didn't doubt that he could put all of his weight behind what they were trying to do. "I'm going to push from the bottom while you lean into the middle of the door."

"I've got the top," Caleb said, catching on to what Rupert had in mind. Now he had them straight. Eddie was thinner and bobbed his head in agreement a lot. Rupert would have made a good farmer with his size and his practical ways. Caleb had heard him mention to someone that he worked on computers and had come to the cabins with his wife so they could experience nature.

"On three." Caleb feared it wouldn't work, but slowly the door gave an inch. By the time there was enough space to squeeze through, they were all out of breath and slapping each other on the back.

"How did it get so high so fast?" Eddie stood in the small hole they'd made from pushing the door out. The snow had completely encapsulated the loading area of the barn. "I don't understand this at all. First the warm weather, then day turned to night, the rains came—"

"Followed by tornadoes," Rupert reminded him.

"Yeah. Then hail, snow, and now a blizzard. It sounds like something out of Revelation."

"It's not the end-times, only a bad storm," Caleb assured him. "It happened here once before, more than a hundred years ago. As far as how the snow has built up, the winds must have shifted. If it wasn't a blizzard before, it is now."

Caleb glanced back into the room, where several of the women, a few older men, and some of the children were watching. "Let's find some buckets and start a line. We're going to have to take the snow into the barn until we can clear a path out. Dump it back against the cave-in."

The work was exhausting, but somehow it managed to raise everyone's spirits. Perhaps because they were doing something constructive instead of simply waiting. Maybe because they were working together. Caleb noticed a few smiles as buckets of snow were passed from hand to hand. When they finally broke through, a cheer went up through the group.

The euphoria didn't last long.

Slamming the door shut, they regrouped inside.

"My iPhone said the temperature is three below zero. Is that a malfunction?" Eddie was staring down at the small screen in disbelief.

"It's probably right. The storm of nineteen eleven did the same thing—" Caleb noticed several in the group staring at him. "In that storm the weather was at first unseasonably warm, then the temperature dropped dramatically and was followed by a tornado and then a blizzard."

"Will we freeze in here?" A woman from the back pulled her child into the circle of her arms, as if she needed to protect her from instant death.

"This barn was built to protect livestock in the worst of our winter weather. It will do the same for us."

The woman nodded and turned away.

Caleb discussed a fifteen-minute rotation of snow clearing with Eddie and Rupert. He knew they would be safe in the barn, but he didn't want their only exit closing up. Come daylight, he wanted to be out and on the road. Emergency personnel would be combing the area looking for survivors. Aaron and the little girl—Darby—needed real medical attention. He wanted to get information about Lydia.

And one way or another, he would find his way home to Julia.

⌒ Chapter 37 ⌒

When Julia woke, the darkness had begun receding from the basement windows. At first she was disoriented, unsure of where she was. It seemed as if her arms were pinned at her side, and she thought maybe it was a dream. If she tried a little harder, she could wake fully.

Then the pain in her left arm became sharper, and Sharon's concerned face popped up in front of her.

"You're awake. I hope I didn't bother you. I didn't mean to, but I was worried. You are sweating even though it's freezing in here." There was the sound of a cloth being dipped into water, and then Julia felt the sweet relief of coolness across her forehead, down her cheeks, and across her neck.

"What—" her voice was a croak.

"Try to swallow some of this." Jeanette was on her other side, lifting up her head and pressing a bottle of water to her lips.

"What happened?" Julia's eyes adjusted to the small amount of light coming through the high windows. She was able to make out the huddled forms sleeping around her, and Tim standing a few feet away. "Where—"

"You passed out when Frances tried to change the wrapping around your arm." Sharon looked as if she were going to cry. "I think...she said maybe you've lost too much blood. Please don't move."

Julia lay back, more because of the panic on Sharon's face than because of the dizziness that she was sure would pass if she sat up for a moment.

"You did lose a lot of blood, Julia, but your pulse is steady." Jeanette raised the jackets someone had covered her with and checked her left arm. "It seems to have stopped bleeding for now, but if you start moving around again—"

Nodding, Julia waved her right hand toward Tim.

"He's bundling up because the blizzard seems to have stopped." Jeanette hesitated as if she wasn't sure how much she should reveal. "The other men are donating what clothes they can spare. Together they have spent the last hour building a ladder of sorts—a way for him to climb out the window."

"But the branches—"

"He'll push his way through. Julia, we can't stay here another day, and it could be some time before anyone finds us. It was right to shelter here through the night, but now it's time to go for help."

"Tell her." Sharon sat back and pressed her fingers to her lips.

Jeanette looked unsure, but after helping Julia to swallow more water, she moved closer and lowered her voice. "The phones are still out, but I was able to catch one news report on my 4G network. It only worked for a moment, and then it went out again."

"What...what did it say?"

"This area took a direct hit. Emergency personnel and first responders have been conducting search and rescue missions. They are not going well. The blizzard conditions have persisted, and everything is moving at a snail's pace. They're saying this is the worst storm since nineteen eleven."

Julia closed her eyes, unable to stop the tears coursing down her cheeks.

Where was Caleb? Why hadn't she told him how much she loved him before he left? Why had she been so stubborn and so cold to him the last night they were together?

Her regrets piled on top of her questions. How many of their *frein-den* had perished? And would Tim be able to find help?

She wasn't surprised when she heard her mother, her voice as calm and gentle as always. She wasn't even baffled by Ada's words. If anything, her mother had always been consistent. But for some reason, this morning her mother's greeting had a different effect on her. Instead of hearing an old woman clinging to words from their Bible, she heard Ada—the one person in her life she knew best, speaking from the very depths of her soul.

This time the age-old words from the Psalms worked their way straight to Julia's heart, past the places that were broken, through the secret chambers where her fears lived, and into the very center of her being. They soothed the ache in her soul.

"I will lift up my eyes to the hills..."

Julia opened her eyes and glanced to the windows that were nearly covered with snow.

"From whence comes my help?"

At this very moment first responders were traipsing through debris and wreckage and snow. But who sent them? Who would guide them to her, to this basement, to this roomful of people? Who would keep Tim safe as he sought a way out of the wreckage? Who would care for Caleb and Aaron and all the others at the cabins?

"My help comes from the Lord." Ada's voice was a caress, more welcome than the cloth on Julia's brow. "From the Lord."

The truth filled her with peace, and the peace was followed by a new courage.

God had brought Caleb to her in the first place. He had kept Ada alive when she might have passed long ago. He had joined Sharon to their family to remind them what second chances were about and to unite them in a special way.

Their help always came from God, even when it came through the hands of men and women.

"Let me speak with him." Julia coughed and wondered if they were all going to be sick with pneumonia. Yet pneumonia could be cured. They had survived the worst.

A look passed between Jeanette and Sharon. Julia had one terrible moment when she was sure they meant to keep Tim away from her. Perhaps they were afraid she would try to talk him out of what he meant to do. But then Sharon rose and hurried across the room.

In a moment she returned, and Tim knelt by her side. Bandit woke, shook himself, and pushed himself into the middle of their small circle. Tim was wearing a black leather jacket. Sticking out from under that she could see someone's Green Bay Packers athletic jersey—the hoodie portion was up and over Tim's ears. A woman's flowery silk scarf was wrapped around his neck.

Staring into his eyes, Julia knew he understood the risk he was taking. All of the layers combined weren't heavy enough to protect him against the cold outside.

"I'll be back soon, and I'll bring help."

She wanted to reach up and touch his face, which was filled with such concern. Suddenly she was too tired. She wasn't sure she could even tell him what had been so important.

What had been so important? *My help comes from the Lord.*

The window. The snow.

"Snowshoes. Cabinet next to the washer." She attempted to reach out and point to where they were stored. There were two pairs. If the strings weren't rotten, they would help him through the drifts.

She tried to point to the area, but she couldn't lift her arm. It was too heavy. She had to struggle to keep her eyes open. It felt as if two strong hands were pushing down on her, urging her to sleep, to rest. Had Tim found them? Would they work?

Her eyes closed and she was down by the creek, watching the fish and laughing with Caleb.

When she opened them again, Tim was standing on the top of the shelves, half out of a window. A cold wind was blowing in, and he'd nearly caught the pack he'd made out of assorted items on the window latch. Reaching back, he freed himself, and that was when she saw the handle of the snowshoes attached to the pack.

He'd found them.

As he disappeared into the branches and snow and then pushed the window shut behind him, it occurred to Julia that he had rather large feet. She had never noticed his feet before.

Unable to hold her eyes open a moment longer, she allowed herself to drift until once more she was beside Pebble Creek. The day was warm—hot, almost—and she was so sleepy that she longed to lie down in the grass. Caleb laughed, took her hand, and assured her that a short nap would be fine.

"I'll sit beside you."

"Until I wake?"

"Yes, dear. Until you wake."

"But I wanted to talk to you. I need to tell you so many things."

He kissed her. "I know what's in your heart, Julia. Words are *gut*, but they can wait. For now you should rest."

"You won't leave?"

"I'll never leave you again. Now sleep, and when you open your eyes, we'll speak as long as you like."

He smiled then, and she knew all was well between them. So she allowed herself to relax and to give up her burdens, with her hand safely tucked in his.

⌒

Caleb wanted to leave alone at first light, but Brenda wasn't having it.

"People might be hurt out there," she said obstinately.

"People are hurt in here."

"And I've done what I can. I'm going with you, Caleb. We can stand here and argue, or we can start moving before that door freezes shut again." She stared at him with her dark brown eyes, and Caleb knew he was wasting time.

He should have guessed that *Englisch* women were as stubborn as Amish women. Tim had hinted as much.

They had decided to leave the horses, at least until they could determine how deep the drifts were. Their first goal was to construct a safe path from the barn to the office, if it was possible to do so. At least the office had a woodstove, as did each of the cabins.

"All right. We'll go together, but we tie one end of the rope to the door. You keep your hand on it at all times. I'll have the other end and go in front. You give it a good hard yank if you're having trouble."

"Agreed."

Scrounging through the supplies usually kept in the barn, they had found gloves, and two of the women had scarves they had wound around their necks. Coats weren't a problem because a couple of work coats were always in the back to be used when mucking out stalls or caring for the animals. They had been extra covering for the children on top of the blankets, and though he wasn't happy about taking them, there was nothing he could do about that.

One woman looked up at him with fear and hope in her eyes. "Thank you for trying to find us a way out of here."

Studying Dr. Stiles as they waited for Rupert and Eddie to open the door, Caleb realized they weren't dressed for subzero weather, but they had done the best they could. At least none of their skin was directly exposed. They would be all right long enough to assess the situation.

The path the men had been shoveling all night was long and narrow. He had the sensation of being underwater, what with the pale and cloudy sky above and the white drifts of snow on all sides. Caleb's boots made no sound against the snow, though he did hear the door slam shut behind them.

Holding a long pole in his left hand and the coil of rope slung over his right shoulder, he allowed it to unwind as he walked up and out of the ramp where they normally steered the wagons to offload hay and feed. He'd cautioned Brenda to keep a few feet behind him, thinking it might be safer if he fell into a hole or came upon something that perhaps she shouldn't see.

But she was a doctor, wasn't she? What would he see that she wouldn't be prepared for?

Caleb thought he'd steeled his mind and his heart against whatever had happened the afternoon before. After all, he'd almost been crushed by the front half of the barn as it collapsed. He wouldn't have been surprised if all of the cabins had been demolished. He had read news reports of what tornadoes could do and had even seen photographs in *Englisch* newspapers.

Yet none of that prepared him for the sight that met his eyes when he walked around the corner of the barn. Reading something and experiencing it was not the same.

He stood in the aftermath of such destruction and felt his world tilt. His legs refused to move. His mind stalled as he looked out on a scene that made no sense at all.

Mouth open, the rope dangling from his right hand, he might not have moved except that Brenda bumped into the back of him.

"Definitely an F4," she whispered.

Half of the shop was gone. They could see into it, giving Caleb the absurd impression that someone had taken a chainsaw and cut the building in two. Its contents were strewn across the grounds as if a child had decided to play with all of the items and left before putting them away. One of the rockers was in a tree, a quilt was hanging from the chimney of cabin three, and a child's toy sat on top of the remaining half of the roof.

Some of the shelves in the shop had items still in perfect arrangement—untouched, unscathed.

The office had taken a direct hit. The porch where they had first sheltered was gone. There was nothing left at all. It had been sheared off at the wall. The doors and windows were blown out.

"You can see the path it took." Brenda pointed past the shed, the office and toward the cabins. "Barn, store, office—"

"Cabins." Caleb counted and then counted again. "Two are missing."

"You mean—"

"Two of the cabins. Numbers five and six. They're just...gone. And number four is—it's been moved." He pointed to the blank slab where the cabin had been. Shuffling forward, he spied the small building down by the creek, looking as if it had always been there.

He turned in a circle, and that was when he actually focused on the front of the barn. Being inside it, he hadn't realized the full force of the destruction. The structure had collapsed like a house of cards, blown over on itself.

Caleb shook his head. The barn structure looked less safe than it had seemed while they were in it. And he could see that as the snow was building up on top of the wreckage, the weight was pushing down on what remained of the roof.

They needed to get everyone out of there. They needed to move them before the rest of the barn collapsed.

Chapter 38

B renda shuffled closer to his side. "I'm no farmer, but it doesn't look as if that roof can support any additional weight. Do you think it's going to snow more?"

"Could." Caleb glanced up. The last thing he wanted to do was move the group currently inside the barn out to the cabins. He was having trouble focusing on any one problem. If Aaron's property looked like this, what did his own house look like, his and Julia's home? "Stay here."

Moving forward, he tested the snow with the pole he'd brought from the barn, jamming it into the drifts until he found a solid path to cabin one. There was enough rope to tie it around the corner post of the porch. Miraculously, the entire structure was unscathed.

By the time he made it back to Brenda, he noticed she was shivering. "Go into the cabin."

"I'm f-fine—"

"Please go into the cabin and check each person as they arrive. I'll send Reuben and Eddie out first—one for the middle of the line and one for the end."

"We can't fit everyone in this cabin, Caleb."

"True. But once a clear path is worn from the barn to here, I'll tie the rope to the next cabin. We have enough buildings still standing to shelter everyone. These cabins have woodstoves."

She was too cold to argue. Caleb realized with a start that he couldn't feel his own toes. What was the temperature? Zero? Below zero?

He'd made it halfway to the barn when he heard her call out to him. He turned back and saw that Brenda was waving her arms wildly and pointing toward the road.

Traveling slowly down it, with bright emergency lights on the front, was a snowmobile.

Caleb released the rope he'd been holding on to and ran toward the road, toward help, waving his arms and shouting. His feet sank into the snow and the wind tore at his face, but he kept running. At first he was sure whoever was driving, covered in snow gear and a helmet, wouldn't hear him. But then the snowmobile slowed and turned into the parking area.

Caleb stopped running, bent over with his hands on his knees, and pulled in deep breaths. Each one felt like a knife carving into his lungs. The snowmobile pulled to a stop beside him. Jack Tate removed his helmet and goggles and dropped them in the snow.

"Are you okay, Caleb? Here, put on my coat."

Before Caleb could stop him, the man had shrugged out of his coat and wrapped it around his shoulders. On second look, Jack had warmer clothes on under his coat than Caleb had been wearing.

Of all the people who could have shown up, Officer Tate was a true godsend. When Caleb had first arrived he'd heard the stories of how Jack understood and worked with the Amish community. He'd helped to find Grace, Gabe's daughter, when she was lost in a blizzard. And he'd dealt compassionately with Jerry Beiler when he'd been caught breaking into Aaron's cabins the year before. No doubt many emergency personnel had been sent out at first light, but Caleb breathed a prayer of thanksgiving that Jack Tate was the first face he'd seen.

He didn't realize until that moment exactly how frightening the last eighteen hours had been. Looking into the eyes of someone he knew, someone who understood what Pebble Creek and its people meant, he allowed himself to voice those fears.

"Everyone's...they're in the barn. Aaron's hurt, and Darby's fever went up during the night. She's young, and the doc says she'll need to go to the hospital. We have to move them out, and I need...I need to get to Julia." The last six words were ripped from his heart.

Jack held up his hand as he spoke into his phone. Why was his phone working? Come to think of it, the phone he was holding was slightly larger and bulkier than the others Caleb had seen. Clicking off, Jack replaced the phone on his utility belt and started explaining as they hurried toward the barn.

"It's a satellite phone. They issued them to all the local police departments a few years ago. When the area cell towers are down, these still work. I called our location in to the dispatcher, who will pass it on to first responders. We've been out since first light—"

He stopped talking as Caleb entered the snow passage.

"Are you sure this won't cave in on top of us?"

"I'm sure it's the only way in, and we have to get everyone who's in there out." Knowing Jack would follow him, Caleb strode forward, pausing to bang twice on the bay doors. He would have tried to open it from the outside, but he doubted he had the strength. It was easier for Rupert and Eddie to push the door open from their side.

When the door had been opened only a few inches, Pumpkin dashed out and raced through the snow. Caleb knew the cat would seek the warmth of one of the cabins.

There was a lot of talk and commotion as the people he'd spent the last night with, surely the worst night of his life, realized they were rescued. Caleb wished he could share in their jubilation. He was relieved that Jack was here, and with his help the job of transferring everyone to the cabins was soon underway.

He stopped him once as they were moving the second group and snow had begun to fall again.

"My place. Do you know—"

Jack shook his head. "If I hear anything, I'll come and tell you. They are checking each property, Caleb. Someone will be there soon. And the minute we finish with these transfers I'll take you over myself."

Three first responders drove up on snowmobiles as they were moving the last of the guests. One was a paramedic.

Brenda had hurried back to the barn, intent on seeing to the little girl's transfer as well as Aaron's.

"Her fever is still up." The young man kneeling by Darby frowned as he relayed her information into his phone.

"Is she going to be okay?" Darby's mom hovered close, keeping one hand on the child at all times.

"I irrigated the wound," Brenda said. "She needs a tetanus shot and fluids, plus a round of antibiotics."

The young man stopped speaking into his phone and glanced up.

"Dr. Stiles," Brenda explained. "Neonatologist."

"Otis Conklin, ma'am. I've ordered transport. Someone should be here within the hour." Two other workers covered Darby with a blanket, loaded her on a makeshift stretcher, and carried her out of the barn.

Caleb breathed a sigh of relief, but even as he thanked *Gotte* for their rescue, his impatience grew.

It was all he could do to stand there.

He hadn't seen Jack in several minutes, but once he saw to Aaron, he was leaving—if he had to, he would take one of the horses which had been moved to an outside shelter.

He needed to go home, even if the only way was to walk.

When Otis had finished working on Darby, he'd moved over to Aaron, who had insisted on being the last one looked at. They were the only four left in the barn. Suddenly the wind rattled the walls, the roof gave a groan as it shook, and snow trickled through.

"It's not going to hold much more weight." Aaron struggled to sit up straighter. "You can do whatever you're going to do somewhere else. Let's get out of here."

Brenda stepped forward. "I don't think you should try to—"

But she was interrupted by debris and snow coming through the roof.

"Caleb on the left. Otis, you get the right. I'll try and make sure you have a clear path."

They hurried outside. It couldn't have been past seven in the morning, but Caleb felt as if he'd already done an entire day's work.

Once they had cleared the structure, which continued to moan but somehow stood, he turned to Aaron and said, "I'll help you to the cabin, and then I'm going to check on Julia."

Aaron nodded, pain clouding his eyes. But he seemed focused on making it across the snow, and although Caleb saw him glance up once, maybe twice, and shake his head in disbelief, he didn't think his friend fully comprehended the destruction he was seeing. No doubt shock had taken hold hours ago.

The good news was that smoke was now coming from the chimneys of the intact cabins, which meant folks were finally getting warm. Food had been brought from the half of the store that was still standing. Everyone was safe and dry. Truly, they had much to be thankful for.

And what of Julia? And Ada? And Sharon? Their names pulsed through Caleb's mind and heart with each step. He wanted to rush Aaron, but he knew that would be cruel. He had the irrational urge to pick up the man and carry him.

They had made it past the office when Jack came rushing back toward them.

"A call just came in. Aaron, Lydia's in labor."

Aaron's face blanched white, and Caleb thought he would pass out. "She's fine. People are with her, but the baby's nearly here so they're not going to transfer her."

"I have to go."

"You can't even walk." Brenda shook her head and held up her hand, as if that could stop him.

Instead of speaking to her, Aaron turned to Caleb.

"It's his first," Caleb said. "If there's any way—"

"He can't ride with me on the snowmobile." Jack ran a hand up and over the back of his neck. "Not with that leg."

"He can ride in the ambulance." Otis shrugged his shoulders and pointed to the parking lot, where an ambulance, complete with winter chains on its wheels had just pulled in. "Darby's injuries aren't life threatening. Where do you live?"

Aaron described the road.

"We'll drive within two miles of that. I say it's in the best interest of one of our patients to stop by there first. Should you...um... change your mind and decide you won't continue on to the hospital, I can't force you."

Brenda almost laughed, but put a finger to her lips as if she needed to hold it in. "All right. All right. I can't argue with three men. But if you're going, I'm going too. I haven't seen a newborn in almost a week. My hands are aching to hold one."

They had moved Aaron to the ambulance when Jack tapped Caleb on the shoulder.

"Still want to go home?"

"I am going. I'll walk if I have to. I caught sight of our property when we moved folks to the farthest cabin. All I could see was the spot where the bridge between our places had been. It's gone. I couldn't see the house from there, couldn't see or tell anything. But I can walk around by the road. Even in this snow, I can make it in an hour, maybe a little more."

He was so keyed up, he felt as if he could run all the way home through the drifts of snow. He stuck his hands in his pockets, or rather the pockets of Jack's coat. "By the way, I still have your coat."

"Keep it. I dressed in layers. And there's no need to walk. I've been cleared to leave this site." He nodded toward the snowmobile. "Want a ride?"

Caleb didn't even have to think about it.

He climbed on the back and they took off at a very safe, very slow speed. Caleb was sure the contraption had the ability to move faster, but before he could lean forward and ask Jack to pick up the pace, he saw a figure walking down what might be the side of the road. It was hard to tell with the amount of snow they had received.

Dressed in an odd assortment of clothes—black leather jacket, Green Bay Packers hoodie, a woman's scarf, and wearing vintage snowshoes, the man began waving his hands as soon as he spotted the snowmobile.

Caleb was off the vehicle before it had come to a complete stop.

"Tim! Our families...are they all right? And Julia. What about Julia?"

With snow matted around his eyebrows, ears, and nose, Tim looked more than half frozen, but he nodded his head up and down repeatedly and tried to form the words. He dropped his makeshift pack on the ground, and Caleb saw the extra pair of snowshoes. Jack had parked the snowmobile, pulled an emergency blanket out of his supply pack, and wrapped it around Tim's shoulders.

"They're okay." He finally managed, but his speech was slurred and he seemed confused. Glancing left, right, and back down at his feet, he didn't seem clear as to where he was or how he had arrived there.

"What happened?" Caleb moved directly in front of him, so that Tim had to look at him.

"Left at first light..." His teeth began chattering violently, and his arms shook so hard that Caleb had to hold the thin, silver blanket around his shoulders. He closed his eyes and pushed out one word after another. "Fell...into..."

He shook his head and pushed on. "Before I put snowshoes on."

Caleb noticed then that Tim's clothes were nearly frozen to him from the knees down.

As he had struggled to speak, Jack had pulled out his satellite phone and called one of the first responder teams back at the cabin. He clipped it to his belt and turned his attention back to them.

"You're suffering from hypothermia, Tim."

The man's shivering became more pronounced as he began to warm up in the blanket.

Caleb heard "Fell. Sorry. They're in...basement." He heard, but he was too busy strapping the snowshoes on over his boots to focus on Tim's words.

Basement. They had made it to the basement.

He stood and tested the shoes. They would hold. He'd used them as a child in Indiana. He'd once been quite fast on the snow.

The first responders pulled up behind them, and Caleb heard Tim's last words "Julia...she's hurt...needs you."

Jack called after him, but he was already moving down the road—clumsy, sliding, nearly losing his balance, but moving forward, unable to wait.

They would stay and help his friend. He needed to be home. He needed to care for his family. He couldn't delay even one moment longer.

Jack had his responsibilities as an officer of the law and couldn't leave Tim until he'd passed him over properly to the group that had just arrived. Caleb understood that.

He understood it as he hurried through the falling snow, and his heart was gripped by a fear colder than any blizzard.

Chapter 39

Sharon knew everyone was worried. She heard their talking, though it occurred in little groups. Most were saying Tim should have been back by now. Some wanted to send another person out to look for help, and others thought that idea was horrible and dangerous.

Frances and Jeanette were keeping a close watch on Julia, who hadn't so much as stirred since Tim had crawled out the window.

"Aren't you afraid?" Sharon had directed the question to Jeanette, but she kept her eyes on Julia. Taking the wet rag from Jeanette's hand, she used it to sponge Julia's face. How could she be so hot when the room was so cold?

"I am, but I know Tim. He said he would find help, and he will." Jeanette shrugged her shoulders and leaned back against the wall. They had tried to turn the portion of the basement against the house into a sleeping area, but only the children had been able to nod off—the children and Julia.

Sharon realized Jeanette was answering her question honestly and not simply trying to alleviate her fears. She did believe Tim would be back for no better reason than he had promised her he would. She didn't doubt her husband for a moment.

"How does that happen?" Sharon whispered. "How do you come to trust someone so completely?"

Jeanette put her arms around Zoey, who had sat up and rubbed her eyes before crawling up into her mother's lap. Bandit now lay stretched out on the floor as if it were his normal sleeping spot. "It takes time and getting to know someone. Tim isn't perfect. He has things he struggles with, but he's a good man."

Running her fingers through Zoey's hair, she stared up at the window, the one Tim had disappeared through hours before. "When he says he'll do something, he does it. I suppose that's one thing that has held our marriage together when so many marriages, especially *Englisch* marriages, fall apart."

"What about love?"

"Trust is a kind of love. How can you not love someone you trust with your life?" Jeanette kissed Zoey on the forehead.

Sharon glanced up in time to see Wess studying her. He rolled his eyes and smiled, as if to say, "Parents! They're so corny!"

A gust of wind caused a branch to scratch against the window, the one his father had climbed out of. When he looked up at it, his expression turned suddenly solemn.

Sharon understood in that moment that the smiles and eye rolls were to lift her spirits. At a time when he had so much to be concerned about, he was worried about her. Was that love?

Wess stood, walked to the end of the room, and fetched more water. He brought it to his mother and sisters, and offered more to her.

He was a good neighbor, a good friend, and possibly he could be more if she wanted him to be.

When she watched how he cared for his mother and sisters, she understood they were a family in the truest sense of the word. Whatever had brought them here, whatever troubles they had faced that had led them to a simpler lifestyle, they were now stronger because of it.

He moved back beside her. "How are you doing?"

Sharon shrugged, but something in his smile caused her to think back to the week they had first started working together and how he had insisted she keep all of the morning tips.

"You never told me what you were saving your tips for."

Wess glanced at his sisters. "Christmas presents."

"*Ya?*" She should have guessed.

"The girls can always use a new doll." His words had the desired effect on her. She remembered the tea party she'd been a part of and thought of Christmas, of the future, which surely God would grant them.

"It's snowing harder," Terra said, resting one hand on Frances and standing on her tiptoes to see better.

"Maybe we should try to leave." Frances sighed. "Maybe Brad's right. I don't know."

Brad had been standing in the corner, trying to put together a small group willing to brave the storm and leave the basement to search for help. At that moment there was a commotion by the stairs on the other side of the door that was still blocked.

Wess hopped up and joined the other adults standing near the door.

"Hello? Can you hear us? Hello?" The muffled voice from the other side of the door sounded as if it were calling from the other side of Pebble Creek.

Sharon's heart started beating a wild rhythm of hope. She couldn't be sure, but she thought she heard more than one person trying to dig them out.

She reached over and grabbed Julia's hand, squeezed it, and looked up at Ada, who had been unusually quiet all morning. "We're found. They found us!"

"We are the people God watches over, child." Ada coughed into her hand and pulled in a breath that rattled her chest and turned her cheeks a bright red. "We are the flock under His care."

Sharon looked into Ada's eyes, and she saw so many things at once—such love and acceptance and hope—that she began to cry.

She'd tried to be brave, but now she didn't feel courageous at all. Fatigue and fear and relief flooded through her in equal measures. This disaster, coupled with Julia's injury, had been too much for her to handle. Sharon suddenly understood that she wasn't nearly as strong as she had thought she was. She didn't even want to pretend to be strong anymore.

She put her head next to Julia's and allowed her tears to flow. So what if people saw her? Who hadn't cried since the storm had crashed through their lives? What did they have left to hide from one another? They had been living and sleeping and eating and even going to the bathroom together in one large room. They no longer had any secrets, and it seemed absurd to pretend they did.

These people really knew her, and it was almost a relief. The one thing she was sure of was that she couldn't keep any of her emotions hidden inside any longer.

She felt Ada's hand on top of her head, her touch a comfort and her words a blessing. And still she couldn't raise her eyes to whatever was happening a few feet away.

What if they didn't find a path through? What if she had imagined their voices, and it was another false hope?

What if Julia died while they waited?

⌒

Julia realized she had slept a long time by the river, but she didn't want to wake. A few more minutes and she would be ready. A little longer to rest, and then she would be strong.

Not yet, though.

Caleb called to her, his voice a sweet gentle presence in her ear. She smiled, knowing he wouldn't mind if she continued to sleep.

Sharon was crying. That bothered her. She wanted to comfort the girl and tell her everything would be fine. Sharon was a good girl, and she would one day grow to be a fine woman and a loving mother.

She thought to turn and speak with her, but suddenly she was standing on the bridge over Pebble Creek—the one Caleb and Aaron had built. The waters flowed underneath at a fast rate, so they must have had rain recently. She reached out for the rail to steady herself, and the wood was warm beneath her hands. The sun was such a comfort. She closed her eyes again, relishing the feel of the light and the warmth on her skin.

When she heard a splash, she looked down and saw fish dashing back and forth in the water.

"This has been a *gut* place—a *gut* home." Ada pointed to one of the speckled fish, a small one that darted into the sun before slipping back into the shadows.

They both laughed.

"*Mamm*, what is the other side of the creek like?"

"Like this side, *dochder*, in many ways. And very different in others. There is more light that comes from the Father, Son, and Spirit. That light is what you feel now, warming on your face."

"And those who have gone before…"

"*Ya.*"

They both looked across to the other side and saw Jonathan waiting there for them, standing in a pool of light. He raised a hand, and Julia realized anew how much she missed her father. It hurt her, seeing him so close and understanding that with a few steps she could be at his side.

"All angels shout, 'Encore!'"

Ada's voice caused Julia's skin to tingle from the top of her head to the tips of her toes—which were barefoot for some reason. She realized Ada wasn't speaking alone, but was joined by a chorus of many voices. Some she knew. Others sounded familiar, but she couldn't place. Together they made a sound that was more beautiful than any she had ever heard.

She wanted to weep. She wanted to dance. She wanted to stand there on the bridge, to stand in this moment forever.

"In awe before the glory, in awe before God's visible power." Her mother's voice was a breathless whisper.

The silence that followed nearly broke her heart. She turned and looked into Ada's eyes.

"We have to go back?"

"*Nein.* The choice is yours, Julia."

A part of her mind remembered then. Remembered the thing she had suspected but been afraid to hope. She placed her hand on her stomach and was assured of the life growing within her. Before she raised her eyes to look at their home she knew what she would see. So she stared down at her hand, which was now covered with her mother's. Stepping closer, she kissed Ada's cheek and said, "Let's go together. I hear Caleb."

"And Sharon."

"They're calling us."

"*Ya.*"

As they walked back across the bridge, she felt her father's blessing following her. The scene in front of her was one of nearly complete devastation. *Englischers* and Amish alike were pulling boards, trees, and what remained of their home from the entrance to their cellar. More people were arriving even as she and Ada drew near.

Then Julia opened her eyes and realized she was still in the dimly lit basement. She could feel the cold air and hear the voices of those on the outside who were coming in and helping the people around her—the people who had been trapped with her through yesterday's long afternoon and the night.

A moment later she was looking into Caleb's face. She wanted to reach up and wipe away his tears, but her arms were too heavy, so instead she whispered that everything would be fine.

The love she saw in his eyes reminded her of all she'd seen on the other side of the bridge. One day they would cross it—together or apart, she didn't know—but they would meet on the other side. For this day, with Sharon weeping at her side, Ada's prayers in her ears, and Caleb showering her with kisses, she was sure she'd made the right decision to come home.

~ *Epilogue* ~

Late December

C aleb walked across the southwest corner of the roof of Tim's new barn. When he'd reached the corner where Tim was perched, he sat beside him. They both looked out over the women and children—numbering more than a hundred—dashing back and forth in what remained of the December afternoon light.

The day had been cool, but not as cold as some Decembers.

Not as cold as that day in November.

They had raised the barn the old way—wood and peg mortise. Caleb had been present when Tim met with Eli Stutzman, who served as the master Amish engineer on the project. Eli lived on the east side of Pebble Creek. He had told Tim they could use more modern methods, but Tim had wanted the old ways.

"Looks *gut*." Caleb picked up his hat and reset it to block out the westerly sun.

"It's twice as big as the one the storm took." Tim shook his head. "I suspect it will last twice as long."

"*Gotte* willing," Caleb said.

"Yeah. God willing."

The small house Tim, Jeanette, and the children shared—what had once been the original property's *grossdaddi* house—had been untouched by the storm. The barn, which sat only a quarter mile from the house, had been reduced to a pile of lumber—the parts they could find. Much of it was simply gone.

In the immediate aftermath of the storm, Caleb, Julia, and Ada had lived with Tim and his family. Although many in their congregation had offered them a place to stay, it had made more sense to stay close. Because their properties bordered each other, it had been easy to share their resources. Sharon had traveled back to Indiana. Wess had slept on the couch, giving up his room to Caleb and Julia. A small bed had been moved into Jeanette's office for Ada.

Over the last six weeks the community had rebuilt each home, each barn, and each business that had been destroyed or damaged. Amish workers had come by the busload, week after week, until the work was finished. Donations had poured in from Amish communities through the United States, which hadn't surprised Caleb—and from *Englisch* congregations, which had.

Tim's barn was the last structure to be rebuilt, erasing the final loss from the storm. Each time Caleb had broached the subject, Tim had explained he was waiting on his insurance agent to process his claim. He had finally given up on waiting and given the go-ahead for the project.

"I saw you meeting with your agent after lunch."

"Russell? Yeah. He's a friendly sort."

"Everything straightened out?"

"Sure." Together they made their way down two ladders that were propped side by side. "He finally brought by my check to begin repairs on the barn."

"You don't say?"

Tim's grin spread from one wind-burned cheek to the other. "I signed it over to Bishop Atlee."

"*Ya?*"

"And I canceled my policy."

Together they headed toward the two women waiting for them, walking past neighbors and friends who called out a word of greeting as tools were packed away and leftover food was carried through the cold to waiting buggies.

"You canceled it?"

"Yeah. I can find better places to put that money. A good friend once told me that God knows our past and our future. I believe I'll put my trust in Him."

Caleb stopped and put one hand on Tim's shoulder. "It's a big step. Our ways are not for everyone."

"I know that. I'm still finding the answers that work for me and my family. Dropping the property insurance might be unwise somewhere else, but here? Here we know our neighbors, and we know they're dependable, good people."

They both turned and looked back at the barn. The wood-frame structure, which had been completed in a single day, rose against a cloudless sky. A small crew of men would return the following week to help with finishing what needed to be done so Tim would be able to use it through the remaining winter months.

Jeanette and Julia joined them as the workers began filing past. Words of thanks and gratitude were given and received—words of grace.

Wess followed Zoey and Victoria into the house. The children had survived the storm unscathed, though Zoey still woke screaming in the middle of the night at least once a week.

When it was only the four of them, Caleb twined his fingers with Julia's right hand. Her left arm had required a long row of stitches, and she still saw a physical therapist once a week to ensure she would regain full strength in it.

They walked across the pasture and down the path that led to their back porch—their new back porch.

"How was Lydia today?" he asked.

"*Gut*, and the baby is so sweet, Caleb. When I hold him, I think of our child and feel grateful." She placed her hand on her stomach as she spoke, as if she needed to caress the child in her womb.

"*Ya?*"

"Miriam says *Gotte* gives us dreams for a reason. I'm so thankful we will have children in our home and that we were able to help Sharon."

They stopped at the pasture fence. Missy and Red trotted over to see if there were raisins. As Caleb reached into his pocket, he marveled that his family and horses had been saved. Structures could be rebuilt, but it was a gift beyond grace to still have each other and the animals they had depended on for so long.

David's place, though close to the cabins, had not even been touched.

Amish Anthem sustained only moderate roof damage. In fact, most of downtown was spared.

Many of the families on the east side of town, both Amish and *Englisch*, had suffered some damage. The homes with more complete destruction, like Caleb's and the Aaron's cabins, tended to be on the east side. And yet there had been no loss of life. Injuries, to be sure, but those folks would heal with time.

Caleb squeezed her hand. They had been through so much together in the first few months of their marriage. He was sure she was right. God was in control of their lives.

They were nearly at the house when she said, "We received a letter from Sharon today."

"*Ya?*"

"I didn't even have to walk to our mailbox. The letter carrier knew how I'd been watching for word from her, so he brought it over."

"Nice of him."

"I think he actually wanted a closer look at the barn raising." She lingered on the back porch watching Pebble Creek, but he pulled her inside, out of the cold.

"I have warm tea ready for both of you," Ada called from the kitchen.

"*Danki*," Caleb answered.

After removing her coat, Julia sat in the chair he pulled out for her, unwinding her scarf but fiddling with the strings of her outer prayer *kapp*.

"So what did it say?" He pulled the *kapp* loose, kissed her cheek, and sat down next to her.

"She wrote she was having a *wunderbaar* visit with her family, and that *Gotte* is still working with her dreams and her fears..." Julia hesitated.

"Any word about the trial of the men who tried to abduct her?"

"I didn't understand all of it, but there will be no trial. There was plenty of evidence against them, and three eyewitnesses from three separate incidents, including Sharon's. The men pleaded guilty in order to receive a reduced sentence."

"So she won't have to testify?"

"*Nein*. She sounded relieved about that."

When she stopped and glanced up, he was surprised to see tears in her eyes. "And she'd like to come back in the spring."

"We'd be happy to have her. *Ya?*"

"We would. I've missed her, and I know *mamm* has as well."

Caleb heard Ada pouring the tea in the kitchen. He stood to go help her but then turned back, ducked his head, and kissed Julia quickly on the lips.

"What was that for?"

"Can't a husband kiss his *fraa* for no other reason than he loves her?"

"I suppose he can."

As he clomped into the kitchen, his muscles already stiffening from the long day of work, he realized he was happier than he'd ever been. And although the storm had taken more than was fair—in lives, in property, and in moments of fear—it had also given them much.

Those moments by Julia's side, when he'd thought he had lost her, were the longest of his life.

He'd seen then, seen as crystal clear as he'd ever seen anything, exactly how precious each moment and each person was.

"The Lord is *gut*," Ada murmured as she set sugar and cream on a tray to be taken into the sitting area—their new sitting area. The home was one story now, with the café in a separate building attached by a breezeway. They would reopen their business the first week of the new year.

"Indeed He is, Ada. Indeed He is."

Author's Note

I would like to thank my friend Bonnie Hinman for being an inspiration to me. She survived the EF5 tornado that struck Joplin, Missouri, in May 2011. The building she was in collapsed on top of her, but she emerged unscathed. Her courage and faith were in the front of my mind as I wrote the final scenes of this book.

The weather described in the last chapters is based on an actual historical occurrence. On November 11, 1911, the Great Lakes Region and Upper Midwest experienced extraordinary weather events. Record highs and lows were broken on the same day. The storm system produced F2, F3, and F4 tornadoes. Rock County, Wisconsin, endured a blizzard within one hour of being hit by an F4 tornado. Many towns were affected by that day's weather. Nine people died in Janesville, Wisconsin, alone. I would like to offer a special dedication to the towns, victims, and survivors of that long-ago storm.

I also would like to note that the recipes included in this story were patterned after recipes included in a very old cookbook from the Nappanee, Indiana, area.

Discussion Questions

1. Ada shares the Psalms, but she doesn't always quote them word for word as we would find in the Bible. It seems as if she is reminding her family of the psalmists' words more than she is quoting them. It's as if she is sharing words from a friend. What has been your experience with the book of Psalms?

2. In chapter 6, David says, "You don't truly know someone until you share your mornings and your nights with them." Do you agree or disagree with this statement? Why?

3. Bishop Atlee explains to Julia, "You are still a child to your parents no matter how old you become." Recall a time you have experienced this sentiment with your own children or from your parents.

4. Chapter 7 contains a conversation between Caleb and his dad. This is very different from the typical view of marriage. What is your response to it?

5. In chapter 14, we see Julia's wedding day. As she waits in

her room, she runs her hand over the double wedding
ring quilt and recalls that "It had gone in the blanket
chest at the foot of her bed, buried there with her hopes
and dreams." But on this day, God is giving her the
dream she'd long ago forgotten. What dreams in your
life has God fulfilled?

6. In chapter 17, Sharon leaves her home upset, confused,
and convinced her family doesn't love her. Have you
been through any situations like this? How did God
convince you that you are loved?

7. In chapter 19, Ada prays over Sharon with the words
of Psalm 23. Have you read that psalm lately? Think of
a time in your life when this portion of God's Word
ministered to you.

8. I love the scene in chapter 26 when Julia and Caleb have
their first big spat. What is causing Julia's short temper?
What about Caleb? How does his attitude make matters
worse? How could they both have avoided the entire
misunderstanding?

9. In chapter 29, we learn that Wess is growing his hair
out so he can donate it to Locks of Love. Discuss this or
another charitable program you have been involved with.

10. Ada describes what happened in Wisconsin on
November 11, 1911. This was an actual event that
included the tragedy described in the following chapters—
record high and low temperatures, storms and tornadoes,
followed by a blinding blizzard. All occurred within a
24-hour period. How does God use such events in our
lives? How does it change the lives of Ada, Sharon, Julia,
and Caleb?

Glossary

boppli . . . . baby
bruder. . . . . brother
dat . . . . father (informal)
danki . . . . thank you
dochder(n) . . . . daughter(s)
eck . . . . corner table
Englisch . . . . non-Amish
Englischer . . . . non-Amish person
fraa . . . . wife
freind(en) . . . . friend(s)
gelassenheit. . . . . .humility
gem gschehne .you're welcome
Gotte . . . . God
Gotte's wille . . . . God's will
grossdaddi. . . . . grandfather
grossmammi . . . . .grandmother
gudemariye . . . . .good morning
gut . . . . good
in lieb . . . . in love
kaffi. . . . . coffee
kapp. . . . . prayer covering
kind . . . . child
kinner. . . . . .children
mamm . . . . mom
narrisch . . . . .crazy
onkel . . . . uncle
nein . . . . no
rumspringa . . . . .running-around years
schweschder. . . . . .sister
Was iss letz . . . . What is it?
wunderbaar . . . . wonderful
ya. . . . . yes

Recipes

Apple-Cinnamon Pie

1 unbaked pie crust
1 cup sliced apples
½ cup sugar
½ cup brown sugar
2 Tablespoons flour
1 cup cream
cinnamon or nutmeg, optional

Place the apple slices in an unbaked pie crust. In a medium-sized bowl, mix together the sugars and flour and then sprinkle over the apples. Pour the cream over the pie filling and sprinkle with cinnamon or nutmeg if desired.

Bake at 400 degrees for 10 minutes, and then turn heat down to 350 degrees and bake another 40 minutes.

Buttermilk Cornbread

2 eggs
1½ cups buttermilk
3 Tablespoons melted lard (or shortening)
1½ cups corn meal
1 teaspoon salt
1 cup flour
¾ teaspoon baking soda

In a large bowl, combine the eggs, buttermilk, and lard/shortening. Add the remaining dry ingredients and pour into an 8 x 8 pan.

Bake at 400 degrees for 30 minutes or until a toothpick comes out clean.

Chicken Casserole

½ lb. uncooked spaghetti noodles
1½ cups cooked chicken, diced
2 eggs, beaten
1½ cups milk
Salt and pepper to taste

Cook the noodles in salted boiling water until soft.

Pour the noodles into colander, drain, and rinse. Then alternate layers of noodles and the diced chicken into a well-greased, oven-proof casserole dish. Mix the eggs with the milk and then pour over the noodles and chicken. Add salt and pepper if desired.

Place the casserole dish in a pan of water and bake at 350 degrees for 30 minutes.

Chicken and Dumplings

1 cup milk
2 cups flour
2 eggs
1 teaspoon salt
1 chicken, cooked and deboned
2 quarts water or meat broth

Slowly add the milk to the flour, stirring constantly to keep mixture smooth. Adding 1 egg at a time, continue beating the mixture. Sprinkle in salt.

Cook the dumplings in boiling salted water or meat broth by tilting the bowl of batter over the pan of water/broth and slicing off portions with a sharp knife. Dip the knife in the hot liquid before each cut to prevent sticking.

Add the chicken and simmer until desired thickness is reached.

Cinnamon Flop Cake

1 cup sugar
2 Tablespoons lard (or shortening)
1 egg
1 cup sour milk (or buttermilk)
1 teaspoon baking soda
2 cups flour
2 Tablespoons cinnamon
1 teaspoon nutmeg

Cream sugar and lard together, and then add the remaining ingredients. Beat until smooth.

Pour the batter into a greased and floured round cake pan or 8 x 8 pan.

Bake at 350 degrees for approximately 30 minutes or until a toothpick comes out clean.

Guey Louie Sandwiches

2 lbs. big bologna (or hot dogs)
1 small onion
½ lb. cheese of your choice
8 medium pickles
1 Tablespoon prepared mustard
3 Tablespoons mayonnaise
1 package of hot dog buns

Grind together the bologna, onion, cheese, and pickles. Add the mustard and mayonnaise. Mix well and the fill the buns.

Wrap each sandwich in tinfoil and bake at 375 degrees for 20 minutes.

Lazy Daisy Oatmeal Cake

1¼ cups boiling water
1 cup rolled oats (quick or old-fashioned, uncooked)
½ cup butter (softened)
1 cup sugar
1 cup brown sugar
1 teaspoon vanilla
2 eggs
1½ cups sifted flour
1 teaspoon soda
½ teaspoon salt
¾ Tablespoon cinnamon
¼ teaspoon nutmeg

Pour the boiling water over the oats. Cover and let stand 20 minutes.

Cream together the butter, sugar, brown sugar, vanilla, and eggs. Add the oats mixture and mix well.

Sift the dry ingredients together, and then add to the wet mixture. Beat all together until smooth before pouring the batter into greased and floured cake pans.

Bake at 350 degrees for 50 minutes or until a toothpick comes out clean.

Frosting

¼ cup melted butter
½ cup brown sugar
3 Tablespoons milk or cream
½ cup nuts, chopped
¾ cup shredded coconut

Mix all of the ingredients together and spread evenly over cake. Put under broiler for 2 minutes.

Sunbonnet Cake

- 1 cup butter
- 2 cups sugar
- 1 cup cornstarch
- 1 cup milk or water
- 2 cups flour
- 2 teaspoon baking powder
- 1 Tablespoon lemon rind, grated
- 4 egg whites, beaten

Cream together the butter and sugar. In a separate bowl, mix the cornstarch with the water or milk and then add to the butter-and-sugar mixture. Stir in the flour, baking powder, and grated lemon rind, and then fold in the beaten egg whites.

Pour into a greased and floured Bundt pan and bake at 350 degrees for 45-50 minutes or until a toothpick comes out clean.

≈ About the Author ≈

 **Vannetta Chapman** writes inspirational fiction full of grace. She has published over one hundred articles in Christian family magazines, receiving more than two dozen awards from Romance Writers of America chapter groups. She discovered her love for the Amish while researching her grandfather's birthplace of Albion, Pennsylvania. Her novel *Falling to Pieces* was a 2012 ACFW Carol Award winner. *A Promise for Miriam* earned a spot on the June 2012 Christian Retailing Top Ten Fiction list.

Vannetta was a teacher for 15 years and currently resides in the Texas hill country with her husband.

Visit Vannetta's website at
www.vannettachapman.com

When she thought her future would never know love...
she saw him.
When he thought his future would forever be empty...
he saw her.

A Promise for
MIRIAM

VANNETTA
CHAPMAN

Amish schoolteacher Miriam King loves her students. At twenty-six, most women her age are married with children of their own, but she hasn't yet met anyone who can persuade her to give up the Plain school that sits along the banks of Pebble Creek. Then newcomer Gabriel Miller steps into her life, bringing his daughter, an air of mystery, and challenges Miriam has never faced before.

At first Gabe just wants to be left alone with a past that haunts him, but the loving and warm Wisconsin community he and his daughter have moved to has other plans for him. After a near tragedy, he hesitantly returns offers of help and friendship, and he discovers he can make a difference to the people of Pebble Creek—and maybe to the Amish schoolteacher.

**A bend in the road can be daunting
...or the beginning of everything.**

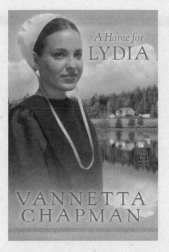

Aaron Troyer simply wants to farm in Indiana like his *dat* and *grossdaddi* before him, but instead he finds himself traveling to Wisconsin to oversee an uncle's small group of Plain cabins nestled along the banks of Pebble Creek. That also means he must work with the cabins' lovely but stubborn housekeeper, Lydia Fisher.

Lydia is the most outspoken Amish woman Aaron has ever met, and she has strong opinions about how the guest cabins are to be run. She also desperately needs her job, and to keep it she must temper her reaction to her new employer. Though sparks fly at first, when danger unexpectedly overtakes them, nothing is more important to Aaron than making sure Lydia is safe.

Together they work to make the vacation property profitable, but can they find out who is causing trouble before more damage is done? And can Lydia guard her heart, knowing Aaron is just biding his time before he can return home to his farm? Or is her dream of a home of her own more than just a wish and a prayer?

To learn more about Harvest House books and
to read sample chapters, log on to our website:

www.harvesthousepublishers.com

HARVEST HOUSE PUBLISHERS
EUGENE, OREGON